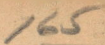

"Don't go over there, Nora."

He sounded tired. "God knows this is bad enough. It'll be worse over there."

She looked up at him, pulling free of his arm. His eyes were turned across the rooftops to the fires in the city. He seemed distant already.

"I can't stay in London. The story is over there."

He snagged two cigarettes from his pocket, and the flare of his lighter revealed a tight smile. Her hand trembled, and he stilled it with his own. "What won't you do for your damned stories and that damned ambition?"

She took a deep drag, and the smoke gave her time to gather courage. "For a long time all I had was ambition. The big stories, the guaranteed bylines. I never figured the future would be much diff'rent. Now I'm not so sure."

For a long moment he didn't move, and she found herself holding her breath. She let the air out softly when he reached for her, gently cupping her face in his hands. His lips were warm but barely touched hers.

"None of us has a future yet."

ELIZABETH QUINN
ALLIANCES

WORLDWIDE

TORONTO • NEW YORK • LONDON • PARIS
AMSTERDAM • STOCKHOLM • HAMBURG
ATHENS • MILAN • TOKYO • SYDNEY

First published March 1987

ISBN 0-373-97035-8

Copyright © 1987 by Elizabeth Quinn Barnard. All rights reserved.
Philippine copyright 1987. Australian copyright 1987.
Except for use in any review, the reproduction or utilization of
this work in whole or in part in any form by any electronic,
mechanical or other means, now known or hereafter invented,
including xerography, photocopying and recording, or in any
information storage or retrieval system, is forbidden without
the permission of the publisher, Worldwide Library,
225 Duncan Mill Road, Don Mills, Ontario, Canada M3B 3K9.

All the characters in this book have no existence outside the
imagination of the author and have no relation whatsoever to
anyone bearing the same name or names. They are not even
distantly inspired by any individual known or unknown to the
author, and all incidents are pure invention.

The Worldwide design trademarks, consisting of a globe surrounded
by a square, and the word WORLDWIDE in which the letter "O" is
represented by a depiction of a globe, are trademarks of
Worldwide Library.

Printed in U.S.A.

For my parents

Many thanks to Anne D. LeClaire, who said I could do it; to Meg Ruley, who helped turn an idea into a story; to Con Sellers, who taught me to write fiction; to Bill Doody and Barbara Haley, who read the manuscript and kept me focused; and, of course, to Jeffrey, who gave me the place and the time to write.

ONE

THE BELLY OF A FLYING FORTRESS wasn't the kind of accommodation Nora had in mind for her first trip to Europe. An outside stateroom on the *Normandie* was more like it, but the French ship keeled over in New York harbor soon after the war started. The other big liners now crossed the Atlantic as troop transports. No matter what the girls back home said, being among a handful of women stranded with a few thousand guys in midocean wasn't the kind of fun she liked. And she was eager to start the overseas job. The camp-out at Mitchell Field waiting for a quick ride over seemed like a better idea until somewhere off Newfoundland when the pilot said their destination was Scotland. By then it was too late to head for the docks.

Now a train swayed her toward London, but the feel of the bomber lingered. Nora eased away from the seat, rubbing back muscles knotted by hours propped against a parachute wedged between the bomber's metal ribs. Daylight brightened outside the train window but left the gray fields and sky a monochrome landscape. Leftover vibrations from the plane's engines still drummed through her head and, although the train's heat came on at dawn, the cheek propped in her hand was cold. Slipping to the floor, she lifted her duffel bag across the seat, legs stretched out the length of the bench as she settled back against the canvas bag.

Glancing at the woman and boy across the compartment, she found them watching her. The woman quickly looked away. Nora's glance held the boy, his eyes round with amazement at waking to find a stranger sharing his journey. An audible stomach growl unleashed a hot flush of embarrassment.

"Will the train stop long enough for me to grab a bite?"

The woman started, looking puzzled. British reserve was no joke. Nora almost gave up hope for an answer until the woman shook her head.

"I shouldn't think so. The tearooms are seldom open."

If the best this railroad could offer was a tearoom, who cared if it was closed? Hot black American coffee was what she needed. Coffee fueled her train trips. Crossing the states as a national writer for International Press made her an expert in railroad coffee. Dining cars on the Challenger to San Francisco served a weak brew. Maybe the lousy coffee should have warned her the desk in New York would butcher the stories on Jap internment. But that system didn't hold up because the coffee on the train to Key West was terrific, especially after the crews changed in New Orleans. And those stories bombed, too. Luck brought her to the navy base the day a training sub sank during depth-charge practice. The censors killed that story. She got used to it.

The whistle blew as Nora trotted down the corridor, working the cramps out of her legs. She dropped to her knees, bracing her arms against the swaying walls as the train sped through a crossing. A young girl straddled her bike behind the gate and waved a red cap when the whistle tweeted again.

English railroads sounded like toy trains to someone used to the mournful horn of freights heading for the Chicago stockyards. The countryside wasn't really all that different from Illinois. More trees but the meadows crept up to the edges of English villages like the grain fields ringing her hometown. Maybe the girl at the crossing sent her imagination down the tracks, too.

Hard times hit when Nora was in high school, and her father put her to work on the soda fountain after school. Between customers she'd read Chicago papers until her fingertips were permanently smudged with ink. As things got worse and the customers griped more often about tough times, the papers became more attractive, especially the scandal sheets. A small part of her wanted to know why she could never buy a new dress and how farmers with acres of ripening wheat became poor men. Mostly, she escaped from the daily monotony of serving the same rotten coffee to the same worn people with the same old complaints.

From the tabloids Nora knew that some people were having good times. Gossipmongers telling that story filled their columns with each rich detail. Although it wasn't a world she could inhabit, a newspaperwoman could see it firsthand. And it wasn't just the big shots, either. Gangsters fascinated her. So did the Cubs at Wrigley Field and even the clowns at City Hall. Chicago seemed wonderfully alive to a young girl trapped in a hick town where hope was dying and dreams were already dead. Each afternoon Nora waited impatiently for the thump of evening papers landing on the sidewalk outside the drugstore. People probably waited like that for the next installment of old-time magazine serials. But the papers were better than fiction because the stories were true and the people were real.

Racketing wheels smothered the sound of the porter's footsteps until he was right behind her. "Is something amiss?" Pipe smoke washed over her when he reached down to help her to her feet. A smoke would do nicely right now.

"I thought the whistle might mean a station."

"A wee one. You're a Yank? Best keep your eyes east for Hadrian's Wall. It's along here soon."

Nora heard voices inside the compartment but they stopped talking when she opened the door. She dug through her duffel for her last Hershey bar. When Nora slid onto the vacant bench just before dawn, the woman was sleeping upright with the kid's head on her lap, their faces pale ovals in the dim blackout lighting. After a night on the train, the woman's blouse was still as crisply starched as her posture, hands folded in her lap and ankles crossed. Nora knew a day and a night on a bomber and a train had wilted her right down to the rugged army getup she wore. She felt like a dishrag but hoped it didn't show.

The boy looked about eight. Only his darting eyes reminded her of American kids. She hadn't seen a boy in short pants at home for years. What was it about her that fascinated him? His eyes rarely left her. Searching down the length of her legs, Nora understood. It was the uniform, especially the trousers. Good thing she had the hips to wear pants. The kid was too young for that to count for much. Slouching along the bench probably made her even more foreign. And if she looked the least bit like she felt Nora figured she could substitute for Bela Lugosi in one of his horror movies. No wonder a boy with that mannequin for a mother found her so strange. She caught his eye and smiled. He grinned back.

Unwrapping the chocolate, she saw the boy's eyes track her hands. All little boys loved chocolate, but the Hershey bar was breakfast. At the rate this milk train moved, she might have to make it do for lunch, too. His eyes begged her.

"Okay, kid, I'll split it with you."

Nora broke the bar in half, glancing to his mother for approval.

"Chocolate is such a rare treat for Teddy. Thank you."

Nora forced herself to slow down after gobbling the first creamy chunk. Hershey bars were best when melted smooth over the tongue. Teddy settled back with a sigh, licking the squares in his fist. His legs swung in rhythm with the train, too thin between wool socks and shorts.

Last time Nora had seen a kid wearing short pants was in Chicago, and he was crying. She'd beaten him to the alley by grabbing a ride in a cop car. Despite the dead man's respectable blue suit, the police left him uncovered. Pooling blood buzzed with the summer's flies. Her inexperience composed the scene as a waxwork tableau until a keening woman fell to her knees and gathered the dead man into her arms. The boy in short pants joined his mother amid the rotting garbage, and the scene took life for Nora. She turned away and was sick. The cops snickered. When she called the story in, the rewriteman laughed too.

"Don't call us with spade stories, Seymour."

Stomach churning at his indifference, she'd snapped back. A man was dead. A doctor, for God's sake, in a slum that needed him.

"Take it easy. You sound like Mrs. Roosevelt. Some people don't count. Better get used to it."

Weeks later the city broiled under the worst heat in memory. Social workers at Hull House said it was killing weather. In cramped tenements the heat took a deadly toll of the very old and the very young. Processions of hearses jammed streets in some neighborhoods. The editors loved that story. Nora believed that one would atone for the paper's earlier indifference. Hope died when her first page-one byline ran off the press under a headline screaming How Babies Are Baked. Those in charge fashioned a vitriolic crusade to pump up circulation. It worked and Nora's star rose.

The train's clatter slowed like a Victrola running down. Maybe Teddy's mother was wrong about the restaurant. She needed the air, anyway. His candy was gone, and he trailed her into the station. The tearoom was shuttered, but a farm woman had a basket of apples rubbed bright and smelling of autumn mornings in the country. Nora took half a dozen and handed over an unfamiliar bill. She recognized King George. The coins that came back weren't pennies or nickels or dimes, but she slipped them into her pocket. English money had as much value to her as the pretend bills in a Monopoly game. Spotting Teddy nearby, she held out an apple.

"Are you a soldier?"

She laughed, pointing to the patch on her sleeve. "I'm a reporter, but they make us wear the uniform, anyhow. You know how far it is to London?"

The boy shook his head, mouth filled with the crisp apple pulp. He swallowed. "Mummy says we'll be in Piccadilly for luncheon."

Mummy finished her toilette before they returned to the compartment. No color highlighted her lips, and her hair still coiled in a tight knot at her nape. A string of pearls now dressed up her gray suit, and the air smelled faintly of lavender. Nora hated the scent. Four bottles of her own perfume stuffed in the duffel were the last of a stockpile hoarded when she'd heard about the fall of France. Even with today's twenty-percent luxury tax, buying perfume was worth it. Sources often forgot she was a reporter when they got a whiff of her Chanel. Maybe four bottles could see her all the way to Paris.

Thrown forward by the train's sudden jerk, Nora checked her watch as she slid down the seat to the window. Past noon, but in England lunch might be later. The train stopped again. Maybe staying on when Teddy had left with his mother was a mistake. No one would meet her, anyway. IP's cable to Will Davies in the bureau said she'd arrive by air. The woman's unexpected offer of help getting into the city had caught Nora by surprise, and she automatically refused. They were probably digging into lunch in Piccadilly by now.

The porter stuck her head into the compartment and waggled the pipe in his fist. "Won't be long now, miss."

She asked what was holding them up. He waved toward the window, but all Nora could see was a tall brick wall.

"The Jerries dropped a few calling cards last night, and a bit of wall collapsed across the tracks. It's cleared off now, I expect."

"I thought the bombing was over."

"Oh, it is. It mostly is. A few planes come over but don't do much damage. At least in London. The worst is over now, miss. Now that you Yanks are helping us finish the job."

So he thought the Yanks were helping. Back in the States, everyone thought the English were doing the helping. A foolish thing to argue about but the stories got big play. Columnists crowed when Eisenhower got the top job. Reading a few London newspapers proved they were miffed over here. That kind of petty squabbling made her avoid the political beat. Assignment to London meant writing similar stuff, mostly from dull briefings or press releases. She'd be off the streets and trapped in routine, but that was the price of her shot at a special correspondency.

Getting bombed wasn't part of her plan. No story was worth dying for. Leading the charge with the soldiers wasn't what she had in mind, even if the army decided to let women near the fighting. Ernie Pyle had sewed up the foot-soldier market, and, of the brass, only Patton's name was page-one magic. For good play every day, Ike's headquarters was the place and that's where Nora meant to be.

The porter disappeared when the train pulled into the station. Nora wrestled the duffel a bit before abandoning attempts to heave it into her arms. Backing down the narrow corridor dragging the bag, she winced as it bumped along and hoped the perfume bottles wouldn't smash. Footsteps clanged across the vestibule floor. Before she could straighten or turn, a brisk spank stung her buttocks and arms closed around her.

"Still got the best bottom at IP, Seymour. The pants really show it off."

Nora relaxed in Will Davies's embrace, freeing herself as she twisted around to return his hug. A tremor ran through the arms and bony shoulders under her hands. Leaning back, she saw deep grooves in his thin gray face.

"My God, what's happened to you?"

The grin was familiar as he shook her off and grabbed the duffel. Two tries raised it to his shoulder, but he slung it to the ground as soon as they reached the platform.

"What the Christ is wrong? You look like you're ready for an undertaker."

A listless hand brushed dull graying hair from his eyes. "I've just spent two years in Russia."

"Doesn't Stalin feed American correspondents? We're sending boatloads of Spam."

"We got the Spam. But there's not enough of anything in Russia these days. We were always a little hungry or tired or cold. And damned little news."

A translucent hand weakly gripped her elbow as Will craned his head around. "Closest we got to Stalingrad was sixty miles and just another Red Army communiqué for our trouble."

"Maybe Ike will make it up to you and let you be the first reporter back in Europe."

Something unfamiliar flickered through Will's eyes. Nora was too busy taking in the scrawny stranger masquerading as her friend to wonder about it.

"Where's that GI driver? Last I saw, he'd spotted a cute little Limey and was tailing her, juggling a couple of oranges. Wait here."

A splotch of moisture hit her cheek and Nora looked up. Jagged fingers of glass strained to close an expanse of smashed skylight. A moment's unease drained off when she saw no anxiety on the faces of other travelers crowding the famous old station. Reassured of safety, Nora dragged her duffel to the closest pillar and waited for Will. No use standing in the drizzle.

A pimply kid in uniform carried her bag to a jeep parked outside next to a small pyramid of sandbags. The rain-washed air was good. Nora wanted to walk once Will promised a tour. Exploring on foot was the way to see any city for the first time. They swung out along the sidewalk, strides matched in the way of old friends used to walking together.

"I'll fill you in on our way to Norfolk House. That's where a lot of the brass work."

Walking loosened the knots in Nora's back, and Will's words sparked excitement as he explained IP's reporting strategy. She kept glancing up at the clouds to reassure herself that no bombers were sneaking in, but finally the parade of dress blues and fatigues, regimentals and khaki overwhelmed her apprehension.

When Will started in on censorship, Nora hardly listened. The rules weren't tough to figure—keep it general and make it upbeat because the customers at home weren't in the market for bad news. What she wanted to know was where all the civilians were hiding, especially the women. London's order of the day seemed to call for a masculine city in military garb. The double-time pace quickened her pulse.

This was definitely the place. It had the serious feel of Wall Street or the State Department. Doing the right kind of work here could give her a special correspondency and all that meant. She wanted respect from colleagues, freedom from routine and orders to concentrate on big stories, the kind that rattle the powerful. Freedom to choose the biggest in politics, business or diplomacy, and all the time she needed to get the story, was the reward she sought. The daily challenge of meeting a deadline was gone, and the subjects were too stiff to be much fun. But Nora didn't mind. Special correspondent was the pinnacle for a wire service reporter who hated editing. Once she finished with the war, special correspondent was the only writing job left.

Will turned off a busy street, and in a few blocks the civilian city emerged battered and gray. A line of people snaked away from a bakery that pumped out tempting aromas of hot breads each time a customer entered under the tinkling bell. The cellar next door sprouted winter-killed weeds and a blackened chimney freed of supporting walls.

"I thought the bombing was over."

"You'll hear the sirens but no one gets up anymore. The worst was over in '42, although rumor says Hitler's got a secret weapon. No one seems too worried, though."

That explained why Englishmen passed through wrecked streets without a sideways glance. Londoners were probably used to threadbare sleeves and patched elbows. Paint peeling unheeded on elaborate Georgian doorways in affluent squares was a familiar and unremarkable sight. But not to Nora. At home outmoded fashions were tossed and the houses got a new coat of paint when the jobs came back with the war. Men sacrificed the cuffs on their pants, but they had new suits. Women jealously guarded their hose, but stockings could be had.

A tide of bicycles splashing down the road stopped them at a corner. There weren't enough cars on the streets to drown the sound of splattering water thrown from the puddles as bicycles passed. The city din of motors and horns was missing except for the silly tinkling ring from the handlebar bells. Nora reached back to smooth her skirt and, instead, found the unfamiliar cloth of government-issue slacks under her fingers. Pants had it all over skirts for hitching a ride on a Flying Fortress. No fussing to straighten seams, either. But why bother even thinking about stockings? By the looks of it, clothes wouldn't be a problem in England.

The thought killed her elation. London was grim, and she was tired of the war. A return to hard times would give no respite from the conflict that had already dominated her working life every day for two years. Leaving the war at the office was easy in New York. There pockets bulged with war-work dollars ready to buy good times and forgetting at a Stork Club floor show or Toots Shor's dinner. Here it might be difficult to escape just for a blessed minute. She might be able to ignore the uniforms, even her own. But as soon as you hit the streets, the sandbags and olive-drab trucks and shattered buildings would bring it back in a glance. All she wanted was a momentary letup, but that didn't look likely.

"It's damned depressing."

Will shrugged. "War's depressing."

"Yeah, sure. But I didn't expect this. In France, yes. But not England."

"You're right. We haven't done much on the people since the blitz. New York wants it, so I'm giving it to you."

Nora grabbed his arm. "Come off it, Will. I've been doing more substantial stuff. I'm off features. I want a piece of the hard news, the brass."

"Sorry, kid, it's your beat. You'll get enough of the generals to be ready when the invasion comes. In the meantime, buck up the alliance with a few tearjerkers and some purple prose."

He reached into his raincoat pocket and dragged out a crumpled cable. "New York's already messaged the members with a promo. They're calling it *The Home Front*, and your share is three pieces a week. You can start with your trip over."

Nora scanned the cable, eyes racing through each demand to STOP. It wasn't so bad. At least she'd get noticed in New York if the columns were picked up by a lot of member newspapers. She'd make sure they got good play. And a few exclusives out of the brass would shake her editors up. IP knew better than to waste someone with good sources on sidebars and color stories. Any decent wordsmith could write that stuff. Only a real pro working all the angles scored major beats.

Smoothed out and folded once, the cable fit neatly into the notebook she pulled from her pocket. Nora saw a girl eyeing the lone pair of dancing slippers displayed in a shoe store window. Her blond head dipped forward as the girl frowned down at her darned woolen stockings. Was there a column in it?

TWO

ANOTHER SIX INCHES HEIGHT would have made it less of a fight, but crossing her arms in front like a cowcatcher helped Nora plow through the herd of uniforms hiding the bar. Getting a refill was a good excuse for ditching the English colonel when she figured out that no matter what he called it, in her lingo he was still just a glorified press agent. So what if his client was a general instead of the ingenue at a West End theater? The brigadier wanted good press and Nora wanted good stories, and never the twain shall meet.

A rangy American stopped her to drawl apologies when ashes from his drooping cigarette floated onto her shoulder. She refused his grinned offer to brush it off and ducked under the raised arms juggling a brace of glasses. After Nora threaded her way to the front row, the white-jacketed barman ignored the men vying for his attention.

"All out of ice, lady."

She took the Scotch neat in a water tumbler, each smoky swallow warming its way down. Except for the chance to drink good Scotch again, the party was a bust. No one she'd sized up so far looked likely as a source. Part of tonight's problem was wasting time with officers too far down the ladder of rank to count. She hadn't been in London long enough to learn what the soldiers' insignia meant, except for the stars on a few shoulders. But as far as she could see, most generals weren't putting in an appearance here, even though the guest of honor was visiting Russian brass. Maybe she should forget work and just enjoy herself.

"—and I brought it in for Ike this morning."

Nora inched through a thicket of elbows toward the trio talking about Eisenhower, all the while scouting for patches on their sleeves. Christ, she'd have to study those army illustrations if she expected to get anything done over here. The emblem for each rank and outfit could instantly clue you in to who a soldier was. The wings above the redhead's chest pocket must mean he was a flier.

"FDR has Fala, and now Ike has a pooch, too. How's it feel to be close to the big man, Red? After all, you're a personal friend of his dog."

Nora veered off as two of the soldiers doubled over with laughter. They looked a lot younger than everyone else. Another burst of laughter from one corner warned her off joining that group whose merriment increased noticeably with every round.

"No friend of mine after the mess he made of my ship. Need to ventilate the fuselage to get the stink out. Krauts'll give me some flak holes, I hope."

Nora allowed a chuckle to bubble over. They were just kids. Nearby heads turned as the boys melted into knee-slapping abandon. Even these greenhorns must know the army acronyms. Before she'd left for England Nora knew SHAEF meant Supreme Headquarters Allied Expeditionary Force because SHAEF also meant Eisenhower and that's where she wanted to be. But what about CIGS or ETOUSA?

"Frightful mess, the estate agent said. Thought he'd the place let, too. Bugger all now. Bloody Jerries."

Learning the English spoken in England was another complication. She studied the man whose voice had stopped her. The thumbnail rubbing his mustache reminded her of a caricature Englishman in a Broadway farce. She hadn't expected England to be exactly like home, but the difference was more than she'd ever imagined. And it wasn't simply calling a truck a lorry or the stove a cooker, although the difficulty in understanding her native tongue jarred enough. Brushing the hair off her forehead left a residue of moisture on her fingertips, and she wiped her hand on the cocktail napkin around her glass. The English were certainly a lot friendlier than she'd expected. But something still made them different. Maybe they were more serious than Americans? Or was it—

"Looking for a friend? I'm a really nice guy."

Even without the New England accent she'd peg that voice as American. An Englishman's come-on would be smoother, less obvious. Nora glanced over her shoulder but had to look up to meet gray eyes crinkled with laughter and sparkling from booze. One of the flyboys, but not the redhead who'd flown in Ike's dog. That dog might make a column on a slow day, and she wouldn't need this kid to get it. But he was cute, just the kind of boy she'd admired across crowded fraternity parties in her one year at college. His body hadn't bulked out with muscles yet to balance his six-foot-plus height, but he wasn't one of the gawky fellows who sniggered in dark corners. He'd definitely been a campus king, and now that she'd caught his eye so many years too late, he'd be easy to brush off. But she didn't have the heart for it. Uncomplicated flirting appealed to her.

"You the kind of fellow who likes older women, soldier?"

The devilish grin he'd pasted on split wider with genuine surprise. "You're American! Great!"

Then his eyes narrowed, dousing the blaze of enthusiasm with a wary squint. "Say, you're not in uniform but you gotta be an officer. And I bet you outrank me. Ma'am. Have I really stepped in it?"

"Relax, will you? I'm not here in disguise."

He snared her hand when she introduced herself and shook it vigorously, visibly relieved that his fraternization wouldn't land him in the brig or whatever the army called it. In the next instant she learned his name was Timothy, he was on his first pass in England, and he'd met these two fellows and brought them to the party when Matt, his brother, already had a date—he was the guy with the two blondes in the corner—and it was a pretty swell party, and he really liked it over here, and how long had she been in England and what did she think of it?

"Whoa, Timothy, slow down."

A red flush crept up his neck, and she instantly regretted embarrassing him. His eyes wheeled across the room to his brother. Nora followed his glance. He was definitely older, early thirties she guessed, with a frame that had muscled into balanced proportions. For a second his size and dark hair convinced her that he was Eric. But common sense assured her Eric was without doubt still in Chicago, safely out of the line of fire and with work suitable enough to quash any rumors of draft dodging.

An older officer drawn by the two fair heads blocked Nora's view, and she looked back to the crestfallen flier. Poor kid—no wonder he'd made a play for her. And a few thoughtless words had ruined it for him already. Maybe she could make it up to him.

"No wonder General Eisenhower trusts you fellows with his dog. You really get right down to business, don't you?"

Praise worked. He grinned again but checked his torrent of words. "I thought you were listening back there. I noticed you right away because of the dress."

His eyes darted below her chin but slid quickly back and the blush returned. "You look very nice."

One hand automatically lifted like a shield but Nora redirected it until the miniature pencil sharpener hanging on the gold chain around her neck bit into her fingers. "I'm glad to hear that since it's the only dress I brought over."

Damn that seamstress, anyway, for dropping the neckline when she removed the shoulder pads and cut the sleeves down. Black was a versatile color when you only had room for a single dress, and it traveled well; one steaming shower wilted the creases. Nothing could wash out the bad memories that soiled it, though.

"Wow, you travel light. My sisters would die if they could bring only one dress to Europe."

"What do you suppose they'd say if they had to fly over in your bomber without even a real seat?"

"Did you really? Wish you'd been with me. All that flying over the ocean's pretty boring. Course it's better than taking a boat. Everyone at home sails, even my sisters. My brother's really good. I get sick but not when I'm flying."

It sounded as if Timothy's sisters were Eric's kind of girls. Why did she have to think of him now? Why couldn't she forget that the first time she'd worn this dress was the night they'd broken up? The only fizz in their celebration of her promotion to New York turned out to be in the champagne. Her glass went flat as he told her why she couldn't take the transfer. He started by telling, then he ordered and finally he forbade her to go. Had that been only three years ago? It seemed longer and ached like an old wound, and yet the sound of his voice rang fresh in her ear. A man in his position at the law firm could explain that his fiancée was killing time until the wedding. But transfers to New York smacked of careerism, which the partners wouldn't like. Before the decision on Eric's partnership, Nora must be at home with a good club membership and an acceptable charity.

A jostling elbow splashed whiskey onto Nora's stockings and wrenched her back to this party. "I say, I am sorry—" someone began before a surge of the crowd washed him past her and pinned her back against Timothy. Taller shoulders trapped her as every head in sight turned in the same direction. She couldn't see why.

"Silly Yank," someone to her left said.

"How'd that kid get in here, anyway?" she heard from somewhere behind.

The next voice was Timothy's, an urgent whisper in her ear. "Holy cow, it's Red. Matt'll kill me. I gotta stop it."

Nora still couldn't see but brought up her arms and headed toward the slurred insults now audible above the party's hum. The higher pitch of her voice sliced enough baritone conversations to part the crowd.

The redhead weaved forward, one hand outstretched to poke the Englishman's chest with each new taunt. "Ya fuckin' Limeys roll over and play dead soon's ya see a Kraut, right, buddy?"

Tim slipped past her as their other friend broke free of the tight ring of bodies crowding the quarrel as if it were a schoolyard fracas. Between them, the pair hustled the redhead away. Timothy's brother left his blondes across the room and followed the boys out the door.

One of the blondes caught Nora's eye and smiled, then headed toward her. Nora noticed the gray in her hair just as the woman offered her hand.

"So much for the alliance." The Englishwoman nodded gravely after the young man but Nora saw a glint of amusement in her blue eyes. "I'm Constance Tolliver, and I think you must be Miss Seymour. Will Davies described you to a T. I'm bunking down the hall from you at the Waverly."

Nora knew the name from hearing it pronounced with respect by serious-minded colleagues, the kind gunning for bylined columns on foreign affairs or national politics. *Manhattan* was too highbrow a magazine for her taste, but she knew Constance Tolliver's letters from London were influential. Her hair and hands, her civilized manner but especially her accent showed Nora right away that this Englishwoman had been born with a big dose of clout in her silver spoon. If the rumpled tweed suit was a little threadbare, it just proved she was too busy to shop. And only someone accustomed to understated elegance called staying at the Waverly Hotel "bunking."

But the best evidence of Constance Tolliver's position was her assurance as she crossed the crowded room. Although she was a civilian woman in a room jammed with uniformed men, there was no question Constance Tolliver belonged. Nora wished she'd stuck with her uniform instead of changing into the damned black dress. Compared to the Englishwoman's tweed suit, it fit in about as well as a Gestapo uniform at Buckingham

Palace. And that last splash of Chanel when Constance Tolliver wore no perfume left Nora smelling like a high-class tart on the prowl.

She panicked for a moment when, after they'd exchanged pleasantries, the dialogue stopped. Her uneasiness melted into gratitude when Constance steered the conversation onto common ground.

"There's a wizard masquerading as a bellboy at the Waverly, and he can conjure up anything subject to rationing. For a price, of course, so everything comes very dear. And he's quite particular about his clients, but an attractive young woman will be a welcome change from aging matrons like me. I'll introduce you straightaway."

A naval officer mumbled an apology as he cut between them. Nora swallowed a yelp when he stomped on her foot, but her words still sounded strangled in her ears. "Sounds like a handy fellow to know. Thanks."

"I noticed you with Colonel Chase's brother, Tim. Charming boy."

That definitely sent the conversation back to her court, leaving Nora grateful that Constance had lobbed her an interesting topic. The way the older brother dogged Timothy's heels like a belligerent terrier convinced her someone was getting bawled out in private and she hoped it wasn't her young friend.

"So it's Chase? We didn't get past first names before carrot-top started misbehaving. The brother looked pretty sore about it."

"I expect he was. He's at SHAEF and likely wants no trouble. He'll tell the boy to mind his manners and that'll be an end to it."

"I hope you're right. Is he—the older one—a flier, too?"

"His name is Matthew, and he was an infantry officer, I believe. He fought in North Africa and Sicily. I'm not quite sure what it is he does at Norfolk House. It's all very hush-hush, you know. But he did graduate West Point."

Nora smiled and nodded. Perfect! If she could snag an introduction, the evening might not be a total waste. Constance half turned away to politely refuse an offered lift. She accepted lunch on Thursday with a distinguished-looking man, a civilian clutching a bowler and umbrella in one hand and her fingers in the other.

Hadn't Timothy said something about his brother's date? Nora studied the Englishwoman over her glass of Scotch and decided she must be at least ten years older than Matthew. And she wore a wedding ring. She could be a widow, after all. Or... Maybe a taste for older women ran in the Chase family.

Rolling the whiskey over her tongue, Nora glanced around the room. God, it was smoky. Chase wasn't back yet. She turned to Constance again and found the Englishwoman returning her smile with genuine warmth. They shared the same business, but Nora was willing to bet the way they operated was very different. Lunching with diplomats was definitely this dame's style.

"You're not the giddy or giggly type, are you, Nora? May I call you Nora?"

Constance Tolliver had her full attention now. She nodded permission.

"London is a schoolgirl's dream—a plague of men. I find it's a bit tiresome, all the uniforms and high drama. Which is why I was delighted to learn you were coming over, and why I'm doubly pleased now I've met you. Most women still living in London are barely out of the schoolroom—lots of gigglers, you'll find. Yet one needs a break from the men and the war, don't you think? I hope we can be friends."

How long had it been since she'd had a real girlfriend? High school, maybe? When she'd started in newspapers, most women working in the city room were proofreaders, secretaries or stuck on the women's page, and an invisible barrier separated them because Nora was a hard-news reporter. In the beginning her isolation from other women bothered her. But the longer she was in the news business, the less she had in common with most women and the more she became one of the guys. She'd been counting on Will to be her buddy in London the way he'd been her buddy in New York. But he was different, somehow. Now Constance Tolliver wanted to be her friend, and she was flattered. With Will acting so strange, she could sure use one.

"Living in the same hotel and working in the same business makes us natural allies, I guess. And if every place in this town is as jam-packed with men as tonight's shindig, we'll both need all the friends we can get. I never could have guessed it bothered you. You seem right at home."

Constance raised her glass but didn't drink. The cocktail shielded her mouth from view as she cocked her head closer to Nora. Both gestures seemed unnecessary as the drone of merged conversations ensured no single exchange could be easily overheard.

"It's a bit like an endless house party in the country, I find, except without the distraction of other women and fashion to take your mind off the men's rivalries."

A graying officer slipped out of a nearby clump of men and smiled tentatively in their direction. Nora stared back, and when Constance kept stonefaced, too, he walked past.

"You'll find that it is war, war, war every moment but these officers aren't interested in winning dirty battles. Their only thought is winning a shining reputation. And your Yanks are as bad as our chaps. Everyone touts the general or scheme that will do him the most good, and I'm sick to death of it."

Nora couldn't help laughing. Usually women put their heads together about men to critique appearances or bank balances or future prospects. After Eric, those forecasts didn't interest her much; future prospects became a lot less important than immediate needs. And now Constance Tolliver had dismissed a room full of powerful men for the very crime men cited to dismiss women—concentrating on the trivial at the expense of the important. She liked the Englishwoman more every minute but didn't get a chance to say so because Matthew Chase was back and heading for them.

He didn't look happy. Darting glances, he worked his way across the room by stops and starts, but his nod of recognition didn't soften the hard line of his mouth. He probably had a cushy spot at SHAEF and worried that the scene caused by Tim's friend might endanger it. Obviously checking the room to gauge how his reappearance went over, he seemed the kind of officer Constance found objectionable. If she didn't like the guy, why was she here with him?

Constance wasn't with Chase, but he couldn't find his date. That became clear after the introductions when their speculation about where the missing woman might be gave Nora time for a closer look at him.

He really was like Eric and moved with the same athletic grace, which always surprised her in big men. Eric had honed his with tennis. Chase looked clubby, too, but the hand around his glass was callused, not polished and buffed. A crease of pale flesh scarring one temple marred the symmetry of his face and blended into the wing of silver streaked through his dark hair. His eyes searched restlessly before swooping down to corner her with his attention.

Constance Tolliver's abrupt departure left Nora fumbling for a ruse to keep Chase beside her long enough to make an impression. The Englishwoman ducked out after warning them that the competitive drinking would start as soon as the vodka for toasting arrived. Chase didn't look eager for more drinking, but his date hadn't turned up yet. Another Scotch was the last thing Nora's waistline needed, but she tossed down the rest of her drink and held out the empty glass.

"Would you blaze a trail for me, Colonel Chase?"

Grabbing the vent in his blouse to make sure she didn't lose him, Nora followed Chase away from the bar. Now she needed an opening. The patch on his sleeve caught her eye. She might as well start learning what the insignia meant right now.

"What's the red number one on your jacket stand for? SHAEF?"

Chase brought out his Camels before he answered. She took one, holding it to her lips while he tapped his against the gold lighter. His words streamed out on smoke.

"It's the insignia of the First Infantry Division—Big Red One, the reporters call it."

His voice carried a tone of challenge, but she ignored it. "I guess I heard wrong. I thought Constance said you worked at SHAEF."

"I do, for the moment."

Nora concentrated on her cigarette. His sharp gray eyes stared her down, making her jittery. She hated moments like this. Feeling the way toward common ground was excruciating, especially when Chase looked as if he knew what she was up to all the time. The worst part of every new assignment was getting started with sources. After a while the reporter could just lay it out. Saying what was needed and hearing it was the way Nora liked to work. Softening them up was tough and too often a waste of time. It felt that way now. But this guy wasn't sent to supreme headquarters for nothing. He might pay off.

"I guess it's quite a change for you. Must be exciting to be right in the thick of it all."

Damn. He didn't like that. Narrowed eyes and a deep drag of smoke underscored his displeasure. Acid etched it in stone.

"I thought you just got here, but I guess war correspondents have to be military experts. Of course you'd understand the insignificance of our sideshow in the Mediterranean. The really tough work is right here in London."

Nora choked on the smoke, and he thumped her between the shoulders, smiling down with cold eyes as patronizing as his words.

"Who the hell are you, Colonel? Maybe you can push your kid brother around, but I'm not your patsy."

"What's Tim got to do with this? Or with you?" Chase snapped back.

Her skin crawled and she clutched her purse tightly. Sounding like a bitch was better than feeling like a fool. No one walked over her with impunity, not after Eric. Only suckers made themselves doormats where other people could scrape off their gripes.

"He's a cute kid, and you've got no right to blame him for what that redhead said. You were way out of line again just now. I may be new over here, but I'm no rube from the sticks."

For a moment he just stared at her. The smile teasing the edges of his mouth annoyed her. He had no right to mock her. He acted as if she'd insulted him with her remark about London. Maybe he was more of a soldier than Constance thought. But even a soldier had to be nuts to prefer getting shot at to the safety and prestige of working for Ike.

"So you're riding to Tim's rescue as well as your own. That's commendable, but forgive me if I don't mention it to him. Since the army gave him a bomber, Tim has the idea he can take care of himself."

Leaping the distance between them, their shared laughter soothed the stab of foolishness Nora felt.

Chase spread his arms and shrugged. "You didn't deserve what I said. Sorry I laid into you."

"Me, too. I didn't mean anything by it. Just wanted to make conversation."

"Can we try it again from the beginning sometime? I have to get out of here before they waylay me for the toasting. But I'll call you. Connie's hotel, right?"

Nora debated leaving as she watched him circle the room again, probably looking for his elusive date. Good thing the girl had ditched him and given her a chance to sound him out. Nora couldn't leave until she was sure Chase had gone or she might run into him again outside. Rushing a source usually backfired, and this fellow was touchy enough to start with.

A commotion near the door spread the crowd as two burly men carried tubs of ice to the bar. The generals followed with the Russian, clapping his hands and beaming smiles, leading less-eager American and British brass. A tray of skidding glasses balanced in the hands of a pleading waiter completed the bar's refitting.

Chase escorted a pretty girl out the door as the crowd surged toward the bar. It was the other blonde Nora had seen him with earlier. She hoped the girl would stick close to him from now on. She liked to keep business strictly business, although once in a while mixing work with fun was okay. But her job in London was too important to her future to take unnecessary risks or let anything get in the way. She needed inside sources of information without any avoidable complications. Matthew Chase looked like a good source, and that was all.

THREE

MOONLIGHT GLISTENING from puddled streets guided Matt as he steered the jeep through the darkened city. The yellow blackout devices atop the headlights weren't enough for a driver unfamiliar with the streets and driving on the left. Even handicapped by inexperience, he found it was good to drive again.

He glanced at the kerchiefed woman beside him. The rush of cold air smoky with winter's fires rouged her cheeks. If living through war rattled her convictions or forced doubt through the cracks in her self-assurance, it didn't show.

Funny that Monique had turned up here. Her name scrawled across the pad on his desk brought nothing to mind. Some old Frenchwoman who knew Mother from her suffragette days, Matt guessed. He returned the call immediately, planning to run the old lady through the hotel suite as interference to the orders that came with the damned invitation. Her young voice threw him off stride and asking her to dinner gave him time to recover. Then she mentioned their night in New York and he remembered it all. It was too late to back out. Picturing her face as he stared at his phone, he listened without giving full attention. Probably Pearl Harbor caused it but, for some reason, he could remember every detail of his last piece before the war. The memory complicated the evening.

Monique tapped the arm controlling the wheel and he braked, easing in the clutch. Her breath tickled his ear as she leaned close.

"It is the next square to the..."

She drew the last word out into a groan as she struggled for the next. Finally she pointed.

"There. That way."

Matt rounded the corner too fast, and the speed flung her against him. He stopped the jeep to prop her upright. Swaying toward him, she smiled an invitation. Grinding gears lurched the jeep forward.

Oh, hell, why not? They both knew what to expect. No awkwardness would mar the pleasure. Monique Diderot was lovely, and he remembered she felt wonderful. But the feeling was all in his fingertips, and it wasn't enough anymore.

Monique signaled wildly with a hand in front of his face, and squealing brakes pitched them forward. Matt hopped out and helped her down. She caught his hand between both of hers as he stepped back.

"Come upstairs for brandy. It is still quite early."

He gestured toward the jeep with his free hand. "Motor pool needs the jeep, and I have a little work left on my desk."

Shadows masked her eyes, but Matt detected the barest whine of hurt in her voice as she thanked him again for dinner. He wanted to explain it to her but couldn't force the words out. A few campaign bars were all the justification most women in England seemed to need to solemnly revere the man hiding inside the uniform. Talk about combat just started them clucking in sympathy.

Sympathy was the second to last thing he wanted from her.

Maybe European women couldn't forget that today's veteran campaigner might be tomorrow's stiffening corpse. If that was the problem, American women didn't share it. Nora Seymour stood her ground, no hint of sympathy weakened her attack. He recognized the moxie in the way she'd followed him without a trace of subservience, confidence unruffled by the leering attention of young officers she'd passed.

She stood out against Monique's simple elegance and Connie's aristocratic coolness. Their blond heads paled next to her hair, so dark and glossy that his first impulse was to loop it around his hand. She was vivid, and so wonderfully American that he realized for the first time that his dislocation came from foreign lands as much as foreign wars.

Matt took it easy on his way to headquarters but still got lost. The buildings dropped away suddenly, and the jeep was over the bridge before he realized what it was. Swinging into a cross street, he downshifted to a crawl and searched for an opening to the river. Moonlight lucked him on to the only dry place on the splintered dock, and he fished out cigarettes and lighter. Oil fumes drowned whatever salt tang made it that far up the Thames. He welcomed the gentle sound of water slapping against the pilings.

Maybe ignoring his natural inclination for sailing was a mistake. Combat in the army juiced you up and the lulls were a real letdown. The daily risks of life at sea probably evened out the low points between combat for naval officers. But dying must be hard after a torpedo, men panicked and helpless in the ocean's grip. Plenty went into the water whole and unhurt but as doomed as the wounded who flailed through pain. Pain was the mercy of the bullet; death easier to accept for a dogface in agony than a tired sailor treading futility in the water. Besides, not one of their ships could make the kind of difference a lone division could and often did.

The butt sizzled out after tracing a glowing curve into the river. He guessed his angle came close to the trajectory needed for maximum distance with artillery. That was another problem with the navy. One mistake could be awfully expensive, a ship and entire crew lost or the wrong target blasted away by guns fifteen miles offshore. His mistakes cost lives, too, but in the army you could try to keep the costs down. Sometimes navy men were helpless victims of circumstance praying for rescue. The navy was worse if only because the sea was a variable no man could control. Control, after all, was the key.

Light tore the darkness outside the motor pool garage when a door banged open in answer to his horn. "Run good for you?"

The soldier's salute was as indifferent as his question, but Matt didn't mind. His arm ached from saluting all the damned ranks above him at Norfolk House. Strictly enforced decorum took a little getting used to.

"Ran fine, but I got lost and used more gas than I expected. I filled up from the can in back. Seen a flier around?"

The soldier cocked his head toward the wall of the house looming over them in the courtyard darkness. "Pointed him toward your office, Colonel. He wanted to know if we got anything heading out toward his base. You tell him I got a truck stopping here in fifteen minutes but it don't wait, sir."

Blackout curtains sealed twilight inside the empty corridors and stairway leading to the basement office. Tim waited by the door, leaning against the jamb, with arms and ankles crossed. The hat pulled low on his forehead showed the free-form flop characteristic of fliers. Removing the internal skeleton in a harmless display of individualism lumped fliers into a new herd. Only thirty-six hours in England and already the kid was shedding obedience to the rigid discipline demanded in his eighteen months as a cadet.

Matt gave his brother's upper arm a squeeze and led the way into his office. Aiming his lamp's cone of light on the desk in the opposite corner, Matt snapped on the radio, twisting the dial until he heard a moody saxophone. Jazz was better thinking music than the swing that dominated the rest of the dial. Good thing the English liked jazz. This station alternated music with cryptic readings even civilians knew were messages to the underground in Europe.

"I share this place with a Georgia boy, Major Hart. The radio is his, and does he ever bitch when he finds it tuned away from the crooners. Says he hates this tribal music as much as he hates the monkeys who made it."

"Sounds good to me, whatever it is. Say, listen, Matt. I feel pretty bad about what happened back there."

"Forget it, Timmy. I just wish I could have talked those MPs out of taking your friend to the guardhouse to sleep it off."

Matt gently pushed Tim into a chair and swung himself onto another he turned backward so he could rest his elbows on the high back. "They'll boot him out first thing in the morning. But he'll think twice about getting that drunk again when he catches hell from your squadron leader for overstaying his pass."

Matt let Tim know he could hitch a ride back to base and asked about his work, measuring the eager bomber pilot against the kid brother he said goodbye to in 1942. That boy's life had centered on what effect Ted Williams's batting average might have on the Bosox's chances for the pennant. When their mother's anguished letter said he had quit Harvard to join the Army Air Corps, Matt wondered if, underneath it all, Tim was simply following his baseball idol into patriotic service. Now, with a zeal typical of his headlong plunge through life, Tim's main interest seemed to be getting started on the twenty-five bombing missions needed to complete his tour. That and comparing the relative merits of English versus American girls.

"She's an absolute stunner, Matt. All peaches and cream on top and really built down below." Matt sank his head into the crook of his elbow to hide his grin when Tim kissed his fingertips and sighed out her name. "Hillary."

"You work pretty fast, Tim. I'm impressed."

"Oh, I haven't met her yet. Just seen her across the tap room. Her parents run the inn and pub near the base."

Tim hadn't been overseas long enough to need an American girl. Maybe he never would. Matt couldn't remember the last time he'd gone out with one. When the division first came to England, before the invasions in the Mediterranean, no Stateside girls had been around. The English were so happy to have America in the war that they invited the boys into their homes, especially the officers. He'd been cocky then, too, loving the adventure and eager to fight. His taste for combat was different now, and he didn't want constant reminders. He wanted to forget for a while, but the English wouldn't let him. Rationed food, wrecked homes and blacked-out streets were their daily lives. He couldn't blame them for being serious when their homeland was the front line. But right now he preferred American girls fresh from the States. Nora Seymour's unaccented Midwestern twang was one way he could get home for a while without taking the trip.

Tim turned down the cigarette Matt offered. "I need all my wind for base running. We'll be playing here in Hyde Park in a few more weeks." He started a detailed description of the Eighth Air Force lineup, and Matt drifted back to Nora Seymour.

Reporting meant she'd know what he was talking about if he mentioned the Red Sox. Her job was okay as long as she didn't expect to mine him for news. Not that he knew anything. His description of the Normandy coast would be a worthless contingency if the army went ashore somewhere else. Connie mentioned feature stories, which wasn't the stuff coming out of Norfolk House, anyway. Better a reporter than a nurse or Red Cross girl who saw the gore every day. But once Nora Seymour got a good look at London she'd need a few laughs. God knows he did.

Tim rattled off statistics of the guys he'd be playing ball with once the season got under way, but Matt couldn't force his thoughts onto the game. Spectator sports were nothing compared to the competition that already existed among army officers in London. No way he'd get roped into another dull party. Dinners were worse here than back in the States, even without the officers' wives. His superiors expected the same deference, and the younger officers touted America's invincibility endlessly. None of them had seen the humiliating mess Rommel left behind when he'd finished with them in the Kasserine Pass or the bloody shreds of American fliers torn out of the Sicilian sky by guns fired from their own ships. In London army officers fought the war with a barrage of files and reports fired from office to office. The men puffed up with their own importance, egged on by English girls who wanted to believe because they had a brother or boyfriend fighting overseas. Matt couldn't imagine Nora Seymour fawning over their boasts.

Tim's chair scraped across the floor and Matt stood, swinging his aside. "I better get going or I'll miss my ride."

Reaching for the hand Tim offered, he nodded and pulled the boy into a quick embrace. "Keep your eyes open up there, Timothy. Let me know whenever you get into town."

Tim was halfway down the hall when Matt turned him back with a question thrown from the door. "Did you see the folks before you left?"

Tim danced from foot to foot. "I saw Mom and the girls but Dad was in Washington."

He looked away and Matt waited for the rest. "We had a nice holiday, anyway."

Matt stepped forward. "You mean he stayed in Washington for Christmas? They weren't in session." Tim shrugged but didn't meet his eyes. "That bastard."

The boy's head flew up. "Don't, Matt—"

The sheen of unshed tears in Tim's eyes held back the fury brimming in Matt's heart. It wasn't Tim's choice to be the battleground between him and his father.

"Get going, Tim."

Matt watched until his brother climbed the stairs, and then turned back to his office. Balancing the light on a corner of the desk, Matt lined up his maps until the shoreline of the nautical chart matched the shoreline on the topographical map. An overlay webbed with roads and villages put the people into his view of the French coastline. He hoped his earlier stop at the river had primed his memory with a fresh waterfront sound or smell to carry him back to that boyhood summer in France. Arms braced at the outer edge of the desk, he drew a deep breath and let it out slowly as he concentrated on the maps.

Nothing floated up. The maps and charts were ludicrous, and so were his orders. One heavy gale could resculpt a shoreline beyond all recognition. And the beach he remembered was free of tangled steel barriers and concrete pillboxes. Numbers and swirled lines blurred as he deliberately unfocused, forcing a clearer picture into his mind's eye. Warm sun, pebbled beach and high bluffs broke free, but the picture was as lifeless as a scenic snapshot. Why couldn't they just listen to French Maquis intelligence instead of expecting total recall from him after one glance at these stupid charts? And how many others were working on similar projects, stupid projects, just because they had once walked what *might* be the invasion beach? Trust the army to double and triple it up for safety's sake. In 1928 he'd spent maybe five minutes familiarizing himself with the few charted hazards between Cherbourg and Le Havre. That summer he'd concentrated on the stinging wind lifting whitecaps across the bow of his ketch as it plowed the English Channel. And on the fruity taste of Norman Calvados Jules had hidden in a hollow log behind the beach.

Where behind the beach? How could it be behind the beach? He remembered the pull of the ketch against his arm as it scraped across the stones to higher ground. He heard Jules shout through a screen of bushes hiding the mouth of a gully. He felt fresh water wash the salt spray from his face. The grass was cool and the apple brandy fiery. They must have followed the gully. But how far? Where did it lead? Would fences trip up men on foot? Could a tank make it through?

A knock fractured the memory and the shadowed gully dissolved. Matt growled at the intruder, a hand held up to stop further interruptions as he bent over the map. His finger found Aunt Ellen's farm and traced his usual route to the boat yard. Jules sometimes finished morning milking early enough to walk along with him. Three ravines opened to their favorite stretch of beach, one arrowing straight for the farm. Knowing he must have waited there for Jules or even taken the shortcut with his friend relieved the frustration. Hell, he'd get it all now. Matt's waggled fingers invited speech.

"Please, sir. Looking for Major Hart's office, sir."

His eyes snapped toward the soldier standing at rigid attention, a trench coat crushed in his black fist. This one was wise to be careful, especially when he opened the door to find an imperious hand raised in silent command. Americans in England were touchy about their Negroes. And Hart's viciousness was notorious.

Waving a hand to relax the soldier, Matt pointed to the desk with the radio. "If it's damp, spread it out. Won't do much good in this dungeon, anyway."

"Yes, sir." The soldier cocked his head toward the radio. "Might bury the music." He hefted the raincoat like a fisherman judging the weight of his catch. "Pretty heavy, too, sir."

The raincoat swung into the desk with a tinny thud when Matt grabbed it. "Sounds like Hart forgot his flask."

ALLIANCES 45

The soldier shrugged ignorance as Matt sniffed the fumes and took a drink. Hart would have hounded this boy unmercifully for wrinkling his coat. His taste in liquor was terrible, too.

"Good thing it's gin. Little water and Hart won't know we've been into it."

He offered the flask to the Negro who hesitated, wiping his hands down his pants. Matt bit back the urge to demand the soldier taste it, but an impatient jiggle of the flask decided it. He gestured for him to drink again, and the soldier grinned. Corking the flask after a final slug, he slipped it back into Hart's coat.

"I'll fill it up from the kitchen, soldier. Don't worry."

The door eased closed and Matt threw the raincoat across Hart's desk. He was a pain-in-the-ass bootlicker, anyway. A stickler for military decorum, Hart never overlooked a tie askew or dusty boot. His whining scolds had grated on Matt's nerves until he finally chewed Hart's ass after he found him bawling out another enlisted man. Hart's love for the mindless paperwork he shuffled efficiently across his desk reminded Matt of his father. The congressman hid his political impotence behind a similar flurry of letters to voters, appeals to conscience and essays published but rarely heeded.

Smoking a cigarette focused his mind on the charts again, but thoughts of the congressman shoved more important memories aside. He should have kept sailing and not cut short his vacation that summer to travel with his father. Hell, none of it mattered now.

Forgetting the past was easy for those eager for the future. Temporary duty in London quashed that. Someone else got his battalion and he ended up promoted to a desk job. Sitting around writing reports from the damned charts would soften him up. The newest replacement would be toughened by the training in the Salisbury Plain by the time he rejoined the outfit. They had to send him back soon, before some green officer had a chance to lead them into trouble.

Scuffing feet outside the door launched Matt for the radio, but it was already off. No, the electric buzz of dead air meant tonight's readings were starting. Major Hart could shove his objections. He yanked open the door and found the colored soldier instead, a canteen in his hand this time.

"Never trust an officer, eh, soldier?"

"You said it, sir, not me."

The radio came alive as Matt drew the flask out of Hart's coat. "Heidi's grandfather milks his goats morning, noon and night except on Christmas Day." The announcer's voice pronounced the words with monotonous precision. It sounded like a book code, which usually took a while. Matt clicked off the radio without retuning it.

"That nonsense not worth hearing, sir. You ask for Joe at motor pool if you want to see that jazz. I know the place."

Matt uncorked the flask and handed it to Joe. "I'll do that."

He watched the soldier sip, wishing he could tell Hart who helped him guzzle his gin. Matt took a mouthful, washing it around before he swallowed. He refilled the flask from the canteen, shook it and tasted again.

"I've had better gin from bathtubs, but it'll do."

FOUR

DRONING INSECTS SWEPT THROUGH the humid summer afternoon of Nora's dream and roused her to a chill winter midnight. A sultry prairie buzz lingered in the London darkness beyond her hotel window. The sound sparked her curiosity, drawing her out from the cozy burrow under the eiderdown. She hunched her shoulders against the cold air of the room and rubbed the blue-striped flannel covering her arms as her curled toes led her to the window.

Before her fingers reached the blackout shade the night erupted. A far-off rumble dueted with a hollow pop-pop-pop until screeches and wails overwhelmed all else. Nora yanked back the heavy curtain and for a moment her dream returned. The distant flashes seemed like lightning heralding a summer storm except for the searing blood-red core of each explosion.

An ocean of dark rooftops shielded her from the threat. Distance lent the inferno a terrible beauty that held her, numbing fear and reporter's instincts. Pillars of light searched among clouds that shimmered pink as the fires below took hold. Flame and light etched silver along the barrage balloons floating between the raiders and their target.

A whine shrieked closer, a sound recognized from a dozen wartime matinees. Why had the plane strayed? Was it really falling, diving toward the Waverly?

"Holy Christ!"

The sound launched her toward the door. Panic built as clumsy fingers fumbled with the key. The engines screamed. Terror hollowed her belly and soured her mouth. The key jammed. Nora dove for the bed. One knee tumbled a bedside stand, shattering a lamp. Glass shards tore her knees as she crawled under. She wedged her arms over her head and howled as the plane roared in.

And passed over, its deafening thunder dissolved into the air-raid pandemonium. Nora's howl drained into a moan as relief collapsed the muscles she'd braced against attack. Her heart pounded on. Fright dampened the hair under her fingertips with sweat and now her scratched knees stung. Her lungs burned. She inhaled a noseful of dust and a sneeze caught her just as a brisk knock sounded at the door. She jerked her head up, smacking her skull against the wooden bed slat.

"Oh, Christ." Remembering the glass, she wiggled out the other side. Holding the nightgown clear of the blood seeping from a dozen scratches, she threw open the door and met Constance Tolliver's startled eyes.

"My dear Nora, what a fright you've had. And all for nothing, I'm afraid."

"Nothing! That damned plane sent me under the bed. You must have heard it."

"I did, indeed, and sprinted the hall to tell you. The bombs are falling streets away, near the Thames basin, I should think. The plane was a bit closer."

Nora raked dusty fingers through her hair. The city was quieter now. "What time is it?"

"A little past midnight, I expect. It doesn't take long, you know. Not like the blitz when it went on and on and on. They haven't the aircraft, so it's over in just a few minutes. But there'll be more later."

"Oh, great." Nora held out shaking hands. "I'll be mush before morning. Shouldn't we go to the shelter? There must be one downstairs somewhere."

"Not to worry, Nora. One gets used to it. One's ear attunes itself and judges the distance."

Suddenly dizzy, Nora swayed against the doorjamb, hands clutching for support. Constance grasped her outside arm with firm fingers.

"You are done in. Let's get you cleaned up in my room while someone sweeps up in here. I'll pour you a nice stiff drink."

The hot tap on the corner basin brought only tepid water, but it was enough to clean the grime from Nora's face and hands. She had tomboy knees again. Complete with iodine streaks Connie insisted on painting there herself.

Dropping into one of the two armchairs in the room, she sipped a whiskey. The first swallow began to melt the knot of apprehension in her chest. The stuff was top drawer. She could hear Connie murmuring to someone outside the door and reached for the bottle on the table beside her. Glenfiddich. She didn't know the brand. Replacing it, her fingers fished between two delicate porcelains and came up with a photograph framed in silver. A young Connie, free of the lines that now crinkled the skin around her eyes and mouth, smiled out from between a man and two children, a boy and girl. The man was a bit older, with a silvered mustache and a belly running to fat under his vest. The children were like children anywhere, clearly uncomfortable posed stiffly for a family portrait. The boy's strain was unrelieved by the impish humor gleaming in the girl's eye.

After placing the photo back among the figurines, Nora surveyed the room, wondering why she didn't rate the deluxe accommodations. She dug her bare toes into a good Oriental carpet spread in the sitting area. It was lots warmer than her digs. Maybe IP was skimping since the overseas staff living on expenses had grown so large. She could do without the yellow-flowered chintz covering the window and bed. It reminded her of the old bedroom over the drugstore. Mom collected those awful figurines, too. She fingered the fragile lines of one and realized Connie's were a lot better china than Mom's dime-store collection. Likely Josie had replaced her cheap stuff with a better grade since the new war plant in Kincaid brought in more customers and more dough. A sudden vision of her father wandering among endless knickknacks filling the big new house on Woodbine Boulevard sent Connie's china piece back to its spot a little too hard.

Nora helped herself to a Dunhill from the box on the desk and glanced over the sheets of longhand piled on the green blotter. A board in the hallway squeaked. She waved the burning cigarette when Connie came through the door. "Hope you don't mind."

Graying blond hair flew away from the Englishwoman's face when she shook her head. "No."

Nora nodded around the sitting area. "You've got all the comforts of home."

Laughter trilled out and the hair took flight again. "Actually, you're right, you know. When I moved here they let me bring some pieces from our house at Wickenden Square. Quite a comfort to have familiar things about."

"You've got a house in London, but live here?"

Settling into the other chair, Connie straightened the lavender cardigan shawled around her shoulders. "A time bomb hit a home adjoining our back garden, so I had to leave until it detonated. My housekeeper took fright at that and moved in with her sister in Devon. To wait the Hun out, she said." She shrugged. "It seemed foolish to keep the place open just for me."

Nora pointed to the photo. "And your family?"

Connie took up the portrait, stroking the frame. "The twins—Geoffrey and Adair—we sent to America in '41 to stay with friends in New York until the bombing was over. You saw tonight why I can't bear to bring them back yet. They're sixteen now. I have a more recent snap."

She crossed to the bedside table and returned with another picture, wallet sized and unframed. "They sent it at Christmas."

Beyond three years' growth, the kids seemed to have a new manner, more relaxed, grown up. Adair was a funny name for a girl, but there was something familiar about it, too. She handed the photo back and dragged deeply on the Dunhill, hoping Connie would fill the silence. She wanted to hear about the man.

"Jeremy's in Delhi, has been since '42." Connie frowned. "When we jailed all the Congress leaders over that 'Quit India' business, a call went out for volunteers to fill the civil service. And off he went."

"That's rough."

Probably it was hard for Connie. Nora was used to living alone and traveling a lot. The only person she'd ever really missed, really longed for, was Dad, and she'd got over that years ago. Once in a while she still felt a twinge and called him at the store. She knew he liked having her all to himself without Mom horning in, even if it was just a phone call. The sound of his voice and their chatter always soothed her. But there'd be no trunk calls from London, that's for sure. And poor Connie—that meant she probably hadn't even talked to her kids in three years.

"You must really miss them all."

"Yes, well, there is much we all miss but we must make do. And what about you—so far from home?"

Nora ground out her cigarette and laughed. "I'm used to it. IP had me trotting all over the map once the war started. I did basic training in the Carolinas, shipbuilding in Boston, airplane factories in California and Jap internment camps in the desert."

Connie grimaced and leaned forward. "Those horrible camps. I read your stories. It must be dreadful."

Nora pushed against the chair, stretching her arms above her head as she fought off a yawn. "I suppose. Seemed nuts to me that the Japs out west are locked up while the ones in New York go about their business."

A vision of freckled faces topped with mops of brick-red hair came to her, and she chuckled. "You know, I met one family they locked up because his grandmother or grandfather or somebody way back was part Japanese. He was as Irish as Paddy's pig and the whole family had red hair and freckles."

"I don't recall reading that."

"You didn't. The desk cut it and ruined that day's piece. They really butchered my copy trying to repair the damage."

Nora pushed out of the chair and thanked Connie for the drink. She paused by the door. "So you read my stuff, huh? I didn't know it was picked up over here."

"*Manhattan* bundles over cuttings. Quite a lot of yours, actually. It helps me gauge America's mood."

"Right, I know. Up the alliance and all that. IP has the same idea for me. I may dig through back issues of *Manhattan* for ideas."

Connie laughed and crossed her arms as she leaned back against the door. "No need for that. You'll find endless opportunities. I'll show you tomorrow. Come with me to the zoo."

For a moment Nora thought she was joking, but Connie was serious. She said Londoners crowded the Regent's Park Zoo on fine days. It was one of the few amusements left in town, although it had been badly damaged in air raids.

"I'm told in the worst days the zookeepers regularly feasted on exotic fare."

Nora felt her face drain of color. There was something about slaughtering those helpless caged animals. "I guess I'd pass on that kind of supper."

"Yes, well, fresh meat is fresh meat. And I imagine more than one keeper attacked his portion with special relish because the creature was particularly nasty to care for. They're not all wildlife lovers, I'm sure."

It might make a good column, at that. And she definitely needed the outing. "Sounds like fun, but I'm still not sure that's what Will had in mind for a 'slice of life.'"

GERMAN BOMBS HAD FLATTENED the Monkey Hill months earlier. Nevertheless Constance stopped beside the crater each time she visited the zoo. She came back because Regent's Park was one of the few happy places left in London. At each turn in the walkway she could pretend the twins had just scampered out of sight, pretend she was not so alone. She told herself she paused at the site of the Monkey Hill to see if they were rebuilding, but she knew nothing like that could begin until after the war.

Sniffing the air for a promise of spring, Constance retraced her steps up the path toward the fork where she'd left Nora. Nothing but fresh ashes and old dust on the gentle wind today. The odor was the main reason she loved the Monkey Hill so, and why the twins preferred other spots in the zoo. The smell reminded her of the monkey tribe that had lined up each morning on the garden wall of Smithson's bungalow in Delhi. That was years before Geoff and Adair were born. Then there had been only Jeremy to worry over. When she'd brought Jeremy to the Monkey Hill she discovered the animal's self-abuse embarrassed him. How that had amused her. Once she'd grown used to their whispered joining, natural things no longer bothered her. But Jeremy went through life constantly verging on embarrassment, poor chap.

She reached for a spidery branch of crab apple and checked for buds. Nothing showing yet, so spending weekends in London didn't mean her garden at Corniche was suffering. She longed to inhale the scent of jasmine grown in her own greenhouse, but those plants were gone. Perhaps Jeremy was breathing in the fragrance somewhere in Delhi. Had he learned yet to appreciate the wonderful smell of India, that heaven and earth mingling of jasmine and excrement?

At the fork in the path, Constance paused to scan the compass until she spotted Nora amid a group of Yank soldiers loitering near the elephant compound. No need to hurry, Nora had a pleasant diversion. She stopped to watch a bird grubbing in the lawn, a tiny wren. Digging out a stale cracker from her bag, she tossed it to the hungry thing. The parrots in India were another delight that Jeremy didn't comprehend. How she'd loved it all. And how she'd hated it, too. He'd found nothing to love—not in Cal' or Lahore or 'Pindi or Bombay. Jeremy had been as shocked as she by their visit to India and had urged her to write that other bloody book. Pure stupidity, that. It just fanned the flames ignited by the publication of *Judgment*.

But that was then. And now—somewhere, somehow—Jeremy had changed. Nothing great, but just enough to make it possible for him to traipse back to India to do his bit for the king-emperor while Gandhi and the rest rotted behind bars. Suddenly he must save the Raj he had despised, and leave her at home alone, without the children or even Wickenden Square. Blast him.

She nodded and waved back across the lawn to Nora, quickening her steps on the gravel walkway. Puffs of dust shot ahead of her feet. Her shoes were sadly scuffed but she hadn't the heart to buy a new pair, which someone else likely needed more. Or to dig out a fresh set from the boxes piled in her closet at home. Nor could she bring herself to donate the lot of those to the needy. It was too late; she'd look a fool for waiting so long.

An elephant trumpeted and Constance slowed. This was the twins' favorite spot, but the huge beasts distressed her. Even today she could still feel the ponderous roll of the elephant ride in Agra, still remember that stab of shame when she saw the Taj that night, lit only by moonlight. What blind arrogance to claim that India was in need of British civilization. The Taj was the image she used to open the India book and that was the night she decided to write it. Thank God no one remembered the bloody thing now that Jeremy had gone back. Living down *Judgment* was difficult enough.

Nora turned toward Constance with a grin and came the last few steps to join her. The shaken creature of last night had vanished. She envied Nora the seamless armor she erected after the air raid was past. Constance was so tired of it all, tired of hearing Mother tell her what an absolute brick she was. She felt more like a scrap of slate riddled with a thousand tiny faults.

A tug at her heel sprawled her into Nora's arms. The heel of one shoe had broken off. "Drat."

She scooped up the piece but it was beyond fixing. "Would you mind popping in to Wickenden Square to get another pair? It's quite near. I could make some tea."

"I'd love that, Connie. I'm even getting a taste for it."

NORA FIGURED Connie probably lived in a swank neighborhood, and she was right. The streets they walked were lined with trees and big houses of brick or stone. A touch of seediness had crept in, though. Rust streaked the granite curb protecting the front yards from the sidewalk, even though the iron fence that fitted into the square holes was gone. Stray papers or a handful of leaves mounded in a corner showed a carelessness with detail not usually seen in ritzy areas. And they hadn't passed any Sunday strollers.

"What's with the fences and where is everybody?"

Connie drew up at the question and looked around slowly, thoroughly. "How quickly we adapt to changed circumstances, like those poor zoo animals quite inured now to air raids. To my eye, everything here is in order. But you see how wrong it is."

Steadying herself on Nora's arm, Connie adjusted her broken shoe. "The fences were melted down for munitions ages ago. And by now all those old barns are surely empty. All these families have country homes."

Around the next bend they came upon the first sign of life, a blue-coated constable who half sat on the barricades blocking a shallow square. Connie tripped forward, clutching her throat. The policeman threw his smoke away when he spotted them and moved quickly to cut Connie off before she could see beyond the barricades. Nora hurried to Connie's side, taking her arm as the policeman told her.

"I'm awfully sorry, Mrs. Tolliver. It must have been stray explosives since they didn't follow with incendiaries. A mistake, in other words, a cruel mistake. With the gas turned off there was no fire to speak of."

Connie buckled for an instant and Nora squeezed her arm gently. But the Englishwoman was smiling when she turned toward her. "That's a relief. With no fire, perhaps we can rebuild."

Squaring her shoulders, Connie walked quickly to the barricade with Nora and the policeman trailing. Nora saw her grab the painted wood with both hands and finally look at the house herself.

The front rooms of the big brick home hung open to the street like an enormous dollhouse ready for a little girl unexpectedly called away. But there was no missing front to fit back on, just a spill of shattered brick and lumber sliced off one corner of Connie's home. One torn wall sprouted wires, a white sink hung free over the front yard and an elegant brocade love seat dangled one clawed foot over the pile of rubble eddied around the lilac bushes. Nora couldn't think what to do for Connie or to say to her and didn't like feeling so helpless.

The policeman cleared his throat, and Nora swung around after Connie. "The inspector's been by, ma'am."

Connie folded her arms and nodded. "What did he say, Spencer?"

The constable swiped off his hat, turning it around and around in his hands. "It's on the list. They'll be taking it down. I'm awfully sorry, Mrs. Tolliver."

Something flashed through Connie's blue eyes. "Well, don't be. Buck up, man. It's just an empty house and we can bloody well thank God the bombs smashed it instead of an occupied home or a hospital or even a mill or shop."

The policeman's eyes widened at her profanity and he cleared his throat again. Nora felt a surge of admiration for Connie. It was a terrific act and probably made them all feel better. She knew she did. Knowing Connie was going to tough it out, at least in public, relieved Nora because she didn't have to find meaningless words. This time Connie's smile even looked genuine.

"Turn your back a moment, Spencer. I'm going to nip in up the back stairs to pick out a few things. I won't go near the edge so you needn't worry I'll fall off. And if you turn away now, you can honestly say you saw nothing."

Neither the policeman nor Connie argued for long when Nora insisted on coming to help load up the half-dozen boxes they found in the garden shed. The force of the blast had tipped over furniture, thrown pictures and mirrors off kilter and knocked small pieces off shelves. After a quick tour downstairs, Connie got down to business sorting through mementos in the bedrooms. Nora lugged the filled boxes back to the shed.

"I'll find someone to cart this down to Corniche first thing tomorrow. I might have to pull a bit of rank. In this instance, don't you think it's justified?"

Nora agreed and took up the last box from the girl's room, Adair's room. Children's books, postcards, ragged dolls, a few seashells and a framed illustration of the Cheshire cat rounded out the treasures of the little girl who was now nearly a woman.

Connie wiped tears from her cheeks when Nora returned. "Silly of me to cry over this house. I've always hated it. It was in Jeremy's family, sticklers for tradition, you see, and he's a younger son."

A gentle hand stroked the satin coverlet on her daughter's bed, stirring up a cloud of plaster dust. "I was thinking about the night before the twins sailed. I combed Adair's hair after her bath, brushed it long after it was dry. 'Mummy,' she finally said, 'shouldn't I go to bed now?' It was terribly late and they had to leave at first light, but I was so frightened I didn't want morning to ever come. I kept seeing a Nazi torpedo sinking the boat. I'm sure I didn't sleep at all until their cable arrived from New York."

Connie spun slowly on her broken heel and surveyed the room a last time. Nora felt like an intruder.

"Let's have a look upstairs at my study."

The desk pushed under the window was tidy and surrounded by bookshelves. Nora almost groaned at the thought of hauling all the boxes down three flights of stairs to clean out this library.

"Damn, I forgot to bring up more boxes. I'll go now."

Constance stopped her with a hand on her arm. "No, I'll go. You must be exhausted. I've only some first editions of my books in here."

Nora studied the shelves, especially a section under glass, and picked out one book with a familiar dust jacket. The colors of the Union Jack had faded but she remembered it from a history course at College. *Judgment of Youth*. The author hadn't been Constance Tolliver when she'd written it. That explained why her daughter's name had sounded so odd and so familiar at the same time. Constance Adair, the outspoken pacifist critic of the First World War.

Opening the slim book, Nora saw that it was the first American edition, published in 1920 in Boston. Connie must have been very young. Nora couldn't remember much about the book except that it was passionate and persuasive and controversial. Had someone close to Connie died over there, or had she gone over as a nurse?

Flipping back to the inside cover to read the dust jacket, she sent an old clipping floating to the floor. Nora was reading the review when Connie came back, and she flushed like a kid caught at some forbidden naughtiness. She didn't know if she was embarrassed for herself for snooping or for Connie's being caught in such a public reversal. All she wanted was to get past this moment. Counting on Connie's good manners to rescue them both, Nora shut the book and offered it to her friend.

"I guess this is one for the box."

Connie hesitated before folding the book into her chest, holding it with crossed hands. "You must think me a monumental hypocrite."

"Forget it, Connie. Times change and so do people. You've got a rave review in there. But the point is I'm sure he's changed his mind, too. That doesn't make him a hypocrite or you, either."

Connie smoothed the clipping against the book. "I'd forgotten Benjamin Chase reviewed it. But you're wrong. He hasn't changed. Don't you remember? He voted to declare war—he's a congressman now—but he condemned it. He said it violated his conscience but was the will of his constituents. Offered to resign, I recall, but nothing came of that. And he was just reelected again."

Nora answered with a shrug. The explanation teased her memory, but those early war days had been too hectic for her to remember anything but her own stories. And she'd always avoided politics, especially national politics.

"Why, you even know his sons. Colonel Chase and—what was the lad's name?"

"You mean Tim Chase?"

"That's it—Tim. Benjamin Chase is his father. And he's no hypocrite. I lost a brother, you see, but as time goes on the hurt lessens, and now Geoff seems like a childhood dream. But Benjamin Chase lost an arm, and I suppose being maimed, living every day with a horrid stump, keeps it all fresh for him."

No wonder Matthew Chase was touchy. He probably got ribbed about his father all the time. It was a good thing to know, but the subject was probably better kept under her hat. Might make him difficult to cultivate for information. After all, with a family connection like that, he was already on guard. Anyone gunning for him had ready-made ammunition with his old man.

"I wonder what he's like? I mean, two sons in the service and he doesn't want to fight?"

Lifting the box of books, Connie led the way out. "I met him in the States years ago and then again just before the war."

She rested the box on the banister, steadying it with one hand. "I didn't lose faith in my earlier views until the Luftwaffe reached Dover, I'm afraid. In any case, Benjamin Chase is very distinguished and very cold. I didn't much like him although I agreed with him. He reminded me of an Old Testament prophet—wonderfully moral, but not much fun."

FIVE

NORA DODGED through the soldiers loitering outside the officers' mess in the Waverly dining room and headed for the elevators. The GI from Oregon had struck paydirt for her column when he found distant relatives still living on the family farm in Kent. But the trip had her running late for her date with Matthew Chase. Now that she had the notes for next week's first feature she could slow down on the column and look for some hard news to shake up the IP big shots back home. Will liked her copy, but no one in New York had cabled her praise. Yet. The elevator indicator showed both cars still near the top of the hotel, so she punched the button again for spite and trotted up the stairs.

The greasy aroma of pork chops faded by the time she rounded the third floor landing. Good thing half a sandwich from lunch was still stuffed in her bag. The cheese was dry to start with, but anything was better than the garbage the army served downstairs. After she'd eaten that for a few weeks, her waist could use the exercise. Snaring the sandwich and her keys, she bit through stale bread as she unlocked the door. It was tough swallowing without a drink.

Half out of her pants, she remembered the blackout curtain and hopped to the window to close it. Connie's cream blouse and her own new blue skirt hung from the mirror. Pushing the clothes aside, she knew at a glance she'd have to redo her face. At least there was hot water in the tap tonight. Her mascara supply was ample but cranking the lipstick up full showed she'd be out of Ridiculous Red soon. Where was her damned footlocker anyway? It had left New York before her and still hadn't shown up. If a German torpedo had sent it to the bottom of the Atlantic, she'd have to bribe somebody for replacements until a package arrived from home.

She snapped the lipstick closed and checked her face. Fast work but a decent job. Begging makeup from whoever handled that end of supply would make her look like an idiot, but she needed it. Her appearance was part of her job. That kid today had let her tag along because he liked having an attractive gal from home on his arm. And it worked out beautifully—the surprised delight of the aunt, the old-world homestead and the new-world boy, hands across the sea, the works.

The silk of Connie's blouse felt wonderful after the scratchy government-issue shirt she'd worn all day. The fabric-covered buttons at the wrists gave her some trouble, and she knotted a simple bow at the neck. Silk and bows weren't her usual things, but she was tired of slacks. Brushing the lip of the Chanel bottle from ear to ear, she moistened her fingertips and combed the perfume through her hair. She slid stockings carefully over the scratches on her knees and reached for the navy skirt. Good thing the girl who'd ordered it was Nora's size. Maybe she'd just forgotten ordering it or had second thoughts and was afraid the seamstress would make her buy it. And the extra inch of length hid Nora's cut knees.

London's drizzle had flattened her hair, but she only had time for a quick brush. Putting it up made her look like a schoolteacher, and anyway, she liked to feel it brush her shoulders. A dressier clip would do better than her sporty tortoiseshell barrette, but all the others were in her trunk. Probably on the bottom along with the damned *Titanic*. Better start a list of what she needed from Mom. A side part suited her narrow forehead, and she wasn't about to crop her hair for convenience. She hadn't joined the army. Veronica Lake was nuts to change her peekaboo style for braids as an example for Rosie the Riveters who might catch theirs in a machine. And look what the new style had done for the movie star's career. Nothing.

Nora took the stairs more slowly going down. Maybe she should have brought a notebook. Carrying one might put Matthew Chase on guard. In a pinch her memory served her well. Even if he could tell her anything important, they wouldn't get to specifics tonight. Tonight was for getting acquainted, finding out what work he did and what he might know. A squabble among the brass or new weapons or a dispute between the Allies over strategy sounded right. There was no hurry, anyway. It'd be nice to be out with a man instead of the guys from work.

The last soldiers were leaving the dining room mess, but Chase wasn't in sight. Buttoning her raincoat, Nora checked in the newsstand and bar before pushing out the revolving door to the street. Matthew hopped out of a jeep and swept his hand toward his wheels like a vaudeville magician saying "Presto."

"I brought you a scarf since I didn't rate a staff car tonight. There's a blanket under the seat if your knees get cold."

"I'll bet you were a Boy Scout."

He laughed and revved the engine, waiting for a knot of soldiers to clear the crosswalk in front of the jeep. The wind blew a trace of his spicy cologne to her. He'd said drinks, but Nora wasn't sure what the plan was.

"Where are we going, Colonel?"

He eased off the accelerator and turned to her. "Cut the colonel, will you? You're not in the army, thank God. I'm Matthew or Matt—take your pick."

"Yes, sir." She snapped a salute and had him laughing again. She liked the sound, rich and easy.

"You newshounds like jazz?"

Nora nodded. There might be dancing then, along with the drinks. "Sounds good if you'll save me a dance."

Matthew grinned. "You've got it. Let's go."

She grabbed for a handhold when the jeep took off but he shifted so smoothly through the gears that she relaxed against the seat, holding the scarf down with one hand and the skirt at her knees with the other. The stream of night air heavy with moisture tingled across her cheeks. She closed her eyes. Riding in the open jeep felt something like joyriding in a windowless jalopy or plunging through air on a Ferris wheel. She yanked off his scarf, and her hair lifted from her neck with a cool caress. A shiver of pleasure raced down her spine. It was like a brisk swim in the ocean without the trouble of getting wet. Nora settled in to enjoy the sensation.

Changing engine pitch warned her that the ride was over before the jeep rolled to a stop. Muffled music drifted through the night air. She scrambled down before Matthew could help her. As her eyes adjusted to the darkness, vague looming outlines sharpened into sagging warehouses.

"Why is it the best joints are always on the bad side of town?"

Matthew took her arm. "If you mean jazz joints, the answer's obvious. That's the colored side of town."

The place was jumping, from the wailing sax on a plywood stage spread across beer kegs to the jitterbugging kids on the dance floor and toe-tapping drinkers seated on mismatched chairs around wobbly tables. Matthew led her through air thick with beer and smoke. At the bar he ordered whisky but settled for ale. He glanced around the club, finally choosing seats in the corner farthest from the band. He tossed his cigarettes on the table and tried to fit himself into the small chair. Nora didn't want a smoke but watched him gently tamp his. His gray eyes met hers as one lean finger flicked a bit of tobacco off his lip. Nora turned toward the band and saw the musicians were all Negro, all uniformed.

She leaned toward him to be heard. "What is this place?"

"Just a club. There must be an enterprising supply sergeant behind it somewhere. I hear an English fellow saw all the black faces in our motor pool and figured there was jazz in there someplace."

Nora laughed and glanced at the other tables. Mostly enlisted men, but the place wasn't 21.

"This is nice. Ramshackle, but nice. I'd make a good story—London's answer to the Cotton Club."

He looked doubtful and pulled his chair closer to hers. His breath tickled her ear. "I think the dress is wrong."

"Oh, no. You haven't been home in a while. Everyone is in uniform, including the women. Red, white or blue with epaulettes is the latest fashion." She gestured at her own clothes. "The only women in gowns are on the stage. Even the fat cats have hung up their tuxedos and put on the blue suit. We're all in this together, you know. You can't even get away with mouthing the national anthem at ball games anymore. Everyone thinks you're a spy."

He gave her the laugh she expected. His eyes warmed. She felt funny leaning toward him while the music buried their conversation. Private yet public, and with a kind of intimacy she wasn't used to anymore.

"What I wouldn't give to see a Red Sox game." He shook his head and craned to see the band. Her fingers pulling his sleeve brought him back.

"Then we're enemies. I gave up on the Cubs when I moved to New York, and I'm a die-hard Yankee fan now."

He snuffed out his cigarette and sat back in his chair as the band headed offstage for a break. "That figures. No one with any sense would ask to be sent over here." A smile softened his words.

Here we go. *What does your mother think of your job?* She smiled back and kept quiet. She didn't owe him an explanation.

"Did you come looking for adventure?"

Nora shrugged, leaning elbows on the table. "I guess. It's the best story around, and that's what my business is all about."

He finished his ale. "And that's it?"

She reached for a cigarette, but his lighter beat her matches. "Oh, every story is more. But I only have about three hundred words and not much time. I leave the pontificating to Walter Lippmann."

He was laughing again.

"Or Connie Tolliver. *Manhattan* gives her all the space she needs to find the deeper meaning. IP wants it short

ALLIANCES

and wants it yesterday. Plenty of hometowns and heroes for the folks at home."

A few hours later, the band swung into a jazzy version of Cole Porter's "Night and Day," putting an edge on Nora's three-ale high. Dancing with Matthew made a new woman of her. Her men never liked to dance, and she seldom found a source ready to hit the dance floor. But she'd forgotten about work and the war tonight. He'd been telling her about slumming through jazz clubs in New York with other West Point cadets on weekend leave from the academy. She'd told him a couple of gangster stories, like the one about the time she ran into Al Capone at the circus just after the Feds had sprung him from the pen in Atlanta. Matthew was easy to talk to, and their silences weren't awkward. His hand rode her hip lightly. She liked the feel of his shoulder under her fingers and the occasional brush of his buttons against her silk blouse as they turned. What she liked most was his not being all over her, grabbing or stroking or squeezing. Definitely smooth. But now the band played a tune Eric had liked to hum, a habit that had driven her crazy. She would not think about Eric or his damned humming tonight.

Nora leaned in close. "How'd you find this place?"

Matthew cocked his mouth toward her ear. "Fellow in the motor pool told me about it. He's up there on piano."

Nora glanced at the Negro soldier playing the battered upright on the makeshift stage. "He's good. What's a piano player doing in the motor pool?"

He shrugged under her hand. "Most likely the army figured he'd be good with his hands and made him a mechanic."

They joined the applause when the band finished the number. Matthew looked at his watch. "Almost midnight. I better get you home before you turn into a pumpkin."

Nora laughed. "Not on your life. Everybody knows Cinderella's coach turns into the pumpkin."

He took her elbow, steering her toward their table. "I never was much for fairy tales. When I was a kid I liked historical stuff. You know, Johnny Tremaine, Francis Marion, Sitting Bull."

He helped her into her raincoat, and she tugged the sleeves of her blouse free. "Sounds like you were rooting for the wrong team. What about Custer?"

He took his hat from a chair and handed over her purse. "Custer was a jerk to get his outfit wiped out."

They paused outside to get used to the darkness. Nearby a soldier pressed his girl up against the brick wall of the old factory. His slurred words carried.

"Come on, baby. I'm going over there any day now. You want me to be a happy warrior, don't you?"

Nora muffled a giggle under her hand and took Matthew's arm. She balanced on tiptoe so her whisper would reach his ear. "Sounds like he saw *Gone with the Wind* once too often. That's Rhett Butler's line."

He laughed out loud. "It worked for Gable."

"Anything works for Gable. All he has to do is show up."

The door banged open behind them, spilling couples into the night. Light spangled across wet pavement until the door swung shut. Matthew led her up the street, warning her away from puddles. He tucked the blanket over her knees and climbed into the jeep. The motor caught on the fourth try, and he let it idle. The flare of his lighter spotlighted his face for an instant. She took the Camel he passed. The image of his frown lingered in her mind.

"Are you staying or going when the time comes?"

The tip of his cigarette glowed brighter. "Staying."

No wonder he seemed gloomy all of a sudden. He'd almost taken her head off when she'd brought up his headquarters assignment at that party. "And you're disappointed."

His butt sailed over the windshield as he gunned the engine, warming it up. "Hell, yes, I'm disappointed. I've been through two invasions with my outfit, and missing this one makes me madder than hell. That sounds asinine, I know. But they've got a job to do, and I want to be in on it. This one will make the others look like a cakewalk."

The jeep jerked into motion, swung around a corner, then steadied into a fast ride. So his outfit was going in first. What had he called it—the Big Red One? Will had mentioned it when the guys in the office talked about the invasion and who'd go first. That division had been over here for the first war. Eisenhower had a special name for the unit, but she couldn't remember what it was. It wouldn't be hard to find out. It wasn't much of a story, but it was a start. Might make a good column. If Matthew was staying in England, he must be doing something important at supreme headquarters. After an evening with him, she didn't know any more about it than when he'd picked her up. Christ. It'd been fun tonight, but not much use.

The jeep swung over to the curb in front of the Waverly. Matthew started to get out, but she waved him back. "Don't bother. This jeep might turn into a pumpkin if you turn it off. Sounds like the piano player has some work to do."

"You win. Listen, I had a good time tonight. I'd like to do it again."

She couldn't see his face, but his voice sounded as if he was smiling. Better leave things on a light note. "On one condition. Next time, pick me up inside. My father never let me go out with boys who honked from the curb, and the rule still applies."

CONSTANCE LAID ASIDE HER PEN and lit a Dunhill. The words wouldn't come right tonight. Writing had never been easy for her, except *Judgment* and the India book. Those sentences had flowed across her pad in a tide of amateur outrage, a youthful enthusiasm that ebbed after washing over the complex muddle of historical truth. She longed for the simplicity of ignorance lost to her when the intellectual set in London took her up. She read the books they gave her and heard the lectures they endorsed but couldn't share their conclusions. The whole lot was a bit too Bolshie for her taste. She wasn't sorry when they drifted away after she started writing for *Manhattan* in 1935. Writing articles for America had seemed safer and certainly easier than continuing to brave the fratricidal battlefields of the political set. The war made writing difficult again.

She couldn't tell Americans that the English were deliriously happy to be overrun with soldiers from New York or Kansas or California. That might be what the Yanks would like to hear, but it simply wasn't true. Not anymore. England's initial excitement at the arrival of those well-fed and well-armed troops had given way on closer acquaintance to wary hospitality. There was some envy from knowing American privates earned as much as British officers and wore khakis that made England's Tommies look like jumble-sale refugees in comparison.

The Yanks' welcome gaiety turned to lawlessness when the Americans filled the towns with drunken brawlers who seduced the girls, vomited in the rosebushes and pelted children with sweets and chewing gum. Only the tots still loved Joe unconditionally. More and more, Constance heard the complaint that the Yanks were overpaid, oversexed and over here.

But it wasn't all bad. Their confidence and great shining trucks spilled across the countryside to boost the spirits of the war-weary English. And Britain now knew that Americans weren't simply another larger nation of Englishmen. The Barzinis and Kowalskis and Steins among them showed America's ancestry embraced all Europe. And there was something to be said for the Yanks' habit of ignoring the inequalities of birth, but she couldn't say it. Her typist expected the work tomorrow. What could she say?

A knock at the door saved her. Maybe Nora wanted to chat. Constance liked having her just down the hall, rather like university days at Oxford with midnight talks over cups of tea.

She opened the door but didn't know the man who thrust an armful of jonquils at her. She sputtered a moment before getting words out. "What on earth . . . ?"

"Greetings from Adair in New York." He grinned, backing her into the room until he reached a table where he counted out a dozen large Hershey bars. "And those are from Geoff. Your kids send their love and promised me a drink in payment. Almost forgot—each sent a letter, and here's a new picture, too."

Dropping the letters and snapshot on her desk, Constance laid the flowers on her bed and turned back to the stranger. An American in uniform, of course, an officer not much taller than she but barrel-chested and looking to be in his early forties, about her age. He pulled off his hat and ruffled his thatch of copper hair.

"And you are . . . ?"

"Peter Ryan, Mrs. Tolliver. Nice to meet you."

She took the hand he offered. His grip was firm, and the air of her room seemed electric with his presence. He made himself at home in a chair, tossing his hat toward the bed. When it missed, he slapped a hand against his knee.

"Never was much of a ball player. Your Geoff is pretty handy, a good tall center. He's a fine kid. Adair, too."

Opening the wardrobe, Constance grabbed a bottle of whiskey and poured two fingers in the glass on the basin. Peter Ryan? Should she know him? He knew the twins and the name sounded familiar, but she couldn't place him. When he took the drink she noticed the physician's pin on his lapel and understood.

"Peter Ryan, of course. You're the chap who shares offices with Tom Dalton. Another surgeon. How good of you to remember the twins when you must have so much to do."

He set the empty glass on the table, and his grin danced across blue eyes. "Aaahhhh, the good stuff. Your kids said you'd have it."

When she turned toward the wardrobe for more, he caught her hand and stopped her. "No more, thanks anyway. I'm on for early rounds tomorrow. Just wanted to get this stuff to you."

Peter pushed out of the chair and picked up his hat, straightening it by the mirror near her desk. Constance met the reflection of his eyes and smiled. He'd just arrived. He couldn't leave yet. It surprised her to admit she wanted him to stay.

"How did you ever find jonquils in London in February?"

Leaning close, he whispered in mock conspiracy. "I've got a buddy from my old neighborhood in New York who's in quartermaster corps. He cased this town the day he arrived, and when I asked—*bingo*—he delivered the goods."

Constance laughed. How could he know she loved gangster films? He even looked a bit like James Cagney. "How can I ever thank you?"

"I'll tell you what. Have dinner with me next week. There must be a decent steak somewhere in this town. How about helping me find it?"

They agreed on an early dinner, Wednesday at six. Constance assured him it wasn't a joke; the pubs did close at eleven. After Peter Ryan had left, she realized whiskey wasn't the problem. She had enough. Finding a beefsteak was the chore.

SIX

MATT COULD TWO-FINGER a typewriter faster than he let on but preferred a slower hunt-and-peck because it drove Major Hart crazy. The Southern officer especially hated the bell on the carriage return, so Matt made sure to crank his page out of the old Royal whenever Hart's favorite chanteuse started in on "Stormy Weather." A whispered off-key rendition of "Inka Dinka Doo" sometimes manuevered Hart into snapping off the radio. A little extra volume in Matt's imitation of the Schnoz usually helped the major remember a pressing reason to leave their office. Today was no exception.

"Excuse me, Colonel, but I've got to run up to the censor's office for a while. I should be back after four if anyone needs me."

Matt glanced up from his typewriter and watched Hart peer in a small mirror hanging above his file cabinet. He straightened his tie and combed a puddle of reeking hair tonic through his thin hair. Looking spit and polish was Hart's main concern. That and wrangling a censorship job, the perfect spot for bullying reporters without fear of retaliation.

"You want messages, Hart, find yourself a secretary."

ALLIANCES

Hart spun on his heel. Matt locked eyes until Hart flinched, biting back whatever he'd started to say. Matt returned to his typing and heard Hart's muttered "Yes, sir" just before the door slammed shut.

As soon as Hart's footsteps faded from the corridor, Matt picked up his pace at the typewriter. He couldn't put off finishing his report on the French coastline any longer. The buck general he answered to expected it on his desk today, before 1700. Technically, finishing today meant Matt could return to division at Tidworth Barracks tomorrow. But the one-star had made it clear that Matt wasn't going back to the First right away. And the old buzzard hinted that leaving London now also meant leaving the First for good.

"Now just take it easy, Colonel," the general had said last week. "We're all eager to win this war, but there's all kinds of ways to fight it." The general punctuated his lecture by blowing streams of smoke from the fat stogie plugged in the corner of his mouth.

Matt heard him out, even though he'd rebutted the same arguments a hundred times in his own mind. He nodded when the one-star said logistics was the key to a successful invasion. He agreed his own record showed a talent for juggling men and matériel. And there might be questions about the Normandy coast he could answer. Yes, yes, he nodded, but his mind echoed with counterarguments. Logistics, yes, but experienced commanders were needed, too. His talent, yes, but plenty with the same talent hadn't been through two invasions already. As for questions, Tidworth Barracks was only three hours by train from London.

When the general had finished, Matt ran through his own argument and it was the older man's turn to nod. He braced his arms on his desk, creating a perch for his bony chin as he listened. When Matt finished, the general just stared and sucked on his Havana. Matt thought it worked that time. Then the old buzzard slapped his hands on the desk and stood.

"You may be right, Colonel. And there must be some outfit that can make use of your special talents right away."

There was no mistaking the threat so, instead of going back to division in a few days, the one-star would find Matt some new busywork. The only outfit he wanted to soldier with was the First. The way invasion plans shaped up meant he could count on getting back right after D day. They'd need replacements then, and fast. Getting back to the war right now meant leaving London just when he'd found a good reason to stick around. Pushing a pencil by day wasn't so bad when he could concentrate on Nora Seymour at night.

What a dame! *Dame* was the exact word—smart and sassy. Throw in good looks and a nice swing to her hips, and you had just the kind of diversion he needed. Matt reached for the phone but relaxed his fingers over the receiver without picking it up. That was...what?...the third time today he'd wanted to call her? First thing this morning he'd thought about asking her to help him type his report—as a joke. Sometimes working women got touchy about jokes like that. At lunch he'd heard about a fellow who might make a good column for her. But he hadn't called then, either, because he didn't want her work or his to interfere with them. Now Matt just wanted to hear her voice wisecracking across the wire. No sense bothering her at work. She'd be waiting tonight like some Midwestern Harvest Queen until he came in to get her. "My father never let me go out with boys who honked from the sidewalk." Just remembering had him laughing again. She was some dame.

And she could write. After they'd gone out, Matt tracked down newspapers from the States and paged through, looking for her column. He'd found enough to prove Nora knew her business and strung words together nicely. She zeroed in on her topic to great effect. He bet her readers' eyes misted over or chests heaved or guts wrenched *exactly* when Nora wanted them to. She didn't provide any fresh information but neither did Ernie Pyle. She gave the reader what he *really* wanted: local color, a good yarn, a boost to morale and hip-hip-hooray. No probing questions, no implied doubts, no rocking the boat. The censors probably loved her.

Pulling the paper taut against the roller, Matt checked his last page for typing mistakes. He sorted the report and copies into piles, fixing problems that he'd noted when he finished each page. He bent over his desk until a familiar voice broke his concentration.

"Typing your own letters, sonny? I thought big shots at SHAEF rated secretaries. Is this cubbyhole really your office?" Lou's voice. "Shit. I seen company clerks at Devins had better offices than this."

Matt grinned at the sergeant standing in the doorway and eased his chair away from the desk to enjoy the show. Lou Caserti dropped his satchel, turned a slow circle into the room and hiked a hip onto the major's vacant desk. He snatched off his hat, running stubby fingers through graying hair as he continued to survey the room. Matt knew it wasn't much. Two beat-up desks shoved against peeling whitewashed walls and a bare bulb dangling above. It'd been a private home once, and Matt figured the fruity smell meant his part of the cellar had been storage. Another unlucky colonel had landed the old onion bin. They all wiped their eyes walking past that door. Lou sighed deeply and shook his head.

"I had hopes this time, high hopes. I figured this was it—the big time. SHAEF is big time—you're at SHAEF. That means you gotta be a big shot, too, right? But no, not you. Perfect setup you got to shine for success among the brass, and what happens? You start bellyaching about getting back to the outfit. What did they teach you snot noses at West Point, anyway?"

"Hell, you know what we learned at West Point—lots of math and dead generals. A cadet doesn't really start learning until he meets his platoon sergeant." Matt shrugged. "Sorry I wasn't a better pupil, Lou."

"Me too. You got the good life here, and all you want is back to mud and marching."

Matt tilted in the chair, crossing his ankles on his desk as Lou Caserti lifted himself to a seat on Hart's blotter. "Who says I want back with the First?"

Caserti dropped his hat on a chair and loosened his tie. "Everybody."

"And what's wrong with wanting back?"

Working a crushed cigarette pack from his pants, Caserti lit a smoke. "Nothing, unless the general wants you to stay put, figuring like you're a spy in the enemy camp or something."

Matt's feet dropped to the floor. "You're kidding."

Caserti pinned him in place with sharp brown eyes. "I never kid about the army, Matt. You know that."

Matt knew it, all right. That the army was no joking matter was the first lesson he'd learned when Sgt. Louis V. Caserti took on the job of breaking in the new West Pointer. Lou had taught him things most boys learned from their fathers. But no boy could live up to the congressman's ideals. Except for the necessary evil of political campaigns, Matt's father thought all forms of competition nurtured aggression. Lou showed him that physical and mental competition helped a man meet his goals, especially if he raced toward the goal and not against the competitor. The congressman's impatience with Matt's intellectual immaturity had smothered the boy's need to share confidences with his father. Lou showed Matt that shared doubts lead to shared convictions. The congressman believed men learned discipline from stern, distant fathers. Lou showed Matt that the best basis for respect was affection. From the time they'd met, Lou had looked out for Matt. And no war would stop him now. It started as a special camaraderie between a good old soldier and a good young officer and served both well. It was more than that now.

Matt nudged Caserti's satchel into the room with his foot and shoved the door closed. No sense advertising this nutty scheme of Lou's. He snapped on Hart's radio, for once leaving it turned to noisy dance music.

"Spill it, Lou. I can't believe the general really expects me to send him intelligence reports on SHAEF."

Lou shook his head. His cigarette billowed smoke in front of his face. "Nothing like that. See, I'm on my way here to look up a guy I know from '18—a Limey ambulance driver with a bum leg. So I stop in the general's office to check if he wants anything from London. When he hears where I'm headed, he brings up your name. Says a friend at SHAEF mentioned Colonel Chase wants out of London and back to the First. Then he says he hopes you'll stick here because he's got nothing for you right now but hates like hell to lose a good man. And maybe, he says, maybe you might hear something he'd want to know about. That's all."

Matt sighed. "That's all? Hell, I suppose I better start nosing around for something to send him."

"Naahhh." Caserti ground out his butt and hopped down from Hart's desk. "All he'd want is warning if the plan changes or something. He don't like surprises. Hey, let's grab a drink at the closest gin mill."

Lou waited in the hall while Matt turned in his report to the one-star. The buck general tucked it into a file without a glance and said he'd found something Matt might think worthwhile. After listening to Lou, Matt knew better than to argue and just said, "Fine."

Midafternoon doldrums left the pub quiet as the bartender cleaned up the lunch mess and got ready for the afterwork crush. Lou raised eyebrows at the genteel paneling and rolled his eyes at the dart board while the bartender drew their ale. They took their glasses to a table in the back.

Screwing up his face after tasting the ale, Lou gulped half the pint. "Hasn't changed a bit since the last war, you know it? They still dish it up warm, and it still don't kill your thirst."

It surprised Matt to hear Lou mention the First World War again. He seldom brought it up except in training and then it was always to illustrate the same point: expect the unexpected. Lou believed in knowing the book first, then throwing it away. He'd lost count of the times he'd heard Lou's standard spiel. It never varied much, and neither did the reaction of the recruits: confused as hell until their first skirmish when it all suddenly made sense. "Most of what I tell you about fighting is garbage," he'd say. "Combat's different for every man. One guy's so scared he pisses his pants, the next guy's so scared he charges a machine gun. No telling beforehand who's who. You'll all be scared, every damned one of you. If you're lucky, you'll remember to fire your piece." By this time the new men would be shaking their heads, figuring as Matt had that only a real dummy could forget to fire his rifle. Combat was never the way you figured it'd be. Matt expected to hate it. He only wished he could.

"What'd you expect the first time you went over the top, Lou?" Matt met Lou's eyes over the rim of his glass, brown eyes that drifted away at the question. He put down his glass. "If you don't mind my asking."

Holding his drink with both hands, Lou stared into the amber ale as he answered. "I don't mind. I guess I expected to get drilled right through the eyeball. Plenty like that rotted out there between the trenches, and guys tripped over 'em. That's what happened. I tripped and went down hard. Woke up after dark, surprised as shit I wasn't dead."

Matt couldn't keep from grinning. "You tripped and knocked yourself out? Hell, Lou, I had you pegged for the only guy in history who pissed his pants and charged a machine gun."

Lou didn't laugh. He took a long pull from his glass and put it down carefully, meeting Matt's eyes head-on. "You expected to hate it, didn't you, Matty?"

Glancing away, Matt nodded and felt for his glass. Hell, why'd he bring it up, anyway? Now he was cornered.

"You expected to hate it, but you didn't. I saw that right off. You liked it. Too much maybe. And it's been eating you ever since."

Matt grabbed a smoke. His lighter flared up on the third try, but the hand holding it shook and he needed both to steady the flame. He dragged deeply and held on to the smoke until it hurt. He just didn't want to talk about it. Not even with Lou.

"You were so jumpy before Sicily that you made me jumpy, too. I figured nerves, but then when we went in, you loved it. You like to fight, and it bothers you. I don't know why. Lots of guys like fighting. Why else are there wars?"

Matt glanced toward the bartender wiping glasses at the far end of the bar and rolled the Camel between his fingers. He was acting like a sullen kid accused of misbehaving. But he couldn't help it. If he didn't talk about it, maybe he wouldn't think about it. Maybe it'd go away. Maybe Lou would shut up.

"I been thinking a lot about this, Matt. I'm worried. You're the best I've trained, and I love you like my own kid. But at the end there in Sicily I got worried. You put a bunch of guys in a crap shoot with long odds against them up in those hills around Troina. It worked but wasn't necessary. There was a safer way but you ignored it. So now I worry."

Matt forced his eyes to meet Lou's and face up to his concern. "You don't have to worry. I'm going to stick around here for a while."

Nodding, Lou reached across the table and clapped Matt's shoulder. "You'll be back with the First pretty soon. And it's okay if you like to fight. You're good so I don't worry too much. Ever since the first time I went out of that shitty trench, I've known you don't get second chances. You gotta take risks, but always remember you're taking 'em for a lot of other guys, too. Keep those other guys in mind."

Each drank another pint before Lou decided it was time to head across town to his buddy's flat. Matt strolled back to his office slowly but couldn't enjoy the warmth streaming down with the rare February sunshine.

No matter what Lou said, liking combat was not okay. At least not the way he liked it. He had gambled with men's lives in Sicily. Waiting out the German garrison in their hill fortifications wasn't fast enough, so he sent men crawling up under their guns to clean them out with grenades. The Germans had been out of water for a week and he had some leeway for mopping them up, but that hadn't mattered. All that mattered was finishing them off, wiping the garrison out, getting permanently rid of as many as he could. Winning counted that day. Winning his way, even if that meant some of his men would never get home.

Someone knocked into his shoulder, but Matt waved the apology away without slowing. Lou was right. He took unnecessary risks with other men's lives. That it worked was no excuse. It wasn't supposed to be that way. Before getting a command, before receiving his commission, before ever starting West Point, he'd known how it was supposed to be. A six-year-old's horror when his daddy returned from war minus one arm blossomed into another kind of fascination. He read and read until he'd visited all the world's battlefields, from Agincourt and Waterloo to Antietam and Verdun. Why was Daddy the only man who understood that war had to stop? That war must stop was obvious even to a serious ten-year-old. By sixteen, he'd known it wouldn't stop and that his turn to fight was coming. And he'd known the part he wanted to play—cautious and patient leadership to make sure most of his men got home.

Movement on the sidewalk slowed, and Matt edged around the shoulders of the crowd. He even started out cautious and patient in Algeria. But later, when things had gotten rough enough to send liquid fire coursing through his veins, he'd known he was in trouble. Hard fighting, balancing on the line between life and death, had boosted him to a tingling peak. Nothing had equaled it; no scene was as vivid, or sense more aware, or moment as endless. And he'd never felt more alive than that day in Sicily when he climbed out of a foxhole to watch his men scramble up a hillside studded with big guns erupting with flame and smoke and death. Small-arms fire smacking hard ground at his feet and warnings shouted by his men had just pushed him higher. They thought he'd get hit, that he was done for, standing like that in the clear. But he knew they were wrong. Heart racing faster, each beat pumped greater life through him until even his skull tingled. He *knew* they were wrong.

Tires screeched and a horn blared. A hand at Matt's shoulder wrenched him back. He'd stepped off the curb into traffic. He jumped back. A taxi driver stopped to shake a fist at him. Civil servants and women in town for the day who'd waited for the light murmured disapproval. Remembering was getting dangerous. But he wouldn't have to remember for long. Tonight Nora would wipe the war out of his mind.

For a while he'd forget where he was and what he was. He'd laugh at her wisecracks and smile into her dark eyes. He'd float in the perfume cloud her hair released every time she ran a hand through it or tossed her head. He'd ignore the urge to squeeze when he put his hand on her waist on the dance floor and fight the need to pull her tight against his chest. And he'd debate just how far he could push and maybe try a kiss to test her. After all, she was the one insisting on propriety, on his coming to her door as if she still lived in her parents' home. She might be a little slow, and he didn't want to spook her. Or then again, she might just be kidding. He'd run the risk of looking like a fool rather than risk scaring her off.

Crossing the street to Norfolk House, he went around the side to reach the stairs he wanted. Hart flashed a shit-eating grin when Matt pushed open the door to their office. Before he could unbutton his blouse, the major leaped to his feet and leaned over the desk.

"There's a real flap on upstairs about your old outfit, Colonel. They killed a story being sent home by one of the wire services. And now they're wondering if the First should even take part in the landing."

Matt slipped out of his blouse and hung it on the back of his chair. "Get to the point, Major."

Hart sat down hard. "No special point, I guess. I just thought you'd be interested, that's all."

"Why'd they stop the story?"

Hart shook his head. "The story said First Division would spearhead the invasion. It's hard to believe anybody's stupid enough to write that, but after meeting a few reporters, I guess it shouldn't be. I still think we should send them all home and then just tell them after we've won."

Scraping the chair up to his desk, Matt anchored his elbows on the blotter. "Are you telling me they may pull the division out because some newspaperman wrote it was going in first? They really think the Krauts are going to be surprised to see Big Red One on the beach, after North Africa and Sicily?"

"It was a wire story—some broad at International Press filed it. And, yeah, that's what they're thinking. At least, that's what I heard they're thinking."

Matt stopped listening after Hart mentioned the broad at IP. He didn't have to hear any more. He knew whose story it was, dammit. And as soon as he wrote to the general at First Division headquarters, she'd get hell.

SEVEN

Two COFFEE CUPS RATTLED on saucers as Nora elbowed through the door to Will Davies's office. He continued to talk into the phone, so she kicked the door shut to let him know how burned up she was. He glanced up, raising his eyebrows as he assured someone on the other end that he'd take care of it today. Nora carefully set one cup amid the cables and copy strewn across his desk. When he nodded toward a file cabinet, she knew he wanted the whiskey in the bottom drawer. He was drinking a lot. She poured a capful into his coffee and slipped the bottle back between the files. The wastepaper basket held one empty already.

Nora settled into a beat-up armchair and watched the IP newsroom through Will's window. The thin partition blunted the din of typewriter and teletype chatter. Norman Cox still smirked as he crossed to a large map of Europe, running his finger through the Low Countries as he searched for someplace in Germany. Probably writing another bombing story, although Cox was too chicken to ride over himself. An English teletype girl joined him at the map, leaning forward as she pointed out whatever he'd found. Watch out, sister. He may look good, but he's a skunk. The girl took Cox's arm as they walked to a map of the Mediterranean. Her finger touched the boot of Italy, and Cox nodded solemnly. He was such a rat that Nora couldn't watch anymore.

Funny the way maps became a big part of newsroom decor once the war came. Or not so funny, really, to watch the Nazis push their border west and south in the spring of 1940. The first map was northern Europe, although the Mediterranean soon filled the blank wall alongside. No one really cared much about the Asian war until Pearl Harbor. A few days later that map had joined the wall display and pretty soon Jap flags dotted the huge emptiness of the Pacific. Now Will had hung little American and English flags in North Africa and waited to push the thick yarn of the Italian front farther up the peninsula. He didn't seem so eager to change the map of northern Europe. Whenever someone brought up the invasion he asked the same question: what difference did the landing site make? No matter where they went in, they were in for trouble.

"Sweet of you to bring me coffee."

Nora jumped a little, spilling the last of hers onto the floor. Will grinned across his desk, waving a hand. "Hello. How's tricks, kid?"

Rising to her feet, Nora walked forward until her fingertips rested on the edge of his desk. "This is no social call, Willard Davies. I'm giving you fair warning. Either you tell Norman Cox to lay off my copy or I'll have to kill him. It's all I can do to sit in the same room with that jerk. If I have to let him touch my work, I'll explode."

Will reached back, pulled the whiskey from the gray cabinet and filled his cup. Christ, he was pouring the stuff down. She met his eyes across the desk and shook her head. He glanced away. "I noticed you two weren't awfully friendly."

"Hardly. You know he resents me because the Chicago bureau hired us at the same time but I got to New York first. What you don't know is that Norm didn't want to come over here. He wanted the job I got in the States and has been out to get me ever since. It took me a while to figure out why. He's a chicken, Will. He's scared to death of this war, probably of everything else, too. And he especially hates me because I'm better than him—me, a woman—and that makes him feel even smaller."

Will stared at his desk. Nora couldn't read the expression in his eyes. He was getting tough to figure. One thing she used to like about him was how his eyes met hers when they talked. And he always gave it to her straight—no games to humiliate her or lies to protect her feelings. He'd broken her in at the New York office, making sure she knew who everyone was, making her feel at home. Now she hardly recognized the man or his behavior.

"What makes you think he's scared?"

Nora shrugged. "He's the only reporter I know who made no bones about wanting to stay home for the duration. You don't see him volunteering to cover the invasion, do you?"

"You don't think the guys in the invasion are scared?"

Nora threw up her hands. "I don't know, Will. All I know is he's butchering my copy, and it's got to stop."

Brushing lank hair from his eyes, Will leaned forward to dig through the piles on his desk. "Your copy has to be edited."

"All right, then you edit it or somebody else. Anybody but Cox. I don't mind a couple of changes. But, Christ, I spend hours getting the most out of these columns and then Cox changes words, rearranges paragraphs, rewrites the lead. He's ruining my stuff."

Will pushed a sheaf of carbons across the desk. "Here's carbons of your originals. Find the edited stuff and attach it to these. I'll talk to Cox in the morning."

Nora grabbed the papers and stood up. "Thanks, boss. I appreciate it."

"How about dinner tonight?"

Will tried for a wolfish leer but couldn't bring it off. It was an old joke between them. He liked family life too much to risk giving his wife, Sylvia, anything to worry about. She'd told Nora the only rival she feared was Will's job.

"I'd like to, but I've already got plans. Maybe later this week."

Before she grabbed the doorknob, it rotated in her hand. The opening door caught her in the hip. A red-faced officer behind it forced Nora to step back as he charged into Will's office.

"Hey, watch where you're going, will you? You almost knocked me down."

The colonel's eyes darted over her, but he stepped toward Will without apologizing. He waved the paper in his hand. "I don't know who this broad Seymour is, Davies, but the Krauts are paying good money for the kind of information she's trying to send home." He balled up the paper and threw it.

The paper bounced off Will's face and rolled across the floor. "We killed this one, and you can be damned sure we'll be reading IP stories very carefully from now on."

Gesturing the colonel toward the armchair, Will picked up a pen and turned it in his hands. "What's the problem, Dick? I guess you two haven't met. Col. Richard Logan, Nora Seymour."

Nora snatched up the crumpled paper and smoothed it out. It was the Tuesday column on Matthew's division. Running through the lines, she saw at once that Cox hadn't touched a word. But he did submit it to the censors before Will had a chance to okay it.

Logan yanked a thumb at Nora to punctuate his complaint. "The problem is this broad announcing to the world that the American First Division will lead off the invasion. That's the problem, dammit."

Logan wouldn't sit, and Will came around his desk to take the column from her. Nora glanced at the censor, wishing she could say something to wipe the anger off his face. But Will wouldn't appreciate her butting in. She'd written the story, but it was his job to defend it in public. Her turn would come later.

Will crossed his arms and leaned against the door until it closed. "You say you stopped the story? Then there's no harm done. Someone here fouled up because I didn't clear it. Since Nora just got here she's still on probation and all her copy has to be cleared through me until she gets the hang of censorship. As you can see, she's still learning."

Nora couldn't stop the heat rising up her cheeks. What a way to start the job. And Colonel Logan wasn't backing down.

"No harm done? You bet your ass this hurts. Right now SHAEF's wondering whether to yank the First out entirely." He turned to Nora, raking her with his eyes. "If this broad knows it, who else does? And I don't even have to ask how she found out. A little pillow talk, probably."

Will grabbed Nora's arm before she could complete her swing. The rotten bastard. He had no right to imply she slept around to get stories. Will's fingers bit deep into her arm.

"That's going too far, Logan. Nora was out of line to write what she did. And she'll be disciplined for it. But it's been common knowledge in every newsroom in London for weeks that Big Red One was going in again. Come on, man, the city's crawling with men on leave from all kinds of outfits. You don't have to sleep with one to know they're going. That's why they're here, and everyone knows it."

The fingers on her arm relaxed their grip but didn't let go. Colonel Logan crammed his hat on his head, and his eyes swept over them again.

"You heard what I said, Davies. From now on we'll be reading stories from this office very carefully. And next time this broad screws up, she goes home."

Logan slammed the door. The sound released the tears Nora had forced back. It was humiliating to stand silently like a piece of the furniture while some jerk said rotten things about you. And aggravating to let Will fight her battles. At least he'd stuck up for her. He always did. "Christ, Will, I'm sorry."

Will's hand slid to her shoulder and he swung her around until they faced away from the window overlooking the newsroom. "Chin up, kid, Cox is watching. Once he sees you've got a heart, he'll really murder your copy."

THE SALLOW GIRL who opened the door was unfamiliar to Constance. Another new maid. Either the recent nights of bombing everyone called the miniblitz had frightened the last serving girl away or some misdeed had Mother bristling again. Either meant tea would be trying. Constance braced herself as she handed her coat to the new girl.

"Your mother is in the drawing room, ma'am. I'll bring tea directly."

Taking a deep breath as she crossed the cold marble foyer, Constance paused before the ormolu mirror sunk into the wall and patted her hair into place. Afternoon sunlight streaming through the fanlight lit a vase of fresh flowers that splashed an unattractive yellow light onto her face. How did Mother manage to find bouquets even in February? Likely she frequented the same supplier Peter Ryan had visited. Trust Mother to maintain her standards, even in wartime. Her approach was typical, if impractical. She'd run through half the servants in London already. Curving her lips into a prepared smile, Constance slid open the door to the drawing room.

"There you are, Constance. I wondered if you'd forgotten."

Bending to reach the woman seated close to the coal fire in the grate, Constance brushed her lips against her Mother's withered cheek, tasting face powder and roses. "Am I late, then? I never quite know which clock to trust—certainly not my own. You know how I forget to wind clocks."

Constance forced herself to lower into her chair slowly, conscious of her mother's careful observation. Folding hands in her lap, she pretended to appreciate the warmth of the fire while the old woman studied her with a critical eye. She'd tolerated the ritual appraisal as long as she could remember. Before she married, such sessions were her only real communication with Mother. Once that great goal had been reached, the point became not catching a man but keeping up appearances. The twins' birth had diverted Mother's attention but, with the children now in America, there remained only Constance for the old woman to oversee.

"You've let your hair go too long between rinses. No matter the circumstance, my dear, one mustn't let go."

The maid's arrival saved Constance the need of replying. She watched the girl nervously set the tray before Mother, waiting for a nod of approval before scurrying back out the door. Declining both cream and sugar, Constance noted her mother's frown and the heaping spoonful the old woman added to her own cup. Real butter melted over the oven-warm scone, and the preserves spread on the sponge cake were prewar rich. They ate in silence for a few moments. When Mother seemed ready to start in again, Constance drew the children's letters from her bag.

A blush of affection warmed Constance as Mother held Adair's blue notepaper at arm's length, nodding and smiling as she read. How could she really expect anything more from an old woman? Married when Victoria was queen and raising her children in the confident security of Edward's reign, what else could she be? Even her drawing room reflected a life lived in defiance of the march of time. Fabrics wore out and were changed and the wallpaper was replaced once or twice, but the heavy tables and chairs and lamps so carefully polished for years now carried a special luster. The stability the room had represented to Constance as a child now unsettled her. No matter the circumstance, Grace Adair maintained her standards and her composure. In the face of progress or world war or the death of her only son, Mother remained unruffled. If she knew the kind of grief Constance had endured at the loss of her twin brother, it never showed. The only change allowed in her daily life then was her mourning garb and her unwillingness to mention the son she'd once boasted of.

"But this is dreadful. You must put a stop to it at once."

Constance turned her attention back to the tea at hand, pouring another cup. "What is dreadful?"

"Geoff writes he is playing basketball. I've never approved of their going off to America and this is why. He should be at Eton playing cricket or polo, or even rugby. He'll return a hooligan, mark my words. You were daft to send those children away."

"Don't be ridiculous, Mother. I insisted and Jeremy agreed. Let's not argue it again now."

Mother set her cup on the tea tray and sat back with folded hands, but Constance noticed she twisted an emerald ring around her finger. "Don't you think it's time they came home? Lady Worth's grandchildren have finally returned from Canada."

Pushing out of her chair, Constance stalked to the window. A neighbor walked by, pushing an open perambulator loaded high with bulging paper sacks. If Mother spotted that, she'd cut the woman dead next time they passed on the street. "Indeed, I do not. In fact I think you should go back to the country yourself now that Jerry is banging away at us again. And you must be bored to tears in London."

Her mother's laughter sounded brittle. "Better bored here than driven mad by Yanks at Corniche. I don't mind living in the gatekeeper's lodge nearly as much as I mind them marching through my garden until it's trod to mud."

"Then stay at our cottage. It's a bit larger than the gatekeeper's, and the Americans never bother coming down our lane. You'll forget all about them."

"Very kind of you, my dear, but I prefer to stay here with Randolph. He needs me."

Folding the children's letters, Connie slipped them back into her bag. Should she ask? It was only Monday, but she'd had absolutely no luck finding a steak for Peter Ryan. If one could be had in London, surely Mother would know where. And it might even make her feel better, show her that Constance needed her help, too.

Her mother's eyes lit with enthusiasm. "I know just the man. But you'll have to dine at Randolph's club. Your father can arrange it tomorrow when he lunches with the member from Maidstone. What time Wednesday?"

Connie frowned. Daddy's club was awfully stuffy. She couldn't picture Peter Ryan sipping sherry in the smoking room or appreciating the hunting prints in the lounge. Yet there was the beefsteak. That should count for something. "Wednesday at six. Better say six forty-five to leave time for a drink in my room."

Constance wanted to bite her tongue when Mother's face stiffened into a grimace. For a Highland woman, she was an awful teetotaler. "Do I take it you entertain men in your bedroom at the Waverly? Really, Constance, that will never do. What can you be thinking of?"

Patting the old woman's hand, Constance chuckled. "What can you be thinking of, Mother? All I've in mind is to save Dr. Ryan from having to choose between bad sherry or worse port at Daddy's club. I'm afraid the only threat he poses is to my supply of good whiskey."

NORA WISHED she could disguise the fact that her Waverly room was a bedroom. Only a woman looking for a good time had the advantage when entertaining a man in her bedroom. Matthew's having a good reason to be angry put her at a special disadvantage. It might be her own territory, but that didn't help. Bedrooms always reminded men of a woman's vulnerability and sidetracked the issue until the discussion ended with his shrug that said, What do you expect? She's just a woman. Underneath his vulgarity, that's what Colonel Logan really thought. She was damned if she'd give Matthew ammunition to help dismiss her like that.

Sweeping an arm across the bureau, she corraled her brush, hairpins, perfume and makeup, sliding everything into the top drawer. She emptied her purse of notebooks and pens to replace the feminine things and grabbed a couple of books out of the bottom drawer to complete the display. Mussing the bed, she scattered clippings on one side and plumped the pillows on the other to make it look as if she'd been working. She pushed the sleeve of her nightgown and an extra pair of pumps into the wardrobe. Should she rinse out the teacup on the sink? Instead, she carried it to the bedside stand and traded the cup for a full ashtray. Wiping that out with tissue, she fished one butt from the wastebasket so it wouldn't look too neat. Satisfied the room was sexless, she lit a Chesterfield and kicked off her shoes.

Now all she had to worry about was explaining the whole mess to him. Running afoul of censorship rules against naming specific units was an honest mistake. She knew the prohibition. It simply hadn't sunk in. The Germans would find out soon enough, but their initial uncertainty might help the Allies. And what Will said about disguising the scope of the landing made sense, too.

The other part of the mess worried her. Some reporters followed an unwritten rule that you didn't use information picked up in a social setting. Conversations at parties were off limits unless the person talking knew you were a reporter and talked to you anyway. Nora always made sure people knew who she was. Matthew certainly did. But she didn't feel right about it now, especially after what that jerk Logan had said.

Snuffing out her cigarette, Nora pulled down the blackout curtain. It was getting dark, and she wanted a light. Her arm ached where Will had gripped it. He'd left a bruise, but that was all right. It proved how good a friend he was. Will always looked out for her. She might not be so lucky if Cox took over in London after the invasion. Cox would have let her slug Logan and then piled it on when the army nailed her. But Will was rational and patient. Logan would think about what Will said and calm down. And Will kept his word to the censor. Nora wouldn't be in the press corps at Ike's Friday briefing or start covering SHAEF two days a week. Since Logan wouldn't see her hanging around for a few more weeks, he'd have time to cool off. It was a fair punishment, and she couldn't complain.

The knock at the door was deceptively soft. She expected Connie to check in as usual but found Matthew glowering down at her instead. He knew all about it. Jaw rigid and eyes cold, he took three steps into her room and stopped.

"You heard. And you're really sore."

He nodded silently as she closed the door. She wanted to look anywhere but into those icy gray eyes. He'd trapped her, snared her with his silence as he waited for an excuse or explanation or apology. But there was no excuse.

"I wish I could say it was a stupid mistake. It was just stupid. Using something you told me was even worse, I

ALLIANCES 101

know. You've got a right to be sore. All I can say is I'm very sorry."

His eyes held her for another second, waiting. The night's first air-raid siren shattered the silence. Flinging his coat on her bed, he doused the light and snapped up the shade. Searchlights fingered the clouds and reflected a glow back through the window. Nora couldn't see any planes when she reached the window. He turned, frowning down at her. "That's all you can say? You're sorry?"

Cars moving along the street below stopped. She could hear the distant rattle of ground batteries. Far off in the east, tracers streamed red against the arriving darkness. Matthew yanked down the shade. "So that's it?"

Nora hugged her arms and turned into the room. What did he want? She'd admitted she was wrong. Did he expect her to beg forgiveness? He could forget it. A half smile touched his lips when he twisted the light on.

"Now you're getting mad, aren't you? You're really something. I come in here determined to chew you out, and you nix that with an apology. Now you're getting huffy because I want something more than 'I'm sorry.'"

Waving her hand, she cut him off. "Hold it. Back up a little. I said I'm sorry, and I meant it. What else can I say?"

Light shot down the streak of silver in his hair as he bent toward her, hands in his pockets. "Try this: 'I won't do it again, Matt. When we're out together, we'll both park our work back at the office.' How's that?"

His smile coaxed her. What had she found out from him, anyway? Just enough to get herself into hot water. Not enough for an exclusive that would count. And now she had to lay off trying for a scoop. At least for a while.

"Okay. Sure."

He came close enough to make her tilt her head back. His smile faded. "Think you can do it?"

The lights flickered and died. Another power plant hit. She found the candle, and he lit it from his lighter. He pushed her hand until the flame hung between them, haloing their faces with light. "I like to spend time with you, Nora, but I'm looking for laughs, not notoriety. If what you want is information, forget it right now."

The even tone and calm manner had fooled her. Someone must have bawled him out about her column. "You're a lot madder than you let on. You think I could get you in trouble with the army."

The flame wavered when his fingers closed around her wrist, guiding the candle aside. He leaned close. "I got over being mad, and I'm not worried about the army. I just don't like being used. I thought we had good times together, but now I'm not sure what you want. It's like getting sucker punched with a velvet glove. The first touch may be soft, but you still end up on the ropes."

She leaned her head against his shoulder for a second before meeting his eyes. "It won't happen again."

He brushed a quick kiss across her lips and took her free hand. "Let's get some dinner."

EIGHT

MONDAY NIGHT WASN'T the test. Nora's real test came today, right now, and it looked as if she flunked. Matthew couldn't miss seeing her standing with his brother's team, talking to Tim when his side batted. He showed up during the fourth inning. Now the game was nearly over, and he still stayed across the diamond near third base. When Tim hollered and waved, he just grinned and waved back. The stocky catcher popped out to center, and Tim's team took the field.

"Heads up, Tim. You've got 'em on the run."

The boy nodded vigorously to her as he ran off, darting in to swat the pitcher's bottom before taking his position as shortstop. Tim danced around a bit but never took his eyes off the batter walking to the plate.

His utter devotion to the game reminded her of boys she'd known in high school. He'd arrived early to chalk out lines and a circle for the pitcher. Today's clear March sky looked like summer in Illinois. The crowd gathered in Hyde Park could have been back home, too. Some spread blankets across the grass, but most stood close in along the baselines, while kids whizzed around the makeshift field. The day's warmth lured tons of people to the park, dotting walks and lawns with strolling couples. Nora almost imagined she was back home until her eye strayed beyond center field to the dark snouts of an antiaircraft battery. Trenches crisscrossing the park to make sure no planes could land added to the strangeness. So did the uniforms. Baseball players had worn overalls and dark tans when she was growing up, and the only machines around had been McCormick harvesters. No one in Illinois scouted public parks for the likeliest spot to grow cabbage, either.

"I hope we're rooting for the same team today."

As she met Matthew's eyes, Nora's insides hollowed just like a kid caught sneaking forbidden treats. Twisting her wrist, she flipped her notebook closed and slid it into her raincoat pocket. "I'll warn you right now that I'm working, in case it bothers you. And I may use a couple of things Tim said in my column."

Matthew shrugged. "That's okay by me. Mind if I hang around?"

He followed her when she detoured past the crowd to reach the boys on the other bench. When she'd finished interviewing the opposing team and was headed back to Tim's side, Matthew fell into step beside her. He didn't seem to mind people seeing them together today. Or, come to think of it, Monday night, either. When the lights came on the other night, he suggested eating in the Waverly mess and even stopped to exchange hellos as they crossed the huge dining room. He made a point of introducing her to people. He hadn't mentioned the censorship snafu when she introduced Will or later when they all followed Connie upstairs to raid her Scotch. Maybe he really wasn't worried about getting in hot water at SHAEF.

Uniformed spectators chanted "Grand slam, grand slam, grand slam" when the opposition filled the bases. Nora tugged Matthew closer to the field. The next batter smacked a line drive out. At shortstop, Tim dove horizontally, snatching the ball into his glove with a matching smack, and finished the game. The teams met near the pitcher's circle to shake hands.

"Play hooky from work and come have a drink with us. Tim's got a club for fliers he wants me to see. It might make a column for you."

"I thought the deal was we parked our work at the office. I don't get it."

He laughed. "You should be a judge, you know it? You're a real stickler for fine shades of meaning." He folded his arms across his chest. "I don't want to interfere with your work. I just don't want to be part of it. You've got a job to do, and you're good at it. That's great, but I'm more interested in the woman than the reporter."

Nora wanted to kill herself for blushing. She couldn't think of anything to say that didn't sound stupid. So she nodded silently and turned away to let her cheeks cool.

Tim trotted up to them and punched Matthew's arm. "How about some beers, guys?" He gave his hand an oo-la-la shake. "You'll really like this place, Nora. The beer needs salting, but what the heck."

Flagging a cab, Tim directed the driver to the Brevet Club. Nora didn't follow the conversation as the brothers sorted through the driver's Cockney while they wheeled through narrow streets. Tim helped her out and pushed open an iron gate. Nora waited under leaded bay windows as they settled the fare. Dropping a polished brass knocker, Tim threw a salute to the servant who opened the door and made for the stairs. Handing their coats to the man, Nora and Matthew followed him down to the lounge. Other ball players draped themselves over stools or girls along the bar. Tim juggled three glasses to the table Matthew chose.

Nora lifted her glass to him. "Here's to a winning season." They clinked glasses, but Matthew cut in before they drank. "Victory in all our games."

Tim drained half and sighed, then finished the beer. Nora and Matthew exchanged grins.

"How's the flying?" Matthew snagged a bowl of peanuts and shoved it across the table to Nora. She grabbed a handful and slid the bowl to Tim. "Had many missions?"

Shrugging, Tim massaged his glove hand. "Just my luck I've got the best bombardier in the air force. He never misses."

A piano in the corner tinkled to life, and Tim nodded in time to the music as he talked. "We did four runs before they yanked us to practice precision bombing. Looks like dry runs until you dogfaces need us. Meanwhile the rest of the guys are off to Berlin."

The target jolted her. Americans bombing Berlin? Since when? Out of the corner of her eye, Nora saw Matthew's eyes flash over her. She cracked open a peanut and tried not to look too interested. He turned back to Tim. "Berlin, huh? If your bombardier's so good, why aren't you going, too?"

Tim shrugged again and added a sigh. "You tell me, Matt. All I can figure is it doesn't count much if we miss target over Germany, but it's trouble if we blast our own guys. Tony's got such a good eye I figure they're saving him for later. Maybe save a few guys on the ground. I don't know."

Sweeping her hair aside as she propped elbows on the table, Nora jumped in. "I don't understand. Why don't they let you fly now and later?"

Matthew's eyes narrowed and his hands stopped working on the peanuts. She'd said something wrong. Tim chuckled. Or was it just a stupid question?

"They figure the odds are we won't make it back sometime. Looks like the only person more worried about me than the air force is my girl. You can't tell Hillary anything, either. I know I'll make it, but she doesn't buy it."

"You been seeing Hillary a lot?"

Tim nodded at Matthew's question and eyed his brother. He turned to Nora for a moment, then settled his eyes on a point midway between them. "I see her every chance I get. I love her."

Nora's chest tightened. Wasn't first love great? Either aching or trembling, one minute crying and the next bubbling over. The first time through that soaring joy outweighed the inevitable crash. Later the scales tipped the other way.

Hunching over the table, Tim shot a glance at Matthew. "I want to get married but not Hillary. She won't even let me have her picture, says carrying it jinxed some RAF guy she knew." A smile brushed his lips. "She's a little wacky."

"You think it's wacky to get to know someone before getting married?" Matt slid his chair closer to his brother. "It's not a great time for marriage, Tim. Things look and feel a lot different in peacetime."

Nora looked from one to the other. Matthew seemed to be holding back, wanting to say more. Tim pushed out his jaw, daring Matthew to go further. He seemed disappointed when his older brother sat back, waving to the barmaid for another round. "You're old enough to know what you want and find a way to get it."

Tim nodded, smiling again. "Thanks, Matt. You'll love Hillary when I bring her down. You'll see why I can't end up like you."

He colored at Matthew's raised eyebrows. "What I mean is, you're kind of married to the army. You worked so hard at that, you postponed living. That may be okay for you but, boy, not for me."

The lights flickered and an air-raid siren wailed. For a minute Nora thought the siren might be her imagination. When it sounded, Tim and Matthew talked on without mentioning the shriek. Bombs fell way off but close enough to hear explosions and feel the ground shudder. Another pair of fliers joined them. No one said anything about the shivers beneath their feet. The piano player alternated Yank and Limey hits from the first war, and the men drank steadily. Maybe some private code kept them from talking about the air raid upstairs. Ignoring it spooked Nora, but she followed their lead. By day she couldn't ignore the men shoveling glass from the streets, or the crowds lining up in midafternoon for shelter tickets, or the fluttering silver streamers strung from suburban trees. Will said the bombers dropped the metallic garlands to make it harder for those on the ground to spot them. And everyone at work still talked about the big bomb that hit St. James Square and riddled Norfolk House with scars.

They waited for the all-clear before leaving Tim at the Brevet Club. A cold and brilliant night waited outside. Tree branches arched the sidewalk like skeletons, stark outlines backlit by a glaring moon that paled nearby stars. The icy iron gate burned her fingers. Matthew stopped outside the gate to button his coat. "It's a bomber's moon. Want to walk, or is it too cold for you?"

Slipping on woolen mittens, Nora voted for walking. Dry nights weren't to be wasted in England. The moonlit city appealed to her. Blacked out and closed up, London looked like an artifact drained of life and ready to be explored. She knew she'd made the right choice when Matthew grabbed her hand.

"Mittens? I thought city girls favored leather gloves."

Nora laughed, spewing out a streaming frost cloud. "I've got both, but mittens work best. I figured that out my first winter in Chicago. The wind off the lake is a killer. Fires were the worst. Your front all toasty and your backside an iceberg."

Their laugh clouds mingled out front until their shoulders plowed the vapor aside. "You're always thinking about the job, aren't you? Even when you're picking out mittens."

"Sure. They don't hand out uniforms to reporters, you know. Most important are shoes. Actually, it's no big deal for guys, but newshens have to be careful with shoes. If the heels are too high, you can't run. You'd be surprised how often I have to run in my business."

A dozen blocks later they crossed a side street clouded with chalky plaster dust. Men in white helmets scurried past hooded lanterns, moving boards and bricks on a heap where a building had stood. An ambulance waited nearby. Matthew dragged Nora toward the civilian defense workers and offered to help.

"We can use an extra hand, mate. Vibrations weakened the house and tonight's raid brought it down. Neighbors think there's a woman and child under there somewhere."

A man kneeling on the rubble shushed them all and bent low in the ruins, pressing his ear to the mess. Workers and a handful of frightened neighbors froze in place. Nora's ears reached out but found only silence. The listening man swiveled his neck until his lips brushed the wreckage. "Don't move, madam. Only answer when we call. We'll get you out."

Pushing back to his knees, the man waved for the others. "To work, lads. We've a live one here."

Matthew stripped off his trench coat and tossed it to Nora before following the workmen. She drifted over to the huddled women edging closer to the rubble. Joining them as the group crunched through shattered glass, Nora shivered. Another deathwatch. They were always the same.

"Tonight's my last in Lilac Terrace, I can tell you," said a woman whose kerchief slipped back over pinned curls when she shook her head. "I'll be moving back below ground in the morning."

Deathwatches began with relief, especially if no moaning relatives were on hand. After relief, reason came to place blame or find meaning or take warning. This group of women was different. No one said there ought to be law or something ought to be done. This group accepted tragedy quietly and calmly laid their plans.

"I'll take my chances with Jerry. I can't abide hiding in the tunnels like a rat," another woman said as her eyes followed the men hoisting smashed timbers.

"Oh, look, they've found something."

A man slithered down a hole into the rubble. The others grabbed small debris pushed out behind him. Nora's nape prickled at a woman's cry. One kneeling man crooned soothing words. The rest hung into the hole, working free first one arm, then the other. And she was out. Nightgown in shreds and hair white with dust, the woman fell beside the hole, scrabbling at shattered bricks as she cried for her baby. A workman lifted her, urging her toward the ambulance. Nora dashed up and swung Matthew's coat around the mother's shoulders.

"I can't leave my baby. Please, don't make me leave my baby."

The civil defense man's face offered little hope. He mentioned the mother's injuries. She looked okay to Nora, except for a few scratches. It was her baby and her deathwatch. And she needed a hand. Nora stepped between them.

"Give her a break, pal. She's got more riding on this than you do."

Neighbor women flocked around, pulling the mother into their circle and driving the man out. They got her buttoned into Matthew's coat, and Nora tugged her mittens onto the mother's bloody hands. When she told the men where her baby's crib had been before their home crumpled, it didn't sound good. The women fell silent, but the mother mumbled on, cooing to her baby and telling them what a rare child she was.

Survivors tried to will life into their lost ones by reciting their shared past. Their urge to share made them naturals for stories.

"And just a fortnight ago she said 'Da' for the first time. Dickie lit up at that. Puffed up, he was."

Tears dripped from the mother's chin. She twisted her mittened hands, but her eyes never left the men burrowing in the wreckage. It would make a swell column. Nora didn't want to risk spoiling things by pulling out her notebook or asking questions. The names and ages didn't matter, and she didn't need quotes. The story was in the men stumbling through the mess while a knot of women looked on, listening to the young mother rejoice in her child as she waited to learn if the little one was lost forever. Mothers like this one welcomed reporters because telling their story made sure the world noticed what they lost. She'd get it down on paper later.

"He's got something. He's found something."

Matthew's voice wrenched Nora's eyes back to the rubble. The mother muttered on about her angel. Someone brought a stretcher from the ambulance. A baby's wail pierced the night. The mother tripped forward. Matthew said something wouldn't fit and threw his jacket into the hole. Kneeling, he reached down with both hands. The child shrieked for Mama. "Mama's here, lovey, Mama's here." Raising himself slowly, Matthew lifted his jacket by the sleeves. Another man pushed from the hem, and the little girl was free. The mother snatched her battered child into her arms. Sobbing as she rocked her baby, she ran for the ambulance.

Nora didn't move until the ambulance turned out of the street. A lantern silhouetted Matthew shaking the dust from his jacket. She wiped her eyes before joining him.

"Tough luck, but the mother walked off with your trench coat and my mittens."

"She needs them more than we do." He grabbed her hands, rubbing them warm between hard palms. "You were terrific standing up for her like that."

The lantern's glow reflected something new in his eyes, something Nora liked. "No big deal. She had a right to stay. And, anyway, it makes a better story."

He dropped her hands when a workman scooped up the lantern. "Thanks for the help, Yank. A good night's work, that was."

Nora agreed and turned back to Matthew. He nodded at the Englishman, but his smile looked stiff. And he didn't take her hand when they stepped out of the lantern's glow and into the darkness.

DADDY'S CLUB WAS absolutely wrong for Peter Ryan. His unease began when the headwaiter showed them to their table. At first Constance supposed it was a question of social graces but his manners were good. He chose the correct forks, thanked the waiters and kept up his end of their conversation. But his eyes drifted. Finally she discovered what drew him away. Time and again he returned to the ornate footed punchbowl centered on the mahogany sideboard with a Regency dandy enshrined above. Likely a founder but too swish by anyone's standards.

"We needn't stay for a sweet if you'd rather leave. Probably tinned peaches, in any case."

His eyes held real enthusiasm for the first time all evening. "Yeah, let's get out of here. I saw a bar a few blocks back."

Constance fussed with her silverware and plate to draw the waiter's attention, but Peter caught his eye with a raised hand. She wanted to kick the old snob for leaving the bill at her elbow. Peter counted out a generous tip despite the insult. He passed another folded note to the doorman who brought their coats and answered the old man's salute. Then, at last, they escaped.

A low-hanging moon glowed among the chimneypots overhead, washing the street with light. Peter steered her along the pavement until they reached the pub. Opening the door, he guided her through, but she paused just inside. The patrons ignored their entrance. A dart game continued in one corner. Peter took a table near the door and helped Constance remove her coat, carefully hanging it over a chair. He topped it with his own and slid into a seat next to her.

"This is more like it." His smile softened as he leaned toward her. "Look, I'm sorry I was such a sourpuss back there. I don't belong in a place like that. Gives me the creeps."

Constance laughed. "You're absolutely right. I must say the place gives me the creeps, too. All those elderly men snoring in the smoking room with a *Times* spread across their face."

A pretty girl took their order. Peter's face stiffened when she turned back to the bar. "What makes you laugh makes me want to cry."

His words startled her into meeting his eyes. "Look, I'll be honest. I hate everything that place stands for—tradition, old money, good family, the whole ball game. All of it's garbage to me."

Glancing away, Constance fastened on an old man slowly pulling coins from a cracked leather purse. His hands shook, and a green patch on his sleeve clashed with the faded blue of his coat. She turned her eyes back to Peter Ryan. His bored through her.

"Ever heard of Hell's Kitchen?"

She nodded. It was the New York equivalent of the East End, a notorious slum, wretched with poverty and disease.

"I grew up there. My old man was a union rabble-rouser. Got himself killed in a strike out west. My mother scrubbed floors to feed her kids. I'd walk her home from the big houses on Central Park. No one had a good word for her. It was always 'Madam expects quicker work, Bridget.'"

The barmaid exchanged their drinks for a pound note and drew a handful of coins from her purse. Peter waved her away without taking any.

"She sounds like a remarkable woman, very strong."

Nodding, he smiled slightly. "You got it. Each time she's knocked down, she gets right back up. Losing my kid brother almost counted her out for good."

Peter looked past her and Constance knew he saw nothing but memories sharpened by time. "I got the old man's brains and Tom got his heart. I worked my tail off at NYU. Tom was a dreamer specializing in lost causes. He found himself a real tramp, cleaned her up, married her and started a family."

The silence lengthened as Peter stared into his past. She didn't know how to recall him and wasn't sure she wanted to. A shiver ran over him. His eyes focused.

"I picked a neighborhood girl named Louise. Never noticed me before I started med school. I took her back to Hell's Kitchen and opened a clinic. Three years later she ran off with a singing waiter, and I wised up, joined a Park Avenue practice."

Peter scratched a match when Constance drew out her Dunhills. He waved the pack away but lit hers. "Tom stayed in Hell's Kitchen. So did my mother. When he died in Spain, his wife went back to the street. I finally got the kids and my mother out of there."

Smoke wound through her fingers. Jeremy's diamond sparkled on her hand. She preferred the school ring on the other hand. Both circled smooth unworked flesh. She'd never scrubbed anything in her life, much less a floor. Her crowning domestic achievement was mixing a satisfactory cocktail to take up to Jeremy while he changed for dinner. She'd never been any good with servants. Too lenient, Mother claimed. Too frightened was rather more like it. She always expected the maid to throw down the broom or the cook to heave a spoon. How it could continue was beyond Constance. That the many did all the dirty work for the few was insupportable. Surely this war would put an end to it.

"I guess what got me back there was those old geezers sleeping behind their papers. Guys like that could have stopped it in Spain. Instead, the fat cats did business with the fascists and to hell with democracy. Now we've got a bigger mess. And my brother Tommy died for nothing."

Constance wouldn't look away. She couldn't. He was right. Hypocrisy deviled him, too. Feeling as he did, his place wasn't here but back in America, back in Hell's Kitchen.

"I can't imagine why you've volunteered. Feeling as you do. Surely you might have stayed in America?"

"You're a great one to talk. How come you're so gung-ho? You'd have gotten a deferment from Uncle Sam for that book you wrote in the twenties."

Her stomach cramped and a chill deadened her limbs. Would they never forget? Constance couldn't look away from the accusing eyes. She was no coward, at least.

His blue eyes softened and warm fingers closed around her hands. "Look, that was a cheap shot. I'm sorry."

Peter's hands renewed her. His touch was compassion, gentle but strong. "I don't see this war as winners and losers. To hell with that garbage." His grip tightened around her hands. "I'm here for the victims, and I don't care if they're Krauts or our guys. I'm saving every damned life I can."

NINE

STABBING OUT HIS CAMEL, Matt flopped back against the pillows, cradling his head with both hands. His eyes traced the cracks in Mrs. Eversham's ceiling but no particular shape appeared in plaster above his bed. It looked ready to let go, just as that house did the other night. Hell, why was he still thinking about that? Why couldn't he just let things happen?

A riser creaked on the staircase outside his door. The nightly procession was on. Matt glanced at his watch although he knew it was nearly nine. His landlady always led off to warm up the wireless in her parlor. Next, Miss Dowd scuffed across faded rugs in worn slippers trying to keep her knitting in one piece. Both old ladies stayed in London because they had no place else to go. A lock snapped into place. Old Titus had a wife in Derbyshire for safekeeping while he did his bit at the ministry.

Matt listened in vain for the click of Miss Charleton's heels. That meant she was spending the night with the married fellow who kept her. If London was raided tonight, she'd say she slept in the subway. If no German bombers flew over, she wouldn't bring it up. The guy must be a big shot to have landed that cushy job for his mistress. Women with good jobs didn't simply get there on their own. Charleton had the brains for it but was the kind who took the easy way up. Plenty of women did, and who could blame them? Unlucky ones ended up old and poor and lonely like Miss Dowd. No one had helped Nora to the top. The steel edges sharpened by her climb showed often. Like when she'd arranged to keep that mother around while they dug out her kid. It made a better story that way. To hell with her stories. Why didn't he just forget it?

Propping himself on an elbow, Matt considered joining the others to hear the BBC's *News of the World*. He usually timed it so he reached the parlor just as Big Ben's chimes started. But no, not tonight. He'd had enough today. He didn't need to hear any more. Mrs. Eversham would squeak when she learned that the Indian Army couldn't stop the Japs at the Chindwin. Miss Dowd would lick thin lips when the announcer described what the RAF did to Stuttgart today. And Titus, the old hand, would tut-tut word of the Red Army's breakout in the Ukraine and remind them all who they'd be fighting next. Everyone in the rooming house was nice enough, but to hell with the alliance tonight.

Matt clicked off the light and swung his feet to the floor. Drawing the curtain aside, he leaned against the casement and searched for stars. Clouds blotted out their light and hazed over the moon, leaving black chimneys and spires sketched against the lighter sky. The raiders weren't coming tonight. Everybody could sleep. There'd be no bombs for London and no stories for Nora.

Sinking into his chair, Matt stared across the darkness to the bar of light under his door. He hadn't expected to see Nora today. Only civilians had Sunday off. With Eisenhower making inspections all weekend, the one-star figured on doing his homework in advance for the questions he'd get asked tomorrow. But the files and paperwork they needed were so screwed up that no one could work. The buck general gave his staff a free afternoon while he went off to play golf. Matt ran into Nora and Connie as they left the Waverly mess after a late breakfast.

"What's on for you ladies this afternoon?"

Connie smiled a greeting, but Nora folded her arms and took a step back. "I'm off to get a story. Just what you wanted to hear, right?"

Didn't she ever take a day off? When they spent time together Matt sensed her sizing up the places and people for stories. She focused on little things like British phrases or customs, and she asked questions that went beyond casual curiosity. He'd get comfortable, and she'd sidetrack him with a remark that took him back to her damned job again. It reminded him of the time he'd showed up for a movie date and the girl had an ugly cousin in tow. Every time he got his arm around his date, the cousin giggled. That was kid stuff, but Nora's work grated the same way now.

Connie laughed. "Don't let's quarrel. The day's too fine to waste on such nonsense." She lassoed his arm with a darting hand.

Connie wrote, too, but didn't let that interfere with friends. He'd been sixteen the first time she stayed with his parents in Washington. His father had sponsored her American speaking tour after she'd written a book the congressman admired. Matt had wound up showing her the sights and couldn't believe how much Connie knew about American history. He'd loved her when her eyes teared at the Lincoln Memorial and again when she saw the Emancipation Proclamation at the National Archives. That was the first time he'd seen a woman cry for the right reason. Later, on the way back to Arlington, she'd pointed to a group of shabbily dressed Negro domestics waiting for a bus and wondered aloud if that was the proper finale for Lincoln's bold stroke.

Connie swung Matt around until she faced Nora, who seemed reluctant to circle his free arm until the Englishwoman insisted. "Do come on, Nora."

Changing her purse to her other hand, Nora linked up but kept her arm rigid through his. Matt smiled a peace offering when her dark eyes darted up to his. She hesitated, then flashed a quick smile. When she bent forward to make a crack to Connie, her arm relaxed under his fingers. That was better.

Sunday afternoon's program started with the speakers lined up under the leafless trees at Hyde Park. Matt counted a Communist, two socialists, some preachers, an Indian and an old-timer ranting about his twenty-year run-in with the Bank of England. Everyone's favorite seemed to be the fellow with the portable podium labeled A One-Man Brain Trust.

Connie wandered off along the sidewalk, pausing to hear each political speaker. Nora stuck close to the brain trust, sidling up to the GIs who stopped to listen to his ramble about coal mining, Welsh legends and the proper bait for trout. Matt joined the laughter at his nonsense but didn't toss off questions with the others. Nora just smiled and got it all down in her book. The way she nodded meant she had a good story in the works. The one-man brain trust didn't seem to mind their derision. He politely heard the crowd's questions but wouldn't let himself be sidetracked into trivial issues like politics and diplomacy or war and peace. For that, Matt followed Connie.

ALLIANCES 121

"And even now the capitalists wage war against the proletariat as England and America delay their second front while the Russian workers' state bleeds from a million wounds." The skinny Communist's eyes scanned passersby, latching on to returned glances with a frightening intensity. "But history is on the side of the Soviets, and we will triumph." Matt had seen the look before, a fanatic's plea for attention. The same agitation had overwhelmed his father when he realized no one listened to his plans for world peace.

A fresh breeze spiced with spring mud wafted across a pair of socialists who couldn't agree on anything but the need for radical change when England finished Jerry. "There'll be no more his nibs starting wars for us to finish. We'll have one of our own as the king's first minister." Few bona fide workers wore high-polished gentleman's shoes or carried an extra fifty pounds in their gut. The fat man's feet had crushed the new grass, scarring the turf along the sidewalk.

Passing up the preachers, Matt joined Connie on a bench near the dead-end path left to the Indian. He figured she'd stop near that fellow. The fire of injustice must warn him despite his thin native clothes.

"Now it is not enough that you quit India." Connie perked up at the man's words. "By holding her so long, you have torn us apart. And we will have Pakistan, Inshallah."

Connie sighed and laced her arm through his. "You men haven't finished this war yet, and already they're working on the next." When Matt frowned, she answered with a gentle smile. "Why can't we all have your father's courage?"

There it was again. The congressman's courage always got rave reviews. People dismissed Hyde Park speakers as eccentrics. Because Boston voters had sent him to Washington, people called Matt's father courageous before dismissing his views. It wasn't so easy for Matt. To him, one man's courage was another man's cowardice. The congressman might have faced up to an enemy at the cost of an arm, but he couldn't—no, wouldn't—face up to reality if the price was his pride.

Nora came their way, head bent as she scribbled in her notebook. Matt wasn't the only guy watching her. An English sailor elbowed his friend when Nora walked by. Wolf whistles from American dogfaces were too much. Matt strode out and took her arm, guiding her to Connie's bench. Nora cocked her head at the Indian for a minute, then shook her dark hair.

"You're wasting your time with the political stuff, Connie. The censors will kill that story."

"I rather think you're wrong. I'm told Roosevelt's patience with Churchill's determination to save our empire has worn a bit thin." The Englishwoman waved a hand at the row of speakers. "I'd wager you can safely quote every one, except the Bolshevik."

Clenching hands together behind his back, Matt lifted his shoulders when Nora asked what he thought. She glanced down the walkway and sighed. "I'll have to see what Will thinks, but I'd better hear what they're hollering about, just in case." Slim fingers touched his sleeve. "You going to stick around?"

Matt liked the invitation in her eyes and the touch of her hand. He nodded and watched her backtrack as far as the socialists. Sinking onto the bench, he found Connie watching him, blue eyes unreadable. Knowing Connie, he'd soon find out what was on her mind.

"Wonderful girl, don't you think?"

Matt didn't answer, but his smile must have encouraged her.

"She was jolly well bucked about that mishap with the censors. Cost her the chance to report from SHAEF. But she's been a good sport about it. And I know she'll not make that mistake again."

Leaving the smile pasted on his lips, Matt bent forward and dangled his hands between his knees. "Are you mending fences or what?" He looked up when she laughed.

"Goodness, you're prickly. My dear boy, I only interfere with good friends. And it's only fair that you understand Nora meant no harm. Hers was an honest mistake."

Lacing fingers until his palms flattened together, Matt glanced away. When he looked back, Connie met his eyes without blinking. "She wanted a story and used me to get it. I don't like being used."

"Neither does she, I'm sure. That hasn't stopped her seeing you, though, has it? A homesick soldier finds a girl from home to chase away his blues? That's what you're doing, isn't it?"

It was a funny question and, eight hours later, he still didn't know what Connie meant by it. Pushing out of his chair, Matt groped for the lamp. The BBC newscast drifted up the stairs from Mrs. Eversham's parlor. Snagging the Camels from his bed, Matt crushed the pack when he found he was out. He smoked too much, anyway. Everybody did.

Connie was nuts. Taking a girl out wasn't taking advantage of her. He wasn't using Nora. She didn't have to date him. She wanted to. He needed something more than work and war. So did she. And even when he'd made it clear she'd get no news from him, Nora still wanted to go out. He couldn't doubt that after today. When Connie left, Nora asked him to go with her to the British Museum.

"I'm scouting story ideas. Have people's tastes in exhibits changed since the war? What treasures were hidden away? Do museum staff solve problems for the army? That kind of stuff."

Trees along the way budded out with pale green nubs dotting the branches. Nora pointed out a bird nest-building on a windowsill in the charred wall of a bomb-gutted building. When she grabbed his arm, he remembered the collapsed house the other night. She didn't mention that. He told her the bird looked like a starling.

"You sure? Starlings flock together. You know—a hundred sharing the same two yards of telephone wire? That one's alone."

He turned away. "Maybe it's the only one left."

"Not for long." She laughed and jerked his sleeve again. "Here comes another. Oh, look, he's got a silver flutter."

Matt swung around in time to see the second black starling swoop over his mate, trailing a metallic strip dropped by German bombers. The smaller bird hopped aside, and the big one dropped into the nest. Together the birds poked the silver strip into the weave of their basket.

Nora seemed entranced and balanced on her toes as she watched the birds work. He followed her eyes, then looked back to her face. One hand held the blue hat on top of sleek hair as she tilted back for a better view. A little smile curved parted lips. She must have memorized the damned birds by now. Brown eyes moved first and her head followed, leading shoulders until she swiveled into his chest. Her fragrance washed over him, fresh and clean. Matt reached out to steady her but missed. The brim of her hat brushed his chin when she lowered her head and stepped back. Her cheeks reddened. Despite those steel edges, he had Nora blushing again. He couldn't figure her out.

"That's something, isn't it?" She nodded toward the starlings. "Those birds don't let our problems stop them."

Civilians managed to find a bright spot in anything. All Nora could see were the damned birds and to hell with the ruins. Maybe the wreckage looked picturesque, good enough for a feature photo. "Birds are stupid, Nora. Next week a Kraut bomb will blast them to bits." The words came harsher than he wanted. Nora stared him down for a moment before pivoting and starting up the street.

British Museum curators had packed away the Rosetta stone and Egyptian mummies for the duration. Right then Matt preferred anything to cultural improvement, but Nora lit up when a guard mentioned how Yanks liked the exhibit of medieval armor. Matt had no taste for chivalry and tried to beg off.

Grabbing his hand, she pulled him along. "Come on, please? It's the closest I'll ever get to a knight in shining armor. Have a heart."

Old stone walls chilled the display room, but Nora didn't seem to mind. Dropping his hand, she made a beeline straight for a row of iron suits standing along a wall draped with heraldic banners and shields. She poked the armor, knocking hard against one metal chest and grinning at the tinny echo. She waved him over.

"Look how short they are. And pigeon breasted. These guys are puny." Stepping next to the largest suit, she measured herself against the iron shoulder. "Not one of these would fit me."

Matt wanted to laugh. She didn't need armor. Nora's came built in.

They walked down the line of vacant sentinels. Nora lifted a visor, peered inside and shivered. "Spooky." The visor creaked going back, and the movement freed a puff of dust.

Nora stopped in front of the last suit, running fingers over the caved-in breastplate. "What did this?"

His hand joined hers on the crumpled metal. Deeper nicks scarred the battered armor chest. "Probably a mace. A spiked one. Feel the punctures?"

Nodding, she slid her fingers down the arm and raised the iron hand. An ancient elbow squeaked, protesting the movement. "It's heavy."

"So's a mace."

Matt fingered the crushed armor. Generations of curious fingers had smoothed the cool metal, except for the deepest punctures of the mortal blow. A printed card fastened to hammered iron feet placed the suit on an unlucky knight at Bannockburn. Laid down hard, that poor sucker never rose and fought again. It took even less today. His kid brother pretended his bomber protected him, but one good shot would pluck Timmy from the sky.

Nora wouldn't believe armored warriors hefted the long broadswords, especially when Matt told her it took two or three men to get a knight on his horse.

"What happened if he fell off?"

"A couple of serfs probably got him on his feet."

A frown creased her forehead. "Could they bend down to help another fellow up when they wore that getup?"

Matt snorted. Civilians liked to believe armies cared as much for foot soldiers as for generals. Dogfaces had been dogfaces forever. "I can tell you learned your knights from fairy tales. Only the big shots wore armor, the aristocrats."

Nora's eyes flitted to a display case hung with pikes and maces and broadswords. "This place bothers you, doesn't it?" She waved toward the armor behind them. "Maybe you wish you could fight like they did."

Something knotted inside him, but he shrugged. "Maybe."

Risers creaked again on the staircase outside his door. The BBC's *News of the World* had signed off. Matt wished he'd picked up some smokes at the Waverly when he dropped Nora off. He needed one badly. He'd have to get over that before he rejoined the First. No telling how long they'd go without resupply once the division started moving across France. The three Phillip Morris cigarettes that came with each C-ration meal wouldn't last long.

Kicking off his shoes, he leaned back on his bed, pillowed by Mrs. Eversham's best goosedown. Maybe he didn't want to trust Nora. He was looking for a reason not to. If she wrote a story about their afternoon, he wouldn't be in it. And what if he was? That wasn't what bugged him about her. It wasn't conniving a better story from that bombed-out mother, either. What got to him was how she knew what he was thinking at the British Museum. Only Lou Caserti knew him well enough to guess what he was thinking. Until today.

Somehow Nora got in too close. He wanted some laughs with a pretty woman and ended up with a mind reader, dammit. He didn't want to find his thoughts in her next column. Hell, what he wanted was to take her to bed. And he didn't need to trust her to do that.

TEN

NORA FOLDED ASIDE the *Times* when Hillary Johns returned from the bathroom. Copper tendrils curled around the girl's face, and her cheeks were rouged pink by steam and scrubbing. Tim's sweetheart was petite and beautiful. No wonder he was nuts about her. Wrapped in Nora's tartan robe, she looked like a child. But when she stepped into her slip, her breasts and hips strained against thin fabric. No one would mistake that for a child.

"Want a drink? You can bet the men are starting without us."

Hillary shivered, hugging herself as she crossed to the suitcase she'd opened on Nora's bed. "Yes, please. That's the perfect capper for a heavenly bath."

Nora grabbed two glasses, poured generous shots and topped the whiskey with water. Hillary finished buttoning her gray wool dress and took her drink. She downed it like a pro. "I believe I floated in that tub. It's miles larger than ours at home."

Savoring the warm glow of the whiskey, Nora retreated to an armchair and watched Tim's girl. The liquor loosened the knots in her back. She hung her legs over the armrest. Something about the English girl bothered her, but she didn't know exactly what. Maybe she'd figure it out before Matthew and Tim picked them up at seven.

Hillary helped herself to another drink. She smiled as she unpinned her hair. "I find London nicer these days if I'm a bit tight."

Nora unhooked a stocking and rolled it down her leg. "What's not to like? No lights after dark, the theaters empty by nine and no one sleeps since the Krauts started coming back. But everyone tells me this is nothing compared to '41." She fingered the stocking but found no pulls. Better save this pair and wear the ones with the run that didn't show.

Laughing, Hillary swung around from the mirror. "Which would Tim prefer, do you think?" She rolled her hair into a chignon. "A sophisticate?" She combed with fingers until her hair brushed her shoulders. "Or an innocent?"

"Either way, he's crazy about you." Nora carefully tucked the stockings into a drawer in the wardrobe and pulled out the damaged pair. She slid her blue dress off a hanger and carried it across the room to her desk. Thank God her trunk had finally shown up. After two months it was almost like getting a bunch of new clothes.

Hillary sighed as she spread her cosmetics on the glass shelf over the washbasin and yanked the chain above the mirror to flood the corner with light. "He's a lovely man, of course. But perhaps he's a bit too far gone on me." Poking her chin in the air, Hillary inspected the line of her jaw. "I expect you'd understand, Nora. You're the independent sort."

Oh, please, no girlish confidences. Nora busied herself straightening the seams of her stockings. She usually got cornered with that kind of opening at work. Hearing people's troubles came with the job. Reporters asked so many questions that people often assumed they had all the answers, too. It disappointed them to find out reporters were more interested in covering all the angles of a problem than in solving it. But Tim was a sweet kid, and he loved the girl. For his sake, Nora would listen to her complaints.

Slipping out of her skirt, she forced a smile in Hillary's direction. "Try me."

"I do love Tim. And short of marriage, I'd do anything for him." Hillary raked a brush through her hair and started pinning it up. "He's not the first man I've slept with, so it's not that. Lovemaking's very special with Tim, but there's more than that."

Nora caught the girl's reflection in the mirror as Hillary sponged makeup base over her face. How could she be sure? Look at what had happened with Eric. His lovemaking mesmerized Nora into believing there was more to it than just physical satisfaction. She needed months, even years, to shake the doubting voice in her head that told her she'd thrown over the only man she could love, even if he was a rat. It all happened so fast that she was under his spell before she really knew him. And she felt guilty as hell for letting him take what Mom called a woman's ultimate lure.

Nora pulled her head through the dress and smoothed the cool silk over her hips. Equating sex with love fouled things up. Wanting to get married made things worse. And now she knew enough to take her time. Once she'd stopped worrying about marriage, the problem disappeared. This time the guy wanted marriage and the girl said forget it. This time, Tim would be the one left hurting. She stepped into her pumps and tried to keep her face neutral as Hillary continued.

"In '39 I'd just finished school, found a little job in London and taken a bed-sitter with a chum. We thought we'd live it up a bit in town before settling down. You know that old story." The English girl snapped open a compact and powdered her cheeks. "But then the war came."

Carrying the mirrored compact to the window, Hillary checked her makeup in the last light of day. The dying sun tinted her face. "I went home to help with the pub when the RAF built an airfield nearby. At first it was great fun with all the fliers coming 'round to make merry. They called it the phony war because the fighting just stopped after Poland." She drew the blackout curtain. "In the spring of 1940 everything changed."

English kids finished school early, and Nora guessed Hillary would have been about seventeen then. Stolen squeezes, tireless dancing and wild jalopy rides filled Nora's seventeenth year. Times were tough, but what a ball she'd had, anyway. Hard times meant something different to this girl. Maybe that's what made her hard to like. There was a distance in her, a shell to protect her from other people and their feelings. "That's when things got hot over here. I know. You had it rough."

Hillary nodded and tugged a Chesterfield from the pack Nora'd left on her desk. "First Jerry ran the army into the Channel. Not much fun anymore, lots of gloomy faces. Then every night the Luftwaffe came, and our boys went up to meet them. I thought I'd go mad with the noise of it all."

Nora figured she'd learned something about air raids in the past few weeks. Everyone dragged through the day, worn out by last night's hell and dreading the next installment. But Hillary was talking about the real blitz four years ago. Week after week of raids as hundreds of bombers had roared overhead and England crumbled below. Scratching a match, she lit a cigarette and studied the girl. The blitz was one story she'd been happy to miss. It sounded as if Hillary wrote the book on it.

"I'd make a keepsake album with their photos. Each night I went through adding dates for the ones killed that day." Hillary ran her hand back and forth through the smoke curling from her cigarette. "Tim didn't like to see it when I showed him. The first night we walked home I told him who'd lived in all the bombed-out houses, but he didn't like to hear."

Nora sighed. No flier wanted to be reminded that his job hurt people. Hillary couldn't love Tim or she'd understand that. If she really had let him inside her hard shell, she wouldn't taunt him with reminders of death. Nora ground out her smoke and stood up. "Don't you think Tim hates thinking about that part of his flying?"

Brushing past Hillary, she crossed to the mirror and started doing her face. She bent closer to mascara her lashes and Hillary's green eyes appeared in the glass. "How can he forget it? I certainly can't." Nora backed off and faced her.

"I've seen girls who married their boy soon wearing black and carting a fatherless baby home to Mum. And there's the other sort, the patient ones who wait. When Jerry or the Japs get their boy, patient girls die a bit, too. They know they held back when he needed them most, and now it's too late. A sorry bunch, the lot of them."

Nora glanced away. Hillary's words brought her back. "I love Tim, but it's the bloody war, you see. It's stolen five years from me, and I'll not let it ruin the rest of my life, too."

She spun away. Nora sighed when she heard whiskey splash into a glass. No wonder the girl was turning into a lush. Hillary would never get another chance at seventeen or twenty.

"If Tim doesn't come back, I'll have lost a man I love. If we married, I'd lose a husband. People would say, 'There's Hillary Chase. You remember, married a Yank? Poor thing's a widow now.'"

Nora turned from the mirror. Hillary's lashes were wet. She wished for once she had an answer. Holding back from the risk of love was something she knew about, all right. A few months ago she'd have agreed with Hillary immediately. Back then she'd kept people at a distance and bared only the toughest skin. Now she simply didn't know.

A faint smile trembled across Hillary's lips. "The war won't rob me of anything more. I'll not put the rest of my life in hock to it."

Nora's doubts about Hillary eased during dinner. She liked the outgoing girl in the restaurant much better than the self-centered woman she'd dressed with. Teaming up with Tim chased away Hillary's ghosts and lit something inside that shone out of her eyes when she looked at her boy. So she wouldn't marry him. At least she loved him. Anyone could see that.

The cab driver leaned toward Matthew and asked directions to the jazz club. Nora wished he'd sat back with them instead of riding shotgun with the driver. She wished it was her hand in Matthew's and her head on his shoulder. Sitting with him in the back of a dark cab might generate enough electricity to shock them into detouring past this damned roadblock. A ride like this might open them both to impulse.

At the club Matthew took care of the drinks while Tim led them to a table. Hillary had him dancing before

Matthew got back from the bar. He set four glasses and a bottle of brandy on the table.

Nora pushed out the chair next to her. "Looks like I was right. The brandy proves it. You were in on Tim's plan all along."

He laughed and passed her a glass. "I had it in my coat. Tim insisted on scaring up the food, so I figured I owed him one."

The brandy tasted sweet and slick on her tongue. She recognized the piano player who nodded at Matthew when a change in tempo gave him time to look up from the keyboard. Tim swung Hillary into his arms as the music slowed, and her copper head fit neatly between his ear and shoulder. Matthew watched them, too.

"What do you think of your kid brother's girl, Mother Hen?"

Matthew shrugged and scraped his chair around until his knees pressed against hers. "She seems nice enough, but they're too young to get married. At least she has the sense to see that."

The crease in his pants flattened out over his knees when he tucked his legs under the chair and leaned closer. Nora stopped playing with the straps of her bag and dropped it to the floor. "I don't think you have anything to worry about." His eyes swooped down to hers. "She's not taking any chances on ending up a widow."

He frowned. "Smart girl. But Tim's determined."

Raking fingers through her hair, Nora propped her arm against the table and rested her head in her palm. "So's she."

"Good." He nodded as he glanced toward the couple swaying on the dance floor. "It's the wrong time to get married."

"Why? What's wrong with getting married if he loves her and she loves him?"

Matthew sighed and picked up his drink. "Is this some secret sentimentality or a joke, Nora?"

Folding her arms on the table, she shrugged. "Maybe Tim's the only one with any sense. He's not running scared. He wants to live in spite of the war."

He studied the amber liquid in his glass. "Plenty of fools are trying to spite the war. But it doesn't always work. Widows are the least of it. What about the basket cases? What kind of happily-ever-after is that? It seems like a pretty big risk to run with someone else's life."

Nora saw his point and agreed with it. But part of her wanted to forget the hard knocks and get back to dreams.

"I guess what gets me is what Tim said about postponing living." His gray eyes narrowed, but she shook her head. "Not just you, Matthew, but all of us. In a funny way we're losing if we let all this stop us from living. Why should people make themselves unhappy now because maybe, just maybe, it'll save them being unhappy later?"

He slid his chair away. "Only a fool expects happiness in times like these. Don't waste your time hoping for a silver lining in this cloud, Nora. Cyclones suck up everything in their path. You just haven't felt the wind."

SHE'D LEFT THE CANDLE BURNING, and the blond hairs of the arm he'd thrown across his eyes picked up the light. Constance wanted to see his eyes but couldn't bring herself to touch him again. Not yet. The smile on his handsome lips must satisfy her for now. How odd those lips were; soft against hers, though they could shape such harsh words. His ragged breathing had slowed into a deeper cadence, but damp curls on his chest gave the game away. How on earth had it come to this so quickly?

Unsteady fingers found a Dunhill. Constance poked the cigarette into the candle's flame, trying not to rouse him. She pulled smooth smoke into her lungs. That was better. Smoking steadied her, no matter what Jeremy said. But don't think of him. Not now.

"Butts aren't good for you, lady."

His arm angled over his eyes as he grinned. "You usually light up after that kind of workout?"

Reaching down to snare the bedclothes, he covered them both as he rolled onto an elbow. His blue eyes bored into her with emotion. Affection? Challenge? Decidedly not indifference, as she'd feared. Thank God for that.

"I'm not...I'm not accustomed to this sort of thing."

He barked with laughter, setting a tremble through the mattress, which rolled her naked shoulder against his naked chest. Gentle lips brushed hers. "Then you're a helluva talented rookie." He took her Dunhill and snuffed it out.

His lips trailed across her cheek and nuzzled an ear. "You're terrific." A nibble followed the whisper and sent a shock racing to her toes. "Damn, you are terrific."

Constance's pulse quickened, daring her to believe Peter's praise. Didn't every woman want to believe she made love wonderfully? And every man, too? Peter Ryan most certainly did. He took her beyond herself into an untouched region, a place she'd glimpsed with Jeremy but never reached. Tonight she'd reached it with Peter. And meeting his eyes she knew with absolute certainty that he'd always take her there.

Sliding a hand to the coarse hair cropped at the back of his broad neck, she tugged him closer. "Am I?"

He leaned into her, his answer a sigh that mingled with her breath as his mouth lowered. "Oh, yeah." Her tingling nipples hardened, rising through the cushion of moist hair on his chest to the hard wall of muscle and bone. His body pressed the length of hers, solid against her cheek and shoulder and breasts and hips and thighs. Strong arms surrounded her shivering flesh with a vigorous promise as their mouths explored.

This time Peter needn't massage away her stiffening fear with tender, unhurried fingers. In his arms, she was pliant and trembling with welcome. This time he needn't gently nudge her thighs apart as his eyes locked on to hers. Feeling his heat, she opened to him instinctively. Where before her eyes closed, this time she smiled as that dear face tightened with passion when she met his thrust.

The glow faded slowly, and Constance kept her eyes closed to hold on until the last flicker. Their legs tangled in the blanket, here meeting warm flesh, there finding rough wool. Every inch of her reached out for sensation, delightfully responsive to each: the coolness of her room, the warmth of her bed, the emptiness when he pulled away.

She squeezed her closed eyes until dazzling patterns lit the darkness behind her lids. His feet padded alongside the bed. She lost track of him on the soft Oriental from Wickenden Square but picked him up again by the squeak of her wardrobe door. He scuffed shoes aside impatiently. Now he rustled papers on the top shelf. Silence engulfed him in the darkness beyond the patterns in her eyes until glassware chimed. The whiskey, of course. Constance laughed as she sat up and watched him carry two glasses back to her.

"That last one deserves a celebration." The bed settled under his weight as he swung stocky legs to parallel hers. She took her glass and waited. "It's been a long time since I pulled off a doubleheader."

Saluting with glasses, they drank. He set aside his glass, pulling her against the pillows. Constance rolled the whiskey over her tongue but found it lacking without Peter's taste mixed in. His arm was nicely heavy across her shoulders and playful fingers tugged at the hair brushing her breasts. She snuggled down into the soft pillows and pulled the eiderdown across them.

Lying here against him seemed cozy and somehow right. This was the way it should be done, with light and frankness and pride. It was never like this with Jeremy, not once. He came to her furtively in the dark, fumbling quickly through his passion as he murmured apologies to her pillow. He never kissed her in her bedroom, only in the public rooms of the house, brushing cool, impersonal kisses faintly across her lips for hellos and goodbyes.

Sharing a bed or a bedroom was not even considered. When an occasional hostess neglected to ask before they visited, Jeremy rolled to his side and presented the feeble barrier of his thin back. Constance now discreetly mentioned his snoring when accepting invitations. Had she ever seen Jeremy naked? Surely not in years. He rarely consented to wear bathing trunks on beach holidays in the south of France. She'd learned to knock before bringing a drink to his bedroom. Her finding him shirtless one time had made him cringe with embarrassment. True, his physique was not something any man would boast of, but she was his bloody wife. His understanding of marriage was hopelessly different from hers, and Constance accommodated herself to Jeremy's wishes out of love and compassion and, perhaps, despair. One shouldn't try to change a man like that. But what a price they'd both paid.

The candle guttered in a pool of wax and sent dancing shadows across walls and ceiling. Constance finished her drink and set it aside. Peter's eyes were closed, and his chest rose rhythmically.

"Are you tucking down here?"

His lids fluttered, and he mumbled agreement. When she pulled out her arm to snuff the candle, warm fingers searched for her. A trace of burned wax hung in the air. She straightened the bed clothes and rolled into his arms. The hair roughly matting his chest was a welcome pillow.

ELEVEN

SCRATCHING OUT a convoluted sentence in Norm Cox's latest SHAEF dispatch, Nora penciled in cleaner language and sighed. His writing might stink, but Cox had the job she wanted. Right this minute, listening to Eisenhower's briefing, he'd be desperate to come up with tomorrow's lead from the supreme commander's talk with the press. In another hour he'd be back to write his story and, as usual, bury the lead. When he passed it to Nora for editing, she'd have the satisfaction of pointing out his mistake. In the end he'd have his name on the story, even though her reporting talent saved him from botching it completely. Just another unsung heroine of IP's report, one whose feature column got taken for granted. IP regularly cleaned up the competition, and her stories were good, damned good. If the New York big shots couldn't see that, she needed to show them fast.

A teletype girl refilling coffee stopped at her desk with a steaming pot. Nora shook her head and covered her cup. The girl grabbed a pile of finished copy and headed back to her machine. Nora studied the hand resting on her cup. Ink stained her fingers from the long morning on the desk. An overlay of smoke yellowed the grime on her right index finger. What a rotten life news could be:

filthy offices, bad food, lousy hours, too much work and not enough praise.

Wadding up the crumbs of her doughnut in greasy paper, Nora pushed it across the desk until it tipped into the wastebasket. Her stomach burned. She needed something in it besides acid. Cox kept gum in his desk, didn't he? That had to be what he snapped in her ear all the time. Rummaging through drawers, she found a piece of Wrigley's buried under some files. The stale gum shattered when she folded it into her mouth. The peppermint soothed her stomach.

Newsrooms settled into a lull every day around noon. Teletype machines slowed and phones jangled less often. Despite the time difference with New York, overseas reporters operated on regular shifts, putting out morning and afternoon reports so both a.m. and p.m. papers back home had fresh stories to fill their news holes. The early report had gone out hours ago, and Nora faced an afternoon of editing filler stories. Editing anything irritated her. Fixing other people's copy bored her no matter what the story was about. With everyone but Decker out of the office, she had no escape. He was too busy answering phones to talk.

Sifting through the stories piled on the corner of her desk, Nora pulled out Will's think piece speculating on Allied plans for postwar Europe. She glanced to the wall map. The black-headed pins on the Russian front had moved a fraction of an inch in the past few weeks. An unbroken wall of Nazi pins lined the coast from the Baltic to the Bay of Biscay. Holding Will's story another day wouldn't hurt.

Tossing it back, she grabbed another story from the pile. "Queen Elizabeth and Princesses Host Tea for Diplomatic Wives." That was better. If the special correspondency didn't work out, a stint as a gossip columnist on a Hearst tabloid could be fun. No one expected Cholly Knickerbocker to edit stories. And his take-home pay probably tripled hers. Nora grabbed her blue pencil and smoothed the story against the scarred wooden desk.

Will breezed in just after one. He patted her shoulder as he walked by. "What's up, toots?"

Nora shook her head and kept reading Decker's story on the army medical corps. Coatrack hangers rattled. Nora knew Will's routine: first off with the jacket, and then loosen the tie. She glanced up just as his hand went for the knot at his throat. He caught her grin and stopped fiddling with his tie, raising a finger instead. "Almost forgot."

Digging into the pocket of the hanging jacket, Will pulled out a paper and sailed it toward her. It floated to the floor behind her chair. "I picked that up for you down the hall. Thought you'd want it for your scrapbook."

Spinning her chair around, Nora leaned down and retrieved the cable. The To and From named a New York editor and the London bureau chief of a rival wire service with offices three doors down. Her last name jumped off the message strip pasted on the telegram.

OPPOSITION BURNING POSTERIOR STOP
IP SOLID PAPERS COUNTRYWIDE STOP
MATCH SEYMOUR SOONEST STOP

What? She went cold and read the cable again, then dropped it onto her desk. The competition griped about getting shut out by International Press and blamed her column. Wiping her forehead, Nora scanned the cable a third time. They'd targeted her stories as the stuff to beat. Her heart thumped in her ears as she raised her eyes to Will. He tipped his hat to her and walked into his office. She ran through the door just as he dropped into his chair.

"Where'd you get this?" She shook the cable as she crossed to Will's desk.

He grinned. "I took it off the competition before lunch. It was on its way to the files. No one will miss it."

Nora hiked a hip onto the desk. "What do you think?"

Tossing his cigarettes and lighter onto the papers spread before him, Will shrugged. "Relax, kid. I already cabled the contents to New York. You'll get your pat on the back."

Nora sighed and read through the cable once more. Too bad it took the opposition's backhanded praise to get her stories recognized. That could work out better, though. If rival wire services saw her as a threat, any holdouts against her at IP would cave in, too. Now that she knew New York would be watching, she'd really have to get down to work digging out exclusives. The column was fine, but feature writers didn't make special correspondent. She had to get positioned at SHAEF, back to hard news.

"Quit gloating, Nora."

She met Will's eyes and smiled. "Sorry."

Shaking his head, Will motioned her to a chair. "Not that you haven't got good reason. But I have to get out of here soon, and I wanted to fill you in on the program for the next couple of weeks."

Flopping into a cracked leather armchair, Nora stretched out her legs. "Where're you going?"

Will sighed. "Wrangling with SHAEF on the press contingent for 'forthcoming operations.'"

Nora raised her eyebrows. "So that's why you visited the competition. Talking strategy?"

Nodding, Will steepled his fingers in front of his mouth. "Spotting that cable was a lucky break for us. While they're scrambling to match your stuff from London, you'll be off on something new. They'll be playing catch-up forever."

Nora folded her arms. It sounded as if she'd better start packing. And, just when she'd lined up something interesting besides work. Matthew turned up whenever she had free time, and she liked it. "What's the plan?"

Will slid a paper from his top drawer and handed it over. His scrawl listed American units and their PR contacts. "I started working on this last week. Gave the army a list of units I want you to visit. Turns out Eisenhower's making inspections, so you can cover him while you're on the road."

Bending forward to scan the list, Nora latched on to First Division. "Holding no grudges, huh? They're letting me see Big Red One?"

Will leaned back in his chair, fingering a pencil. "That's the best part. You start with them the first of April. And Matt Chase kindly offered his escort."

His grin lit a fire across her cheeks. He liked to rib her about men. Usually it took more than a smile to get her going. Traveling with Matthew sounded fine, except... "Whose idea was that?"

Will's mouth took a wicked twist. "His. I ran into him last week, and we grabbed a beer. I asked him which units were worth visiting. It took off from there."

Matthew's precious First Division. No question he planned to keep tabs on her. Maybe Will had the same idea. "Since when are you two so chummy?"

He chuckled. "Since we raked your past over the coals." Gripping the armrests, Nora half rose. He shielded himself with his hands. "Take it easy, will you? I'm kidding. He didn't ask, and I didn't offer anything." Will checked his watch. "Hey, I gotta get out of here."

Pushing up from the chair, Nora led the way out the door. At her desk, she slipped the folded cable into her wallet and stuffed her purse back into a drawer. She started Decker's story from the lead. The opening sounded clumsy now. Reading it again, she couldn't spot the problem.

Will crouched next to her chair. "I don't know what's got into you. Moping isn't your style."

Raking fingers through her hair, Nora propped an elbow on the desk and waited for the rest of the lecture. "And neither is Matt Chase. You used to like guys you could lead around by the nose. Matt's used to being in charge. He's no patsy."

With that, he headed out the door. Nora watched Will's shadow through frosted glass as he straightened his hat. She sank her chin onto her hands. She didn't need Will to tell her about Matthew. Starting today the opposition was after her, and New York was watching. And if she stumbled over Matthew, she'd be the patsy.

CONSTANCE CARRIED her teacup into Jane Ludwig's tiny back garden and found a seat on the porch steps. She needed fresh air. The faint medicinal odor that clung to Jane absolutely pervaded her East End surgery. The physicians wouldn't miss her. Jane adored chatting about her slum practice, and Peter'd been wanting to meet her. Let him quiz her old school friend and poke a bit in the dispensary. Peter and Jane were so alike. Both had to be doing every minute of the day.

Finishing her tea, Constance sniffed the air from the Thames. Even from two blocks away the tang of river muck promised spring. Small wonder that Jane's bulbs had poked out on either side of the crushed-shell path leading to the back gate. Oyster shards crunched beneath her feet as Constance paced off the path, counting the steps to the wooden door. Just twenty, imagine that. At Corniche she'd barely reach Jeremy's blessed roses in twenty steps, yet in summer Jane's tiny garden gloried far beyond theirs. Bending, she crumbled a clod of earth stuck to the spade Jane had left propped against the wall. The soil was as poor as everything else in London's East End. Jane found haven in this garden, but just over the brick wall grew the rank bloom of wretched poverty. Dirt sifted through Constance's fingers into a wisp that dusted her shoes.

The porch door banged open. "There you are." The steps shuddered under Peter's bulk, springing back when he reached the path. "Looks like Jane's got work to do. She's on the phone now."

Connie stopped before him and searched his eyes. "Will you stay to watch?"

Peter grimaced and shook his head. "No, thanks. Someone's timing contractions on the other end. You only need one doc to catch the kid." He glanced over the garden. "Nice spot. How far's the river? I'd like to see that."

On their way out, Jane invited Peter to return some evening to visit her patients in the deep shelters. Connie shuddered, remembering the stale air, squalling infants and trapped desperation of her one night underground during the blitz. Jane's fingers closed around her upper arm. "I could use you, too, Constance, whenever you've time. Perhaps you could talk sense into those silly girls who insist on staying in town when we've fresh air and cozy beds waiting for their children in the country.

Nodding, Constance mumbled a vague promise and escaped into the street while Peter and Jane settled on a date. What a coward she was. The sensible thing would be to march right back to Jane and say it. Say that she couldn't bear to spend a single minute in those fetid tombs stinking of sweat and boiled cabbage where lights burned all night and the piped-in wireless echoed cheerfully across huddled families.

Peter touched her arm, steering her toward the river while reviewing his plans. Clearly, he expected her to go with them. And if she waited, begged off later, he'd rate her a worse coward than she deserved. If she explained now, perhaps he'd understand. After their night together, she found a new gentleness in him, a hint of tenderness in his eyes.

"Oh, Peter, I can't. I simply can't." She braved his eyes, hoping for neutrality and not disappointed. "I can't bear going down there again."

Constance closed her eyes and shook her head. She sucked in air, tasting oil and salt and muck. A barge whistled from the river, and she opened her eyes. Peter frowned and pulled her gently onto a quay. She leaned against a splintered piling and waited.

"What are you afraid of—the shelter or the people in it?"

She turned away from his narrowed eyes and watched the barge plow through choppy water. "I'm afraid of both. Can you understand that? I'm afraid my last breath of air will reek of their sweat. And I'm afraid they'll turn me into the streets and let Jerry do the job for them."

"Connie, Connie." He shook his head, holding her eyes with his. "Pretending not to see won't make it go away."

She sighed. "If only it could."

Wrapping arms around her stomach, Connie turned back to Peter. "When I was young, after the last war, I burned at the injustice of life. I thought if people knew, it would stop." Her laughter tasted sour on her lips. "What an utter ass I was. I wrote *Judgment* and another book on India. Oh, the applause, the ovations. They read the books, discussed my argument, and wondered what cook had for dinner. And on it went, wretched lives eked out in the East End, in India, in America, everywhere."

Peter reached out, but she brushed his hand aside. Let him hear it. "You know, I've a cousin of sorts, a curate in Devon. His wife adores doing good works. She signed up for two boys bombed out of London and put them in her second-best bedroom. Fancy that."

Peter didn't smile. His eyes were solemn. She looked away. "The night they arrived, she left them to get undressed and said she'd return to put out the light. When she came back, the boys were gone. But they weren't, you see. They were tucked down *under* the bed. 'Isn't this our place, then?' they asked. Poor Drusilla. Such consternation. She refused to believe that in England in 1940 there were children whose rightful place was on the floor beneath their parents' bed."

Constance blinked away tears until Peter's face no longer blurred before her. "Perhaps that's the only reason we can be grateful to Adolf Hitler. He's taught us a lesson we won't soon forget. He's shamed England's ruling class by showing us how the multitude lives." She tightened her arms and dug her back into the piling. "But I am without shame, Peter, because I've always known and I've done nothing."

He touched her then, gentle fingers brushing the line of her cheek and chin. "I've spent my life hating people like you. Now, I should hate myself for loving you, Connie, but I can't."

AFTER HER SHIFT, Nora stuck around the office, waiting for Will. She didn't want him thinking she was mad. She wasn't anymore. Maybe a little scared, but she wasn't mad.

She glanced at the clock above the maps. Almost five. What was keeping him? She flipped *Stars and Stripes* open, found Mauldin's cartoon and laughed. That soldier had a future. He made a good story but not for her. Will had other plans for her. So did Matthew.

A snort from Norm Cox brought her eyes around. He glanced at the army paper laid across her desk and curled a lip. Christ, she hated him. "What's your beef, Normie?"

Squinting his pig eyes, Cox cleared his throat and bent over his typewriter. He hated being called Normie. Cox dressed like a dandy, from the polished links in his cuffs to the shine on his tasseled shoes. With his high-priced college diploma, he sneered at the poor stiffs who had to work their way into reporting jobs, reserving special abuse for GI newspapermen. He even prided himself on his educated typing, although the newsroom's two-finger typists beat him every time.

The last of the night shift pushed through the door, with Will on their tails. The new overnight teletype girl started an excuse. He pushed by her and into his office without shedding his jacket. The door slammed. Nora followed him through the window. He went straight for the whiskey stashed in his file cabinet. Her knock on the glass stopped him. He glanced over his shoulder and waved her in.

"Look, Will, I'm sorry."

Nora leaned against the door until it snapped shut. Will took the bottle into the corner hidden from the newsroom and tipped it up to his mouth. She grabbed his arm, spilling the whiskey on his coat. His eyes flashed wildly for a second, then fixed on her face. She tugged the bottle. He gave it up and crumpled into his chair.

"All right, let's have it." She capped the bottle and shoved it back into the files. "You keep that up, and we'll be distilling your damned blood."

Palms to his head, Will rubbed his temples. His hands shook, and he folded them into his lap. "All right." He bent over the desk. "All right."

Nora pushed a pile of books off the straight chair in the corner and pulled it next to his. She grabbed his hand under the desk and checked through the window. Everyone was back to work. She squeezed his fingers, meeting bone too soon. Will lifted his head and tried to smile. Fumbling his hand free, he searched through a pile of mail and pulled out an envelope. Nora recognized Sylvia's handwriting. He pushed the letter at her hand. "Read it."

She took the letter and squeezed again. "You tell me."

Will sighed raggedly. "Right. Well, Sylvia's had it with me being overseas. Two years in Russia and now this. No end in sight. She's been building up to it for months—moaning that she's lonely, the boys miss me. Now she tells me a friend of ours is trying to make time with her. And she sounds kind of happy about it. You know, excited."

Nora looked at the picture pinned on the wall next to Will's desk. Nice-looking kids, one grinning gap-toothed at the camera, and Sylvia kneeling behind them with every hair in place and her mouth curled carefully under a perfect coat of lipstick. Will's wife loved him, worshipped their kids and hated his job. Oh, boy, did she hate his job. Two minutes after meeting her, you knew that.

"So she wants you home. You can't blame her, Will. It's got to be tough raising kids alone."

Will's air whistled out on a sob. "And what am I supposed to do? Tell New York I want out? SHAEF gave us spots in the invasion press pool today. Guess what I landed—a front seat in the first wave. If I tell New York I want out, I'll get tagged a chicken for sure. That would finish me with IP."

Will knew his masters, all right. With his seniority, he'd get the first boat home for the asking. When IP assigned him to the desk, they'd explain about not having enough notice. When a stinker job opened up in East Jesus, they'd ask him to take it anyway, and give them a hand. And when his pride screamed "Enough," he'd walk away. He'd have no choice. IP didn't need an axman to fire unwanted employees. They just kept sharpening the blade until the fall guy slit his own throat.

Tucking his hand into hers, Nora forced Will to meet her eyes. Pain and tears muddied his. "I don't know what to say, Will, except you're in a helluva jam. You really think Sylvia's serious?"

Will breathed deeply and let the air leak out slowly as he nodded. "You know Sylvia. She thinks reporting is a job. Fifteen years of marriage and she hasn't learned.

I'm not telling you anything you don't already know, kid. For some of us reporting isn't what we do, it's what we are."

TWELVE

BETWEEN THE BLOWER pumping out hot air and wipers slip-slopping over the windshield, the staff car was too noisy for conversation. Matt didn't mind. He wasn't in the mood for more talk. Anything he said would just antagonize Nora again. His mind spun too fast, churning up fresh grudges against her and England and the whole damned world. All because mangled rails forced them off the train and into a three-hour delay. He'd been unreasonable when he snapped at her back at the railroad station while they waited for the car to show up. From the way she held herself now, aloof from him and the driver, Matt figured she was still steaming. She'd stiffened every inch of herself except for one black tendril defiantly curling to break the smooth line of her hair.

Matt lifted his arm from the seat back behind Nora's head and checked the time. They should make it with a few hours to spare. If they didn't, the general would get official word tomorrow, along with the other division commanders. Matt wanted to let the old man in on the alert a day early. He counted on the general to remember the favor next time the outfit needed a battalion commander.

The skinny GI at the wheel slowed the car and eased it toward the shoulder. A row of steel bays packed with artillery shells flanked the country road, hidden from German reconnaissance by overhanging branches. A while back they'd passed a field sprouting precise ranks of half-tracks and Shermans which disappeared over a distant rise. Ike had the men and the matériel alerted starting tomorrow. Now all they had to do was wait for the date. The car jerked to a stop between two ammunition bays. "What's the holdup, soldier?"

Spitting a toothpick into his fist, the scrawny kid pointed through the windshield. "Looks like a company from our outfit, sir."

A haze of moisture fogged the window, but Matt made out legs and arms swinging through the rain in unison. Nora brushed his shoulder as she slid forward to wipe the windshield with her hand. She shook her head. "They picked a bad day for marching."

Matt snorted and popped open the door. Only civilians figured soldiers could pick and choose when to march. The men strode closer, quiet on rubber soles. Pushing the door shut, Matt lifted his foot to the running board and propped hands on hips. The soldiers were big men with the matched gait of rigorous training. No shoulder slumped or foot dragged despite the steady rain. At their officer's command, all eyes snapped left while a captain Matt didn't recognize offered a salute. Fit and disciplined and they damned well better be. Matt touched the brim of his hat. Soon these men would be called upon to expend that stamina and self-control.

A shorter column of British infantrymen followed the company from First Division. The heavy tramp of boots announced the Tommies before Matt could see them. He didn't need to stand in the rain watching English soldiers. He wouldn't command any. Matt didn't subscribe to the officers' club notion that American muscle would set things right if the English missed their mark. That seemed unlikely. Five weary years into the war, the English were still tough and ballsy and damned hard to beat.

After knocking a warning for Nora to shove over, Matt swung back into the car and slammed the door. He tossed his dripping hat onto the back seat and caught the driver's eye. "Think you can nudge those Tommies aside, soldier?"

"Sure thing, sir. The English already say us Yanks are kind of uppity." The driver ground through the gears, searching for first. The car bucked forward, scattering the ranks of marching Englishmen. The driver grinned. "Works every time, sir."

Beside him, Nora sighed and flopped against the seat as the car moved forward. She turned to the side window. A water tank posted with warnings to use hologen tablets slipped behind the car as it picked up speed.

"Those poor boys were soaked right through. I wonder how many will come down with pneumonia from this rain?"

Clenching his hands, Matt swallowed a gust of angry words and forced himself to make allowances for civilian stupidity. It was damned hard. If Nora hadn't tagged along, he'd have already met with First Division's commander and made certain he got the first available job. All she wanted was a story, some silly tearjerker about poor boys marching in the pouring rain. Matt waited until his pulse evened into a slower beat. "Wars don't get called because of rain."

Nora's eyes sharpened and a frown tugged at one corner of her mouth. The staff car nosed into an ancient village with narrow streets and muddy lanes. The place looked no different from a hundred other European towns, each a tactical nightmare of twisting alleys and hidden snipers waiting to stall the advance. The car spun around a cramped corner, startling a young girl who hurried away under a black umbrella way too big for her. You never knew when you'd run across civilians and get mixed up with locals too proud or scared or stupid to run from the battle.

Suddenly the car wobbled, bounced twice and then settled into a steady bump as a front tire deflated. The GI driver braked and scrambled out the door. Nora dropped the hands holding her clear of the dashboard and wiggled arms into her raincoat. The back seat dipped as the soldier worked the spare free.

She grabbed her purse and glared at him. "Are you really going to make that boy jack you up with the car? Or does common courtesy get called off on account of rain?" She slipped across the seat and out the driver's door before Matt could say a word.

The kid had found the lug wrench when Matt stepped from the sedan. Nora sheltered under a leafless hedge behind the car. Her matches wouldn't catch, so Matt flicked his lighter and lit her cigarette. "Thanks." She turned up her collar with her free hand.

A couple of cows eyed them from a pasture across the road. With foliage, Matt figured the hedge would have hidden the small cottage from passersby. A wisp of smoke rose from the chimney, and a light in the front room glowed through the rain. A small face appeared in the window, low down near the far corner, and then a second popped into view, higher than the first. In a moment the door opened and a woman holding a coat above her head sped down the front path.

"May I help in some way?"

Nora glanced at him. Matt shook his head and smiled. "Sorry to bring you out in the rain. The driver'll have the flat fixed in no time."

Under the tented coat, the woman smiled. "Well, I won't have you standing out here when I've a pot of tea brewing right this minute. Come along." After two steps, she turned back and frowned. Raised eyebrows conveyed more displeasure than the firm tone of her voice. "I insist."

Sighing, Matt took Nora's arm and followed the Englishwoman into her cottage. Two round-eyed children waited by the fire as their mother ushered Nora and Matt into the front room. A book of nursery rhymes lay open on the hearth. The little boy plugged his mouth with a thumb when Matt pulled off his raincoat. The older boy watched with solemn eyes. Nora smiled at the children and tried to interest them in their book, but neither boy took his eyes off Matt. Their mother pushed a strand of faded blond hair from her eyes and smiled gently. "I'm afraid the officer reminds my boys of their father. Poor lads never knew him, really."

A kettle sang in the back of the cottage, and the woman trotted out with Nora on her heels. Matt spotted the photograph on the mantel and brought it down. He crouched until his shoulders drew level with the younger boy. "I'll bet this is your dad."

The little one stepped closer without replying. The older boy nodded but kept his distance. "Was our da. He's dead."

The enlisted man grinning at the camera stood open collared and sweating in the glare of a desert sun. One hand shaded his eyes and the other rested on the armor side of a Crusader. Egypt? Libya? Did it matter where

ALLIANCES

their father had died? The older boy watched him closely.

"He drove this tank?"

The little boy stared. His older brother shook his head. "He kept the engine running. Sir." Thin shoulders straightened under the black sweater.

Matt nodded and glanced at the boy. "Ah, he was a mechanic. Bad luck for us, I guess. It's tougher to keep a tank running than to drive one. We need men like your father."

A smile ghosted the older boy's lips until his mother swept back into the room, loaded down with a tray of tea and cups. The younger boy's fascination with Matt ended when he saw the plate of cookies Nora carried through the door. He sidled up to his mother with pleading eyes, but she silently shook her head. After listening to her whispered instructions, the boys ran from the room. Matt did without any of the widow's precious sugar or cream. So did Nora. The women had introduced themselves in the kitchen and seemed pretty friendly for just a few minutes' acquaintance.

Mrs. Burley was telling Nora how she managed to keep her small farm going without a hired hand. Nora's eyes darted over the room as she listened. Her brown eyes fixed momentarily on the picture Matt had returned to the mantel, a radio in the corner, books stacked on a table. When she tipped her head to read the titles, Matt realized what she was up to. She'd found another war victim's plight to entertain her readers.

Matt pretended not to notice when the boys slipped back into the cottage carrying an empty beer bottle. He listened to the women without hearing their talk, smiling and nodding when it seemed appropriate. Their words pierced his isolation without warning and catapulted him back into the conversation. "Wait a minute, ladies. What did I just agree to?"

Mrs. Burley smiled. "To take supper with us, Colonel. The joint of spring lamb will be on the table in three-quarters of an hour."

Setting aside his cup, Matt stood and shook his head. "I'm awfully sorry, but we can't stay." Nora's mouth dropped open, and Matt smiled as he took the widow's hand. "I have pressing business. You're kind to offer, but we should get back on the road."

Nora's eyes iced over when she looked at him. They thanked the widow, said goodbye to the boys and picked their way down the soggy path. The rain had stopped. Nora's hands were jammed in her pockets, and she kicked a twig blown down by the storm. Matt tensed and waited for her to blow.

"You've got some nerve." She stopped, but he kept walking. She jogged up to his side. "You were damned rude and lost me a good story to boot."

The GI driver threw open the door at their approach. Nora caught Matt's arm, forcing him to stop. "What harm was there in having lunch? You might be a little later getting to your base, but I'm sure you won't miss the invasion."

Matt shook off her hand. "Doesn't your work in London feed your ambition enough? You have to use widows, too?"

She reddened and stepped back. Matt came after her. He flicked a glance at the driver and leaned close. "That spring lamb she offered was probably her meat ration for the week or the boys' pet. You'd never know it from the life you live in London, but the war has cost this country plenty. She's already lost her husband and put up with us tramping around the countryside in droves. We don't have to take her food, too."

Nora's eyes widened. Matt struggled to dam his anger. Don't say a word. Just take it now or you'll take worse later. Her brown eyes flashed. "I seriously doubt—"

A fury sliced through him with a tide of adrenaline jangling every nerve until he had to lash out. "You forget rationing? This is your first trip outside London, right? In town you're at the Waverly or SHAEF. Don't worry, though. There's no rationing at First Division. We've got a helluva mansion to put you up in and plenty to eat and drink. Better get going or you'll miss the start of the party."

Spinning on his heel, Matt forced himself to stop. He wished he could whisk them back to the train station in London and start the day over. Had he managed to temper the contempt in his voice? Deliberate humiliation was something she wouldn't forgive.

The soldier opened his mouth. Nora cut him off by stepping in front of Matt. He waved the soldier back into the car when he saw the look on her face.

"Christ, the war isn't my fault."

Hearing the outraged innocence in her voice, Matt stopped trying to hold back. "No, it's not your fault, Nora." He grabbed her shoulders and gave her a little shake. "But you're enjoying it."

MATT SIDESTEPPED A PUDDLE tinted orange by the setting sun. A burst of laughter echoed between enlisted men's housing and drowned out the Andrews Sisters' harmony from a nearby radio. He'd given up trying to find Lou in the maze of Tidworth Barracks. He should turn back toward the big house for dinner.

A soldier rounded the corner of a two-story brick barracks and threw a reluctant salute. The troops hated officers nosing around their side of camp. Ordinarily Matt respected their need for a measure of freedom and privacy. Armies supplied little enough of either. But this afternoon his need was greater. He needed the hoarse shouts, the measured steps of guards walking the perimeter and the bugler sounding "Taps." He'd been gone too long to take any of it for granted. Brushing fingertips along the rough and solid barracks wall, he savored familiar things. Damp earth packed by a thousand boots and oil spread carefully over a thousand carbines were sweet to his nose. He found relief here and a certain satisfaction. Maybe it was simple, like lacing up boots already broken to your feet; the fit was everything. He'd spent too many years shaping himself to the army to live comfortably outside it for long.

Circling a hut, Matt came out close to the mess. He didn't need to hear the GI griping about more damned chicken to know what was cooking. Hell, half these men ate better in the army than they ever had at home. Every one of them ate better than the English. Starting tomorrow they'd be shoveling in all the hot chow they could fit. Any meal might be their last hot feed for a long time. And they could forget hot showers, clean socks and regular mail from home, too. He just hoped the First's men were as tough as they looked. They'd had a nice rest, but Ike was putting them back in business. Three invasions in just twenty months. The army wouldn't demand performance like that from any outfit but Big Red One. Soon it'd be his outfit again. Letting the general in on the alert a day early guaranteed that.

"Hey, Major!" Matt ignored the running footsteps behind him until he heard his name. "Major Chase?"

He pivoted and recognized Anton Mendoza, a wiry New Bedford fisherman from the rifle company Lou had led in Algeria. Mendoza squinted at him through gathering darkness until Matt nodded and smiled. "Sure. It is you!" His grin flashed white against olive skin. "Geez, colonel now, huh? You back here for good?"

Matt counted to three before Mendoza tacked a "sir" on the end of his question and flapped his hand into a halfhearted salute. "Just visiting. But don't get too cocky. I keep tabs on the outfit from London."

Mendoza fell into step beside him. Military decorum gave the soldier a little trouble, but everyone overlooked that after North Africa. Mendoza was the wiliest fighter Matt had ever seen and the best shot. The fisherman had a talent for knowing where the next Kraut would turn up and squeezed off his round before anyone else spotted the enemy. Lou figured the sixth sense developed as Mendoza gazed across the waters of the George's Bank, learning where the fish schooled. When he heard Matt mention a summer crewing on a trawler out of Provincetown, Mendoza forgot his officer's insignia and treated him like a hometown boy. They never got much beyond fishing and fighting, but it was enough.

"You mean it? You ain't coming back?" Mendoza scuffed a stone aside. "Shoot. I like familiar faces, you know? These new guys are all right, I guess. But can you depend on them? I don't know." Matt caught his sideways glance just as the last light faded. "That's the thing. I want to know who I can depend on if we're going in again. And we are. Boy, you can make book on that, sir. We are going in again."

Breaking stride, Matt fished out his cigarettes and offered one to Mendoza. When the soldier tucked the smoke behind his ear, Matt pushed the whole pack on him. "I can't believe you're broke, Anton. You get a crap game going in every bivouac. Five months in barracks means your setup should rival Havana."

Mendoza grunted. "I sent home a little too much last month and shorted myself. I got a rule never to touch the proceeds. Live on your pay, send the bootleg home. I make it back to New Bedford, I'll have enough for a couple of new trawlers. My old man will, anyway, no matter what."

No one knew how Mendoza managed to get his money back to the States. The army restricted enlisted men to sending home the amount of their paycheck. Officers had no restrictions and, for a percentage, some handled money for the ranks. Matt didn't blame the GIs, especially doughboys facing long odds and high casualty rates. When it was over they'd have to go home and restart interrupted lives. A nest egg might make that easier.

Reaching the last barracks, Matt drew up beside the drill ground. Mendoza's shadow stopped, too. Across the dark expanse, he picked out the scuffing boots of a soldier plodding through a punishment march. Matt flicked his butt away, following the glowing tracer until it sizzled out in dewy grass. He turned to Mendoza. "Keep your head down over there, soldier."

"Sure. You know me." The rifleman laughed, but the sound rolled heavily from his throat. "The rougher it is, the better off I am. I even let a couple of guys list me as their beneficiary instead of paying off now. I'll never see a dime unless they catch one over there. Funny world, huh?"

Matt listened until Mendoza's retreat blended with rattles and sighs as the camp settled down for the night.

ALLIANCES

The men were still trading on those damned $10,000 GI insurance policies. Business heated up on troop ships where soldiers swapped promises and dreams and fears in the long wait for H-hour.

A guard shouldering his gun swung a salute to Matt as he turned onto the roadway outside Tidworth Barracks. A twenty-minute walk would take him to the house First Division used for visitors and top officers. He needed to exercise his legs if he expected to lead an infantry battalion. Matt stopped and felt for his Camels until he remembered giving the pack to Mendoza. Damn. He didn't want to face Big Red One's mansion or Nora just yet. They'd have a feast laid on, and some wiseass would be sure to toast the absent owner whose wine they'd "borrowed." Someone was probably selling the aristocrat's wine cellar dry on the black market. Gas, nylons, booze, eggs—you name it, the Yanks had it and so could the English, for a price. Make the best of the war. Make a buck from it.

Clearing his throat, Matt spat and started walking. Hell, where did he come off so high horse? Why was it okay for Mendoza to make a buck but not the officer who risked his career to get the fisherman's dough home? Sure, more GIs than officers got planted under little white crosses in graveyards far from home, but no one had it easy. None of them asked for the war. What was wrong with making the best of it?

Matt shook his head. That was Nora's argument and he'd nailed her for it. He got riled up whenever he watched her use people's troubles to further her own ambition. What made it worse was realizing that she enjoyed the war, watching her thrive on it. She had a special sparkle in her eyes, a special animation when she worked. She was having a good time, dammit.

A double-decker bus rumbled behind him and sent thin snakes of light darting across the road. Matt avoided a lungful of diesel exhaust by stepping to the shoulder and waiting for it to pass. Pinpricks of glowing cigarettes hung in the dim interior of the civilian bus. Routes to Andover and Salisbury pulled in at Tidworth. A rebel yell touched off a series of happy shouts and yips that hung in the road after darkness swallowed the bus. Those soldiers were off to whoop it up in the closest gin mill. Hell, for too many it was just another Friday night.

Why should he blame Nora for making the best of things? Everyone made use of the war somehow. Nora built her reputation and so did he. At least she stuck to the fringes. He preferred war's bloody heart.

A sentry challenged him when he approached the gravel drive to First Division's big house. He endured a moment's flashlighted glare in his eyes before the soldier waved him on.

Gulping night air, Matt picked his way over small stones in the drive. When had he turned into a Yankee Puritan? He sounded as smug and self-righteous as the congressman at his finger-pointing worst. And for a lot less reason. Father brandished his stump like the Medal of Honor and ensured that no one questioned his high-toned ideals closely enough to detect the fear. Even though the old man was fooling himself, his war at least left him something to believe in. For himself, Matt didn't know.

A shadow moved across the flag-stoned terrace fronting the old brick house above him. Matt knew those curves. The dark silhouette paced from the shrubs walling one end of the terrace to the shrubs walling the other. Matt climbed the twisted flight of stairs from the drive as she passed and caught her fragrant wake of sunshine and flowers.

At least Nora knew what she wanted. He hadn't bothered to ask himself that question since he started West Point. Joining the long gray line meant forgetting what he wanted and accepting what he got. Once he realized that another war was unavoidable, his future was decided. Now they were winning it. And if he made it through, what would he be left with? Suddenly the future loomed as dark and empty as England's blacked-out night.

THIRTEEN

THE STEWARD HELD her coat. Nora slid into it and threw a last glance around the drawing room. The energetic major who'd dogged her all afternoon grinned across an acre of polished mahogany and young American officers. Nora forced a smile. The major turned back into the huddle of newsmen and soldiers pawing over smutty pictures. The men whooped like adolescents when they discovered a fresh supply of girlie magazines had arrived. Starting right then, First Division's borrowed mansion reminded her of frat houses back at college.

Pushing out the door to the flagstoned terrace, Nora cinched the belt of her raincoat tighter and turned up the collar. The showers had stopped and a few stars peeped out between clouds, but the night air was chilly.

The blackout curtain covering the French doors from the dining room gaped open an inch. She pressed her cheek against cool glass to watch preparations for dinner. White-jacketed waiters working in tandem under glowing chandeliers set the long table with heavy silver, translucent china banded with gold and crystal goblets filled with starched napkins. Two long buffets spread with lace cloth and empty chafing dishes guaranteed that tonight's meal wouldn't be the army's usual mess-hall fare.

Nora dug through her pockets until she found the Chesterfields. She lit up and leaned a shoulder against the house. The young officers came from America's campuses, just as the soldiers back at Tidworth Barracks came from America's factories and farms. Officers and soldiers didn't start from the same place and didn't end up together, either. The boys in the mansion played at war here, just as they played at life back home. Training in England offered the rough games, ample booze and towny women they enjoyed in civilian life.

Drawing smoke deep, she held it a second before gently blowing it out. Back at Tidworth, eating out of battered mess kits and sleeping on straw mattresses, the GIs lived lives similar to those left behind, too. Instead of worrying about the factory shutting down or a killing drought, the young soldiers worried about the whims of the high command that could order them home to safety or back to combat. Though accustomed to outside forces controlling their lives, no working stiff or GI enjoyed being a puppet whose strings were pulled to match a tune whistled by the big shots.

Nora had shared their impotent fury and recognized that explosive pressure in a kid from Brooklyn she'd spotted earlier that day. He was glaring into space from a bench near a mess hall. A hint of awkwardness in the angle of his crossed legs and the soft fuzz covering his cheeks made it hard to believe he was a soldier. Nora figured he was just off a troop ship and feeling a little lonely. In other words, he'd make a column. She didn't expect him to hand her a major exclusive.

When she plopped down beside him and asked if he minded, a deep crease ran between the fine arch of his brows, and his hazel eyes remained flat with indifference. "Free country, ain't it?"

The voice spilling from the corner of his mouth was pure Flatbush, and she grabbed that accent like a lifeline, since the usual soldier's enthusiasm at the appearance of a woman hadn't worked. Angling around until she could prop her elbow on the back of the bench, Nora flashed him her flirtiest smile. "Sounds like you're from Brooklyn, soldier."

He folded his arms and gave her the once-over with cool eyes. "Yeah? What's it to you?"

"Listen, mac, I'm not looking for an argument. I just saw you sitting here, thought you looked interesting and decided to sit down. If it bothers you, I can leave."

He shrugged and looked at the ground between his knees for a second. Then he pulled out a pack of gum and offered her a piece. "Stick around if you want. How'd you know I'm from Brooklyn, anyway?"

Jimmy from Flatbush Avenue thawed enough to tell Nora he'd been with the outfit since enlisting at seventeen in 1940. She asked if that meant he'd been in North Africa and Sicily, and the boy nodded silently. A deep throbbing hum lifted his eyes to the sky. Far above, crossing a break in the clouds, flew a formation of planes.

The young soldier snorted. "Listen to this crybaby feeling sorry for himself 'cause Uncle Sam says he's gotta hit the beach again."

Nora's eyes dropped to Jimmy shaking his head as he watched the planes. "Them airborne dummies got it even worse." He jerked a thumb at the sky. "Guys jump out of transports like that. They're sitting ducks up there, you know? Nothing to hide behind, and sometimes they get shot down by our own guys." A deep sigh whooshed from him. "We killed a bunch in Sicily. A couple hundred, at least."

Taking a final drag from her Chesterfield, Nora paced along the shrubs that lined the side of the terrace. The cigarette glowed brighter as she inhaled. She tossed it at the bushes and turned back across the flagstones.

That's where the exclusive had started. Jimmy told her all the details he could remember. Nora didn't bother telling him she was a reporter since she needed confirmation from higher up to get the story past the censors. Jimmy thought at least twenty U.S. transports carrying paratroopers got knocked down by American Navy guns. He remembered how everyone raved when the naval gunners went into action after the division's artillery bogged down, how they cheered when shipboard guns blasted targets miles inland and got things moving again. And he remembered standing on a ridge swearing helplessly at the Germans as smoking American planes spun to earth and dissolved in fire. He remembered the helplessness of seeing them go down and the helplessness of learning American hands had triggered those guns. Friendly fire. That's what Jimmy from Flatbush Avenue called it.

Her heels clicked on the stones paving the terrace, shattering the heavy silence of the night. She didn't care how it happened or who was at fault. It made little difference if the boys died because someone was careless or because someone was trigger-happy. Those boys were dead, and they shouldn't be.

An ember of outrage flared inside her as she tried to visualize the grief of three hundred mothers. She remembered a line of hearses burdened with small coffins, an endless black chain of death that twisted through Chicago's meanest streets after a killing heat wave.

Those mothers ended up with empty arms. Uncle Sam would give the paratroopers' mothers a few thousand in insurance and a gold star for their sacrifice. And they'd never know the truth.

Nora's elbow caught on the branches of a hedge as she spun back across the terrace. She yanked free. She'd give it one more day. From what Jimmy said, plenty of people at Tidworth Barracks knew the story. With confirmations tomorrow morning, she could phone it in to Will after lunch. She wouldn't trust anyone except Will with her exclusive. He had the savvy to get the story through censorship without claiming credit in the byline. If she roughed out the story tonight after dinner, she might be able to phone it in to IP before noon. And if Will worked fast, her exclusive might get okayed in time for the next day's news report.

A brief exchange of deep-toned voices floated up from the darkness somewhere along the drive. Nora glanced at the staircase twisting down to the gravel but could see only the tall silhouettes of sturdy trees. Slowing near the wall of bushes, she noticed a red glow on the ground. Her cigarette must have bounced off the hedge. She scuffed the butt across the stones with a foot and turned.

A shape broke free of the shadows on the terrace and moved in her direction. Nora took a deep breath and jammed hands in pockets as she walked. She knew that easy stride, that tall shape tapered from shoulder to hip. Surprise or apprehension shortened her breath. Matthew had some nerve. First he'd given her hell because the damned train was late, and then he'd laid into her over Mrs. Burley's damned lamb. Arriving at Tidworth Barracks, she'd been so burned up that she wanted to spit.

ALLIANCES

Their paths converged, and Nora forced her hands into fists inside her pockets. So maybe there was a little truth in what he said. She was so wrapped up in work that she probably did look insensitive to someone outside the news business. Her heart tripped into a faster beat. But he was wrong to accuse her of enjoying the war. What she enjoyed was her work, not the war. He jumped to an unfounded conclusion, and this time he owed her the apology. She'd cooled off a little, but he could still go to hell.

Veering out of his path, Nora tried to detour around Matthew. His arm shot out at waist level, erecting a barrier she couldn't bring herself to step around or brush aside. She stared into the darkness.

Matthew sighed. "Look, Nora, I guess I was pretty rotten to you back there on the train and at the widow's house. I had a lot on my mind. Which is no excuse, I know, but I am sorry."

The arm blocking her dropped, but she didn't move. Instead she turned her head up to him. A beam of starlight freed from drifting clouds fell across them and streaked down the bolt of silver in his hair.

Nora shivered and hugged herself against the chill. "Let's just forget it, all right? I owe you one, anyway." Turning until her shoulders lined up with his, Nora took his arm. "Mind if we walk? It's too cold to stand around yapping, and I can't stomach another minute inside with the college boys."

His fingers closed over the hand she rested on his sleeve. "I take the first London train tomorrow morning. When do you get back to town?"

She shrugged, liking the touch of his hand. "Depends on you guys. I've got a couple of things lined up, but all my plans are off if Ike starts on his."

Making small talk felt so nice after their argument that she overlooked the danger when he steered their conversation onto hazardous topics. She listed the outfits on her itinerary when he asked. He wanted to know the kinds of stories she planned to write, and she described a couple of her ideas. Simple carelessness trapped her in the end. Will wanted a few pieces on airborne outfits, claiming the public thought of paratroopers as modern swashbucklers. She told Matthew that and was surprised when he abruptly stopped walking.

"You aren't planning anything foolish." His fingers tightened around her wrist. "You're not going to try to talk your way into a parachute or even onto a transport, are you?"

"I hadn't thought of it. Why?" She smiled under cover of darkness. "You may have an idea, though. Sounds like good copy."

The pressure around her wrist increased. And she knew what he'd say before he spoke again. She wanted to clap a hand over his lips and hold back the words.

"Promise me you won't go up. Airborne outfits are unlucky. They get dropped in the wrong place or blown off target or shot down before they jump." He gave her arm one firm shake. "I know what I'm talking about. In Sicily the navy shot down our own airborne troops. I saw it, and it wasn't pretty."

The weight of his words slumped her shoulders. She felt like a child whose bright toy balloon had snagged on a thorn, horrified by the tear and helpless against the insistent leak shriveling the fragile dream.

THE GENTLE SPLASH of raindrops streaking down windowpanes and the hiss of green wood laid upon glowing coals perfected the moment for Constance.

They had escaped London and its urgent demand for work. Peter's black-market wizardry had stuffed the fridge with meat, the likes of which she'd rarely seen since '39. Her own foresight had ensured enough wine and whiskey for a hundred stolen weekends. As soon as they'd arrived, they tested the sturdiness of her bed upstairs and found it met the challenge of sheltering two bodies instead of the usual one. All those things totted up left Constance with a wonderful feeling of rightness, of completeness. He was here with her, within reach of her hand.

Weekending with Peter at Corniche felt anything but wretched. At first apprehension had tugged at her happiness when he agreed to spend a few days in the country. But soon the need to show Peter something of her other life had won out over the fear. The cottage at Corniche was her special place, from the leaping dolphin wind vane atop the slate roof to the clippings and dead flowers mouldering into compost for the gardens. In all seasons, by day and by night, Corniche offered her refuge and promised her safety. She wanted Peter to know Corniche, too.

Still, she'd snatched the photos off the bookcases and hidden them in the cabinets below. It seemed as if Jeremy's eyes had accused her from the gilt frame of their last family portrait before the war. But he had no right to make accusations. He'd been the one who had abandoned her and run off to the safety of India's vastness when Nazi bombs exploded across England like firecrackers squandered on a lavish Guy Fawkes Day celebration. He'd left her to bear it all alone. If there was fault to parcel out, his came first. Constance pulled the cardigan draped around her shoulders. She wouldn't think of Jeremy now.

Beyond his blasted roses, Corniche wasn't Jeremy's place at all. Corniche was her place, and Geoff's. Whenever she returned, a deep thread of mourning for her brother ran through her happiness. She couldn't pass the village sweet shop they'd haunted as children without thinking of him. Whenever the church bells rang, she remembered the time she'd shamed him into climbing the bell tower and how Geoff accepted responsibility when the curate caught them. Each pasture and lane, each fishing hole or secret swimming spot brought him to life again, always laughing and young.

The fire crackled, popping an ember across the hearth and onto the carpet. Peter sprang from his chair beside her and kicked the cinder back into the flames. She studied the line of his back as he propped one arm against the mantel and poked a toe into the grate to bank the fire. He sighed, and she noticed the clenched hand hanging at his side.

What a ninny she was to expect him to enjoy an afternoon spent warming himself before the fireplace. He was a creature of cities, of horns blaring in the streets and crowds marching shoulder to shoulder between errands or appointments that couldn't be put off an instant. The rush of life stretched him as taut as the strings of a violin. He needed some kind of activity, something that challenged him even as it gentled him.

"I don't suppose you'd mind mucking through a bit of rain?" He turned to her, and the fire cast a ruddy tint across his cheeks. "I thought we might see if we could catch a fish course for our supper."

His eyebrows ran together when his forehead creased. "You want fish when we've got that big sirloin in the kitchen? I don't get it."

ALLIANCES

Constance laughed and caught his hand as she stood up. "Don't frown so, Peter. The fun of fish is landing them. And I know exactly where they'll be biting."

He grumbled a bit when she insisted he put on the gardener's moth-eaten sweater and old mackintosh. With an extra pair of socks, the boots fit, but he absolutely refused a hat until she offered him Jeremy's old tweed cap. After she brought two rods from the shed, he even helped dig through rotting leaves for worms. When they'd filled an old tin with bait, she led him through the back gate to the pasture. New green shoots twisted through the winter stubble, and mud sucked at their heels in the puddles.

Peter turned his face up to gray skies. "I always liked the rain. When I was a kid, I liked to feel the drops hit my cheeks and watch the water splash through the grates into the sewers. Tommy was the neighborhood champ at damming gutters. He'd flood the street, and we'd have a ball before someone kicked in his dam and chased us back home."

He took the rods when they reached the stone fence. Constance muddied a knee climbing over and studied the water of the river. Someone might see them from the bridge, then Mother would hear. But trout hid in the deep pool under the arch, and Peter must catch one if their outing was to be a success.

She pointed toward the road. "By the bridge, I think. The fat and lazy ones are there, hoping to steal our worms and send us home empty-handed."

Peter slid down the grassy bank to the rock she pointed out and reached back for their gear. Warm fingers closed around her hand to steady her as she joined him. He dug into the bait tin, came up with a worm and slipped it onto her hook. "Okay. Show me what to do next."

Constance laughed. "I expect you know from the way you handled the bait."

He shrugged. "I'm a surgeon, lady. I've never fished in my life."

Lines placed, Constance sank onto the mossy rock and dangled her booted feet into the pool. Peter smiled when she offered him the flask from her pocket. He tipped it to his mouth and passed it back. "Is booze standard for fishing or something special for me?"

"Oh, it's standard. When we were children, my brother said we'd finally arrived when Daddy offered us his flask. Wearing long pants and swigging brandy were sure signs of growing up, Geoff said."

"You fished here when you were a kid?"

Constance nodded. "All along here. My parents' country house isn't far."

Peter's eyes narrowed. "I'll bet they'd love it if we showed up for tea." He pulled a twig from a lilac bush growing close to the stone bridge. "But how would the butler announce us? 'Mrs. Tolliver and her Yank'?" The twig splashed into the water.

Cheeks burning, Constance bent over her pole and wound in her line. "They're in London. The house was given over to the army for the duration."

Her hook came in empty, and she reached across him for the tin of bait. He caught her line and jabbed another worm on. "And your brother? Does he still live here, or is he doing important work for king and country?"

His words knifed open that tender wound. Was it important work for king and country that had killed Geoff? Nothing had changed when he died, and yet her world had never been the same again. Geoff hadn't died for something noble or good or worthy. He just died.

Scrambling to her feet, Constance cast her line into the river. "No, Geoff has no important job. He's still here. He's buried next to our grandparents." A sob broke free, and she let the tears run down her cheeks.

Peter took her rod and dropped it to the grass. He pulled her into his arms, running strong fingers up her back and into her hair. "Connie, Connie. I always hurt you, dammit. The country houses, the fishing, the big shot father. I don't know what to do with you."

He drew her head against his shoulder and rubbed his cheek against her hair. "You're like the beautiful china dolls in the window of a Fifth Avenue toy shop. When I was a kid, I wanted one of those stupid dolls, all bright and clean with shiny hair and lace clothes."

His voice deepened into a harsh growl. "I didn't want a train to play with. I wanted something pretty to look at. But I knew the only way I could get a doll was by smashing the window and making a run for it."

Constance tried to lift her face to him, but his hand kept her pressed against the shoulder of the gardener's coat. The damp wool scratching her cheek smelled of earth and smoke. "Don't, Peter. It's not you. It's me, and fishing here, and remembering other times with Geoff. You haven't hurt me."

He shuddered, and the movement ran through her, too. "But I have, and I will. I don't want to hurt you, but I will. You're like that damned doll. My mother held on to her dreams. She begged a cast-off doll from the house where she worked, said it was for her daughter."

Constance pulled back, twisting free of his hand and snarling her hair in his fingers. "Ten years she worked there, and they didn't know she had only boys."

The planes of his face looked hard and tight. His eyes dropped to the gold strands caught in his hand. "She brought it home and put it on her bed. And she looked at it. I watched her eyes go dreamy when she looked at that stupid doll. I hated it. I didn't believe in dreams anymore."

With a painful jerk, his hand pulled free of her hair. "So one night I took the doll to the alley and smashed that pretty face against the tenement wall."

Constance caught his hand, squeezing until she drew his eyes. "I told her what I'd done. She cried, and I told her why. I told her having one pretty thing doesn't make your life pretty. She just cried harder."

STRETCHING A LEG through now lukewarm water, Nora snagged the chain between her toes and jerked the stopper from the tub. Draining water pulled against her calves. She folded her legs and stood up. The radiator had warmed the towel she'd draped across it, and she wrapped herself in thick terry. The peach towel hung below her knees, and she wondered whose bathroom this had been before the war. The flowered paper above the scrubbed tile lining the walls looked girlish. The towels and unopened packages of lotion and dusting powder were definitely not government issue.

She unscrewed the cap of the lotion and sniffed. The barest hint of roses drifted up. The hot bath had worked the kinks out of her arms and legs, and only a Puritan would insist on Jergens when something nicer was available. She massaged the slick lotion into her shoulders and caught a glimpse of herself in the mirror. Her eyes gave her away. Too big and too bright always meant she was excited. Christ, was it Matthew or the exclusive, or having to choose between them? Why couldn't she have both, like the girls in fairy tales or Hollywood movies?

Bending to sit on the edge of the tub, she reached down to work the lotion into her ankles and calves. All through dinner and her bath she'd been going around and around. The friendly fire story would be big. It was the kind of story that had to get out sometime and, when it did, the reporter who broke it would be noticed. She'd been looking for this exclusive for three months.

Nora unwrapped the towel and massaged the lotion into her belly. They'd had it out about her using Matthew for a source weeks ago. He'd made it clear then she had to choose, and she had. Except that it was no choice, really, since she hadn't learned anything from him again. Until today, dammit. And if he hadn't blurted out that warning, she'd have been home free.

Shielding her dark hair with an arm, she dipped into the powder and dusted her neck and shoulders and breasts. What was wrong with her, anyway? She never had trouble making decisions. In her position, she couldn't afford second thoughts or compromises. Will always said reporting might be a game without rules but there was one law chiseled in stone—anything for the story. As a woman in a man's job, she couldn't break that law, especially not with a scoop like the one she'd lucked on to today. Why was she letting Matthew hold her back now?

Nora folded the towel aside and slipped into her robe. She unpinned her hair and brushed it smooth around her shoulders. Snapping off the light, she pushed open the door to her room. She'd forgotten to switch on the lamp by her bed, and the change from lit bathroom to dark bedroom blinded her for a moment. She felt her way across the room and nearly reached the bed before spotting the cigarette glowing above her pillow.

"I brought you a brandy."

She caught her breath and stopped in midstride, raising her arms like a shield. But as her eyes adjusted to the dark and the shadow formed into Matthew, she relaxed. He lay propped on an elbow, offering a glass with his free hand. She thanked him and sipped, still standing.

"You really annoy me, Nora."

"I'm not surprised." Nora sank into a chair beside the bed. An hour ago everything had been forgiven. What was the problem now?

Matthew sat up and swung his legs to the floor. He leaned close. Too close. She threw up a wall of words. "I annoy plenty of people. Partly, it's my job. The rest is just me. I'm not the kind who never meets a person who doesn't like me. I meet plenty."

He held out a cigarette, but she shook her head. She could see his smile now. "I'm always annoyed when I find myself preoccupied. And you've caused me a lot of annoyance lately."

She looked at him steadily as he leaned closer and slipped a hand under the loose hair at the back of her neck. A shiver ran down her spine.

"I've been wondering about your hair." He raked his fingers through gently, lifting until his hand ran out and it fell back to her shoulders. "I knew it'd be soft."

He touched her chin, raising it, brushing her lips lightly with his thumb. "And your lips. How do you taste?"

The kiss was soft, light and lingering. He straightened and drew her up from the chair. He reached for the knotted sash at her waist. "And that's not all I've wondered about."

Cool air licked softly across her breasts as the robe opened under his hands, but she stood still. His eyes held hers as warm fingers closed gently around the curve of her waist. She sipped air through tight lips and closed her eyes to hide from the question in his. The tips of strong fingers brushed lower. She dropped her head, snapping the bond of doubt that had held her motionless. Her eyes opened and gave Matthew the answer he wanted.

Nora moved into him when his hands slid across her willing flesh, one reaching behind to pull her close while the other circled a breast. He caught her bare legs between the cloth covering his and the buttons of his shirt ground into her belly. And then she was falling, until the mattress rose to cushion her back as his mouth swooped over hers. Brandy mingled on their tongues as she kissed him. When he tried to draw away, she clung with greedy lips and dug through the thick hair on his head, holding him closer still.

But in an instant it wasn't enough to touch just his head when he touched her everywhere. As he searched the length of her body with teasing fingers, Nora wanted more, too. She tugged the knot at his collar and used both hands to free him of his shirt. He sucked air hard when she touched the flat stomach above his belt, but her fingers plunged on, tangling in the curling hair on his chest as she pushed her way up. For a long moment his eyes caught hers as he hovered, bare chest above her bare breast. Then she pushed at the elbow bracing him and, at last, drew him down as her mouth tilted into his.

He sighed, and she breathed him in. His lips ran along her chin and down the length of her neck. She reached for him again, fumbling at his belt with unsteady fingers. He rolled away and, when he came back, lifted her and pulled away the blankets. Icy sheets cooled her only until he dropped onto the bed and held her.

As he whispered against her hair, his hands stroked lower and lower. She stretched against him, melting into his arms without answering, pressing tight against him from chin to knee. His words blew against her temple again. She pulled his mouth to hers and lifted her hips, fitting herself around him. His soft groan echoed counterpoint to her trembling sigh.

He filled her as if they were practiced lovers, and an ache of pleasure spread through her as they rocked. She looked into tender eyes and turned her lips into the gentle hands brushing tangled hair from her cheeks. He smiled down, and she smiled back.

The roll of his hips slowed into a tantalizing dawdle. "Maybe this will cure my preoccupation with you." His lips brushed a nipple. "But I doubt it."

His teasing words and mouth and hips were too much. She lured him faster with swaying thighs and tickling tongue. Her fingers coaxed, and his mouth closed over hers, robbing her of breath. A delicious panic crept through her as the moment lengthened and still his lips gripped her. Her weakening fingers clasped iron shoulders as he drove her on and up against him. His harsh pants broke against her mouth, rasping quicker to match the pulse beating in her head, the pulse throbbing through her limbs. And then the pulse rose into a wave that rushed through her on an unstoppable tide.

FOURTEEN

NORA FINGERED the satin edge of the blanket tucked around her hips and tried to concentrate on her problem. There was no avoiding a decision now. Matthew had pressed a last kiss on her lips at first light, leaving her happy and sad and definitely in a fix. If it had been out of bounds to report things he told her when their friendship was casual, how much worse would it be to report the paratroopers' deaths now?

"Lots worse."

The sound of her voice focused her mind on the predicament he'd left her. What if she explained, told him she knew the story before he mentioned it? A cool draft brushed across her shoulders, and she wiggled back under the covers. Offering an explanation might square things with Matthew. Or it might not. She'd be gambling.

Turning on the pillows, she breathed in the spicy tang he'd left in her bed. The dent he'd left in the pillow drew her, and she closed her eyes as she burrowed into his scent. Without his arms around her, she found that the sheet's embrace chilled, and the vacant spot beside her was too empty to bear. She wanted time to get used to their new intimacy, time with him to find out if he shaved before he showered and if he liked his eggs scrambled or poached. She wanted to watch him dress and comb his hair and tie his shoes. She wanted to look up from her coffee to find his eyes on her and see the gleam that said she was special, and they were wonderful together. But the only time they had was stolen from his work and hers and the damned war.

The water in the tub was tepid, so she hurried through her bath and into her clothes. She stuffed her belongings into the small suitcase and left it outside the door when she went down to breakfast. The grinning major had reminded her last night that he'd lined up a busy morning before her train pulled out at noon. She gulped coffee and studied her itinerary. The schedule put her with an airborne unit in two days.

"Are you nearly finished, Miss Seymour?" The major pulled out the chair next to her at the long dining table. "Hope you got plenty of rest. We'll keep you hopping until train time."

Nora searched his blue eyes for a hidden snicker but found nothing except the slick phoniness of an experienced press agent. The major mentioned working for a big Madison Avenue outfit before the war. The forced brightness of his smile came with practice and was not a dirty joke at her expense. Trust Matthew to be discreet.

"I hope you left time for me to file a story."

"You bet I did." The Madison Avenue smile widened. "I even know your deadline so you'll have plenty of time."

He explained the structure of an infantry division on the ride back to Tidworth Barracks. The regiments, battalions, companies, platoons and squads were just numbers until he brought up Matthew. She knew officers of his rank commanded battalions. But she didn't know Matthew was getting his own battalion and soon. He hadn't said why he was visiting his old outfit, and she hadn't asked.

Nora shook her head. "But he's assigned to SHAEF."

"Sure, for now." Madison Avenue spread his hands. "But that's just temporary. The general wants him back. Since the old man always gets his way, it's just a matter of time until Colonel Chase has another crack at the Germans."

Damn Matthew! Nora knotted her fingers together and stared out the staff car window as greening spring meadows slipped by. He was going to run out on her whether or not she reported the friendly fire deaths. The real question was how soon. If she wrote the story, he'd be gone tomorrow. But even if she held off, Matthew was going. Everyone expected the invasion soon, by summer at the least. Will said the timetable hinged on the weather. Already tree limbs were fringed with the pale green lace of budding leaves, and yellow splashes of forsythia blossomed in gardens they passed. How long did they have? A week, a month?

The major reached out to help her from the car's back seat, but Nora brushed his hand aside. The morning sun cast a bloody glow over the lines of old brick barracks. She turned her back on the enlisted men's housing and took the steps to the briefing room at a trot. Madison Avenue was right behind her. Unless she shook him, she had no chance of getting the friendly fire deaths story confirmed. She didn't like his type but figured he was good at his job. A good publicist knew reporters' deadlines. If the major knew hers, he also knew how to cut off questions that might have embarrassing answers.

A half dozen reporters lounged in folding chairs pulled into a chummy circle in the briefing room. The coffeepot, scarred desks and brace of telephones shoved in one corner completed a reporter's requirements. Nora recognized a couple of men from last night's dinner but couldn't remember names, only affiliations. The grizzled hack from Chicago talked up stories about hometown boys making good overseas. She didn't see the paunchy writer from *Manhattan* who had spent time with the First in North Africa. He was the intellectual type who used initials instead of first name in his byline, but she liked him. The other reporters were second-raters from minor league papers. Working for International Press gave her the biggest audience. That explained why she rated the personal escort. She dropped into a chair and flipped open her notebook as the major cleared his throat to signal the start of the briefing.

Smoky halos hovered around the bent heads of the other reporters and the scratching of their pens combined into a chorus as he explained infantry tactics. Nora's mind strayed. She could get the same information out of a book if she ever needed it. The civilian reporters all wore uniforms and even had regulation haircuts. They were probably careful to make a show of taking notes so they wouldn't have their snouts pulled out of the army feedbag. Not one of them had the gumption to dig out a story like the friendly fire deaths. The old-timer from Chicago might have chased it down years ago, but he looked too tired now.

Nora sighed and smoothed her skirt. Maybe choosing between Matthew and the exclusive was out of her hands, anyway. She wasn't going to get a chance to find those confirmations before her train pulled out. Madison Avenue droned on about the division, promising a peek at the weapons he described and hinting at a chance to fire a round or two. Big deal. The other reporters could fill their notebooks with the garbage he called background. She had to come up with a scheme to rescue the friendly fire exclusive.

Hanging back when the other reporters filed from the briefing room, Nora tried to lose the group by slipping out another door. The major proved his worth by finding her when his head count came up one short. She returned his thin smile and shook her head when he asked if she needed the convenience. As they walked across Tidworth Barracks to the training grounds, Nora worked on a story for Will in her mind.

She backtracked to avoid a muddy spot and laughed when the major glanced around in panic after finding her gone from his side. He reddened and shrugged, and she knew she'd scored a point. Now she could insist on privacy to phone Will and wouldn't need secrecy or codes to disguise the friendly fire exclusive from snooping ears. But she still had the problem of her byline. Will would use her name on the story or demand to know why she didn't want credit. Telling him the truth about Matthew might backfire. She didn't want her boss thinking she was going soft.

The other reporters flocked around the guns the major brought out at the firing range. Nora clapped on a pair of mufflers and moved far back from the line but still ended up with ringing ears.

Back at the briefing room, the Chicago hack found a typewriter and spun a clean sheet of paper around the roller while the other reporters drained a fresh pot of coffee. Nora drew out a Chesterfield as she watched the Chicago newspaperman pound out a page of copy. He'd just slugged the story name on the top left of his second sheet when Madison Avenue touched her arm. "I've arranged to have you use a private office whenever you're ready."

"Thanks." Nora drew in a lungful of smoke to give herself time. "Yeah, thanks a lot, Major, but I won't need it. I don't have a story lined up just yet."

CONSTANCE RUBBED HER HAND across a window and studied the filth smudging her fingertips. Mother would be speechless with rage if she saw the grime and dust in the old nursery. No matter that the room had been shut up before the last war and never used since.

Moistening her handkerchief with the tip of her tongue, Constance wiped the dirt from her fingers. Peter had a right to his anger. But it made her happy to know their weekend together had managed to burn off a bit of his hatred and resentment. With time and love and patience, she could free Peter of the small enraged boy chained within him. It had been too long since she'd felt pain like his, and she hoped visiting her childhood home would stir memories of youthful emotion.

Dust stirred by her exploration tickled a sneeze from her nose. The day had turned fine when she waved Peter off on the London train, and she detoured past the village. It wasn't until she reached the gates that she remembered that a hush-hush Yank intelligence unit had taken over the house.

The gates stood open, so she walked through, only to be met on the drive by a stern young American who ordered her to fall in, then led her to his superiors. The hard-faced colonel wasn't having any of her explanation until she pulled a copy of *Judgment* from Daddy's trophy case and pointed to the jacket photo. He apologized then, and told her to stay as long as she needed. Now she was free to wander through the rooms of her childhood but wasn't quite certain what she was looking for.

Opening a cupboard under the nursery bookcase, she sifted through a stack of old books but found no treasures. Soft pine floorboards still showed the ruts left by Geoff's crib when he'd pushed it across the room so he could be closer to "'stance." Nana Carberry had frowned when she discovered the change and warned them not to tell Mother if they wanted the new bed arrangement to remain. How they wept when Mother decided the four-year-old twins were old enough to move into separate bedrooms on the floor their parents shared. Mother caused another flood of tears when she exiled Geoff to boarding school. But when he came home on holiday they were inseparable again.

Constance brushed the dust off the raised hearth and sat down. Perhaps the nursery drew her because in this room she and Geoff had created a separate world until Mother tore them apart. Mother thought their attachment was unnatural. For a time after his death, Constance wondered if she was right. Her grief was so great, so unceasing. But when she had twins of her own, their special closeness mirrored what she'd shared with Geoff.

What would he think of her today? Twisting away from the thought, Constance hugged herself. The world was different now. He'd been a golden boy showing such breathtaking promise that everyone agreed he'd go far. But France had changed him. His letters to her grew bitter, cynical and grim. He stopped writing to their parents altogether. Constance supposed later that Geoff had blamed Daddy for the war. He kept his last leave secret and never once visited their parents, preferring to meet Constance for meals in town and never saying where he stayed. He called the war legal butchery but told her nothing else of life in France. And then he was dead. Just like that—dead. That was when she stopped believing in God.

Constance wondered if Peter believed in God. Not bloody likely. Poor boys rarely had leisure to ponder intangibles, and bright ones rejected the notion that poverty was their cross to bear. But he believed in something. Peter believed in himself and in medicine. Geoff had believed enough in his principles to go back to a war he hated, even if he couldn't return to the home that had nurtured him. What did she believe in, really believe in? Certainly not pacifism, if she took her *Manhattan* articles into account. If she truly believed in social justice, she'd have jumped at the chance to help Jane minister to patients living in deep shelters. And if she truly believed her marriage vow sacred, would she now ache for the touch of her lover and glory in her adultery?

Geoff would despise her today. The truth chimed through her mind with the thunderous peal of Westminster's bells and sent her racing from the nursery. She slipped on the worn carpet in the servants hall but righted herself before she tumbled. She clattered down the wooden stairs and into the kitchen. A young man swathed in an apron looked up from a steaming kettle as she bolted past. He called out to her, but she slammed through the door and across the barren kitchen garden without hearing his words. At the line of trees, she stopped and gasped air into burning lungs.

Sinking down against a tree, Constance shuddered and admitted she couldn't outrun the truth. She'd made a botch of things, as usual. She'd always lacked Geoff's single-mindedness and strength. When they read tales of King Arthur as children, Geoff admired the noble purpose of the myth while she sighed over the star-crossed romance. On lovely summer days he insisted they visit their aged nanny at the gatekeeper's lodge, though Constance preferred to ride or fish. Geoff had always done the right thing.

Sunshine filtering through green-budded branches drowned the woods in underwater light. She couldn't face that stern boy on the drive again. As she pushed to her feet, Constance spotted a clutch of violets at the foot of an old elm and picked them. She cut across the path toward the road and came out near the old family burial ground. She looked at the flowers in her hand. Violets had once been Geoff's favorite.

The sun dipped behind a cloud as she rounded the high stone wall, and the morning turned cool. Geoff's grave was in the back, behind the mausoleum. They'd buried him on a brilliant summer day. Birds had trilled in the oaks when the coffin was lowered into the earth. Today the birds were silent, and the graveyard looked dirty and unkempt.

When she stepped past the mausoleum, the sun reappeared and lit the plot. A scream strangled and died in her throat when she saw the boy. For a moment the shock of yellow hair on his forehead and dark uniform clothing long legs haunted her.

Sanity returned. It wasn't Geoff.

Stealing closer, she studied the unlined face pillowed by a haversack. The nose was straight, almost chiseled, and thick lashes fanned over high, ruddy cheeks. Even as he slept, the line of his mouth and chin were firm. No, it wasn't Geoff, just a weary Yank.

Constance placed the violets on the grave and backed away from the sleeping American. When tears came, she wondered who they were for. Whether for Geoff or Peter or the unknown boy, it hardly mattered. She had tears enough for all.

NORA FLIPPED THE BUTT of her cigarette across the tracks and checked her watch again. Christ, the train was nearly an hour late already. She wished she hadn't given in to the impulse to send a wire to Matthew asking him to meet her. All week she'd had butterflies from remembering their night together, and the note he'd written set those velvet wings fluttering faster. An intimate dinner was the reunion she had in mind, not meeting bleary-eyed in a deserted London railroad station in the middle of the night.

But he'd be there to meet her. She knew that for sure. She could make all kinds of excuses for not tracking down the friendly fire story, and now it was too late. The man from Chicago reported it two days after she left Tidworth Barracks. Maybe that was the story he'd been working on the morning she left, the morning she hesitated because of Matthew. She missed her exclusive, and so did IP. But she had Matthew, at least for now. His note made that much clear. She didn't know how much time they had left, and suddenly it didn't matter. Neither did the lost exclusive. Matthew meant more to her than any story, and she wanted to make the most of every hour they had left.

Grabbing her suitcase, she retraced her steps along the short platform and peered through a small window into the station. The other passengers gave up hope earlier and now had seats on hard wooden benches. In the far corner a porter spread his hands and shook his shaggy head at a frowning woman before moving on to the next bench. The passengers looked up when he pointed at the clock over the ticket counter. A harried mother of two fussy toddlers exchanged disgusted glances with the frowning woman. Nora pushed through the door in time to hear the porter apologize to the last group of passengers.

"At least another hour, I'm told. Very sorry, but we must expect delays with the war, you know. The tea shop across the square is quite comfortable, and I'll simply dash over when the train arrives."

Damn. Several passengers took his advice, but an hour of sitting didn't appeal to Nora. Her bottom was numb from endless briefings, dinners and train trips in the last week. The aching knots in her legs felt like overwound rubber bands. She trailed the porter back to the ticket window and touched his shoulder as he opened the door. "Can I leave my suitcase?" She smiled at his raised eyebrows. "For safekeeping. I'd like to stretch my legs." His thick brows knitted together over wary eyes. "I'd like to take a walk but don't want to lug this around."

Outside the station she paused. The shops lining the square had a seedy look from the empty trays in the butcher's window to the dusty cards noting the number of ration stamps needed to buy the ordinary hats displayed by a milliner. The place looked worn out and tired. On the platform she'd sniffed the springtime perfumes of mud and manure from the meadows across the tracks. Nora turned her back on the town and crossed the tracks to follow the road that promised fresh life and new beginnings. For the past week she'd felt like a draftee as she was hustled from one army camp to another. Finally the stops merged into a spooky waking nightmare featuring infinite numbers of green-clad men marching to the staccato rhythm of rifle fire. She didn't need any more reminders of the war.

Spring's sudden arrival had drawn villagers in the west of England out of their homes and into their gardens. She answered the smiles and waves of an elderly couple cleaning winter's last leaves from garden beds bracketing their door. The flower boxes needed a fresh coat of paint, but the cottage looked trim and tidy. The small house reminded her of the widow's cottage where Matthew had embarrassed her so. Maybe the old couple had a treasured photo on their mantel and another sad story to tell. The thought almost turned her back to find out. Walking lightened her mood, and another tearjerker would just put her back in the dumps. Besides, she already had notes for two weeks of columns.

A row of poplars lined the twisting road, and the breeze carried the lowing of cattle from a nearby pasture. She spotted three cows pressed against a wooden gate up ahead. The animals turned grave eyes toward her when she returned a moo and stepped to the fence. The cows backed off. From the look of their udders, someone had forgotten the milking this morning. The neglected chore didn't jibe with the bells hanging from thick necks or the carefully mended gate. The breeze stiffened against the curls on the broad heads of the cattle and blew a grit of ashes into her mouth.

Around the next bend in the road, Nora found the tardy milkmaid, an old lady propped against her milk can and sobbing into her hands. A hundred yards across the meadow, a thin wisp of smoke rose from the wreck of a large stone farmhouse. The blackened skeletal tail of an airplane jutted from broken timbers and masonry. A shattered wing hung from a tree in the meadow just beyond a muddy scar torn through the lush grass that showed where the plane had touched earth before plowing into the house. Workmen in heavy gloves and boots slowly picked through the smoldering ruins. The way the fellows took their time meant survivors had already been pulled out.

Nora angled around until she could approach the woman from the side and deliberately scuffed a foot to draw her attention. Work-roughened hands brushed tears from her plump red cheeks when Nora stopped a yard away. "I..."

Jamming fists in pockets, she tried again. "Can I do something for you? Telephone someone?"

The milkmaid turned tragic eyes from the wreckage. "Nothing to do, no one to ring." Strands of gray hair pulled loose from the bun at her nape as she shook her head. "They had no one, poor lambs, no one and nothing. Just me and Maisie, a couple of old grannies who cooked and cleaned. Now Maisie's gone, too."

Nora stopped trying to puzzle through the riddle of words when a shuddering sob bowed the old lady over her hands. She crouched until her eyes came level with the woman's tears. "For you, I mean." The woman's hand was ice. "Your hands are freezing. How long have you been out here without your coat?"

Watery eyes clouded at the question. "I came out at first light to do my milking. Then came the motor sound, just as I opened the gate."

Nora waited, but she said nothing more. Knobby fingers twisted and knotted as she watched a man carry a black bundle from the ruin and set it down among the wreckage on the drive. "That'll be Joey." Tears splashed unnoticed onto twining fingers.

A shiver swept across the withered flesh of her thin arms. Nora stood. "Take my coat. Please. You're shivering."

"I'm not cold." The old lady nodded toward the drive. "I gave my sweater to little Alice. After the awful noise, I came running to the fire and found her in the garden. She had only a nightgown so I gave her my sweater, poor lamb." Her voice trailed off as another sob shuddered free.

Sighing, Nora considered returning to the railroad station. Her watch showed at least a half hour before the train arrived. Maybe the gray truck in the driveway had food or clothing for the old lady. It was worth a try. Someone had to do something for her. A workman stopped by the cab and pulled a bottle from his pants. As he pulled a mask from his face in order to drink, Nora realized all the men wore masks. That fellow had the kind of bracer the old lady needed.

Following the slope of the drive, she tried to place the sweet odor that rose from the place. The smell stirred a memory, but no recollection floated up. Still, it left her uneasy. Something roasted, something she didn't like—but what? She moved to a shoulder to avoid debris the men had carried from the ruins. She tossed a glance at one little bundle, but her heel punched through soft earth and nearly tripped her up. Fire didn't leave much worth saving. She concentrated on her footing until she got to the truck.

The cab was empty. A stout man jumped from the rear at her approach and reached back for something inside the truck. "Excuse me." He spun to face her. "That woman out there needs help. She's awfully cold."

"She would stay, though we said no. Her orphans, she said." The mask muffled his words. Nora realized she'd been breathing through her mouth, closing nostrils to the stink. What the hell was it? The workman nodded at the open door as he drew out a stretcher. "In the far corner, then. Clean blankets. Mind, keep to your right. The others is bloody."

Inside the truck, canvas stretchers hung in tiers from each wall. She sidestepped down the narrow aisle and reached for a blanket. Her fingers touched wet, cold and sticky. On the right, the man said keep right. Pulling a square of wool from the pile, she backed out and wiped the blood staining her hand on the edge of a cot. A shiver chattered her teeth and she gulped the sunlit air. She gagged, twisted toward the shoulder of the drive and nearly stepped on the fuzzy pink sweater in the gravel.

And then she knew. She tried to look away, but her eyes were glued to the sweater, tracing the pattern of cables running from... Oh, Christ. A strand of dark hair. A slender bulge beneath the sweater. A small pale foot, bare and lifeless. Nora fought the nausea, tightening her throat against the bile. Little Alice.

Feet scraped gravel behind her. A workman knelt carefully, gently placing his burden on the stones. The tiny charred hand looked like a silhouette against the lighter gravel. The workman tucked the blanket over the little body and raised his head. For an instant, their eyes met. And then she was running.

Running with the blanket hugged tight against her chest. Running over ruts and through her stumbles. Running until her breath came ragged, torn from her lungs like a soundless scream.

FIFTEEN

MATT CORNERED NORA as soon as closing doors sealed them alone inside the elevator. Bracing hands beside her shoulders, he waited until she lifted her eyes to his. He knew she was tired. Drooping eyelids and pouting lips told him that. And she was due at work in half an hour. He knew all that, but still he wanted her.

He showed up at her hotel an hour early, hoping to find her sleeping so he could crawl into bed beside her. Instead he found her drinking tea with Connie. That still left them time to be alone for a while if they rushed dinner. But Nora dawdled, and he kept checking his watch. She ran into a newspaperman from Chicago in the hotel lobby, and getting reacquainted took fifteen minutes. By the time they got in line for dinner, the queue stretched to the dining room doors and waiting cost another half hour. His hopes shot up when she got right down to business with her food. But then she decided to drain a pot of coffee all by herself and took her time drinking it.

The elevator ride was the longest they'd been alone together in a week. She was working double shifts and he was exhausted, all for a lousy forty-eight-hour leave he'd wrangled from SHAEF despite Eisenhower's orders canceling all leaves. In the six weeks since she'd returned from touring American bases, she'd become a tough habit to break.

"I've got a bad feeling about this scheme of yours, Nora. Looks to me like a few more twenty-hour days will have you so worn out you'll snore your way through my leave."

A tired smile curled her mouth as she opened her eyes and shook her head. "I'll sleep on the way to Connie's."

Leaning in closer, Matt brushed his mouth across her lips. "We could just forget it, you know." He tasted the silky skin of her jaw. "We could lock your door, tell the desk to hold your calls and—"

The elevator jerked to a stop, bouncing his forehead into the wall. Nora's smile widened. "Naughty boy."

He rubbed the sting above his eyes as she brushed by him, tossing a wink over her shoulder. "Looks to me like divine retribution."

After sprinting through reclosing doors, he slowed to watch her walk. Thick carpet absorbed the no-nonsense click her heels made on harder surfaces. He liked the natural swing of her gait, liked watching the silk skirt of her dress tighten and loosen with each stride. Most of all, he liked remembering how neatly her curves and hollows fit against him, like finding a lost piece of a jigsaw puzzle that falls into place and completes the picture.

At first Matt thought she stopped to wait for him to catch up. Cocking her head, she half turned. Her frown deepened, and then he heard it, too. The solid wooden door of the guest room muffled words, but a man's deep rumble penetrated the barrier. Muttering rose into barks of laughter that drained away into a choking sob. Trembling fingers closed around his sleeve when he stopped next to her.

"It's Will."

Four rooms down, a door opened and a florid woman popped out her head. A couple of civilians stepped from the elevator and stared in their direction. Nora's fingers bit into his wrist.

"My God, Matthew. He's on a bender. I've got to do something."

She'd mentioned Davies's marriage was in trouble. Nora's boss poured down two drinks in the time it took most drinkers to finish one fast. After he'd had a few, the haunted cowering look disappeared from his eyes, and he smiled more. Liquor usually had the opposite effect on broken hearts—the more drinks, the more she done him wrong.

Nora's fingers loosened. She flashed a smile at the snooping neighbor as she raised her hand to the door. The muttering stopped when she knocked. The civilians shot them a last glance and walked into the opposite corridor. Four rooms down, the disapproving head vanished.

Matt gently shoved Nora aside and whacked the numbered door with his knuckles. The polished brass knob jiggled and turned. The door eased open an inch. Behind the crack, Davies's red-rimmed eyes widened. He moaned and tried to force the door shut against Matt's hand. Shouldering through, Matt blocked a roadhouse right with his forearm and plowed the reporter back onto the bed.

Davies cringed into the mattress, tossing his head from side to side. "No, I'm not going. Not over there." Puffy lids closed over seeping eyes. "Not for anything. I'm not going in."

Grabbing a pinch of sunken cheek, Matt twisted until the reporter's eyes opened. "Davies, it's Matt Chase." Behind him, the lock snapped into place. "Nora's here, too."

Terror and panic drained from bloodshot eyes. Matt had seen that fear before. Every soldier had. He'd seen it when the muzzle-flash of a big gun pierced the darkness on a troop transport anchored off Algeria. He'd seen it in rigid men waiting inside rocking landing craft in the pink light of a Mediterranean dawn. He'd seen it on the sweat-grimed face of a young rifleman crouched inside a foxhole carved out of rocky Sicilian soil. Every soldier knew that fear.

Waiting did it to a man. Knowing what was coming and having to wait tied knots in every soldier's guts. In transports or landing craft or foxholes, soldiers knew it was just a matter of waiting a little longer. Then shore batteries would growl a murderous answer and machine guns would spew death and a crack shot would notch your kill on his piece. A waiting man in combat usually felt like a sitting duck. Forget stories about wily prey. It always *felt* better to be the hunter. And the best hunting was hunting men.

Under Matt's hands, Davies struggled to sit up. He looked like hell. His hair was ragged, he'd nicked himself shaving and he reeked of cheap gin. He wasn't sloppy drunk—not yet. His eyes still focused. The reporter climbed to his knees when Matt let go. Nora's shadow flickered across the bed as she walked to the corner basin. Liquid splashed into the sink and Matt turned. "Don't pour it out."

She raised the bottle just enough to stop the flow but kept a pouring angle above the sink. "Why the hell not? He's already a mess."

Matt tossed a glance at the bed. A lock of limp hair curtained the face sunk between shaking hands. Sucking a lungful of air, Matt forced it out between stiff lips and crossed the room to take the bottle. He looked around for the cap, and Nora handed it over. "You better get to work. I'll stay here and keep him out of trouble."

Her eyes flashed, and she raked a hand through smooth hair as she walked to the door. "It's a little late for that. He's in big trouble already. He's turned into a lush, and it's starting to show at work."

Her voice was too loud, but the man on the bed didn't move. "I've got an idea what's bothering him. Talking it out might help."

"Christ, I hope so." Tears washed her eyes, and she sighed. "Talking to me hasn't helped him much." She opened the door, pressed her mouth against his cheek and was gone.

Gin and cigarettes overpowered the lingering summer fragrance that had teased him all through dinner. He turned into the room. At least baby-sitting her boss was better than drinking alone. Dragging a chair to the bed, Matt sat down and hoisted the gin to his lips. Raw booze burned his throat, and he coughed. When Davies looked up, Matt handed over the bottle. After a moment's hesitation, the reporter tilted a gulp into his mouth and passed the bottle back. Capping it, Matt set it on the floor next to his chair and leaned forward.

"Davies, I've known you—what?—three or four months?" The reporter shrugged without answering. "Not long, but I've known guys like you before. There's tons of guys like you at West Point."

Scraping his chair closer to the bed, Matt studied the man flopped against the mound of pillows. Will looked like a corpse, flattened and drained of life. He closed his eyes, turning away from Matt, mumbling for him to come back later.

Why did they try to fight their fear? Beating it back wasn't the answer. Fear couldn't be beaten. But it could be sidestepped. Matt sidestepped his every time he went into action. Each time he froze until the crack of the rifles shattered fragile ice and freed him. In that instant he was past fear and heading for pleasure. He'd take the fear over the pleasure any day.

"I don't know what it is about guys like you." Bracing arms behind his head, Matt leaned back and addressed the ceiling. "Take a drink, you have to get drunk. Throw a punch, you have to kill the guy. Get laid, it has to be love." Cocking his head toward the bed, Matt snared Davies's eye. "For guys like you it's not enough to have the balls to overcome the fear. Go into battle, you have to be fearless. What a crock that is."

Davies's eyes dropped away. Matt gave him a ten count. Then he gentled his voice and spoke softly. "But here's what I can't figure. Usually you don't run into problems the first time in. The first time you fool yourself into believing you're fearless. It starts eating you later, when you know you're not."

The red eyes were back and Matt held on, silently urging. "I've known I was gutless since Russia." The eyes clouded and shut. "One good look at hell and I lost my nerve."

Matt kept quiet and still. Nora's boss had scratched the wound but not enough to open it. A tighter squeeze would split that festering sore, but the reporter had to do the squeezing.

"Moscow wasn't so bad. When the Heinies got close, the Reds sent their capitalist allies to safe haven outside the city. We barely heard the guns. The Russians were mad, determined to hold. That was early on."

Davies elbowed himself up and reached for the bottle. Matt nudged it closer with his foot. The reporter swallowed an inch of colorless gin before rolling back onto the pillows, cradling the bottle in his arms.

"Stalingrad was worse. We never got into the city—what's left of it—just a fast tour of the surrounding countryside. We stopped by a field strewn with dead. The bodies were frozen, German and Russian, and wolves or dogs had been at them. The Russians didn't care. The head honcho said the Red Army didn't have time for burial details and, after all, it was just butchered meat." He shook his head and caught Matt's eye. "Just butchered meat."

Matt kept his eyes leveled on Davies as he twisted the gin bottle in his hands. "Russians are sentimental about things like burying the dead. Used to be, at least."

Slowly, Davies unscrewed the cap on the gin. "You could see it in the eyes in Leningrad. I got into the city for two days last winter. Their eyes scared me."

He took another pull on the bottle, and Matt didn't blame him. The Krauts had Leningrad under siege for nearly three years.

"You know what happens to people who have to feed their kids sawdust for a couple of years? Makes 'em cruel, like maniacs. War's drained the joy out of Russia and replaced it with hate."

Davies looked at the bottle in his hand for a minute before recapping it. "I'm scared, all right. I'm afraid I'll try to run. I'm afraid I'll get killed."

He held out the bottle, and Matt took it. "And I'm afraid I'll fill up with hate like the Russians, hate that kills your soul."

He pulled up from the bed and swung his feet to the floor. Reaching for a cigarette, he offered the pack to Matt. "I guess I'm luckier than you. Civilians like me don't have to go. Soldiers have no choice."

Matt found his lighter and scraped up a flame. Davies dipped his smoke into the fire. The reporter was still kidding himself. What about ambition? What about self-respect?

Snapping the lighter closed, Matt caught Davies's eyes through a wisp of smoke. "You're right. Guys like me don't have any choice. But neither do guys like you."

MATT FED DRY TWIGS into the flames and rocked back onto his heels. Smoke corkscrewed toward the darkening sky, rustling through the leaves of a rosebush. The heat might wither Connie's flowers, but the Englishwoman wouldn't mind. She'd suggested he scoop a fire pit in the garden when he asked where to grill a steak at her country place. A cast-off fireplace screen propped on bricks from the garden shed worked as a makeshift barbecue. All he needed now was a decent bed of coals.

Grabbing a handful of larger sticks, he leaned into the smoke. When he added the wood, the fire died down for a second before surging higher as the new fuel crackled and caught. Orchard fruitiness scented the smoke.

He liked fires, always had. The driftwood he'd burned on Cape beaches gave off salty smoke and glowed with dancing rainbows on summer nights. The fir he'd burned in the mountains after a long climb sizzled and snapped, a warm friend as he stretched out under a vault of cold winking stars. Even brief gasoline flashes boiling GI canteens on stony Algerian hillsides were welcome. There was comfort in those fires: rest and warmth and a full belly.

He added a spit length of oak to red embers and reached back for his beer. The bottle came cold and slick with droplets. Connie really delivered the goods. She'd promised a local girl would make up a bed and stock the fridge. And someone had, right down to fresh eggs, a couple of big bakers and a dozen beers chilled American-style in the back of the icebox. Add Nora and a thick black-market steak and he had the makings of a perfect leave. At last.

Before returning to the house, Matt idled the jeep into the gloom of the garden shed and latched the double doors. He didn't want any reminders of the war to spoil his weekend with Nora. He wanted to pretend for a while that they had time, that this was just the first of many country weekends they'd spend together.

For too long the war had dominated his life. For too long he'd needed more time. Soon, in a year or two, his war would be finished. With some luck he'd have time then for everything he'd missed, for Nora. Except he didn't believe in luck. Matt drained the bottle and turned toward the house.

In the kitchen he pried open another beer and checked the potatoes. A wave of heat from the oven burned his face. He opened a can of green beans into a pan and set it on a burner. Unwrapping bloody paper, he plopped the steak onto a plate and dusted salt and pepper over both sides. Easing through the swinging door, he crossed the hall and stepped into Connie's parlor.

While he'd been outside Nora had settled deeper into the chair. The blanket he'd tucked around her an hour ago had slipped from her shoulders. He tugged the soft wool up to her chin. She sighed and rolled her head, releasing an invisible cloud of summer from her hair. Sleep softened her face and wiped away the vivid blaze of life that had first attracted him. That sparkle had pulled him in despite her steel edges, drawing him the way a thrumming beehive drew a hungry bear. Like the bear, he'd risked getting stung for a chance at sweet reward, and he'd won.

Matt sank onto the couch facing Nora's chair and studied her as he sipped his beer. Now more fighting, dammit. Having Nora, wanting her, didn't change that. Her special vividness, that zest for life, might pull him like a magnet but just for now, just for today. Tomorrow he'd go back to the war, and in another few weeks he'd ship out for a new fighting front. But he'd take part of her with him over there, the best part, the part that left him homesick in this familiar yet foreign land, the part that made him mad as hell to be fighting over here when he'd rather—yes—he'd rather be home in the States, lost in her arms.

In a strange way she was home to him. Her defiance and damn-your-eyes independence, that curious mix of cynicism and inexperience was part of what home meant. The wisecracks, the so-what shrug of her shoulders, the snap decisions and quickly drawn conclusions stood out in England as brash Americanisms, exasperating and endearing at the same time. He'd been fighting for an abstract ideal, but now he'd tacked on a human face, Nora's face. And he hoped she made things different for him over there, where it really counted.

His first skirmish had tarnished his ideal of humane soldiers and just wars. He'd found no meaning in combat, only death. He'd looked at the first bullet-torn body from his outfit and felt only relief that he wasn't that poor sucker. Soon fighting had become a special drug that he craved. He had to keep testing the thin line that separates life and death. He'd pushed against that line, sometimes reckless with his life and the lives of his men, until the only emotion left was disgust. Disgust with war and with death and with himself.

Now he could feel again. Like the stinging throb of blood returning to a numb arm, Nora brought him back to life. The Mediterranean invasions had soured him on life because the world seemed intent only on death. In the thrill of combat he sought his own. But now there was more to the world than death. Now there was Nora. She made a difference today, and he hoped she'd make things different when he crossed the Channel to hunt death again. He was counting on her for that.

He looked up to find her watching him with a sleepy smile. Uncurling her legs, she stretched stockinged toes and polished fingers with a slow grace that brought him back to the real point of their weekend. But first, dinner.

"I hope you've had enough sleep to last through dinner." He grabbed her hand and pulled her to her feet. "I've got potatoes about done, and the fire should be ready for the steak."

"Is cooking another of your secret talents?"

"Of course." He pointed her toward the kitchen door across the hall and swatted her bottom lightly. "I've heard career girls can't even boil water, so I saved setting the table for you."

A loose hinge squeaked as the kitchen door swung shut behind them. Matt lit the gas under the beans, adjusting the flame while Nora rummaged through cupboards and drawers.

"Matthew?" She pointed to the small kitchen table with a hand filled with cutlery. "Do you mind if we eat in here? There's something nice and ordinary about eating in the kitchen."

Shrugging agreement, he scooped up the steak and went out to the fire. The fire pit glowed in the deep twilight of Connie's garden. The sirloin hissed as the hot fireplace screen seared the meat and drops of melted fat flared into small flames on the bed of coals. The rattle of silverware and clink of glasses carried through the open door to the kitchen. A rectangle of light flooded through the doorway as she lit a lamp and brief jangles of music meant she was tuning the radio. She settled on a lush romantic symphony. The music twined around the perfume of Connie's roses, lifting his mood. Or was it the ordinariness of grilling a steak while Nora rattled around the kitchen, the Saturday-night ordinariness of a million couples? Maybe it was knowing the finer dish that would follow their meal, knowing for once he could stay past tomorrow's sunrise.

He flipped the steak and poked his finger into the broiled meat. "You like it rare, medium, or what?"

Her shadow loomed into the flood of light. "Whatever." She folded her arms and leaned against the door frame. "That's some grill you rigged."

"Connie mentioned a cupboard of wine somewhere." He prodded the steak again. "Want some?"

She rolled her head against the door. "Nope. No way I'm passing up ice-cold beer. Besides, beer's more homey."

Her mood matched his, then. Nora wanted to pretend for a while, too. When the steak was cooked just past medium, he discovered she'd set the kitchen up perfectly, right down to the slab of butter on a cracked saucer and folded dish towels for napkins. She grinned as she scooped beans onto their plates straight from the saucepan and wrapped her hand in the skirt of her apron to snatch steaming potatoes from the oven. He sawed the steak in half while she poured two glasses of beer.

Crickets chirped to life in the garden as orange faded to black in the western sky. A cool breeze lifted the curtains at the window over the sink, and Nora ran upstairs for a sweater. Matt closed the door and window and returned to his meal. He couldn't remember a better steak. There was a special warmth in the light of Connie's kitchen and a strange beauty in the pattern of flowers dotting the oilcloth spread on the table. The radio's soft music completed the mood.

Nora'd been gone too long. He drained his beer and went to find her. The dim light of a candle burning in the upstairs hall guided him up the stairs. Another light glowed from the door of the room she'd chosen. He stopped on the door sill and waited for an invitation. Their eyes met above the bed. She raised her hand from the satin comforter and beckoned. "I decided not to wait for dessert."

SIXTEEN

WAKING UP BESIDE HIM with sunshine slanting across the bed was pure luxury. His arms held her loosely, and the steady rhythm of breath tickling her ear meant he still slept. She closed her eyes and concentrated on the touch of his chest along the length of her back and the hard legs tucked behind her own. They fit together like fine silver spoons nestled under soft felt in a mahogany chest.

She'd never liked sharing a bed before. With other men, even in all those nights with Eric, arms tangled and legs bumped and neither slept well. Sharing a bed with Matthew was easy and natural. Curling into the safety of his arms after making love as he whispered against her neck brought another kind of satisfaction, not fierce but gentle.

Breakfast in bed was Matthew's idea. Nora wanted to cook but he insisted on doing it himself. It was delicious to nuzzle into his pillow with brilliant spring light streaming through the window and the rich scent of blossoms on the morning air. She hadn't stayed in bed past nine in months or, more likely, years.

The squeak of a loose board announced breakfast a second before he rattled a large tray into the room. Nora elbowed herself up against the pillows and took the tray while he slipped under the covers.

Matthew settled the plates on the blanket and grabbed the teapot. "Even with real eggs, the best I can do is scrambled." He poured a cup and handed it over. "But I'm famous for my coffee."

The food disappeared fast. Nora settled back against the pillows with a second cup. "Famous for coffee and what else? I don't know much about you."

Draining the pot into his cup, Matthew grinned. "What is there to know?" The brush of his mouth across her bare shoulder shivered up goose bumps. "You know about last night. That's all that matters."

Reaching for a Chesterfield, Nora tried to frame the right question. There had to be more between them than lovemaking. And there was something deeper, something they never named. But they needed to know more about each other to end that conspiracy of silence. Today and tomorrow didn't bother her; she wanted to know about Matthew's yesterdays. Not the superficial details like girls he'd loved or books he'd read or things he'd done. She wanted to know the intimate and private parts of his yesterdays that made him the man he was today.

She cocked her head over his lighter and saw the scar again. "I'm not so sure. That scar, for instance. How'd you come by that?"

He fingered the pucker of flesh at his temple. "How do you think?"

"The question sounds like a setup. All right." She shrugged. "You were wounded."

"Yeah, but not in the war. I sailed as a kid and got nailed by the boom. I caught a cleat as I went over the side."

Nora ran a finger along the wing of silver streaking back from the scar. "You must have been hurt pretty bad for it to gray your hair."

He laughed as he caught her hand and turned the wrist up to his lips. "Just a coincidence, sweetheart. That streak runs in the family. Look Tim over when we see him tomorrow. His is starting to show, too."

Her curiosity returned later as he led her across a meadow toward the river. He picked a buttercup and held it under her chin. The long grass buzzed with insects, and he knew the name of a butterfly she spotted drifting and fluttering in the sunshine. A common type, he said, and mentioned a boyhood collection.

"You collected butterflies?"

"Butterflies, rocks, stamps, baseball cards—anything to fill time and keep me busy."

She took his hand. "You were lonely."

Plucking a stem of grass, he studied the edge. "I guess so." He met her eyes. "Yeah, I was. I was an only child till I was about eight. My parents were...preoccupied."

Nora glanced at the river shimmering with jewels of light. She gently squeezed his fingers and turned back. "Your parents, your father..."

A flare of defiance changed his eyes to steel. "What about him?" The bitterness snapped, biting through his words.

Dropping her head, she hugged his arm against her chest and looked at the hard fingers twined with her own. "I'm sorry to pry. I shouldn't, I know, but it just seems so strange. You in the army with a father like him."

His fingers slipped from hers and he turned away, shoving his hands in his pockets. She waited, giving him time. It couldn't be easy. She knew that much.

He pivoted back, holding himself stiffly. "It is strange. I grew up believing what he believed. But he wanted me to think for myself. And when I did, I stopped believing in perfection. The congressman's right about a lot of things, but his ideals don't work. Ideals never work."

Matthew pulled his Camels from his slacks and drew out two cigarettes. She took the one he offered and met his eyes. "You sound so sure, Matthew. Look, I'm not sticking up for your father. But you've got to admit it takes courage to do what he's done, holding on to his beliefs right to the end."

A stream of smoke snorted out at her words. "Courage? A kind of courage, maybe." He took a quick puff. "But the only beliefs he respects are his own. If you agree with him, fine. If not, forget it. He'd rather have his sons rotting in a federal prison or as conscientious objectors treated like dirt than see either of us follow our own beliefs." His cigarette sailed into the long grass on the riverbank. "Connie seems to think my father's some kind of saint. Well, to me he's just a fanatic. Neither one is easy to have in the family."

Taking his hand again, Nora led him to the riverbank. Frowning, he stared into the water until she tugged his hand. She turned her face up to the sun as they followed the river toward the arch of an old stone bridge.

Connie'd said Benjamin Chase reminded her of an Old Testament prophet. Matthew's description amounted to the same thing. In Nora's family, Mom was the difficult one. Josie Seymour had wanted more from life than a small-town druggist could give her and never bothered to hide her disappointment. She berated Dad for giving credit to hard-luck families, even when the bill covered medicine for a sick kid. Dad was the gem of her family, the original good neighbor looking out for his friends and his hometown.

Nora understood how Matthew felt. Mom still hadn't forgiven her for throwing over Eric. She'd only met him once, but when Eric squired them to the theater and to his country club, Mom's eyes nearly popped. *That* had been the kind of life Josie wanted and, if she couldn't have it, then Nora would. No matter that Nora didn't want Eric or his life. Mom had been so disappointed when Nora told her about the broken engagement that she wondered if her mother had planned to install herself with them in Chicago after they married. Maybe she'd insist on helping with the first grandchild and never leave. Whatever she'd had in mind, Mom had been cool with her ever since. Nora figured she knew something about difficult families.

As they neared the old bridge a bird squawked close by. Wings flapped overhead, and Nora ducked as the bird dove toward her face. With a jerk, Matthew pulled her away and laughed. "We must be too close to the nest."

"I'll say." She raked a hand through her hair and looked up at him. The steel in his eyes had melted back to silver. "She doesn't want us around."

Halfway across the arch, she paused to watch the water and spotted movement in the rushes shadowed by the bridge. Another bird tried to rise from the grass but fell back. The first swooped over again, but its mate couldn't fly up to meet it. She touched Matthew's elbow.

"Look, that bird is hurt. Oh, the poor thing."

He bent over the low stone wall. "Not hurt, caught. Looks like he's tangled in some fishing line."

Nora trotted back across the bridge. "Let's get him out." But as she tried to climb down the bank, the first bird dove for her again. Frantic wings touched her shoulder.

"You stay here and keep that one occupied." He slid down the muddy bank. "Okay, birdy, okay. I'm not going to hurt you."

Nora dodged another aerial attack and shot a glance at Matthew. Cupped hands moved in slowly as the bird struggled against the line snagged around its foot. He circled the frightened bird with one hand and gently loosened the fishing line. When he'd freed it, he raised the bird in his hands. "Looks all right. Okay, bud, off you go." He threw up his arms, and the bird flew free.

Something inside Nora took flight, too. He really was a wonderful guy. She remembered the birds they'd seen nest building in London. He'd been different that day. *"Birds are stupid, Nora. Next week a Kraut bomb will blast them to bits."* That harshness was gone now. He'd shown her a gentle side, and she liked it.

Reaching down a hand, she steadied him as he climbed the bank. When he stood beside her, she wrapped her arms around him. She pressed her lips into his neck and breathed in his special spice. "You were wonderful."

His arms tightened around her shoulders, and his hand tilted up her chin. "You're pretty easy to impress for a big-city career girl."

Nora smothered his gibes with her mouth, happy to be pulled so close that his buttons bit through her sweater. Maybe he was right, after all. Maybe she shouldn't worry about anything but this. The rest would take care of itself.

CONSTANCE WATCHED THE DARKNESS invade her room until the only light came from the red glow of her cigarette. Her stomach growled, and she sipped whiskey to silence it. Dining tonight with Mother and Daddy would have been unbearable. Mother would only start in again on having the twins home from America. While their school term was nearly over, Constance couldn't bring herself to summon them home. She couldn't, not since Peter. A cramp knotted her abdomen. She'd only begun feeling unwell when she rang them up to beg off dinner. She hated to lie and didn't do it well. Something in Mother's voice told her she'd failed again this time. As she replaced the receiver, the notion took her that perhaps something else was responsible for the brittleness of Mother's voice. Perhaps they'd heard....

Stabbing out the Dunhill, Constance bent forward and pressed her temples with shaking fingers. That was the trouble—perhaps they'd *heard*. And that was why she hadn't written to the twins, either, though their latest letters had been waiting on the corner of her desk for a week. What could she say? *My lover has been keeping me busy, darlings—a wonderful man you're sure to adore.* Was it unforgivably selfish of her to keep them safe in America while she spent whatever time was left with her lover? The time left to them was short. Everyone knew that. Leaves canceled, bombers flying across the Channel every night, engagements premised with a cautious *if*—everyone knew the balloon was going up soon.

And Peter would go, too. Without a word of warning, he'd be gone from her life to the hell of France or Belgium or wherever the bloody invasion landed. He'd told her his life wouldn't be in danger. He'd promised her that. But danger or no, the end was the same for her. Her life would be empty again.

Tugging at the sweater shawled around her shoulders, Connie crossed to the window and pulled the heavy curtains shut. She switched on a lamp and picked up her drink. He wouldn't come to her tonight. He knew her dinner plans and wasn't happy. She'd had to hush him in one of the Tate's galleries when he protested. He grabbed her hand and pulled her close. She looked up to see Susannah Blake watching them from across the room, watching them again. The one woman Constance couldn't abide in Jeremy's circle of friends had seen her with Peter—again.

That was the real cause of her gloom. Jeremy. He'd learn of it soon enough. She was certain of that. Susannah would discuss the matter with Melvin tonight. "You won't believe who I saw today at the Tate, darling. Constance Tolliver with that awful Yank in tow." Stuffy old Melvin would suck on his pipe and scratch his head while she gave him all the dirty details. When she told him she'd mentioned it in her next letter to Emma Smithson in Delhi, Melvin would protest but only mildly. Susannah would win in the end. The story would circulate on the sly through the club in Delhi until some good soul convinced himself that Jeremy *should* know.

Jeremy's hurtful eyes stared out from the gilt frame in her hand. Heavy lines of concern creased the corners of his eyes. His hair had already gone gray when the photo was taken. He'd worked hard all his life, provided well for her and the children. In most ways he was the model husband. He deserved better than the condescension of some well-meaning Colonel Blimp who would return to his bungalow to regale his friends with the story of how well Jeremy Tolliver had taken the bad news. He deserved better than the malicious glances and sympathetic whispers he'd get.

Glancing at the twins' latest photo, Constance replaced her husband's portrait in her desk drawer. They deserved something better than a mother behaving like a bitch in heat. After the war when they all were reunited, Jeremy and the twins would expect to return to their old life. Jeremy would want the wife he'd had for twenty years, and the twins would want the "good sort" of mother they'd always claimed she was.

How could she be that woman again? The world was utterly changed. Peter had awakened her to a life she'd missed, an existence full of the joy and juice of living. How could she go back to the sterility of their earlier life in Wickenden Square? That quiet routine of reading over breakfast in the morning room and writing after lunch in her study, a drink with Jeremy before dinner and his daily recitation of the latest intrigues at the ministry when they'd finished their meal. That quiet life that had once seemed fine now was dreadful. The only life in their home came when the twins banged home from school on a rare weekend, and they were almost grown now. Soon they'd go up to Cambridge or Oxford and would never really return. There'd just be Jeremy then, and that dreadful routine.

When she'd met Jeremy the year *Judgment* created such a sensation, she'd been terribly young and still wounded by Geoff's death. Despite her book's forthright denunciations of the past, she hadn't a clue what the future should be, for her or for England. Jeremy had known that women would be emancipated and that the Empire would be lost. And he knew what he wanted to do. He'd carefully chosen his spot in the ministry, a job beyond the whims of voters who sweep governments in and out without a thought for continuity. Jeremy and all the other civil servants provided the continuity and therein lay their power. She thought him very clever to choose such a position. She'd thought he shared her views on justice and pacifism, too.

Dropping into a chair, Constance lit another Dunhill and finished her drink. How could a woman live for twenty years with a man and fail to know him? Yes, he was clever, but more, he was cunning. He didn't hate the Empire and love justice. He was a realist who knew the Empire was lost and was determined to disengage gracefully, quickly, without loss of lives—English lives. She'd read liberalism into his distaste for bloodshed, when in reality it came from the value he placed on English lives. For twenty years Constance had seen only the placid surface Jeremy presented to the world. Underneath, a patriot boiled and only his realism tempered his chauvinism.

Drawing in the last stream of smoke from her dwindling cigarette, Constance arched back in the chair. How could she go back to that life? How could she take up life again with the stranger she'd married? Yes, he'd been a good husband, a good father, a good provider. He'd been all that. But was he a good man?

NORA'S EYES kept coming back to the map hung behind the kerosene stove in the tin-roofed hut Tim shared with officers from three bomber crews. The fliers had marked the destinations of their missions, studding the Low Countries and Germany with cartoon bombs inked red over the pale pastels of the grade-school map. Tim claimed credit for his share, describing more memorable raids to his brother as Nora lounged in a wooden armchair. The boy scratched his head as he searched for a particular destination and came up empty.

"Darn, I must have forgot one." He bent closer until he found the name he wanted. "Yup, I did." He grabbed the red pen tied on a string tacked to the wall next to the map. "My formation left a big hole there."

The setup reminded her of a boys' camp: cots along each wall and chests of drawers between, wooden armchairs that looked straight off the shady porch of a summer hotel and, except for the map, walls covered with calendar pinup girls. Betty Grable was obviously the favorite.

Outside, a rutted road led to the village across meadows filled with cows and haystacks and serenity. In the opposite direction the muddy road led to a large Nissen hut, runways and huge Flying Fortresses looming inside shadowed hangars. In that direction any similarity to a boys' camp ended.

The planes looked different to her today, not at all like the one she'd ridden over from the States. She knew from the start that Tim piloted a bomber, but somehow that didn't sink in until he reached up and patted the belly of his plane while giving them a tour. The engine was exposed on the plane he'd named Hillary. Tim squatted next to a mechanic cleaning parts on the floor to ask when his bird would be ready to fly.

The soldier wiped a greasy hand across his forehead and frowned. "Wish I could tell you, sir. I've stripped this engine down and put her back together three times since last week, and she still cuts out on us. I'll find the problem, but I can't say when."

"Well, dammit to hell, anyway."

Tim's language startled Nora. She'd never heard him swear before. In that instant he changed from a cute kid into a fighter. And his Flying Fortress changed from a huge marvel into a deadly menace. The fliers were too young. They looked as if they should be working on merit badges instead of dumping bombs on Europe.

All afternoon she'd watched the kid-stuff horseplay of a high school locker room. When a formation of planes towing gliders flew overhead, they all paused to follow with eyes brightened by something she didn't quite understand. They joked about flak holes and limping home to base. They relished each retelling of threats survived and enemies outsmarted. But when one freckle-faced navigator mentioned the time Steve went down, a momentary stillness dulled their eyes until another flier released them from mourning by saying what a good man Steve had been. The fliers nodded and brightened and went on. But they weren't men. They were just kids. And Nora hoped the engine of Tim's plane would stay in pieces in that hangar forever.

Matthew seemed unaffected. He'd followed Tim like a proud father visiting his kid's classroom on parents' night. His eyebrows lifted when Tim described having to fly under the flak because his engines didn't have the power to lift him above it. He patted Tim's back when the boy admitted that he loved his bird, *really* loved her. Nora trailed them, wondering how Matthew could hear about Tim's close calls so calmly. He was just a kid, an innocent young kid, but he killed every time he went up and couldn't wait to fly again. She didn't get the chance to quiz Matthew until they'd climbed into the jeep to return to London.

She waved as Tim walked slowly away. A group of airmen carrying baseballs, bats and mitts came out of a hut. Tim stuffed his cap in a back pocket and trotted after them.

"Christ, he's just a kid."

Matthew sighed and took her hand. "They're all kids. Boys always fight the wars old men make."

She squeezed his hand. "Doesn't it scare you?"

"I can't protect him. And I can't let him interfere with my work."

He sounded so cold and reasonable that she shivered. "So you just forget it?"

He slid around to face her. "I try to. Sometimes the work is so absorbing that I get carried away and forget how many boys will die. We send them in with three days' supply and figure maybe seventy percent will need resupply."

She looked toward the makeshift baseball diamond. "Jesus." Maybe Tim was better off flying.

"I just hope we do that well."

SEVENTEEN

THE BELL OF A BUOY RANG across the empty harbor, breaking the stillness of the night. Matt scraped out his smoke and tossed it onto the pile of dead butts on the dock beside him. Underneath him, the sea lapped gently against pilings bearded thick with barnacles and weeds. In the east, toward Calais, a sliver of gray hinted at dawn, but his eyes were drawn back to the southern darkness, to Normandy. The formation of tow planes had returned without the gliders hours ago. The bombers should be on their targets now. He searched for flashes he would not see and listened for thunder he would not hear. Portsmouth was too far from France even in perfect weather. Portsmouth was too far away, and so was he.

Sinking his head onto a cocked knee, he rehearsed the voyage in his mind. They'd get a good dinner for once, steak and real eggs or plenty of chicken à la king. The "last meal" was always good. The men would split up into squads after eating, and a card game would start. A few would write last letters. Others would see the chaplain again. The bookworms would have their noses in paperbacks, and the Romeos would take out snapshots one last time. Experienced fighters would be too cool to talk about it and green recruits too scared. But they'd all be thinking about it. All the way across the Channel the only thing in their minds would be the invasion. And then it would be time to go. Lou or some other sergeant would roust them for one last equipment check and remind them to be careful not to break the rubber when they unrolled it onto the rifle barrel.

A breeze stirred his hair, and he stared across the water. He didn't have to be on those ships to know what was in those backpacks. He'd filled those packs in list after careful list, crossing off the extra shorts and adding ammunition, generous with C-rations one day and stingy the next. A few necessities no one argued about: the entrenching tools and canteens and ponchos. Someone questioned the extra socks—weren't two pair enough? Luckily the one-star got a bad case of trenchfoot the last time he'd seen France. He ended that argument quickly. Everyone knew no amount of ammunition or food was too much, but no one knew how much was enough. They'd all find out today.

Pushing to his feet, Matt lit another Camel and leaned against a piling. The men would welcome the fresh air on deck after the stale cramped quarters below. The fleet would fill the sea in all directions, two thousand ships tangled up off the coast of France. They wouldn't be able to see the beach until daylight, and even then not until they'd climbed into landing craft and headed for hell. Sailors would start the loading as sergeants ran around counting heads, checking that rifles were protected and nothing important was left behind. The boat would smack down into the chop, bucking wildly until the coxswain steadied it into the wind. They'd hear the bombers before they could see them and cheer when bombs started falling. When the battleships opened fire from farther out, they'd whoop. And as the landing craft moved into open sea, circling the troop ship as other boats were filled, the men would heave that good dinner into their helmets and wonder how much worse it was to die.

He glanced to the line of pink in the east, a pale scar on the night. Not long now. In another hour they'd find out if the plan was brilliant or a botch. So much could go wrong. And something would—something always went wrong. They'd know by noon if Overlord was working. By lunchtime they'd claim success or admit defeat. If things went right, Portsmouth harbor would stay empty and the supplies would go straight to France. If things went wrong, the fleet would limp back to Portsmouth and other Channel ports until they could try again.

Flicking the butt into the water, Matt rose and walked back toward shore. His steps echoed through the gathering dawn, beating a lonely retreat that mocked him and all he'd worked for. There'd be nothing for him to do at Southwick House, nothing he could do except wait for the latest report. He should be sending those damned reports. He should be over there with them, puking and praying as the landing craft bobbed toward shore. He should be with his outfit hitting that beach and climbing those bluffs.

His job at SHAEF was finished, and he'd be over there soon. But next week was too late, tomorrow was too late. What counted was today. He wanted to be over there right now with the acrid cordite smoke burning his nostrils and the steely taste of fear on his tongue. Before he reached shore, liquid fire would shoot through his veins and armor him against the fear. Hidden savagery would shred his human costume and free the wild beast who loved the fighting and the dying and the killing. And he did love war, better than anything. No minister's sermon on the evils of war or reasoned demonstration of the stupidity of war could change that. Every argument against war failed because nothing and no one could explain that away. There were men who loved war, and he was one. Nothing could change that, not even Nora. He envied Will Davies's fear and the congressman's outrage and came close to hating both men for his own deficiency. But mostly he hated himself.

His foot touched the solid mass of the old stone quay, and Matt checked his watch. Six-thirty. They were going in.

THE LANDING CRAFT PITCHED UP the crest of a wave and slid into the trough as a thunder of explosions rolled out from shore. He couldn't think, and he couldn't hear, and he couldn't stop puking. Crawling past the coxswain's boots, Will Davies pulled himself up the gunwale and heaved the rest of his dinner into the sea. A reviving spray washed his face as the floating vomit fell behind the landing craft to be buried in the bubbling stream of the wake that arrowed back to the transport. Other landing craft spread out in lines beside them, and the big ship looked smaller. . . .

Shit, we're heading in.

Struggling to his knees, Will stared into mist—not mist, smoke—billowing from shore. He glanced at the coxswain, but the sailor was too intent on his job to notice him. Sliding across the stern, he pulled to his feet and shouted his question.

"How far do you take us?"

The young sailor's eyes remained fixed forward. "Close as I can get without hitting an obstacle. Better get down with the other guys if you want to get off. I won't be staying long, I'll tell you that."

Below, in the landing craft's belly, a huddle of officers conferred by the ramp. At their shoulders, a boyish lieutenant hung from the gunwale and yelled down to them. The roar of wind and guns smothered the words before they reached Will's ears. Sergeants moved through seasick infantrymen grabbing helmets, dumping out the slop and dropping the dripping steel hats on bent heads.

A scream punched out of the wind and shuddered through him. Ten yards out from the landing craft, a man bobbed in the chop, crying for help, begging for someone to help him. The coxswain shrugged off Will's hand. "We aren't a rescue ship, sir."

Watching the flailing soldier fall behind, Will fought the urge to go over the side. He spotted another man facedown in the water, tossed by the tide, moving slowly toward the beach he'd never see. Omaha Beach they called it, and this landing craft was heading for Easy Red. That was a laugh.

He counted the other landing craft heading toward shore and felt a little better. There were lots of guys going in, lots of targets besides him. A clear spot drifted through the smoke, and he saw bluffs above and huge black spiders of metal awash in the surf below. There were men on the beach and men in the water. But none of them moved.

To the right, a landing craft exploded with a terrific flash bang, showering bits of men and boat that splashed back into the water. Will's horror spilled over when a smoking torso—headless, legless—splashed down near his perch. He gagged on bitter juices, choked on despair.

ALLIANCES

"All right, let's move it! Move it!"

The infantrymen down below pulled themselves up and moved toward the ramp.

Too late, damn, too late.

A sergeant patted his leg. "Coming, Davies?"

Will forced the bloody torso from his mind and met the sergeant's steady brown eyes. He didn't look scared. Will straightened and stepped down. He nodded.

"All right, then." The sergeant grinned. "Better fasten that helmet and move it up there with the rest of the men."

Clawing for the chin strap, Will took a few jerky steps before the steady voice stopped him. "Whoa, Davies, don't forget this." The weight of his typewriter pulled his hand. "You don't want to take this swim for nothing, do you?"

The front of the landing craft fell away. "Time to go, men. Let's move it." The soldiers swarmed toward the ramp, pulling Will on, pushing him out.

He slid down the ramp. Water pulled his legs, an icy claw reaching for his crotch. He stumbled forward. The howl of the guns blended into a constant deafening roar.

The man ahead went down. Will dodged right to avoid him. A zippered line of holes tore into the water to his left.

He tried to run, lifting dead legs through a ton of water. Another man fell screaming. He had to go faster, faster. On the left a tank burned with a blessed smoke. He angled toward it, fighting the water at his knees.

A floating log blocked him. He reached down to clear a path and his hands met cold flesh. Pushing the thing away, he dove the last yard to safety.

Hugging the dead tank, Will crouched in the water and fought for breath. Smoke stung his eyes and burned his lungs. The bulk of the tank hid the beach.

Lifting his typewriter to a dry perch, he looked back. His landing craft was gone but others were unloading. The seabed shuddered under his feet, and the tank under his hand trembled. Up and down the beach, fountains of sand and water rose toward the clouds. Will cringed at the splash behind him until a hand touched his sleeve.

"Lose your rifle, buddy? Tough luck." The boy grinned and waved his own. "Not me, friend, not ever."

The tank bucked, and a wave poured over them. Will spit saltwater and sand. The young soldier shook his head. "That's our cue, friend. Heinie's got his sights on this tank."

The rifleman crept the length of the tank, then dashed for the beach. As his feet hit the sand, he twirled along the shore and went down. The soldier got to a knee and fought his way up the sand, cradling an arm and dragging a leg. Will held his breath until the boy topped a small rise and rolled out of sight. It was his turn now.

Pulling the typewriter's bulk against his chest, Will forced himself to follow. He crawled the length of the tank and paused to plot his route. Sucking a lungful of oily air, he dipped his head and started running.

Water tore at his calves and then his ankles. Spongy wet sand gave under his feet. He slid on small pebbles, hearing nothing, seeing nothing except his feet flashing out and up. The rise slowed him. As the sand leveled off, the typewriter slammed into his chest, and he somersaulted down into a hollow.

He breathed in a noseful of grit when his wind came back. He pushed up on palms scraped raw and saw the kid sprawled in the sand. A medic had his shirt open, packing a bandage over his oozing chest. Behind the corpsman lay three other moaning men. Will rolled across the sand.

"Is he bad off?"

Tearing strips of adhesive with his teeth, the medic shrugged. He finished the chest and started on a leg. "Don't know. He's breathing." The medic tore bloody pants from hip to knee and fingered ripped flesh. "He'll be taking the white boat home."

The gun roar sorted into distinct sounds. Rifles cracked across the jittery stutters of machine guns, and bigger guns shook the ground. A cloud of sour smoke clung to the edge of their hollow, their safety.

Another man dove in on a spray of sand and rock. Ripping the clip off his rifle, he tossed the empty aside and slapped in a fresh one. A sergeant bellied into the hollow, and a radioman slid in behind. Three more tripped in fast. The sergeant crawled to the medic. "How's it goin', doc?"

"Lots of business. How's it look out there?"

"Not so hot." The sergeant pulled out a can of chewing tobacco and stuffed a wad into his cheek. He suddenly stilled, head cocked. "Get down."

The explosion lifted Will off the sand and stunned him for a minute. A crumbled wall of sand half buried two wounded men who tried to shake free of the weight. The other man lay motionless, entombed.

The sergeant slapped Will's shoulder and grinned. "Hey, Davies, you made it." He kicked the typewriter at his feet. "Don't expect the doc to put this back together."

Will pulled the typewriter onto his lap and stared at the smashed case. He pried the top off and touched mangled keys. A flattened blob of metal rolled free. He folded the still-warm bullet into his hand.

The sergeant made a quick head count of the men in his squad, then looked at the bluffs ahead. "You know our objective. One by one, hit the bluff. Move out."

They went out of the hollow separately, each man crouched and ready when the sergeant slapped his ass. Will crawled up to watch them zigzag away toward the bluff. When the last man rolled behind the next piece of cover, Will looked back at the wounded. The medic was gone, moving down the beach toward other piles of motionless men. A big white cross was pinned to the kid's shoulder. At the foot of the bluff, the first of the squad grabbed the long grass and started up. Ducking, Will bent into a crouch and left the hollow's safety behind.

THE THROB OF ENGINES pulled Nora to the open window. Anchoring a hand on the casement, she leaned out over the street. She could finally see the planes crawling across the sky like dark insects. Everyone in London had heard them for hours, wave after wave roaring out of the night, through the dawn and into the morning light. Most of the formations were heading home, not flying away to the south, to France.

The Allies were landing in Normandy. She knew that now, and once the censors passed IP's stories on, so would everyone else. She'd been up all night making sure they had every angle covered. The sound of the planes woke her about midnight. Tired and groggy with sleep, she snuggled under the sheet and tried to not hear, but it was no use. The planes kept coming. As the sound of one formation faded to the south, the whine of another grew louder in the north or east or west. And then she figured it out and jumped out of her bed.

She hammered on Norm Cox's door forever before he finally woke up. As she talked he shook his head and asked "What? What?" so often that she wanted to clobber him.

"It's on, Cox. The invasion's on. Get dressed and down to SHAEF pronto."

"Was it on the radio? What'd they say?"

She pointed at the ceiling. "Can't you hear the planes? They've been going over for an hour. Believe me, it's the invasion. Will's gone, remember?"

Will had disappeared without a word, just as he said he would. The invasion reporters had packed their gear weeks ago and warned their offices that they wouldn't show up one day. That's the way the army wanted it. When Will missed work, she checked his hotel room and found a letter on his desk. She put his belongings in storage, settled his bill and moved into his office as acting bureau chief. That was last week, Monday.

Matthew disappeared on Thursday. She'd expected Will's vanishing act, but not Matthew's. He wasn't in the invasion. Matthew never talked about the landing, but for weeks she read it in his face. When his answers were too sharp or his eyes drifted or his mouth fell into that grim line, she pretended not to see. But she knew him now and understood how he felt. He wanted to be with his men, needed to be part of the invasion. Matthew was missing out on the landing he'd spent a lifetime preparing for. His anger and frustration had been building since their weekend at Connie's place.

That last night he tried to hide the anger but couldn't. He spent the night with her and his bitterness knotted him. She slid her fingers up his back, trying to smooth the stiff ridges of muscle. Finally he pulled her into his arms and buried her concern under his hard mouth. In the morning he woke her with a caress and joked over morning coffee. And then he disappeared. She called his rooming house. His landlady said she expected Colonel Chase back but didn't know when. Nora heard the same story when she called again this morning. If the old lady was playing straight, he was coming back. Of course he was. He *had* to come back.

Shy fingers touched her sleeve and Nora looked up. The new teletype girl fidgeted with the pencil in her hands. "I thought you'd want to know, Miss Seymour. I rang up my mum at St. Luke's. She's matron there. They're emptying the beds, sending anyone home who can go."

Nora nodded and raised an eyebrow. The girl flushed and dropped her eyes.

"She said not to wait supper for her. They expect the first trains this afternoon, and it's worse than they thought. They're calling all the staff in."

Pushing up from the window, Nora spotted Decker hanging over Cox's desk. She walked over and interrupted their gab session.

"They're bringing the wounded to London by train. Get on the horn, Cox, and find out what station they're using."

He shot her a surly look but picked up his phone. Nora walked toward her office and nodded for Decker to follow. She stopped at the door. "Anything from Will yet?"

"Not a word."

Nora looked at the map on the wall across the room. She'd pinned the Allied flags on the Normandy coast right after the first write-through on the invasion had been sent. She found the pile of little flags in Will's desk, next to a pile of letters from Sylvia. He was over there somewhere. Maybe he was already on his way back in a stretcher. Or worse. She forced the thought away and met Decker's eyes.

"Find out if the competition has heard anything from their guys yet. Then talk to the censors. Keep checking in with the office. I don't want to be the last to know."

Crossing to the wall maps, she scanned the bulk of France reaching toward England. The small rank of Allied flags looked like a puny annoyance the Germans could easily swat away. The Allies were back on the continent to stay, Churchill said in his broadcast. And this morning the spokesmen at SHAEF sounded upbeat and confident. When a broadcast reporter asked about expected casualties, the spokesman lowered his voice. "Every success carries a cost." But who was paying the price?

EIGHTEEN

NORA PICKED UP the last stack of cables on Will's desk and glanced through the pile as she chewed an antacid tablet. Each message strip demanded specific information or a story, and IP's New York office wanted everything SOONEST. Will's latest dispatch described the slow and dangerous work of clearing the Germans out of Normandy's hedgerow country. Cox was at SHAEF tracking down rumors that Montgomery wanted supply priority for his Tommies. Decker was meeting another source from SHAEF for a drink and hoped to get a clearer picture of where the Allied Expeditionary Force was headed now that the beachhead seemed secure. Her interview with wounded men back from France and description of the miracles of modern battlefield surgery was being cleared by the censors right now. The London office was doing a great job covering the invasion and New York still wanted more SOONEST. The antacid left a chalky film on her tongue but eased the discomfort in her belly.

Dropping the cables back on the desk, she stretched her arms over her head and glanced through the window at the clock over the maps. Almost eight. New York would just have to wait. None of the staff had grabbed more than three hours' sleep since the landing in France last week. Everyone in the newsroom was punchy with fatigue, and if she didn't ease up now, there would be breakdowns later. She wasn't the only staffer griping about bellyaches.

She lit a cigarette and sorted through papers heaped on the In basket. Only the SHAEF letter soliciting requests for assignment to France needed immediate attention. She spun the form into Will's old typewriter, added Decker's name requesting immediate reassignment and spaced down to fill in her own. Army policy had been that women reporters need not apply to work at a fighting front, but gossips at SHAEF predicted the army would let women go to France soon. Will had talked about her coming over before he left and cautioned that it wouldn't be easy for her. The men would expect to have priority in everything from meals to transportation and filing their stories. Hearing that didn't surprise her much. Eyebrows shot up when the rank and file press in London heard she'd be filling in for Will. Getting ahead in her job always involved a fight. She'd get to France. Not just yet, though. She wasn't leaving London until Matthew left. But she might as well start asking now. Nora added her name to the form and typed "you tell me" in the space for the reassignment date.

Folding the SHAEF form into an envelope, she dropped it in the Out basket and grabbed her bag. She marked herself out on the sign-in board and crossed the newsroom to the teletype machines in the corner. The new girl looked up.

"Who's on for tonight?"

Rose pointed to the schedule pinned to the wall. "I am, Miss Seymour. And Mr. Cox." A crescent of gray drooped under each eye and her skin was blotchy from too much greasy take-out food. The poor kid was beat.

"When Decker gets back, tell him I said to go straight home and get some sleep. Tell Cox to call me at the Waverly if he comes up with anything. I'll be in at six to relieve him." She flashed a smile. "And you, young lady, will stretch out on the cot in Will's office whenever there's a lull. Okay?"

Rose nodded shyly, and Nora felt better. Not one of the staff had let her down, not even Cox. New York could wait, and if tempers flared back there, she'd take the heat. IP's stories from Europe were getting picked up by papers at home twice as often as the competition's. With a little extra effort, she could satisfy New York and take care of her staff.

On the stoop outside, she paused to scan the empty sky. Hitler's new secret weapon usually announced itself with a droning whir, but no one in London took silence for granted these days. After three days of buzz bombs, the whole populace had acquired the habit of frequent glances toward the cloudless sky. Everyone had blessed the good weather helping the armies in France until the robot bombs started. But the experts said even bad weather wouldn't stop the doodlebugs. Bad weather wouldn't stop the launches, and the Germans didn't care where the bombs fell. In fact, the more civilians hit, the better. Everybody knew the target was London, though no one, least of all the censors, wanted to admit it. Tonight only the barrage balloons anchored high above the rooftops marred the darkening sky, and even those grim reminders seemed harmless as they drifted lazily on the warm summer breeze.

On the sidewalk, Nora brought a bouquet of blue cornflowers mixed with red and white peonies. She buried her nose in the fringed peonies as she turned the corner. The patriotic bouquets appeared after lunch the day of the landing, and the flower sellers sold out before dinner. The English reaction to the invasion was odd. During the day people lined up to buy newspapers and paused to listen to the king's broadcast, but there was no cheering or bell ringing. Decker had filed a nice piece on the tributes laid by shopgirls and bowlered businessmen on the tomb of the unknown soldier in Westminster Abbey. Bars and movie houses were empty that night and business was still off. Yet the English were happy about the landing. There was a new spark of quiet pleasure in their eyes and a new pride in their carriage as they went about the usual business of life.

The heat of the day still radiated from ancient brick walls lining the street, and she opened the collar of her blouse. She nodded at a man across the narrow street, the first pedestrian she'd passed since leaving the flower seller. Suddenly London seemed empty. Before the invasion the railroad stations had been jammed with soldiers, fit men kissing girls goodbye or sharing jokes with new pals. Now trains painted with red crosses pulled into those same stations and waiting ambulances soon filled with stretchers of wounded men, white faced and still.

She'd listened to their stories but couldn't make sense of them all. One boy had breezed ashore that first morning and spent three fruitless days looking for Germans until a hidden mine toppled the truck he was riding in and shattered his leg. Another man had been hit as soon as he touched the sand and headed back to England before sundown the first day. She listened to their stories, read the communiqués and studied the maps, but none of it made sense to her. Hundreds of thousands of men were fighting small battles, and the hot spot one day was replaced by a new threat miles away the next. Even Will's stories were spotty when it came to the grand design of the invasion.

As she neared the hotel, she picked up her pace, and her bag hit against her leg. At least Will was okay. He hadn't got his first story out for nearly thirty-six hours, and she'd been frantic until it arrived. When Matthew had phoned that night from somewhere in the south of England, he told her Will was assigned to the First Division. The rush of relief in learning Matthew was safe hadn't lasted long. News from Big Red One was tragic, the casualties enormous. The division had made it ashore and carved out a toehold in France, but the cost was high. Until Will's dispatch arrived, she couldn't go home. Writing updates, answering phones, even editing Cox's stories were welcome jobs that night. The next morning no one in the office mentioned him, and by lunchtime she was hammering on doors at SHAEF demanding to know something, *anything*, about Will's fate. But no one at SHAEF had news of him or the time to find out. So she walked back to the office and slumped behind his desk, not daring to meet the eyes of his wife and children in the photograph on the wall. Finally Decker answered a phone and yipped, giving her a thumbs-up through the window. Relief drained all the strength from her limbs and, for a minute, she couldn't push out of Will's chair.

That was nine days ago. Today getting Will's dispatches from Normandy seemed routine. But the wounded were still arriving, one day a trickle and the next a flood, but always more. And tomorrow the pale, silent face on the stretcher might be Will's. Or Matthew's. They didn't have much time left. The crippling losses on Omaha Beach guaranteed he'd get his command soon.

Trotting up the Waverly's granite steps, she swung through the revolving door and glanced around the lobby for Matthew. The dining room was dark, and the lounge shuttered. She dug in her bag for her key, but her door was unlocked. He had a drink in one hand and the paper in the other and, when he looked up, his smile almost stopped her heart.

She kicked off her shoes and knelt by his chair, resting her head against his thigh. Gentle fingers slipped under her hair and kneaded the nape of her neck. She arched against his hand, liking their silence and his touch. They were so good together, so natural and right, that she ached at the thought of him leaving her.

Matthew's presence in her life showed her the emptiness of those years since Eric and the emptiness of her ambition. She could become a special correspondent, but what good was it? In the end she'd have boxes of faded news clips and an empty heart. Eric's kind of love suffocated her but Matthew's transformed her. His love expanded her, pushing out the bitterness and resurrecting the warmth and tenderness she'd buried along with her pain. But it was no good; Matthew had come too late. He was her chance at something more than a lifetime of grimy newsrooms and endless deadlines and strangers' beds. And he was leaving, going off to fight and maybe to die. By losing him, she'd lose the best part of herself again and shrink back to the emptiness of bitter ambition.

Air-raid sirens shrieked to life across the city, and the thigh under her cheek turned to stone. Nora reached for the hand knotted in her hair and forced down the urge to run. She'd gotten used to air raids, just as Connie had predicted. But the buzz bombs were unnerving. Matthew's hand slid down her arm and he pulled her to her feet. "Let's go up and watch."

Night shrouded the city, but on nearby rooftops she made out burning cigarettes glowing in the dark. By day and by night, the city paused to watch the pilotless planes, inhuman and fearless amid the exploding flak. The bombs flew on unwavering until the flames shooting from the tail disappeared. Then the robot arced toward the city with a terrible silence. She still wanted to believe that the invasion meant the war would be finished soon, but people said the buzz bombs could change everything. When she asked Matthew, he nodded and slung an arm around her shoulders.

"Robots make it easy to bomb without risk. Today they hit London from France. Soon it might be Berlin to New York. There'll be no safe distance, no hiding from war."

For Nora the doodlebugs carried a special horror. It was such a cold and impersonal way to die. But that was stupid. It didn't make much difference whether a human hand or a machine guided the bomb. Dead was dead. She reached up for the hand on her shoulder and turned in to it, rubbing her cheek against his knuckles.

"Will you be spending your time on rooftops after I'm gone?"

His words hit like a fist in her belly, stealing her breath and leaving her desperate for air. When she could manage, she asked how soon.

"Next week. Sooner if I can swing it."

She looked up at him, pulling free of his arm. His eyes were turned across the rooftops to the fires in the city, and he seemed distant already.

"Don't go over there, Nora." He sounded tired. "God knows this is bad enough. It'll be worse over there."

"I can't stay here. The story is in France."

He snagged two cigarettes from his pocket, and the flare of his lighter revealed a tight smile. Her hand trembled, and he stilled it with his own. "What won't you do for your damned stories and that damned ambition?"

She took a deep drag, and the smoke gave her time to gather courage. "For a long time all I had was ambition. The best stories, the big bylines. I never figured the future would be much different. Now I'm not so sure."

For a long moment he didn't move, and she found herself holding her breath. She let the air out softly when he reached for her, gently cupping her face in his hands. His lips were warm but barely touched hers.

"None of us has a future yet."

MATT WELCOMED the gentle monotony of Nora's heart beating through the soft mound of breast rising and falling under his cheek. A narrow strip of dawn edged the blackout curtain on the window. They weren't sounding the all-clear yet, but he hadn't heard a V-1 fall for close to an hour. Maybe the RAF was shooting the doodlebugs down over the Channel, or the men launching the robots from Pas de Calais had targeted another town for a change. The night's alert was the longest so far, and when the explosions got thick around two, he lost count. But the total had to be past three hundred by now and, after last night, he was betting the panic would really be on at SHAEF.

Shifting his legs carefully, Matt rolled onto his back and closed his eyes. Nora must be exhausted to sleep through that. Of course, the three quick Scotches probably helped some. He wanted her tipsy, figuring he'd talk her out of going to France. The ploy was a bust. She seemed close to agreeing but wanted a promise in return that he couldn't give.

He opened his eyes and elbowed up to look at her. A sweep of dark hair covered her face, leaving only the firm line of her chin for his eyes. She was too damned stubborn. He drew a light finger along her jaw. So soft and so stubborn. But what else could he expect? She'd spent years getting ready for France, just as he had. Their jobs were different, but soldiers and reporters had that much in common: battlefields provided the ultimate test of their skills. And, unless he had something better to offer, her job was all she really had.

Antiaircraft batteries chattered to life in the distance. The lull was over, and the attack on again. Matt eased out of bed and crossed to the window. He pulled the edge of the curtain, taking care that the stripe of morning light didn't fall on her face. Her window had a good view of the skyline, but he didn't see any buzz bombs in the pink-streaked sky. Hasty footsteps slapped across pavement somewhere below. A man couldn't outrun a V-1. The RAF put the doodlebug's speed at close to 400 mph, and fighters had to chase them all the way from the Channel to get a good shot. The Germans packed them with high explosives for maximum blast. SHAEF had reason for concern. With enough time and buzz bombs, Hitler could level London. Civil defense had already spotted a pattern in the bombing and was evacuating whole sections of the city. The shelters under the streets and trains heading for the country were stuffed with homeless Londoners, and injured civilians had to compete with the wounded from France for hospital beds.

Turning from the window, Matt peered through the shadows at Nora curled up in the bed. He didn't want her in France, but he didn't want her in London, either. She wouldn't even use the damned air-raid shelter at the office, claiming the alerts sounded too often to get any work done. He came close to begging last night, wanting to send her home to the States but not having the right. Maybe the fighting in France would keep him too busy to worry about the danger she faced.

He took three steps toward the bed and stopped. Not likely. He'd never had to leave someone important behind. No other woman had counted too much. Nora counted, and if it was hard to leave her, the forgetting would be even tougher. Especially since he didn't want to forget her. He wanted to remember every moment, to pull those memories out when things were bad over there and savor every detail. He wanted to remember the golden gleam sparkling through her eyes when she laughed and how his chest ached when her soft fingers traced his spine. He wanted to think about the weight of her head on his shoulder, and the new smile she had just for him. He wanted his mind filled with memories of her, not fear for her.

Lifting the bed clothes, he slipped in next to her. The movement drew a gentle sigh from her lips and she snuggled close, trailing limp fingers across his belly. He pulled her into his arms. There wasn't much time left for them, just enough to build a few more memories.

NINETEEN

CONSTANCE PAUSED near a pyramid of sandbags outside the deep shelter and sipped the warm summer air. She couldn't bear going below ground again. Perhaps it wouldn't be so bad tonight. Surely one grew accustomed to these urban foxholes. Closing her eyes, she willed herself calm.

It was far too late for a change of heart. Hadn't she cabled her resignation to *Manhattan*? Hadn't she steeled her spine for the decision by announcing it to Mother and parrying each objection the old woman raised? She'd even dashed off that note to Peter, trilling with pride like some infatuated adolescent seeking approval from a first love. Too bloody late now. She was trapped like a fox turning to meet the hounds, too tired to run and too weak to fight. Yes, she must go down there again.

Straightening her coat, Constance dug through her bag for the shelter pass. Fresh reassurance swept through her at the ordinary task. Routine, that was the ticket. When she had that the spells of panic would stop. Her own relief helped some. A wonderful sensation of release came from doing after all those years of talking. Talking, writing and feeling low-down. But she'd put that behind her now, along with her job. She couldn't guess what else might fall behind as well. Her marriage? Her children? No, never the twins. And no need to worry about her husband yet, not with Jerrys' V-bombs putting forever back into the whole bloody war.

Edging around the shoulder of the crowd, she flashed her pass at the civilian defense man. He checked his list and motioned her ahead of the people waiting for the lift. She looked over the jumble of women, young and old, and a full range of children from swaddled infants to gawky youths. Fatigue etched their faces, and their shoulders slumped beneath ragged sweaters and threadbare coats. Their limp hands clutched worn string sacks and battered carpetbags. She glanced down the sleeve of her crisp mackintosh to her smooth leather bag and slipped it under her arm. Lift wires groaned, and the crowd strained forward as the little box of stale air rose toward the surface.

Constance shuddered and stepped past the civilian defense desk. "I rather think I'll climb down tonight."

The official frowned as he plucked a pipe from his mouth. "You must be daft. It's eight hundred steps by my count."

Constance waved a hand. "Still, I prefer to. My thanks for your concern."

Easing through the door to the staircase, she checked her watch by a caged bulb flickering over the landing. Nora should be waiting. Perhaps after visiting air-raid shelters, she'd see reason and forgo reassignment to France. Matt was right—Normandy was simply too dangerous. Constance envied her friend's ease and assurance, but going to the front was too much.

Moisture popped out on her forehead, and she stopped to lean against cold concrete. Still, there was a new uncertainty in Nora's manner. Would it undermine that confidence that seemed so common in Yanks? Peter,

Matt and the other Americans she'd met all shared that certainty that things would come right for them. Their innocence was at once heartening and terrifying. The convolutions of history and complexities of politics be damned: America would set things right and have things her way. The Yanks were cocksure.

Constance pulled the scarf from her neck and continued down as she folded the silk into a neat square. Even so, the war was changing Nora, or was it Matt? Either way, she seemed softer now, less guarded and freer with laughter. And with tears. How shocked she'd been by Nora's tears the evening Matt had sailed for France.

She knocked aside an old carton with her foot. Nearly down now. A jangle of voices and music floated up to her. Perhaps the wretched shelters would convince Nora. Fleets of British Lancasters flew off each night followed by American Fortresses by day to pound the continent. Not just Germany, but Holland and Belgium and France endured their own terror. It was madness to think of going there.

The light in the shelter blinded her as it glared off metal shelves fitted along the walls for bunks. She blinked and let the familiar horror wash over her. The place reminded her of the regimented and antiseptic future portrayed in prewar films.

She spotted Nora wandering along the corridor and beckoned to her. A scratchy version of "Blue Skies" wafted from a speaker overhead. Nora jerked a thumb toward the box. "What is with this music? I've been listening to the hit parade all day. Every shelter has one of the damned things."

Constance laughed and took her arm. "It's trying but the occupants quite like the records. And if they find solace in it . . . ?" She shrugged.

For the next hour Constance led Nora through the warren of corridors as she tried to convince elderly widows and young mothers to accept safe housing outside the city. The Londoners huddled in the shelters were determined and defiant. One old lady was typical. A buzz bomb had wrecked her flat but since her oven still worked, she wasn't leaving.

Nora grinned as they walked away. "She thinks she's put something over on the Krauts. As long as she has that hearth, she has a home. Don't let her worry you, Connie. She's a tough old bird."

Nodding, Constance turned toward the young mother she'd made a habit of avoiding. Despite earlier fears that the shelter inhabitants would dislike her, Constance had found most friendly and warm. Only Regis Wilde despised her simply for her class. The girl's lip curled and a mocking light brightened her eyes every time Constance came near.

The young mother rocked a pram with her foot. "Going to have at me again, Mrs. Tolliver?"

Constance ran a finger across the baby's face, silken cheeks far too pale. "Have you taken little Vivien to see Dr. Ludwig? She doesn't look well, you know."

Regis leaned over the child. "She's right as rain."

Constance motioned Nora closer. "What do you think?"

Nora studied the baby for a moment, then turned her palms up. "She's a skinny little ghost and no wonder. She's living in a hole filled with crummy air."

Regis reached a shaking hand and stroked her baby's head. "I only came back because of the noise. CD had us next to an airbase with bombers coming and going at all hours. Viv just fretted there. Where could we go?"

Constance ran a finger down her clipboard. "What about Bath?"

"The seashore?" A different light danced in Regis Wilde's eyes. "I've always wanted..."

Constance smiled. "Well, there you are."

She allowed herself a triumphant grin as they took a table in the canteen. Nora matched it when she finished scribbling in her notebook. "Nice little squeeze play, Mrs. Tolliver."

Tapping a Dunhill from her box, Constance offered the cigarettes to Nora. "Now if I can only make *you* see reason." She scratched a match and lit their cigarettes. "I'll not give up on you, you know."

"It won't work, Connie." Nora took up a *Daily Mail* abandoned on a nearby chair, erecting a barrier between them.

Pouring tea, Constance recalled a similar scene years ago. The other cup had belonged to Jane that day and Constance was the woman determined to go to France. Geoff's death had already transformed her life and working behind those endless trenches finished the job. She'd been such an innocent, so earnest and naive, until the double blow of death and battlefields. Witnessing Nora's change had already resurrected painful memories of those days of upheaval. The grieving innocent who had sailed for France had returned an outraged fury.

It was then she took her first false steps toward living to fulfill the expectations of others. She hadn't wanted the intellectual fame or the burden of bearing the standard for this cause or that, no matter how worthy. She'd only realized her mistake by seeing Nora determined to follow her own false path.

Crushing out her cigarette, Constance pushed Nora's hand, shoving gently until the newspaper barrier collapsed. "At least let me warn you, my dear. Twenty-five years ago in wartime, I too had a choice to make." She stretched her hand across the table. "I made the wrong choice, one I bitterly regret today."

Folding aside the paper as she leaned over the table, Nora reached out. At her touch, Constance closed her fingers. "I never considered what I wanted, only what I thought I must do. So I wrote that bloody book and the outcry propelled me into a public life I didn't want. I married the wrong man."

At the squeeze of Nora's hand, she shook her head. "No, I see that now. I made that mistake, married the wrong man and from that day until this, every step I've taken has been false. In twenty-five years, the only right thing was the twins. Everything else had been wrong."

The concern in Nora's eyes wrapped around her like a snare. "Maybe it's not too late, Connie. You can still have the life you want."

"Can I? Perhaps, and perhaps not. But you do have time, Nora. Don't make my mistake. Be certain you know what you want. You do, don't you?"

For a moment, something new veiled Nora's eyes, and the fingers around Constance's hand slackened. "I'm not sure anymore." She withdrew her hand to pull a fresh cigarette from the pack. "I thought I wanted to be a special correspondent. Maybe I'm kidding myself."

She lit a match and studied the flame. "Maybe I've been kidding myself all along. Going into newspapers—did I want to be a reporter or just escape my hometown?"

Smoke curled across her eyes as she leaned closer. "I've been gunning for special correspondent so I wouldn't have to look at where I am and what I want. Now it *is* too late. Matthew was right about that—the future is indefinitely suspended for all of us."

Constance didn't want to believe it—not for Nora or for herself. Yet it was true. They were all pawns to the war, robbed of freedom and sentenced to a random destiny. Some would live, some would die and all would be changed.

FORCING HERSELF to ignore the smirk on Norm Cox's face, Nora crossed the newsroom with deliberately slow steps and retrieved the wad of copy lying by the teletype machines. She'd tossed the crumpled ball with a gust of fury and now regretted venting her frustration in front of the whole IP crew. Will always kept his cool, always. She didn't know his secret so she'd have to fake it when she confronted Colonel Logan about the shelter story. She couldn't let this hatchet job by the censors pass without protest. If Logan had it in for her personally, fine. That would just be another reason to get to France ASAP. She sure wasn't doing IP any good in London.

Back in her office, Nora smoothed the shelter story Logan had killed and called his office. The clerk told her the colonel would see her immediately, so she ran a comb through her hair, grabbed the story and headed down the hall. She was tired of London and tired of her job. With Matthew gone and Connie spending every night in the shelters, she had no one to talk to and no way to escape the monotonous routine she'd fallen into. Sometimes she felt like a rifle-range target jerking down a track until hit, then jerking back up the track until the next shot connected. *Ding*—go to work. *Ding*—check in at SHAEF. *Ding*—back to the Waverly. Even if she didn't have the fire of ambition in her belly anymore, she needed a new challenge.

Logan kept her waiting in the outside office and made a few calls after inviting her in. He wasn't budging on the story and, as usual, offered no explanation. Nora clenched her fists in her lap but managed to keep her face impassive.

"Can you at least explain what the problem is? You guys are killing so many stories we're having a hard time getting out a decent report."

The censor rubbed a hand through the stubble of hair fringing his ears and propped his feet on the desk. "Come on, Seymour, we've been over this before." His eyes rolled. "The V-1s are off limits."

"I know, I know. V-1 stories might help the Germans improve their aim. But this story never mentioned the damned buzz bombs."

His feet dropped to the floor, and he smacked a thick finger against the desk. "Maybe not, but you've been warned before. By saying the robots are driving London underground, we're telling the Krauts their strategy is working. Until we knock off their launch sites, we're keeping quiet."

Glancing away, she took a calming breath and started again. "Right. But how long can you keep this thing secret? You've had three sets of congressmen through London in the past two weeks. You know they'll blab it around Washington, and it'll be the Patton thing all over again. Some hotshot will scoop the whole overseas press corps, and we'll end up looking like jerks. You guys, too."

Logan shrugged and raised his eyebrows. At least he wasn't yelling this time. And it didn't look as if he was out to get her. But, the buzz bombs were the only good story left in London. Anything else was just a routine dispatch from SHAEF.

"Okay, I'll drop it. But maybe you can save me some time. This afternoon I'm set to talk to a crippled veteran from the last war who makes artificial legs for the new amputees. You know, a feature piece. Any problem with that?"

"Not today. But tomorrow, who knows?"

Nora sighed and pushed out of the chair. "Thanks, anyway."

He stopped her at the door. "There's been some talk upstairs about encouraging more stories like that. Getting people back home prepared for the worst."

She nodded and thanked him again. At least her whole day wouldn't be wasted. She could grab a quick lunch in the mess downstairs, then find someone who knew where Maybrick Street was. The old man's directions were confusing, and she didn't want to be late. He'd been curt on the phone, reminding her that he must be at hospital by three.

The bus wound through unfamiliar sections of London, detouring past wrecked streets and burned-out cars. Except for the soldier necking with a girl in the last row, Nora was the only passenger riding upstairs. The view up here was better, especially for surveying the devastation. Occasionally a wisp of smoke drifted from a shattered building or a helmeted fireman hosed down a street. It was hard to tell blitz rubble from buzz-bomb wreckage. Did it matter? Everyone knew the buzz bombs were beating the hell out of London.

The conductor called up the stairs and she climbed down. He held the bus long enough to draw a map to 841 Maybrick Street and warn her that bombs had fallen in the neighborhood last week. Nora wasn't worried. The city had been quiet since the all-clear sounded at nine that morning.

After spending two nights in the shelters, Nora welcomed the sun on her arms. How did Connie stand it down there every night? She'd tried to talk her out of quitting *Manhattan*. Maybe they were both too stubborn for their own good. Connie's moods had swung crazily in the past few weeks, but once she'd started working down there, she evened out. When she was with Peter, she brimmed with happiness, hanging on his words as tightly as she hung on his arm. Peter was good for Connie. That much was clear. But back at the hotel, when Peter was working and she had to write her column, Connie was glum. She said her work was a waste and her writing didn't matter. Nora threw the usual argument at her, that the reader had a right to know the truth, but Connie just waved it aside. She was happier now and seemed to feel useful.

At the shriek of the air-raid sirens, Nora hunched over her bag. Stepping into the street, she searched the empty sky. She checked the address in her notebook and glanced at the numbers on the brick buildings: 568, 572. Still a few blocks to go.

Somewhere to the south guns chattered to life. She quickened her steps. Shades were pulled in every window. The houses looked abandoned.

A whine cut across staccato fire from antiaircraft batteries. There they were. One, two, three—oh, Christ, too many. As long as those engines hummed, she was safe. Silence meant the bombs were coming down.

Breaking into a trot, she scanned the street, looking for an open window. Didn't the English like fresh air? Someone had to be home, someone had to live on this street.

The pitch of the motors changed and she spun, skipping backward up the road. The first robot curved toward earth, glinting in the sun as it fell. Not that one, thank God—too far away.

At the corner she checked both side streets. To the left, streetlights tilted over a blast crater. To the right, blank windows overlooked an empty street. The light flashed red as she ran underneath and spun to check the sky again.

Sparks shot from the tails of the missiles scattered across the sky. Antiaircraft fire exploded in puny puffs. A brass plate numbered 722 gleamed on a red door. It wasn't far now.

Crossing to the odd-numbered side, she kicked up dust in the gutter. Her heels smacked furiously along the sidewalk. Far above, an engine sputtered. She screamed as the fire at the tail of the bomb died.

"Is anyone home? Is anyone home?"

She dropped her bag and bent low to scoop handfuls of stones. Her hoarse shouts echoed along the street as she showered the empty windows with pebbles. A shoe flipped off but she ran on, screaming and throwing, begging the doors to open.

A voice called out. "Here, here. Back this way."

Turning took her into the middle of the street. She darted back toward the walk, not daring to look at the sky. A blur—a waving arm—drew her. Her bare foot scratched across rough stone. A plump woman backed into the gloom as Nora leaped a low hedge and vaulted the stoop to the open door.

Sturdy fingers caught her arm. "Downstairs now. This way."

Blinded by darkness, she hesitated. A firm hand nudged her shoulder, and she tripped down a narrow staircase until she touched damp earth.

Something brushed by, stirring up cool dust. A hand yanked her arm. "Hurry, under the stairs."

Crouching low, Nora scurried toward safety. "Get down now. Head down. That's fine. All right, then. Shield yourself with this."

She groped and caught the cold metal, resting it on her head and holding firmly with both hands. The silence was awful, terrifying. She concentrated on the ragged sound of her own breathing, wanting the woman's reassurance, needing to hear that calm voice.

A brilliance of light flashed through the gloom. A rush of hot air stung her cheeks. An invisible cyclone lifted her up and threw her against the basement wall.

TWENTY

NORA SHOVED THE MUG to the center of the table. The fried eggs wouldn't settle in her stomach, and the coffee was making things worse. Pushing out of her chair, she stretched her arms for balance and tilted toward her duffel in the corner of the wardroom. Braving the cold breeze on deck was better than waiting for the inevitable in the belly of the ship.

She sorted through her gear, trying to balance the load, and hefted the bags. A polite sailor offered his help, but she settled for directions. She might as well get used to lugging her own gear. There would be few niceties in Normandy.

Choosing a sheltered spot by a funnel, she plopped on her duffel and checked her equipment. Stuffing the black dress in was against regulations but at least she had all possibilities covered. Even though common sense told her the chance of a quick reunion with Matthew was slim, she was ready.

Her fingers brushed over the bumps in her makeup case. Vanity, at least, was satisfied. Carrying a portable typewriter and her supplies was a pain, but having a good stock was essential. She pulled out her field glasses and scanned the white-capped water. A bank of fog hugged the coast, but sun burned through mist to spotlight trawlers dragging sweeps before the convoy. Binoculars had a civilian life and maybe the mess kit did, too. The canteen and tin dishes looked like the kind Boy Scouts used. But the helmet: well, that was the real item. The helmet was serious business.

Undoing the chin strap, she settled the metal hat on her head. The fit was a little off, she guessed. Either the front tipped over her eyes or the back rim bounced against her neck when she moved her head. She didn't mind. After her afternoon on Maybrick Street, she understood why helmets were standard issue.

Her head ached at the thought, but remembering still brought a smile. Christ, what a pair they'd been. When Nora came to, she looked at Clara Partridge and yelped with laughter. The old lady's face was smudged with ancient dust knocked free by the bomb, but it was the headgear—a frying pan with the handle at full salute—that set her off. Clara looked like a yokel from *L'il Abner*. Nora laughed until tears streamed down her cheeks, falling in grimy drips to her collar. Mrs. Partridge's eyes went from narrowed concern to twinkling blue in seconds, and they'd both released their pent-up fear in a torrent of giggles.

"You'll not have all your fun at my expense, young woman. Upstairs now to freshen up." Mrs. Partridge squirmed out from under the stairs and reached back a hand. "But first, you'll have a look at yourself."

In a lavatory off the kitchen, Nora saw the white enamel pot she was sporting and collapsed on the john. When Mrs. Partridge scurried in with fresh towels, Nora could do no more than gasp her thanks before doubling over again. She finally got cleaned up and took a seat at the kitchen table, but whenever her eyes met Clara's over their teacups, they started laughing again. And later, after they'd inspected the smoking crater in the next block and she'd watched the crippled veteran carefully sand a wooden leg that could never replace flesh and bone, remembering the laughter had made her feel a little better. She patted her helmet and lit a smoke.

An hour later she slung the field glasses around her neck and climbed into a dispatch boat headed for Cherbourg. The boat bounced through swells thrown up by a stiff breeze clearing the fog from the harbor. Dozens of ships swung at anchor and tugboats nosed derelicts into a makeshift breakwater. A curtain of fog clung to the town but she spotted a narrow tower piercing the mist. Lifting her glasses, she focused until the blur sharpened into a jagged finger reaching for the morning sky, rising charred and useless from a tumble of wreckage. She scanned left and then, more slowly, to the right but finally stopped counting jagged edges and stopped searching for something intact. The destruction seemed complete.

The coxswain pointed her down a twisting path bulldozed through the rubble. She struggled her equipment forward on sea-wobbly legs. A dog dozed in a patch of sunlight, and a young matron shelled peas on her doorstep while she watched a little boy circling a parked army truck. Bullet scars dotted the old stone buildings and shattered glass littered the gutters. The U.S. flag hung outside a café across the small square.

Inside, a lieutenant checked her name against his list, stamped her credentials and pointed to the truck outside. "You can grab a lift on that deuce-and-a-half. We're putting you ladies up with the nurses from the hospitals. I'll make sure your boss knows where to find you. He'll brief you."

The driver threw her gear in the back of the truck as she hoisted herself in the front, gently nudging a rifle aside. The GI wasn't interested in small talk, which was just as well. She couldn't think of anything to say as he swung the truck through town, dodging wreckage and whistling at every pretty girl they passed. Nora was glad when they left the rubble of Cherbourg behind and sped down country roads lined with thick hedges. She opened her window. The warm morning air was thick with the stench of death. Groaning, she closed her eyes.

The young soldier laughed and thumped the steering wheel. "Just dead cows, ma'am." He slowed at a corner and pointed through an opening ripped in the hedge. Flies swarmed over bloated carcasses strewn across the lush meadow grass like boulders. Nora gagged.

"Got 'em bad. Don't guess there's much milk left hereabouts. When they get done with the boys, they'll likely start on these."

Nora fought nausea. The villages were as wrecked as the port, but the countryside was peaceful. Women fed chickens in courtyards of ancient farmhouses, and she saw a farmer in muddy boots carrying a brimming pail of milk from one barn. Some cows had survived.

The driver turned the truck onto a narrow dirt road lined with poplars. The trees didn't look right. The branches were clipped, uniformly sheared off for twenty yards. She craned to look as the truck slowed, tires crunching through withered leaves.

The driver caught her eye. "Machine gun."

She didn't understand. He nodded to his left. A blackened tank lay dead in the ditch, tipped and missing a tread.

"Bazooka got it, though."

The swastika jolted her. It was the first signature of the enemy she'd seen. The world suddenly seemed unreal. Somewhere outside a bird called, and the sun was warm on her face. All around the earth burst with midsummer's bloom amid the dead things of war.

"IT'S A TERRIBLE THING, lad, terrible."

Tim nodded and brushed past the old man. He had some time. Fred would fend them off for a while. They could string a rope around the crater. They could holler for him to get out of there, shout until they were hoarse. But it wouldn't work. He had to see for himself. They couldn't just tell him Hillary was dead and think that finished it.

He stepped over the rope and walked toward the hole. A wisp of smoke coiled up from the back. Melted macadam dripped from the rim into sooty puddles trapped in the wreckage. He glanced back toward his copilot. Fred and the old fellow turned away.

Stripping off his jacket, he tossed it aside and slid down through the mud. His foot snagged on a twist of wire and he jerked free, tearing his pants. Scrabbling for handholds, he worked his way over the wreckage. Someone shouted but he ignored the voice. Fred would cover for him.

About noon, they'd said. She'd have been in the kitchen then, fixing lunch for her kid sister. Had she heard the sirens or was she singing along with the damned radio? He slapped a stinging ember off his hand. Or maybe she decided to wait for Susy, knowing the girl would be scared.

He kicked a broken timber from a mound and uncovered the top of the fridge. Jumping down, he cleared a place in front of the door. He wrestled the handle but

ALLIANCES

couldn't budge it. He fingered a darker smudge on the smoke-stained enamel. Was she standing here when it hit?

They could be wrong. How could they be sure it was her? Maybe she'd gone to town for the day and taken Susy with her. She did that sometimes without telling anyone. Not as much anymore, but sometimes. The house next door was flattened, too. What if the Kelly sisters were thrown over here by the blast? They found only pieces.

Tim slumped. Don't think about that. Don't think about what happens when the bomb explodes. God, he'd spent the past two months forcing his mind away from the thought every time his bombardier cried, "Bombs away!" He didn't look down to see if their load hit target. He didn't want to see the cities burning below, not Munich or Stuttgart or even Berlin.

A gust of wind flapped through a frayed rag. The splash of red drew him across the wrecked kitchen on hands and knees. He'd bought the scarf for her in Dublin, picked the finest Irish linen. He tugged it free, rubbing fingers along the charred edge. She wore it all the time. But not today. It was too hot for a scarf today.

He couldn't stop his searching hands. His mind screamed to stop but still he dug. The bricks came free easily and the hole deepened. He worked by touch, feeling for her softness among the shards of her home. The scarf didn't mean anything. Maybe she'd gone to town...without telling anyone...with Susy...sometimes she did... too hot today.

"You lousy bastards."

A minute ago the air around him had been dead. But now it breathed of her and he knew.

"Lousy rotten bastards."

He buried his face in her scarf, drowning in the rich spice of her scent. Hillary. Gone.

They were such cowards. Cowards launched robot bombs, cowards who risked nothing and slaughtered innocents. He let tears spill.

The weight of a man crunched through rubble behind him. Who would Fred let through? God, not the chaplain. He couldn't stand listening to any crap about God's will.

"You want to go home, Captain Chase? You're only a mission short."

Tim wiped his face with Hillary's scarf and pushed to his feet. Taking a breath, he turned and faced his CO. "No, sir. I'm staying."

He met the stern eyes without flinching. Think of Hillary. Think of Matt. Think of Dad.

"You're sure?"

"Yes, sir. I'm sure."

The CO turned away, but Tim called him back. "I still want to stay. Once my tour's up, I'll switch to fighters."

At the raised eyebrows, Tim held his ground. He had to stay now. "Don't let emotion dictate your decisions, Chase."

Dipping his head, Tim wound the scarf around his wrist. When he met his commander's eyes again, the smile came naturally. "I won't, sir. I'm a damned good pilot. And you can use me."

THE FORCE OF MATT'S SHOVE sailed the map halfway across the room before it floated to the floor. Held in reserve. Dammit to hell. They'd sidelined him again.

He scraped his chair back and crossed to the window. The old farmhouse had a good view of the target area, a couple of tree-topped ridges to the east. Matt frowned.

ALLIANCES

Three divisions were dug in up there waiting for the dust to clear, waiting for the order. Two hours of pounding from 2,200 bombers and then those soldiers would bust through the German lines. The race would be on and the First hadn't made it to the gate.

Hell, pushing paper for SHAEF was better than this. He'd spent two weeks crouched in a foxhole in Caumont as the Germans peppered the town with artillery. Two panzer divisions primed for attack and what had they done? Sent in a shower of goddamned leaflets. The bullshit about medical care for the wounded was stupid. So was the crude pornography. Two weeks the First had waited for the attack but it never came. They got orders instead: reassigned to VII Corps and held in reserve.

The door squeaked open, but Matt didn't turn. Only Lou had the right to barge in unannounced. "My watch makes it another five minutes." Tin clinked against wood. "Have a cup of coffee."

Matt sighed and turned from the window. "Your coffee is lousy, Sergeant." He took a steaming gulp. "But thanks."

Lou swept the map from the floor and rolled it up. He snapped a rubber band around the map and dropped it on the desk as he walked to the door. "Want company? Davies is back."

"Send him up."

Davies was okay when he wasn't drinking. And he wasn't hitting the bottle in France, although the rest of the correspondents were swimming in Calvados. Maybe the IP man just reminded him of Nora. Will didn't have her sass, but the same curiosity brightened his eyes. And, like Nora, he didn't kowtow to rank. He asked a straight question, expected a straight answer and usually got one. Matt didn't mind him hanging around.

Motors hummed overhead as the door opened again. "Here they come. This should be some show." Davies joined him at the window.

A stream of heavies came in from the north, swept over the far ridge and curved off to the south. In seconds the concussions set Matt's shirtsleeves fluttering. Puffs of black smoke from German antiaircraft guns dotted the sky and parachutes bloomed white against blue as a crew bailed out.

Another formation flew in from the south and turned over the closer ridge. Eruptions of smoke and dust towered into the sky, curtaining the target area. Matt stepped back from the window and glanced at Davies. "How was your trip?"

"Good." The correspondent crossed his arms on his chest. "I saw Nora. She got in yesterday morning."

Matt smacked a closed fist into his palm. "Oh, great. She coming up to the line?"

"Hell, no. Don't worry about that." He pulled an envelope from his pocket and passed it to Matt. "I'm sure she'll tell you all about it. She's got the same restrictions as nurses or Red Cross girls. She's bunking at one of the hospitals and can't leave without an officer escort."

Tossing a glance at the scrawl of his name, Matt tucked the envelope into a back pocket. If she followed orders, she'd be safe enough. The Luftwaffe harassed behind the lines at night but didn't do much damage. In the past six weeks hidden snipers back there had been flushed from their roosts. As long as she kept well back and didn't wander around alone, she'd be all right.

Davies gave him a stack of old stateside newspapers he'd lifted from the PR boys in Cherbourg. The euphoria of invasion hadn't worn off yet back home. The editorial writers would swallow their rah-rahs fast when news about the V-1s finally got out. As usual, columnists like Lippmann and Pearson were second-guessing Ike and sniping at Montgomery. As Matt turned to the sports page, the door banged open.

"Trouble, Matty." Lou trotted across the room to the window. "They're hitting our own guys."

Matt trailed him to the window and squinted against the noon sun. The curtain of dust hung closer now as the bombardment crept down the nearest ridge. Another stream of bombers whined overhead.

Davies moaned in his ear as the planes dropped their loads. "They're walking it in the wrong direction."

Turning away, Matt pulled his chin. "You notified division." Lou nodded but it wasn't a question. "Get the officers over here fast. I want someone on the horn to VII Corps right now. And tell him to stay on that line until he's got us an okay to jump off. Send one of the new men—someone you trust—back to Divarty. I want to know what their spotters see the minute the planes get down."

Lou spun off toward the stairs, but Matt called him back. "I'll need you to fill me in on the replacements before they get here." He nodded and was gone.

Matt leaned over the desk and sorted through a stack of papers. Tugging the rubber band off the map, he smoothed it across the desk. No telling which outfit they'd pinch-hit for. His fingers traced possible approaches on the map as he double-checked the objectives listed on mimeographed sheets.

Were they hitting the Germans at all? His eyes closed as he sifted the din of bombardment, searching for German fire. Nothing. The Kraut gunners were either dead or out of ammunition. He'd find out which soon enough. In person.

TWENTY-ONE

NORA SANK BACK as Peter eased the jeep away from the hospital. Having him around was the only good thing about her billet. The trek to the men's press camp meant she was first up and last to bed in the tent she shared with a couple of nurses. Not that she was getting much sleep. When the helmet she wore to bed didn't keep her up, the air raids it was supposed to protect her from did. Most nights her mind spun over the daily briefing again, comparing explanations of the day's objectives with the progress marked on huge wall maps. She'd hoped coming to France would give a clearer picture of the war, but the skirmishes and bombardments and advances still didn't add up for her. The army wouldn't let her near the fighting and good stories didn't come from secondhand reports.

"Hold on."

She grabbed for the steel frame above her head as Peter turned a corner and gave it the gas.

"Want the windshield up?"

She shook her head and he grinned.

"Good thing, sister. The Krauts aim for the reflection. But I guess if you've got the stomach for this trip, you don't mind having your hair mussed."

Sliding a knee across her seat, she angled around. The jeep left dust hanging as it sped along. It was good to be away from the hospital without an officer escort. Peter had signed her out but that was just for show. He'd warned her there might be snipers, and she still asked to come. No PR escort would let her near the frontlines.

"Why do you go out like this? I can't believe the medics leave wounded behind."

"Not intentionally, but it happens. The doughs have been rolling forward for five days now." He squinted against the sun. "Things get screwed up with an advance that fast. Ask your boyfriend next time you see him."

Nora looked down to hide the blush. She felt like a kid when he said things like that. The big-brother approach wasn't reserved for her. He ribbed all the nurses that way, and they loved it. So did she, really. It was nice having someone familiar to lean on in all the confusion.

Chaos reigned in the wake of the advance. Even the reporting was all wrong. Only Will and a few other correspondents stayed with the fighting troops. The rest listened to briefings, dashed forward to grab a few quotes, then shot back to the press camp to file their copy and sleep in safety. No foxholes or bedrolls for those guys. Once in a while they hung around the front long enough to pick up a sidebar on life in the line. None understood what was happening any better than she did and most didn't care. Nora couldn't see risking her life for a story but still believed in knowing the score before writing it up.

The jeep slowed and she raised her head. Wires dangled from high broken poles and coiled across the gravel. Charred craters pitted the rural intersection, and an overturned wagon blocked the road near the smoking ruins of a stone windmill. An eerie silence blanketed the crossroads. Peter swung the jeep along the grassy shoulder beside a slow-moving river.

"Too many hats." He pointed down the road. "That's what the French say when casualties are high."

Punctured helmets and broken rifles lay scattered among sprawled bodies and pooled blood in the shadows of elms. The jeep crept forward, dodging around dead men and broken machines. Bodies clogged the ditches, heaped in some spots, strung out in others. She spotted a smashed airplane in a field behind the trees.

Peter cut the engine and sniffed. "Not a whiff. They're fresh." He reached under the seat for his bag. "Stay away from the buildings. I doubt there's any snipers but you can't tell." He moved off down the ditch, kneeling to check the bodies.

Nora forced her fingers around a pen but fumbled over the notebook cover. Her eyes kept returning to the ditch. Taking a deep breath, she counted bodies. *Three, four, five.* They didn't look dead. The boy with a hand under his cheek might be sleeping. Except for the blood staining the grass. *Twelve, thirteen.* She couldn't look at faces, couldn't bear those staring eyes. At least they were mostly German. *Twenty-one, twenty-two, twenty-three.* Her eyes strayed past slumped shoulders but snapped back as the insignia registered.

The red number one on the shoulder patch drew her out of the jeep. It couldn't be First Division. Nora dropped the notebook and knelt beside him. She traced the cool thread of the patch with a trembling finger. His pack had spilled when he fell, tumbling a Bible and a sewing kit, socks and packet of letters under the trees. She reached for the letters but picked up the Bible instead. "Pvt. Daniel Cornell, Erie, Pa." When she leafed through grimy thumbed pages, a snapshot fell out. A pretty girl laughed up at a tall young soldier. Slipping the photo between the pages, she tucked the Bible next to his body and picked up her notebook.

Taking notes steadied her as she walked down the road. The cluttered scene dissolved into a series of stray items. A bloody shoe. A trail of crushed cigarettes. A dented first-aid kit propped on a grenade. Helmets and rifles everywhere. Odd things, too, that might have tickled her if she could remember how to laugh. A banjo abandoned by a tree and, farther down the road, a tennis racket, a Wilson clamped in a press. The grand strategy detailed in maps and communiqués might elude her, but this she could understand. The briefings about skirmishes and hot spots meant nothing without the human element. Since that morning in Cherbourg she hadn't been able to shake a feeling of strangeness. Nothing about France had seemed real. Until now. Pvt. Daniel Cornell of Erie, Pa., was real.

"Get the jeep. Bring it here."

At Peter's shout, she swung around. He dug through his bag as he crouched next to a motionless German. Nora trotted to the jeep and drove it alongside him. He didn't look up when she jumped down.

"See if you can get that stretcher down. And pull out some plasma from the box behind the seat."

She wrestled the stretcher off the frame and helped lift the wounded soldier on. Peter jabbed an IV needle into a bloody arm and gave her the bottle to hold. He dusted sulfa over the boy's shredded belly and started a bandage. The soldier's eyelids fluttered.

"*Wasser.*" His head rolled as he croaked again. "*Wasser.*"

Nora looked at Peter for help. "He wants water."

She used her free hand to snap the canteen from her belt.

"Shit, don't give him any. He's gutshot." Peter pulled a syringe from his bag. "This will shut him up."

The boy groaned when Peter pulled the helmet off his head, fingering the scalp and neck. His hands slid over limp shoulders and he flicked the twin lightning bolts on the German's collar. "The kid's SS." Nora cringed at the hate in his voice, but Peter's hands moved on, prodding and squeezing their way down the length of arms and legs. Finally he looked up and met her eyes.

"All right. Let's get him up."

The weight of the stretcher staggered her as they heaved it on the frame atop the jeep. She climbed into the jeep as Peter strapped the German down and secured the stretcher. When he swung into his seat, she couldn't hold the question back. "Will he live?"

Peter grunted as he revved the engine. "Maybe. His pulse is good and the bleeding's stopped." He spun the wheel and the jeep jerked around spitting gravel.

Back at the hospital Nora paged through her notes as she walked to her tent. She had to fashion a story from those scribbles. Throwing together a five-hundred-word piece from the daily briefings was simple. The PR guys provided the pieces and all the reporters had to do was shuffle the information into order. Every day the stories were the same—units from this or that army had pushed the enemy back five miles here and two miles there. But stories like that left out the human element. Those stories ignored the French who'd learned the cost of their freedom was the destruction of their towns and villages. Those stories rarely mentioned filthy and exhausted soldiers dragging themselves into rest stations for a day before returning to battle or the Pvt. Daniel

Cornells whose reward was a shallow grave in foreign soil.

The nurses were on duty, so Nora had the tent to herself. She tied up the flaps and dragged a table in front of her cot. Spinning a sheet of copy paper into the portable, she slugged her name at the top left and stopped. What would she call this story? "Battlegrounds." She locked down the shift key and typed it in. Yes, that was good. If only the rest would come that easily.

Half an hour later, she'd rejected a dozen leads. The only words the papers strewn across her cot shared were her name and that title: "Battlegrounds." But finally she had a good start. She'd typed half of a second page when Peter stopped outside and knocked on the tent post.

"I've got some coffee and a flask. Want a drink?"

She nodded and motioned him to a chair. She moistened her mouth with the strong brew and asked about the German boy.

"You're softer than I figured, worrying about an SS officer." He tucked one of the nurse's pillows behind him and leaned back on her cot. "He'll do all right. Our belly man is working on him right now. I just fix heads."

Peter glanced through the false starts strewn across the blanket.

She couldn't guess how he'd react to her story, not after seeing him work a few hours earlier. That Peter despised the boy he'd found was obvious, yet he saved him. For a minute back there when he pointed out the SS insignia, she thought he might leave the boy to die after all. But he drove like hell once they got the stretcher on the jeep and hustled him into the operating tent without a word to her.

"I don't understand you. You brought him in but you hate him. Why?"

"The suckers who got drafted I feel sorry for, even the Krauts. But that guy's different. He's SS because he bought Hitler's crap about supermen. He asked for it."

"So why'd you save him?"

Peter shrugged. "I knew how." He pulled her first page from the table. His eyes zigzagged down. "You're right. This is great."

Nora leaned forward and scanned her words. "You really think so? I'm feeling my way with the story. I'm not sure what I want to say. Maybe I should stick to official briefings."

"Naahhh." He sat up to read the page still in the typewriter. "This is the real stuff. Maybe people don't think they want to read it, but they will. The official version leaves out heart. You give them the heart and they'll be crying for more."

AS THE CLOSING HYMN built to a crescendo, Constance stepped from the church's cold shadows into afternoon brilliance. The sun's heat didn't smooth the gooseflesh on her arms, and she shivered. She'd given up going to funerals during the blitz. There were simply too many and each left her feeling a hypocrite. She followed along, bending her head and kneeling, but had no prayers to offer up to an empty heaven. She'd only come today because there was no one else. However hypocritical, she couldn't leave Tim Chase to face this memorial service alone.

The scuff of feet across old stone warned her they were coming out. She slipped down the steps and across the grass before the first mourners reached the vestibule. The vicar had a supporting arm around the mother. The father came alone, dazed and lost. Tim towered over the three, his face so rigid that Constance's cheeks ached at the effort required to keep those hard planes and angles from shattering. He was holding up well for such a young man. When he strode up the aisle before the service, his gait was stiff. Perhaps he'd never be young again. Great sorrow murdered youth. Geoff's death had murdered hers.

She dug through her bag for a Dunhill and returned the vicar's glare over the flame of her match. The crowd filed out slowly, pausing to say a word to the family and nod in Tim's direction. Constance hadn't asked about the burial but saw no grave dug in the cemetery beside the country church. Certainly that made the day worse, the ceremony more difficult.

The last kerchiefed woman took up the mother's hand, shook her head at the father and Tim, and it was over. The vicar drifted back into the gloom of the church, leaving them stranded on the steps. The father's shoulders shook as the woman reached up a hand and patted Tim's cheek. For a moment, he covered that worn hand with his own. He walked them to the gate and turned back toward Constance.

She fought the quiver in her legs as he came toward her, arms rigid and legs stiff. What could she say? Still, he could have been her son, and words were required. A feeling of helplessness surged through her as he closed the distance between them. She caught his arm and squeezed through his jacket. "What will you do now, Tim?"

He lifted his hat and swept a hand across his forehead. "I've got a week's leave and then start training."

She gripped tighter. "Training? For what?"

He patted her hand. "Fighters. I flew my last bombing run yesterday and asked to be reassigned. I'll be up again over Germany in a Mustang in a few weeks."

"Oh, Tim, why?" She tugged back when he started for the gate. "You've done your bit. Have done with this bloody war."

For the first time a gentle curve tilted the corners of that stiff mouth. "It's not that simple, Mrs. Tolliver. I thought my war was almost over. It's not. It's just getting started."

"It is that simple." His eyes drifted away, and she raised her voice, trying to recall him. "You've flown your missions and lost your girl. You've paid your due. Have done with it."

His eyes swooped down, eyes quite like Matt's. Constance had never noticed before, though Nora claimed they were. She glanced away before he spoke.

"Have I paid? I don't think so." He searched his pockets until she offered her cigarettes. He coughed a little as he sucked in the smoke. "You know what I've done over here? I've piloted my own crop of bombs over the Channel and dropped them in towns like this."

He pulled her out the church gate and pointed to the wreckage down the street. "I did that. In Holland and in Belgium and in Germany. Oh, there were war plants and airfields. Oh, yes." His laughter rang bitterly in her ears. "But there were homes, too, and schools and goddamned kitchens."

She winced, trying to pull free, but he tightened his grip and steered her toward the crater. "Look at that hole. Jesus, would you look at that hole? I left plenty like that, bigger than that."

Yanking him to a stop, she forced him to meet her eyes. "Then why are you going back?"

She didn't need to hear his answer. She didn't need to see his rage and hatred as he stood at Hillary's grave to understand his need for vengeance and atonement. So many years before she'd stood at Geoff's grave on a bright summer day, stood beside a hole that was smaller but just as bottomless as this crater. Her parents hung back as she stepped forward to drop a handful of clay that echoed hollowly against his casket.

"I have to do it right this time. I have to do it right for her."

Constance looked up, but tears blurred her eyes. That's what she'd told herself, too. But what difference did it make if she persuaded Regis Wilde to take lodgings in Bath for the duration when in the end the girl would return to a filthy flat in a wretched slum? She blinked back the tears until his young face came clear.

"Don't you see? In a fighter, I'll know my enemy. He'll come up to meet me. And I'll be ready for him."

TWENTY-TWO

NORA LEANED against the tree and eased down the trunk to a shady seat. She couldn't believe the raves. The onion-skin paper in one hand trembled, and she set her tin cup in the long grass. She was actually getting fan mail. For the first time in her career, fan mail! Not that she'd seen any letters. IP was too cheap to pay the freight to send her mail overseas. But "Battlegrounds" was a hit. The New York office had sent excerpts from the letters and, backed by the strength of the reviews, Will figured he could spring her from the hospital to a billet with the rest of the press corps.

She sipped the hot coffee and reread New York's letter. The column started slowly with the story about the young German Peter had saved. Only a dozen papers picked that up. The piece on the old Frenchman digging through the ruins of St. Lo added a bunch more, including a big Midwestern chain. By August, four hundred papers featured "Battlegrounds" with more signing up every week. And she had Peter to thank for it. Readers loved the column.

Nora shook the last drops of her coffee toward the fading arc of sunlight near her feet and clipped the cup to her belt. Folding the letter into her pocket, Nora glanced around the press camp. The male reporters barely tolerated her. Hanging around would spoil the moment for her. She glanced toward the censor's tent. Will had been in there a long time. It figured that Colonel Logan would show up just in time to say no and leave her stranded with the nurses at the hospital. But she could work around him. She'd proved that and a whole lot more.

Nora snagged a cigarette from her pocket. The first drag left her light-headed, but the buoyant euphoria came with all the hot air from New York. She was back on track for a special correspondency. Someday, after the guns and the dying stopped, there might be something different with Matthew. She wanted him in her future, needed him in her future. But they couldn't find a future together until the fighting stopped. For now, all she had for certain was her work. With "Battlegrounds," she'd rediscovered how much reporting meant to her.

"Through gloating yet?"

Dry grass snapped under Will's feet as he grinned his way toward her. She grabbed his hand to help her up. "What did Logan say?"

Will picked up her helmet and gave it to her. "He wasn't too happy but couldn't say no. Even the brass like 'Battlegrounds.' But you better watch out for him and stay out of trouble."

She tucked her helmet under an arm and followed Will across the dusty camp as he described the new setup. Will couldn't get her absolute freedom of movement, but she'd have a jeep when she wanted one. The driver wouldn't take her close to the action and might try to yank her back if something started on a front she visited. But she'd get a tent in the press camp and be treated like just another guy when it came to lining up for meals or censors or transmitting stories. Promises always sounded good, but Nora expected to twist arms before she got delivery. So did Will.

"Make a stink if you have to. 'Battlegrounds' will get you the goods. Let's drink to it."

The orange sun dipped toward the horizon. Nora shaded her eyes and looked up at him. Will was himself again. Three months ago she'd cringed when he wanted a drink, but not now. Matthew's letters made it clear Will wasn't hitting the bottle, but Nora knew just by looking. Even a stubble of beard couldn't hide his healthy color, and the hollows of his cheeks had filled in. Maybe he'd worked things out with Sylvia.

He gulped from his flask and sighed before passing it. His pocket had warmed the metal. The brandy went down sweet and easy. She lifted herself to a seat beside him on the stone fence. "Everything fixed up with Sylvia?"

He took another pull on the bottle. Nora waved away the flask. He shook his head as he screwed on the cap.

Nora frowned. "Then clue me in. You were falling apart in London."

A sweep of too-long hair fell over his eyes when he tilted forward onto his elbows. "That wasn't Sylvia. That was fear." He met her eyes. "I was scared, kid. I'm still scared, but not the same way."

She touched his shoulder. "I was scared for you."

He melted into a grin and swung an arm around her shoulder. "I know you were. Logan said you were a real pain in his butt until my copy came through."

The hug felt good, and she leaned into him. It was hard to imagine Will scared. He was always so cool and controlled. Even a big story breaking on deadline didn't fluster him. Admitting fear must have cost a lot.

"Why are you afraid now? You made it through Omaha."

"I didn't know what to expect then. It was dumb fear. I figured the worst would be to look chicken or freeze up. I'm smarter about it now. The worst is getting killed."

Nora blinked through the setting sun and searched his eyes. No story was worth dying for. Will knew that. "You're not taking stupid chances, are you?"

He laughed and gave her a quick squeeze. "If I do, it's all your fault. You're the one who introduced me to Matthew Chase, the demon colonel of the First."

The curve of Will's mouth didn't match his serious eyes. She started a question, but his hand stopped her lips.

"Don't start raving. He's got a job to do, and he's good. Very good. But the job's risky for the worst colonel and dangerous for the best."

Nora pulled his hand from her mouth with a jerk. "What do you mean?"

She didn't like the way he wrapped both hands around hers or the solemn light in his eyes. Was he telling her Matthew was hurt? Was he telling her Matthew was...

"Matt's fine. He knows his business, Nora, and his business is war. He commands a thousand men with orders to kill. He didn't get that oak leaf for nothing. He got it because he's right up there with them. And that can be dangerous."

Nora swallowed hard and looked away. No sense getting hysterical. Will was simply warning her. She jumped down from the wall and set her feet in meadow grass. The sunset glowed with a bloody fire, and a ghostly mist rose from the fields. War's ugliness even robbed the beauty from a summer twilight. Will stepped down behind her and pulled her arm through his.

"Matt's got his war, and we've got ours. Which reminds me. I cleared it with Logan. If and when the army takes Paris, the bureau is yours. I'll have the title but you'll run it. They'll be setting up shop in the Scribe Hotel, and you've got a right to be with the first ones in."

An artillery battery three fields away belched flame into the darkening sky. She cringed toward Will as the gun's thunder rolled over them. His arm slid up her back and around her shoulders.

"You're moving up front, Nora. Better get used to the guns."

She nodded as she watched jeeploads of reporters returning from the line. Something had gone wrong. Will had given her Paris and "Battlegrounds" would give her a special correspondency, but the elation was gone. The war had stolen it from her.

TIM CHEWED THE CAP of the pen, struggling to find words. How do you tell the man who practically raised you that you don't need or want his advice anymore? He looked at the pile of crumpled paper by his chair and sighed. Matt had always been there for him—always. When bigger kids jeered because he couldn't keep the baseball in his mitt, Matt consoled him. When he had to face Mom's wrath after a shopkeeper caught him swiping a Nehi from the cooler, Matt helped him. And when he finally found the courage to ask why some people snickered about their father, Matt explained things. Matt was always there for him, but Tim didn't need him anymore. He was his own man now and made his own decisions.

He tilted back in his chair and closed his eyes. He'd made the right decision. He knew he was born to fly fighters the instant his new bird got airborne. Flying the

Mustang was effortless and smooth, and he became part of the machine. After the slow weight of the Fortress, the P-51 flew magically, dipping and gliding, tumbling and cartwheeling across the cool blue English sky. The instructors weren't happy with his first flight, but Tim was delighted. They called it aerobatics and stunting, but he knew different. Rolling wingtip over wingtip taught him the limits of his new bird. He knew the most she could give him and the least. And he needed to know both to pay the bastards back for what they'd done to Hillary.

Matt just couldn't understand the whole thing was about Hillary. He had a reason to fight now, a reason to hate and a reason to kill. The Germans had killed Hillary. It was as simple as that.

God, he missed her. He kept hearing her voice call across the pub, clipping his name even shorter than it was. At night in his cot he heard her whisper "Timothy," sighing out his name in a tone rich and warm with pleasure.

He wiped his eyes and checked the letter for teardrops. But it wasn't only that the Germans killed Hillary. He'd done the same thing to their girls, to their mothers and sisters and babies. All those flights, taking off before dawn, watching the sun rise over Belgium or Holland, and seeing the smoke towering up behind after their load dropped. Factories burned, railroads twisted, dams busted and more. He'd piloted his squadron over farms and homes to smoke-draped target areas high above city centers and market squares.

He stared at the map from his old unit. A few of the cutout bombs fell off when he rolled it up, but he'd pasted them back on. The new fellows thought he was crazy or showboating. But he had to remember. He couldn't forget what they'd done to Hillary or what he'd done to them. Shit, those last missions had been easy. They hadn't really needed to find the targets. Who could? Between the RAF at night and the Eighth during the day, Germany looked squashed, pounded flat, blown to bits. How did they keep fighting?

He blotted the pen tip and scratched a few more lines. Now he wouldn't take the easy way, flying at twenty-five thousand feet and dropping the load wherever. Not anymore. With the Mustang, he could do it right, put his neck on the line every time he went for a kill. And he wouldn't be targeting civilians. He'd have the best of the Luftwaffe in his sights. The best they had left. And they had enough left to pay for Hillary.

Tim folded the letter into an envelope and scrawled Matt's address. No use sealing it tonight. He might find better words tomorrow or the next day. Better, but not easier.

He shoved the envelope away and his eyes caught Nora's photo atop her new column in *Stars and Stripes*. Where had they found the picture, anyway? He'd never seen her smile like that, all stiff and pained. She grinned easily. No wonder Matt was nuts for her. And that stupid helmet. You could see they'd faked it, drawn it in later.

Tim stared at the picture for a moment, then grabbed the envelope. He added a few words and tore off the top of Nora's column. A smear of Lieutenant Dennison's Brylcreem would hold it. The glue of the envelope bittered his tongue. He smoothed the flap carefully and glanced at his watch. Just enough time to make the last mail run.

A couple of new guys tossing balls outside the huts asked him to play, but he shrugged and turned away. He didn't have time for kid stuff anymore. The instructors promised a hard day tomorrow, and he had to be ready. He wasn't going to wash out of fighter training. He hoped Matt would understand. The picture of Nora might help.

TWENTY-THREE

WHAT A JOYRIDE! The jeep crept down the wide boulevard through swarms of cheering people. Nora thought the whole population must be on the street singing and dancing, kissing cheeks and pumping hands, throwing flowers, waving flags and smiling through tears. She quit taking notes an hour ago. Words were useless today. IP would want a five-hundred-word wrap-up and she'd do her damnedest, but it would take more than words to capture the spirit of Paris on Liberation Day.

The city-wide hysterics beat anything she'd ever seen back home, even the ticker-tape pandemonium New York put on for Lindbergh in 1927. Never mind the muffled explosions that might mean the Germans were blowing bridges over the Seine. Never mind the rattle of machine guns in the distance or the whistle of shells overhead. The French didn't care. With the Boche running and the tricolor flying, Paris was free. And even though she risked big trouble with the army for hooking up with LeClerc's Second Armored Division, Nora didn't care, either. History would remember August 25, 1944, as one of the world's greatest days, and so would she.

Hiking her hip onto the seat back, Nora pulled herself up for a better view. The jeep swam through a sea of waving arms. An avalanche of people buried the leading tanks. Young girls in summer pastels crawled over dusty metal to kiss their heroes. Mothers raised babies to be kissed while old men saluted and children danced rings around the stranded tanks. Determined not to miss her turn with the soldiers, an elderly woman in black stockings pulled a stepladder through the crowd and spread her kisses from the top rung.

Nora nudged the shoulder of the reporter sharing the jeep's back seat. "Come on up, McManus. They're going crazy!"

He tilted a stubbled face smeared with lipstick. "You can tell me about it later, Seymour. I don't want to get out of reach."

The surging crowd brought the jeep to a stop and suddenly hands reached for Nora, tugging her arm, touching the Stars and Stripes on her sleeve and pressing cheese and flowers and bread into her hands. The booty soon overflowed her lap onto the seat between her feet.

A weeping veteran pulled the red-white-and-blue cockade from his black beret and raised gnarled fingers to pin it on her shirt. *"Merci, mademoiselle."* Hot tears dripped on her hand. *"Merci."*

Before she could speak, he was swept aside by a young woman who pressed a firm kiss on each cheek, then turned toward the soldier at the wheel. Nora smiled and waved at the throng, knowing she didn't deserve their cheers. She was simply there, one of hundreds who rode army machines into Paris after it had been delivered from occupation. The crowd pressed forward, rocking the jeep in its frenzy.

Suddenly the crowd hushed and eddied back as a woman and two children pushed forward. The girl tugged her blond hair as she curtsied and held out a bouquet of vivid blossoms. The boy was younger and placed a heavy bottle in Nora's hand. The woman dipped her head and smiled. *"France ne vous oubliera jamais. Jamais!"*

Nora nodded. The crowd buzzed. *"La comtesse. Vive la comtesse."* The shout rang out and carried through the crowd. *"Vive la comtesse! Vive les Américains! Vive la France!"*

The woman turned slowly, hands on the shoulders of her children, and smiled. *"Oui. Vive la France. Toujours."*

Fresh tears fell as the Parisians picked up the cry, echoing it down the street until it built beneath a multitude of voices. Somewhere behind the jeep the cry turned to music as hundreds joined in "La Marseillaise."

McManus elbowed her as he hauled himself onto the seat back. Nora raised her eyebrows, but he shrugged. "Who knows? I don't speak the lingo."

She hefted the large bottle but couldn't decipher the label. McManus leaned over and ran his hand up the slim green neck. "I may not know much, Seymour, but I know this, Frenchies call that a magnum—a nice big bottle of champagne."

Nora held on to the bottle when she and McManus climbed down from the jeep. The driver had disappeared into the crowd, so they were stuck. She stuffed her pack full of goodies and searched the crowd.

McManus touched her arm. "We better hole up and start writing. But where?"

Nora grinned. "The Hotel Scribe. I don't know where it is, but that's where we're supposed to be after the surrender."

She elbowed her way through the crowd toward the sidewalk. She caught a stray kiss and shook a few hands. McManus hissed in her ear. "Who says?"

Laughing, Nora caught his arm and pulled him on. "SHAEF says. That's the plan, Hal."

He snorted. "Who let you in on it?"

She spun around, planting her feet. "SHAEF did. I'm taking charge of IP's Paris bureau so Will can stay with the troops."

He tried to mask his surprise, but his eyes widened. "You!" McManus coughed. "If that ain't something." He feinted to the left, but Nora caught his arm. His head dropped, and he scuffed a foot. "Okay, okay. Your column's terrific. Everybody says so. But in this business, great work usually means squat." His grin seemed genuine. "Congratulations, Nora."

At the hotel, most of the Scribe's staff had deserted their jobs before making up the rooms, so Nora and McManus set up shop in a lounge. In the next few hours more reporters drifted in and, as night fell, censors arrived with dispatch riders to carry the stories behind the lines for transmission to London. When her "Battlegrounds" column and straight news story cleared censorship, she sketched out items for a sidebar until someone flipped her notebook closed.

"Hey, what—"

"Just thought you might want to call it a day, kid." Will brushed rough lips across her cheek. His mouth hovered at her ear. "I brought you a present from First Division. May not be gift-wrapped but he's out in the lobby."

Wrapping a quick hug around his neck, she grabbed her pack and streaked for the door. She looked for a dress uniform but couldn't spot him among the soldiers crowding the lobby. Then the line of his back caught her eyes. He leaned against the empty newsstand, flicking ashes into a tall brass cuspidor. She tripped forward a few steps and stopped. The taper from shoulder to hip drew her, but nothing else was familiar; not the helmet with a single stripe or the short jacket snugged to his waist or the holster slung from the web belt.

Nora walked up behind him. "Matthew?"

The pack dropped from her hand as he swung around and crushed her in his arms. The helmet shadowed his face as his lips caught hers. Her hands searched his rough cheeks and strong neck. But she already knew. The kiss stole her breath as only his could. The hard arms, so fierce yet so gentle, held her as only he could. And her head nestled into his shoulder, fitting only Matthew's shoulder with such perfection.

His arms loosened, and she heard clapping and whistles and stomping. Cheeks burning, she took a step back. Matthew cocked his head and stared down the soldiers group by group. The ovation faltered. Eyes dropped. A knot of GIs still poked one another and grinned. Nora picked up her bag as Matthew raked the boys with steely eyes. One boy coughed and grabbed his buddy, quickly swinging around and out the door.

"Let's go, sweetheart." Matthew swung her pack over his shoulder and bent close. "I got you a room."

She wanted to ask why he was in Paris and how long he could stay. A concierge carrying a smoking oil lamp led them up two flights of stairs. Matthew asked questions and translated for Nora.

"No hot water. No restaurant. Electricity only during the day."

She laughed. "Of course—just when you need it. I've got some food and a very big bottle of champagne."

He squeezed her fingers as the concierge unlocked the door. The Frenchwoman swept in first, lighting the candle on the bedside stand. Light flickered across the bed. A hat lay in the middle of the rumpled spread, and the concierge gasped when Matthew picked it up. An eagle gleamed silver against black. The German hat skimmed by Nora's ear. He fired rapid French at the concierge who nodded, spread her arms, nodded again and stuttered *"merci"* as he folded a bill into her hand. He picked up the candle.

Nora backed out the door and grinned. "I hope she checks the closets."

His frown melted into laughter. "God, it's good to see you." He pulled her close with his free arm. "I know just the spot for a moonlight picnic. What've we got for food?"

"Oh, a bottle of wine, a loaf of bread, a little cheese, and . . ." She tugged his hand.

"Let me guess. C-rations?"

She tried for his lips, but their stride threw the kiss to his chin. "So much for the poetry of romance."

Candle flames danced in his eyes. "Just wait."

The rising moon bathed the river in shadows and twilight. Laughter echoed across still water. Nora liked a spot closer to the bridge, but Matthew said the bridges could be mined. She followed him into the dark shadow of a tree.

Thank God for shadows. She caught a glimpse of herself in a mirror as they left the Scribe and nearly sank through the floor. A film of road dust coated her hair, and the shapeless fatigue jacket made her look like a fat cabbage. She hadn't seen him in two months and had hoped to be sleek and sexy when she did. She could kick herself for leaving her one damned dress behind when she'd followed her hunch that LeClerc's Frenchmen would be ordered into Paris.

"Where's that bottle?"

Nora groped through her pack for the champagne. As Matthew wrestled with the cork, she found her knife and sliced cheese. The apple and pear she discovered in the bottom of the pack felt too soft, but she cut the fruit, anyway. Champagne shot from the bottle after the cork, splashing paving stones under the tree. They drank it warm, straight from the bottle, and layered fruit and cheese on pieces of *baguette*. He picked up her knife and tested the blade.

"Looks like you've learned something about soldiering." His fingers sifted through her hair. "Might not have recognized you except by smell."

"I didn't recognize you." The butt of his gun dug into her side. "Think you could put that cannon somewhere else? What is it, anyway?"

He leaned aside and slid the gun free, holding it in his palm. "A .45. Standard issue." Steel clinked against stone as he pushed it aside.

Nora leaned into his shoulder, nuzzling his neck. His arm tightened, and his lips brushed her ear. "You're getting famous, I hear."

A delicious shiver ran through her at his kiss. She didn't want to move or talk. All she wanted was what she had—his arms around her. "Who says?"

"Tim, for one."

Nora's heart lurched. Tim.

"Last letter I got he wrote 'love to,' then pasted the picture from your column on the page." He lifted her chin. "Where'd they get it, anyway? And that cartoon helmet."

"Someone in New York did that." She squeezed his hand. "Can't you stop him, Matthew? Won't Tim listen to you?"

He pulled her hand against his cheek. "I'm not even going to try, sweetheart. Tim has to fight his own war."

She tugged her hand free. "You all say the same thing. I'm sick of hearing it."

His lighter flared, and he passed her a smoke. "Come on, Nora. You know better than that now. It shows in your writing, and that's why you're getting the recognition."

She sucked in a lungful of smoke. "I *don't* know better. That's the problem. The more I see, the less I understand."

He rested his elbow on a cocked knee. "It's pretty simple."

"Yeah, I know—whoever kills the most wins." She flicked her cigarette toward the river.

She lifted the bottle and bubbles of fizz dissolved across her tongue. Why were they talking about war? They didn't have time for philosophical discussions. If Matthew wouldn't try to talk sense into Tim, fine. He should, but she couldn't force him. Yet she couldn't hold back the next question.

"Christ, Matthew, all the little villages in Normandy are wrecked. Grave's registration stacks the bodies. The air force is beating the hell out of Germany. For what? Your father is right, you know. It can't go on, and yet it does."

He rubbed his jaw and sighed. "Last time I was in Paris I came with my father. I thought he was the greatest man on earth. He'd traveled all over Europe—London, Berlin, The Hague—getting support for a treaty to outlaw war. I was sixteen."

Nora wanted to take his hand. She wanted him to talk now. She needed to know this part of him.

"Everyone agreed. All the foreign ministers signed. But in our suite, after the official meetings, his assistants and the embassy men argued on, telling him the treaty was absurd. In the morning the foreign minister signed, but in the afternoon the defense minister stockpiled ammunition. The congressman wouldn't listen."

He leaned forward and stared at the river. "I didn't understand, but I listened. Peace was just a word. It wasn't real, and it wasn't possible. Later I learned why. You can't stop war because men love to fight."

He laughed and she flinched at the bitter sound. "It's just that simple, Nora. No matter the cost, some men love war."

She took his hand then, but didn't speak. *"Some men love war."* He didn't have to tell her he was one of them. She could see that now, read it in his gestures and his stride. There was a difference in him, a resonance he didn't have in England. She didn't understand why he loved war, but he did.

Gunfire rattled in the distance. She pushed to her feet and tugged his hand. "Let's go back now."

At the hotel, she ducked into the bathroom when Matthew unlocked the door. There was no soap, so she scrubbed her face with cold water. Bending over, she shook out her hair, raking with her fingers and wishing again she'd brought her gear. Even a dab of perfume would help.

The candle haloed the bed. Nora slung her fatigue jacket over a chair and sank into the soft mattress. He lifted her feet to his lap to unlace the heavy shoes and pull off the thick socks. She sighed when he kneaded her foot. "That feels wonderful." She leaned back and closed her eyes.

His hands slid under her pants, massaging her calves. "You feel wonderful." He dropped his hands and pressed her into the pillows.

She opened her mouth under his and tasted champagne. His rough lips left a tingling path down her neck. She rubbed her face against his cropped hair and trailed slow fingers over his shoulders.

When his hands fumbled over buttons, she nudged him to his back and rolled on top. She wanted to heal him as he'd healed her, to soothe his pain as he'd soothed hers. His arms tightened around her shoulders when she whispered against his ear. She pushed him down with a kiss and worked open his clothes.

When she pulled off her own, he reached for her. She held him off, and his sigh wrapped around them like a cloud. "Oh, God, Nora don't tease me."

Knowing his hunger exceeded his patience, she came into his arms. His need was larger, fired by the deaths he'd seen, the deaths he'd caused. She tore breathless kisses from his mouth and urged him on with feverish hands, smoothing and giving, soothing and healing.

His back tightened under her fingers as he filled her and pressed deeper still. She thought only of him and his need until he pulled her hips against him and buried her mouth with his. She arched into him, rocking slowly toward a dazzling whirlwind that swept her beyond his need or hers as they became one.

TWENTY-FOUR

ACROSS THE PLATFORM, a jet of steam hissed from the locomotive. Constance leaned against Peter's shoulder. The old station was December cold, but the block of ice frozen around her heart came from knowing he was leaving again. Peter was leaving too soon. They'd had so little time and so much to say. And he was leaving with so much unsaid between them. A porter wheeled a cart of baggage by the bench and loaded it into a compartment.

Peter's hand slid across his lap to pat her knee. She marveled at those skilled hands. That's why he'd come, to train others to produce miracles of healing. Peter said his new technique was simply a shortcut, a faster way to fix a damaged head in an operation where increased speed increased the chance of survival. He'd trained surgeons in the field and in London and, when the war was over, he'd train other surgeons in the States. It all made her feel a bit small and useless.

He lifted her hand and squeezed. "Are you working in the shelter tonight?"

"I suppose so." Constance sighed. "I'm not much use, really. More a nuisance, I'm afraid."

"What's wrong?" He tilted her chin until she met his eyes. "You sounded enthusiastic in your letters."

"Oh, Peter." She rubbed her cheek against his hand. "What good do I do? What good can anyone do? We're all like rats in a maze down there, except rats like me don't have to stay. Poor rats have no choice."

She looked away from his steady eyes. The first passengers entered the train. "And when it's over, when they climb out of the shelters, they'll find their wretched homes gone but nothing else changed. And they'll have to work even harder to replace the little they had."

He brought her eyes back to his with a painful tug of her hand. "Then do something, dammit. Do something useful. You see a problem and give up without even trying to find a solution."

Peter made it sound so simple. Perhaps doing the right thing was simple for him. Hadn't he taken care of his mother, given a home to his brother's orphans, worked his way out of a slum? He'd done all those things of necessity—because he'd had no choice. He couldn't understand that having choices didn't make it easier to choose.

A girl with a Red Cross armband strolled by, offering doughnuts to waiting soldiers. And yet, Peter did the right thing, even when doing right was somehow wrong.

Constance smiled. "You're the doctor in Nora's story, aren't you? You're the one who searches the battlefield." He shrugged, but she knew she'd got it right. "And is that really the only reason you saved the German boy—because you knew how?"

He nodded. "That's right."

She squeezed his hand gently. "You saw a problem and knew how to solve it."

He laughed softly. "Yeah, that's it. My philosophy of life."

"But you see, Peter, I don't know how. I don't know where to start."

His eyes went stern, and he folded his arms. "Oh, come off it, Connie. No more excuses. Start with your connections—your father, for one. And what about your writing? You've got an audience and you're persuasive when you believe in something."

She frowned and shook her head. "I don't—"

Peter cut her off. "No more don'ts, no more buts. You're shrewd, lady. You know how things work in this country. Start making them work the way you want them to."

A whistle blew. Passengers thronged the doorways. A tardy few scurried across the platform. Peter stood and pulled her up. His hands reached for her shoulders as he stared into her eyes. "You're right about those shelters. You're trying to stop a hemorrhage with a Band-Aid, and it won't work."

He glanced at the train. "Today's not the problem for those people. Tomorrow's the real trouble. You've got the time and the money and the connections to make a difference. You'll figure out how."

The last passengers filed up the stairs into compartments as he pulled her into his arms. For a moment she clung to him, burying her face in his shoulder. He wanted so much more from her than any man had ever asked. And he'd given her more than she'd ever thought possible.

His lips brushed her cheek roughly. "One last thing, Connie. When the war's over, I'll be back for you."

She opened her mouth, but he cut her off with a hungry kiss. When he pulled away, he left a finger across her lips. "Don't give me your answer now."

He lifted his bag and back-stepped toward the train. "I've made up my mind. The rest is up to you."

She covered her mouth with a trembling hand and forced back tears. Peter swung up the stairs and waved. A porter closed the door and, with a sigh, the train rolled forward. She couldn't move, even when she saw his face behind the glass and watched the window open. The train picked up speed but his voice rang above the clatter of wheels and echoed through the deserted station. "Don't let me down, Connie."

WILL LOOKED at the rolled clothes left on his bed and admitted defeat. His duffel already bulged like a sausage. He'd have to leave the rest behind. Heaving the bag onto his shoulder, he picked up his typewriter and carried the load to the street. A GI detached himself from the group across the road and wandered in his direction. After the soldier stashed his bags in the back of the jeep, Will said he'd meet him at headquarters and returned to his room. He pulled the case off a pillow and stuffed in the rest of his clothes. He could always leave it at the village church if nothing better came to mind.

Stray flakes of snow drifted from the clouds as he walked toward Matt's billet. Chill air stung his nostrils. The low clouds had threatened snow all week, but he'd get to Paris. It wouldn't be like last time, a city crazy with joy at liberation. Luckily he hadn't missed that story. It was something to tell grandchildren not yet born and sons not yet men. If he didn't lose those sons.

A pimply youth swung around a corner and dodged out of his way. Will called him back, waving when his meager French failed. The boy smiled brightly, lighting the sullen day. Everyone smiled at the Americans except German prisoners. Maybe the Belgians had passed a law.

He pressed the pillowcase into the boy's arms and pointed first to himself and then touched the kid's shoulder. "From me to you, buddy. You know—Christmas?"

What did they call it over here? No Santa Claus or little reindeer maybe, but he knew they had Christmas. The strains of an old hymn floated through his mind. *Noël.* Yeah, *Noël.* "*Joyeux Noël,* kid. Merry Christmas."

The boy grinned and shouted the words back before swinging around the corner. The brief glow Will felt disappeared with him. Maybe the village would be pretty in peacetime, with the laughter of boys like that one wafting through the old streets and their grandfathers sunning themselves over glasses at the café. There'd be laundry drying in the yards and flowers climbing ancient stone walls. The village would be pretty then—on the surface. Underneath, the ugliness would still seethe, ravaging and festering until it boiled over. Every village was the same, every town in the whole world. War just stripped the mask of peace away to reveal the ugliness.

He stopped for a minute and sniffed the air. The storm would hold off until he made Paris. At least he wasn't running out a coward. He'd proved that much. He went in on June 6 and stayed in until—what was today? December 16? And it sure as hell better not be too late for Sylvia. She'd threatened so often that he got tired of reading her letters. First threats, then pleas, then coy hints about other men, but always the same message—come home. She'd never understood why he had to stay. No woman understood, not even Nora.

Morning chill penetrating his coat sent him around the last corner toward Matt's billet. He'd be leaving Nora in a fix, but she'd understand Sylvia's legal papers just as he had. Sylvia wanted it all—the house, the bank accounts, the boys—and was going after it starting January 1. Happy New Year, 1945. He'd wire from London in case he got held up. Sylvia would hold off then, wanting to do the curtain scene in person. But it wasn't curtains for them. He'd make her see that.

The sentry at the old hotel smiled a greeting and waved him through. Will took the stairs without checking the lounge. Matt didn't hang around with his men much. He relied on Sergeant Caserti for that.

The door was open but he knocked, anyway. Will held out his hand when Matt looked up from his desk. "How's the song go—'I'll Be Seeing You'?"

Matt grinned and pumped his arm. "Looks like bad weather for traveling. You may get caught in the crush."

Will shook his head. "We're going to swing out a ways, toward Malmedy. It's pretty quiet out there."

Matt nodded and folded his arms. "It's been a pleasure having you around, Will. I mean that."

"Same here." Will turned for the door.

"When you see Nora—" Matt glanced away to finish "—give her my love."

"Sure thing."

Going down the stairs, Will smiled and almost turned back. Why not tell Matt he'd soon have his own chance to give Nora his love? But no, Nora made him promise to keep her visit a secret. She'd been bugging him for a month. He only relented after he got Sylvia's letter and decided to go home. Maybe he'd see her on the road. Not likely. She'd be coming up through regular channels while he skirted far behind the lines. There was little chance of running into anything interesting out there and just as well. Since June, he'd had enough excitement for a hundred lifetimes. All he wanted now was Sylvia and the boys.

SITTING OUTSIDE was uncomfortable, but Nora didn't mind. Heat rose through the jeep's hood to keep her bottom from freezing while the smiling GIs huddled around her perch helped her forget the cold nipping her bare hands. And from here she'd spot Matthew as soon as he returned to his quarters.

Another GI sidled up to the group. She flashed him a grin. "What do you want for Christmas, soldier?"

The boy opened his mouth, but a rough-looking corporal interrupted. "Bet you can't print what he asked for."

The young GI blushed and dropped his eyes. The corporal elbowed a pal and lowered his voice into a stage whisper. She'd asked the same dumb question at every stop and got the same guffaws every time. Only one soldier came right out and said he just wanted a girl in his bed. Who could blame them? Earlier, a tank commander said he'd asked Santa Claus for enough fuel to get his Sherman to Berlin, and an infantry officer wanted good weather and hard fighting. A German surrender, a long hot shower, a real turkey dinner—they all might sound good, but none of them matched the hunger in the soldier's eyes.

The knot of soldiers around the jeep talked among themselves. Nora kept an ear on the conversation comparing French and Belgian girls and glanced down the street. No sign of Matthew yet, and Lieutenant Simms, his executive officer, wasn't sure when he'd be back. An inspection, Simms said, certainly not white-glove, but the colonel wanted to check in with each company.

Turning to a fresh page, Nora added a few notes on the look of the town and tried to frame a better question. Christmas with the troops wasn't up to her usual standards for "Battlegrounds," but at least Will had given the okay to come to the front. Where was he, anyway? With Matthew, she guessed. He'd been with Matthew's battalion since summer.

Nora wasn't the only newshen covering the European theater now, but the other girls relied on official briefings and produced dull stories just like the men. Running the Paris bureau made it harder to come up with good material for her column, but the other IP staffers helped. Decker, especially, relayed the kind of vignettes her readers wanted.

The corporal's voice slashed through her thoughts. "If that ain't a sight to warm a Heinie's heart. One good burst would wipe out all the battalion's officers."

Nora followed the thumb he jerked over his shoulder. Her eyes searched the huddle of men coming up the street. *There he was.* Matthew's head was half turned away, cocked toward an eager young officer whose hands flew faster than his mouth. Suddenly Matthew stopped and swung around. The young officer dipped his head and took a step back. Matthew turned toward another man in the group who nodded once quickly before trotting back the way they had come.

Forcing herself to sit still, Nora watched the group reform around Matthew. The eager officer fell behind. The soldiers around her melted away at their approach. Matthew's eyes flicked over her and back to an older sergeant at his side. She reached up and pulled off her helmet. Her hair swung against her shoulders as his eyes veered back. He touched the sergeant's arm, and the group stopped. She slid off the hood of the jeep as Matthew walked the last five yards.

"Dammit to hell, Nora. What are you doing here?"

Her arms came up at the harsh tone, and she searched eyes as cold and steely as the winter sky. She winced as the fingers he wrapped around her elbow bit deep. What was wrong? "Matthew, I..."

She couldn't say she wanted to see him, not when he obviously didn't want to see her. "I've got a special assignment."

Shaking his head, he propped his hands on hips. "Great. Just great." He took her arm again, then released it.

She followed him into the old house and he pointed her up the stairs. Everything was fine, wonderful, in Paris four months ago. What was wrong now?

"Room on the left. I'll be right up."

She gently closed the door behind her and shivered. Embers glowed in the shallow fireplace and drew her across the room. Tugging a chair close, she sat huddled in her coat. The heavy sound of shuffling feet carried up the stairs.

When Matthew came in, she didn't look up. She wouldn't look at those frozen eyes again. Her ears tracked him across the room until he stopped beside the chair. The hand pulling her chin up might be gentle, but his eyes were flat and his voice tired, almost bored.

"Look, Nora, I'm sorry."

This was it, then. She'd got it all wrong somehow. She'd made a mistake, made a fool of herself by coming.

He crouched at her feet and took her hands in his. "You shouldn't be here. What are you doing here?"

She needed a deep breath before she could trust her voice to be steady. "I've got a special assignment. Will approved it. I'm finishing a week's tour."

He looked so hard, so worried. Well, she'd make it easy for him, easy for her. Laugh it off. She willed her lips into a smile. "I didn't know I needed a reservation at your bivouac."

His eyes widened for a second, then scrunched into a frown. "What?"

Nora pulled her hands away and stood up. "I'll clear out right now. My driver's downstairs."

When she tried to brush past, he blocked her with an arm. "You're right you'll clear out. But not just yet."

She pulled back as his arms closed around her until she felt the touch of his lips. She leaned into him and her fingers raced up his broad back to grip his neck.

His mouth slid along her neck to an ear. "I'd like to push you down in my bed and make love for a year."

She smiled. His eyes didn't matter anymore. His lips told the story, gentle lips that pressed against her neck and cheek and hair.

He sighed and held her at arm's length. "But we can't dammit. You can't stay." He pushed up his sleeve and glanced at his watch. "Hell, it's close to two already. You'll never make it back to Paris today."

"To Paris? I'm not going back to Paris." She followed him to his desk. "Matthew, this is crazy. I just got here. I'm not due in Paris till the day after tomorrow. What's wrong?"

He jabbed a finger at the map on his desk. "There's movement behind the German lines—here and here and here. Look at the distance—easily seventy miles. I don't know what they're planning. No one does. But you're not staying around to find out."

Nora laughed. "Oh, come on Matthew. Nothing's going to happen. There's no way SHAEF would have let me come up here if they expected trouble. Or Will, either. Where is he?"

Matt glanced up from the map. "Gone home."

She started a question but he held up his hand. "Just listen. I know SHAEF thinks everything is quiet, and it is—for now. But I think SHAEF's too optimistic. So do some other good soldiers. And in case I'm right, I want you safe."

He wasn't kidding. Concern tugged grooves around his eyes. But the whole thing was crazy. None of the briefings she'd heard in the past five days had mentioned renewed fighting. No one else was worried.

He muttered as his finger traced the roads to Paris. "You'll be fighting convoys the whole way, and you'll have low priority. Maybe if you took back roads like Davies—just get south fast and then worry about getting east. That'd work. As far south as Bastogne, then cut toward Paris. That looks good."

Nora touched his arm. "Did you say Will's gone back to Paris?"

"New York." He shrugged. "I guess his wife finally convinced him. He packed up this morning and left. If you get back to Paris fast, you'll probably catch him."

Nora frowned. "His kids are okay? His wife?"

Matthew nodded. "Nothing like that, sweetheart. He said the last letter was a classic Dear John and he hates the name. What's your big deal assignment, anyway?"

She looked away. "Don't laugh. Christmas with the troops. But I didn't care what it was, as long as I got to see you."

He didn't come close to laughing. He pulled her against him, and the worry in his eyes kept her silent. "I want a promise this time, Nora. You have to head south and stay south until we know for sure what they're up to. Promise me?"

She nodded and laid her head on his shoulder. Touching him made her ache, and she wanted to stay. She pulled back her head and caught his eyes. "What do you want for Christmas, soldier?"

"Snow." His smile didn't reach his eyes. "A ton of snow, a blizzard, enough snow to freeze those bastards in their tracks."

TWENTY-FIVE

MATT ADJUSTED the lantern flame and rubbed his forehead. When he opened his eyes, the map blurred. The battalion's position looked good on paper. He had the high ground with men digging in deep among the trees. No matter what the Germans threw at him, they'd have trouble getting up that wooded slope.

He splashed tepid dregs of coffee into a tin cup and sank back against the hay bales piled against the stall's outer wall. The terrain was really all he had going for him. Linking his flanks to other units stretched the line too thin. Once that line was pierced—*if it was pierced*—a new blitzkrieg might roll straight to the North Sea. With no units left in reserve and bad weather grounding air support, the Allies might be in real trouble.

Draining the cup, he blew out the lantern and stepped out of the stall. The old barn wasn't an ideal headquarters, but no one scouted up anything better before night fell. He didn't have time to be choosy and neither did his men. Once the officers positioned their rifle companies just below the ridge, the men dropped their guns and started digging. First Division veterans didn't need to be told to make their foxholes deep.

Matt checked with communications, but the phone lines weren't strung, and dense fog left radio communications with division patchy at best. He sent a clerk in search of a runner and checked the big map hanging from the rafters. The picture looked spotty since no one had solid information on enemy movements.

He snagged a cigarette from his pocket. On the road down to Butgenbach, the news he heard was bad. Fresh replacements broke and ran when tanks emerged from the smoky dust clouds of the initial barrage. A rumor about English-speaking Krauts wearing American uniforms meant endless delays at every crossroad as sentries tried to outsmart would-be imposters with trick questions.

A shadow flickered over the map, and Matt glanced back at Fred Simms. He wondered how the major kept that perfect crease in his pants. Even getting rousted from the sack at 3:00 a.m. for twelve hard hours of driving hadn't dusted over the shine of his boots. Matt couldn't trust Simms unless he discovered substance under the spit-and-polish exterior. He couldn't trust anyone until he'd seen them under fire.

"Looks good here, Colonel. I'll go out now and check the line."

Matt shook his head and waved his cigarette at the map. "I'll check the lines. You stay here and fill in the blanks. If everything looks good then, I'll want to hear about it."

The earth under his heel crunched when he stamped out his smoke outside the barn. He looked up, but fog obscured the sky. The cold had come, but not much snow. A good storm might make things uncomfortable for men in foxholes, but it would slow down the Germans. He peered up the hill, searching for a rock or tree to get his bearings, but the night was too black.

Pointing his hooded flashlight to the ground, he snapped on the dim light and picked his way forward. The grenades on his belt swung with each stride, thudding against his hips with familiar heaviness. He'd probably never pull the pin, but he welcomed the weight. A wisp of fog spread under his feet as he climbed the ridge. If he angled to the left a hundred feet, he'd find Lou's squad.

The gritty scrape of a shovel hacking earth led him the last few yards until a familiar voice barked, "Douse that light, dummy."

Matt snapped off the flashlight and followed the voice. "Come again, Sergeant?"

Lou brought him in with a grunt. Matt crouched beside the thick shadow at the base of a tree. "What do you hear?"

"Mendoza's listening down the hill. I was just going to check him."

A thick cushion of pine needles muffled their steps as Matt followed Lou down the slope. Figured Lou sent Mendoza forward. He was usually the best man for any job that counted. Lou kept suggesting him for promotion, but Mendoza always refused, saying he wanted to finish the war and get back to his fishing trawler in New Bedford.

Matt shouldered aside a heavy branch, wishing these trees touched limbs like those in the man-made Hurtgen Forest. That woods favored the defender, masking every natural advantage with bushy limbs. When Lou stopped short, Matt groped forward until their shoulders brushed. On Matt's left, a man hissed for quiet.

Darkness swallowed the thousand men behind him, smothering every sound. The silence of the hillside raised gooseflesh on his arms. His ears strained to hear

Lou's breathing. He started at the touch of his shoulder and then heard it, too; heard the squeaking clank of treads somewhere in front. *Tanks.*

A shadow crept to his side. "Hear that, Sergeant?"

Lou stepped behind him and whispered urgently. "How many?"

"Eight, nine." The numbers whooshed out on a sigh. "Enough. More than enough."

Matt groped for Mendoza's arm. "How many, dammit?"

Mendoza stiffened. "Sorry, Colonel, should have known you'd hike down here." Matt gave him time. "Nine, I guess. Gives me the creeps hearing 'em. I might have lost count a while back. I snuck down to try and pinpoint the spot. But, shit, this fog sucks up sound one place and spits it out another. No telling where they are."

"One's too many, Mendoza." A spurt of excitement raced up Matt's spine. A couple of tanks could blow trees down around their heads. A dozen wouldn't have to bother. "Make sure you stay hidden. And keep listening."

He led the way back, and Lou followed him to the top of the ridge. While a runner alerted the company commanders, Matt squatted over Lou's flask and considered the possibilities. A patrol might stumble into the German lines and draw an attack before he was ready. The men needed a breather now to have staying power later. And the Germans, wherever they were, didn't know his position. He had the high ground and the trees and experienced fighters.

When the last officer filtered in from the dark, Matt laid it out. The company commanders wouldn't be happy but so what? "Gentlemen, we're hearing tanks out front. A bunch of tanks. Fog plays tricks with sound, but count on a wallop when they start moving."

A man on his left groaned. Matt tried to make out his profile—another replacement. "It's tough luck, but there's no changing it, so don't bother griping." The new man coughed.

"We'll try to stop them. Keep a man forward to watch but don't send a glory boy. I want those men well hidden and careful. If we can't stop the tanks, then heads down and let them through. They'll have infantry following close, and we'll get the foot soldiers. When we've finished them, we'll worry about the tanks."

Matt knotted his hands and heard out their objections. Of his company commanders, only Santino had been at Kasserine. As a buck private, he'd watched his division quiver when armor approached and run when the tanks came close. And he'd seen his buddies slaughtered.

When the rest had talked themselves out, Santino had his say. "Fighting tanks head-on is suicide. From behind, it's simple, especially in trees. A tank can't maneuver in woods, can't come around."

His voice brightened. "Colonel, what about turning some men after them—say every third or fourth? Knock off a tread and they'll come out. Or if not, we'll have some nice bonfires."

Matt liked Santino's spirit, and so did the others. Suddenly, it sounded so simple, almost easy. Stop the tanks and torch them. And even though Matt knew his officers understood that stopping tanks was never simple or easy for riflemen, he let the mood build. Confidence had a role in war, even overconfidence. When they'd talked themselves into it, Matt sent the officers back to their companies.

Lou emerged from the shadow of a tree to reclaim his flask. Matt took another sip and handed it over. "You heard?"

"Yeah, I heard." He smacked his lips after his drink. "In my book you hold the line no matter what. Nothing gets through unless everything gets through. I'm no gambler."

Matt frowned. Every fight was a crap shoot, but his way at least bettered their odds. They had nothing behind them except a long flat plain that led to the sea. And who knew what the Germans would throw at them? Tanks, yes, and infantry. But how many tanks and how many men? He couldn't hold off his decision to find out the answers.

He turned away, but Lou caught his arm. "I lose when I gamble, Matty. Mostly you don't. Let's hope your luck holds."

NORA HOPPED OUT of the jeep and darted across the road toward the red brick seminary. She dodged two GIs with sooty faces and red eyes stumbling down the middle of the street. Something clattered against stone, and she glanced back. One of the soldiers had dropped his rifle.

"Hey, you. Soldier!"

The rifleman didn't look back. He wasn't the first sleepwalking American she'd seen today. Plenty of fellows with the same dead eyes clogged the roads, begging for rides. Her driver, Frank, had picked up a few but, when the jeep stopped, the soldiers wandered on down the road. By the time she trotted out and grabbed the carbine, the GI had vanished.

Thinking about those sleepwalkers worried her, so she concentrated on finding an easier way to carry the rifle.

She slipped the strap over her shoulder and leaned right to balance the weight. This wasn't the first time she'd felt like slugging her driver today, either. Or yesterday, for that matter. Once he convinced himself the planes buzzing overhead last night were German, he pulled the jeep into a thicket of brush for the night. Today, he stopped at every burg to cross-examine townspeople about the German positions. As far as Nora could tell, none of them knew any more than Frank. But they all shook their heads and shrugged wearily, so her driver slowed to a crawl as they approached Bastogne.

She glanced down the empty street once more before stepping into the seminary. In the chapel, the setting sun blazed through stained glass and splashed rainbows across the stone floor. On the other side of the entry, dusk filtered down from a skylight to silhouette ranks of thick columns. She shivered at a creak on the stairs and spun.

Frank hesitated until she stepped into the fading light streaming through the open door. He finished the stairs in a hurry. "What's wrong?"

"You tell me. Can we make it to Paris tonight?"

He brushed by her and poked his head out the door. She came up behind him, and the stock of the rifle bumped his arm. He looked back. "Where'd you get the carbine?"

Nora frowned. "A guy dropped it in the road and kept walking."

He nodded and pulled her toward the stairs. "Good. We might need it. Got any clips for it?"

The words stopped her head in midshake, freezing the words in her mouth. She tried to think as he nudged her up the steps. Matthew had said Bastogne was safe. VIII

Corps was headquartered in Bastogne, after all. Her heart pounded. "Where's the headquarters?"

"Gone, Nora. They pulled out a few hours ago."

She tripped and he caught her arm. "But don't get worried yet. The 101st Airborne is heading our way. Should get here pretty soon."

Nora leaned into a wall for support. She shook her head. "Why should we wait for them? Let's start for Paris right now."

His eyes dropped for a second. "Can't do it. Not tonight, for sure, and probably not tomorrow, either. The Germans caught us with our pants down this time. No telling where we'd run into them."

Flattening her palms against cool plaster, Nora closed her eyes. She tried to convince herself that Frank was kidding her. Usually he loved to tease her. But not this trip, not since yesterday.

She opened her eyes and fumbled for a cigarette. Her first drag tasted terrible. "So?"

He straightened slumping shoulders and tried for a confident smile. "So we wait. Maybe things will blow over. VIII Corps' pulling out could be just a precaution. And there's some armor out there, setting up a perimeter around the town."

Nora tried to flick ashes from her cigarette, but her hand trembled so hard that she dropped the butt. "Who told you that?"

"Would you believe a nun?" His grin came easily. "They've got a bunch of orphans here, and the sisters take care of them." He patted her arm. "Look, I'm going to get our stuff out of the jeep and pull it into a shed out back. No use advertising we're here. Go on upstairs. There's a bunch of food left in a big room on the top floor."

This time he took the stairs slowly and eased his head out the door carefully. Nora shivered and hugged herself. The chatter of fingernails against metal drew her eyes to the rifle. As she sank onto a step, she lifted the strap off her shoulder and folded the carbine across her lap. The darkness thickened, and a bell tolled somewhere above the seminary.

Her fingers tightened around the rifle.

WILL FINISHED his soup and pushed the bowl away. The café served good food but not much hospitality. He pulled out his billfold and sorted enough francs to pay for the meal. The slovenly woman behind the bar raised her eyes and scooped up the money without a word. He smiled anyway and tossed another bill across the counter. He wouldn't need francs in New York.

He buttoned his coat and sliced through an exhaust cloud to climb into the jeep. His driver raised his eyebrows and grinned. "Colder inside than out, huh?"

"Can you blame her?" Will nodded at the moon-faced concierge staring through the window. "How many armies you figure she's forced smiles for in her lifetime?"

Lynch shrugged and eased the jeep into gear. "An artillery observation outfit just drove through. I'll try to catch up."

Will maneuvered his legs into a comfortable position and lit up. The German offensive had cost him a day's travel yesterday when he swung out to Spa to check with First Army headquarters. No one knew much or seemed worried, so this morning he headed back to Malmedy and the road to Paris. Covering the war wasn't his problem anymore, and making the detour irritated him. He couldn't afford to be sidetracked, not now. Extra efforts like that were Sylvia's main complaint. If he wanted to keep his boys and his wife, he better change his ways.

A high-pitched whistle alerted him just before Lynch yanked the wheel and sent the jeep into a skid. Bracing hands on the seat and windshield, he leaned over the icy road and looked back. A tank topped the rise beyond the café. Shit. The snout of a second tank rolled into view. "Get moving, Lynch—there are fucking tanks back there."

The driver grabbed his coat and yanked him back into the jeep. "Up ahead, too." Lynch slid to the ground.

Will rolled out the door as machine-gun fire zipped overhead. He looked for cover. Snow worked into his coat as he crawled for the ditch. A tangle of American trucks blocked the view ahead. He glanced back and saw a third German tank slide up the hill. No way out.

He bellied over a fallen branch and crept toward the American trucks. A quick squeeze on his calf told him Lynch followed. Ahead, a few of the artillerymen returned the German fire, but it wasn't enough. After a few minutes, a bayonet topped with a white handkerchief poked up among the trucks. The gunfire trailed off. One man stood with his arms up and then another. Will glanced back at Lynch and nodded toward the field next to the ditch.

Lynch shook his head. "Don't even think about it, Davies. No cover and running gives 'em a nice excuse to shoot."

He nodded and climbed out of the ditch. Sticking his hands in the air felt melodramatic, but he took his cue from the American soldiers ahead. He walked slowly toward the group as armed Germans surrounded them. Fear tightened the artillerymen's faces. His cheeks felt numb.

ALLIANCES

Behind their guns, the circle of hard-eyed Germans waited stiffly. An American major stepped forward to speak. A German pointed a Mauser at his belly and forced him back. *"Still."* On Will's right, a man coughed. The German swung around. *"Still!"*

He looked beyond the guards to a knot of officers wearing black SS uniforms. His stomach wrenched. Storm troopers. A young officer nodded and turned out of the huddle. He muttered to one of the guards, and the circle closed in.

"Los gehen wir." Rifles waved at the café down the hill. *"Schnell."*

He forced his legs into a walk and memorized the slanting shoulders of the soldier ahead. He stumbled on an icy patch but caught himself. He dropped his eyes to the road to make sure he didn't give anyone an excuse for anything. His arms ached.

A guard motioned them into the snow-dusted field opposite the café. He caught a glimpse of the woman barkeep as she bit her fist and turned away from the window. His feet kicked up fine powdery wisps. At least he'd eaten. He probably wouldn't get another meal for a while. The Germans had to be moving fast to get this far. It would take time to get camps set up for prisoners.

The men around him broke into low-voiced talk. This time no one shushed them. Maybe Sylvia would feel different once the Red Cross notified her. She wouldn't go through with the divorce. She'd look bad divorcing a POW. The boys would be scared but thrilled underneath at having their dad held by the enemy. No one could convince little kids that POWs had more bad luck than courage. At least he'd get officer's treatment—whatever that meant now.

A shot cracked out, and a man on Will's left crumpled. The men squeezed closer. Someone shouted hoarsely. "Stand fast."

A German half-track stopped on the road. An SS soldier in back lifted a machine gun from his side. Will closed his eyes at the hacking burst and tried not to scream.

TWENTY-SIX

THE RISING SUN at Matt's back cast a bloody tinge up the snow-covered slope. Oily smoke coiled through firs shattered by German artillery. A white-draped figure broke from the trees and raced for the covered trench. Matt nudged a clerk-turned-infantryman, who poked his head up and waved an arm.

The sprinting soldier dropped to his knees at the frozen edge of the trench. "Tigers coming, Colonel. I need ammo."

Matt waited for Mendoza to catch his breath. Lou had warned him he'd send Mendoza for a bazooka when things got tight. Mendoza's instinct for when and where to shoot was better spent knocking off tanks than riflemen.

The unlucky clerk hoisted a box of armor-piercing rockets toward Mendoza, who nodded his thanks before finishing his report. "Someone from Baker Company torched one, but I count five still coming."

Matt picked up his phone. "How far?"

Mendoza tugged the scraggly thatch on his chin. "Five hundred yards maximum."

"And the infantry?"

"A ways behind. Make it six hundred." Mendoza danced awkwardly from foot to foot and slapped his hands together. Four layers of blanket mittens muffled the clap. "The infantry's moving slow and careful."

Matt waved Mendoza forward to his new foxhole while waiting for Lou to come on the line. A string of curses echoed over the wire before Lou snapped "Yes" in his ear.

Tucking the phone between shoulder and ear, Matt pulled himself up the side of the trench and scanned the trees. Nothing moved. "Can you hold?"

"No, sir."

He'd expected the answer. Yesterday German assaults chewed up soldiers already weary from three cold nights in foxholes, but the battalion held their line. The German barrage started this morning just after one, but return fire from Divarty stopped it for a while. A second German barrage began just before four and cut communications with division, so there'd be no repeat performance. Yesterday's luck made today's trouble inevitable.

Matt dropped back into the trench and finished with Lou. "Let the Tigers through. You have cover handy?"

"Shit, yes. They blew the whole woods down around our heads already."

He motioned a runner to his side. "Fine. I'm sending a runner to the rest right now. Send your men back."

Lou grunted. "Those Tigers will be all over you."

Matt sighed. "Yeah, I know. I'm ready."

He broke the connection and turned to the runner. The soldier eyed him and fumbled with the carbine in his hands. The last bit of bravado hadn't worked. Even the eight balls knew no one was ever really ready for tanks. Two days ago the runner had been a cook safe in a field kitchen, but today his life turned hazardous.

There wasn't a man in the battalion who wasn't a combat infantryman today.

Matt gave him a stiff grin. "You're on, Cookie. Keep your head down and alert the company commanders to send their men back. Then find a foxhole and when the tanks clear your position, start nailing the foot soldiers."

He helped the other men position fir boughs to mask the trench. He wanted it to look natural—a tree toppled into the field. One felled tree the Germans could target easily, but four would make it a guessing game. He hoped to hell he'd guessed right. He dragged an ammo box to the trench's wall and stared out through severed branches.

The chatter of rifle fire died, and a ghostly silence enveloped the ridge. Over the whispers of the men sharing his trench, Matt strained to hear a warning sound. The barrage had finally rousted a few birds lingering in the winter forest. He fingered the grenades on his belt and glanced at the Thompson propped near his hand. The growl of engines raised the hair on his arms. And then he froze, imprisoned by the familiar momentary fear, the awful waiting.

A whizzing bolt of fire split the barn on his right. The Tiger's machine gun sputtered a spray of lead through the burning ruin as the tank nosed out of the trees. Matt pulled up the submachine gun and thanked God the second shot had melted his fear. Again.

Three other tanks crashed from the woods. Mendoza had guessed wrong. One looked like a Panther. Matt searched for the last tank until a cone of flames brightened the woods and shot toward the treetops. On cue, the rearguard fired scattered rounds, covering the bazooka men bellying out of their holes.

Someone in the trench snapped a clip into place and Matt hissed, "Hold your fire. Don't draw theirs."

A Tiger's machine gun burst thudded into the nearest bazooka man and rolled him down the slope. Another man rose from the dead man's foxhole and fired his rocket. The Tiger smoked fitfully before spilling flames. Matt slapped frozen earth with savage joy.

When rifle shots cracked up on the ridge, he grabbed his phone, but the line was dead. The lead Tiger swayed left and clanked down the slope, spitting snow from iron treads. Another man—Mendoza?—knelt in its path and fired. The rocket glanced off the hatch. The soldier stumbled trying to escape and screamed as the massive treads ground over his legs.

The Panther wheeled around, seeking safety but heading for a grave in the trees. But the Tiger came on, chewing down the slope on a tide of lead. The stream of bullets cut down the last bazooka man. Matt glanced at the men beside him. Terror glazed their eyes. He snapped a grenade from his belt and pulled the pin. "Let 'em have it."

Two men squeezed off rounds as Matt scrambled up the wall. He aimed a kick at the third who froze. The soldier's carbine spat fire as Matt cleared the trench. He hurdled the fallen tree and crouched into a run.

The Tiger swung around, trying for a shot. Bullets shredded fir limbs inches behind his feet. His yell thundered in his ears as he tossed the grenade in a low arc. Another man's war cry joined Matt's as a rocket tore into the Tiger. An explosion lifted the tank and sparks flew into the morning sky.

Matt tripped across the broken tree. The bazooka slid from Mendoza's hands, and his head fell over his crushed legs.

NORA TRACKED WORDS with a pencil as she counted. She'd scribbled enough notes for a book, but the switchboard had orders to stop dictating her stories after four hundred words. By writing tight, she kept under her limit and managed to save a hundred-word reserve each day. So far she hadn't needed those extra words.

She yanked the copy out of her typewriter and threaded around desks to the situation map. The positions marked on the clear overlay hadn't changed much in four days, except on the German side. American armor and airborne outfits formed a loose circle around the city. With the continued arrival of Germans outside the ring, the defense circle looked more like a noose. Was she saving those hundred words for Bastogne's surrender or annihilation?

The GI on the switchboard looked up when she stopped by his chair. "Just set it down. I'm not sure when I'll get to it."

Nora shrugged. "No rush. Did you manage to send anything last night?"

The clerk tugged the headset off one ear and covered the mouthpiece with his hand. "Sure did. Wouldn't want you stuck here for nothing, Miss Seymour."

She smiled and patted his shoulder. "Thanks. At least you guys are getting credit. Need some coffee?"

He shook his head, tugged out a plug and jammed in another. Nora hoped he didn't take her remark as false flattery or buttering him up. Bastogne had enough food, so things weren't quite desperate, but unceasing German assaults dwindled hope. Low clouds prevented resupply by air, and the larger map of the whole Ardennes squashed expectations of quick relief.

At the gas cooker, Nora snapped the tin cup from her belt and filled it. She checked the coffee level and started a fresh pot. At least she wasn't scared anymore. Or maybe she just got used to fear. Seeing truckloads of the 101st Airborne Division roll into the city had soothed her jitters the first night. A new spirit had infected the whole town. Civilians opened warehouses of food, a group of stragglers formed their own Combat Team Snafu and Negro artillerymen stuffed their pants in their boots and joined the airborne. The first night, things had looked good.

When the coffee perked, she lowered the flame and checked her watch to time the pot. She was the only reporter in Bastogne. Back home every IP paper must be using her dispatches. It was the best work she'd ever done. The word limit combined with her fear to sharpen the stories into razors of prose. Every sentence stung with a distinctive edge, the edge characteristic of special correspondents.

She checked her watch again and turned off the gas. "Fresh coffee, guys."

A few men raised cups, and she made the rounds. She tried to come up with a wisecrack for each but fell back on a smile when the jokes failed. At Ed Morris's desk, she set the pot down and waited for him to finish a phone call. The intelligence officer raised his bushy eyebrows in invitation. Keeping an eye on her added to his troubles, but he'd been a good sport so far. That might end right now.

"When you make your rounds today, I'd like to come." She had up her hands before he could object. "Come on, Ed. I'm stuck here, too. At least let me see what's going on."

"I'll need an okay from the old man." Nora held her ground but added a flirtatious smile. Morris sighed. "Okay, okay. I'll ask him."

He reached for the phone, but she stopped his hand. "Do I have time to run downstairs?"

Morris nodded and picked up the phone. "But just a half hour. If you're not here, you're out of luck."

Nora took the stairs two at a time and checked the seminary dining hall before descending into the cellars. The reedy strains of singing children guided her to a small storeroom. Four nuns waved arms to mimic a maestro and circled the children seated on mattresses. When she didn't spot Sister Marguerite, Nora backtracked down the corridor, checking every room. In the largest cellar, she found the elderly nun supervising the older children spreading mattresses across the floor. Sister Marguerite crossed the cold stone floor with whispering skirts and took her arm.

Nora smiled, careful to speak slowly. "Do you need anything? I'm going out with Major Morris today."

The old woman folded a hand against her chest. "Such care you take with us. Each day the same question." She glanced at the supplies beside the door. "Yes, perhaps some buckets."

Nora wondered if Sister Marguerite's strong accent mangled her words. "Buckets?"

"Buckets, yes." Her blue-veined hands clasped as she searched for the explanation. "For waste."

Of course. Toilets were already a problem at the seminary. She surveyed the blankets, canned goods and boxed candles stacked along the wall. The Franciscan nuns had rounded up more than enough for twenty orphans and eight sisters. She touched the rough wool of a blanket. "No sheets? These blankets scratch."

Sister Marguerite's hands disappeared inside her habit. "Our sheets are for the soldiers so they may hide against the snow."

"You mean for camouflage?" Sister Marguerite nodded and so did Nora. "Just buckets, then. How many?"

The nun's eyes widened and gestured at the mattresses. "Enough buckets for two hundred, or three. Now we shelter all those who need safety." Her hands slipped out of the black cloth and spread wide. "From today we are required to live in the cellars. All of Bastogne, your general says."

Nora left the nun to her work and relayed Sister Marguerite's needs to a supply sergeant who promised to scare up some buckets. Morris looked disappointed to find her waiting but didn't complain. While the jeep warmed up, she asked him about the order to move into the cellars.

"Everybody goes downstairs tonight. Sometime the Krauts will figure out that a poke here and there doesn't work. When they do, they'll really let us have it." He gunned the engine a couple of times. "I hear they found a private broom closet for you."

For a minute, his wisecrack broke the knot of tension in her chest, but Nora's laughter choked into something close to tears. She'd rather hole up in a broom closet underground than take her chances as a German prisoner. Sister Marguerite's stories about German treatment of prisoners sickened her. She wanted to believe the nun's horror stories simply resurrected phony atrocity tales from the last war. Similar rumors about the fate of Europe's Jews and Gypsies and Communists had sounded unbelievable in London but not anymore. After six months in Europe, believing the worst about anyone seemed easy.

She stared ahead as Morris swung the jeep into the empty street. An icy wind bit through her mittens. She tucked her hands into her armpits as the jeep wheeled through the city. Civilians had followed orders to stay inside. The GIs manning big guns throughout Bastogne wore blankets over their coats. When the town's cluster of buildings fell behind, Morris turned down a snowy lane. The jeep bumped through muddy ruts, forcing Nora to brave cold hands to keep her balance. Stray flakes of snow drifted from heavy clouds.

"Krauts scared us good over there yesterday, but we held 'em off." Morris pointed to the north. "You heard the guns?"

Nora raised her field glasses. Black craters pocked the snowy field, but nothing moved. Except for the craters, the fields as far as she could see reminded her of a Christmas card. But Santa wasn't coming this year. She pushed the thought away and asked a question instead. "Where's the line?"

"Dug in just below the ridge. You can't see them. Can't see the Germans, either. They're in the trees."

The intelligence officer scrambled out of the jeep and called back over his shoulder. "Follow me."

Morris angled for the shattered stone wall of a cottage. He crouched into a run as a hiss split the air. Nora darted after him. The explosion tossed her headfirst into his knees. She shrank against the cottage as shells whistled overhead.

He screamed against the roar. "They're moving! Let's go!"

The yank on her arm hurt but she followed at a trot. She slammed into his back when he stopped short. A peek over his shoulder showed mud and snow fountaining around the jeep. Morris elbowed her against the cottage and crept back along the wall toward the ridge. At his nod, she slid up behind him. The building thunder of explosions buried his words, but she understood the gestures. At his signal, she tore down the slope. A narrow trench gaped behind a stone fence, and she jumped in. Morris slid in fast and gave her a thumbs-up.

Icicles of fear stabbed her as individual explosions melded into a continuous roar, drowning men's screams. Blasts shuddered the earth and knocked her against mud walls. She panted frosty clouds, unable to think but grateful for breath. She cowered lower, but the barrage ended as suddenly as it had begun. She thought the terror had lasted for hours. Her watch made it just ten minutes.

Morris poked his head up and eyed a gap in the stone fence. Her ears throbbed, but now she could hear him. "I better get you out of here."

Nora tried to pull herself out of the trench but her quivering arms had no strength. She shook her head. She couldn't climb that slope for anything. "Forget it. I can't make it just now."

Morris just stared down until she held up trembling hands. He looked back through the fence. "Here they come."

Nora struggled to get up until, finally, he dragged her. He propped her with one hand and widened the hole with another. She pressed her chin into the cold mud lip of the trench and raised her binoculars.

Just beyond the trees, the snow seemed to move. The black snout of a tank slid from between the branches. As the machine edged forward, the moving snow stood and became soldiers draped in white camouflage. The ghostly infantry fell in behind the tank as it flamed to life.

The shell hit another stone wall, closer to the trees. The explosion and screams were familiar now.

Nora kept her glasses trained on the tank. The big gun wheeled left and right, searching out targets as the tank came on. A machine gun sputtered below the tank's gun, but the German soldiers stayed safely behind.

The silence from the American lines spooked her, and she gripped Morris's elbow. "Why aren't they firing back? Where's the artillery?"

"Ammo's rationed. Ten shells per gun. They'll wait until they can't miss."

Nora hoped silence frightened the Germans, too. On the left another tank broke from the woods, and more infantry fell in behind. A whistle pierced the air, and the lead tank bucked forward. A bloom of flame ringed the turret.

Morris grabbed her hand. "That's good shooting." A second, smaller explosion knocked off a tread. "Bazooka."

The tank's rear flamed high, and the hatch popped open. A man appeared, silhouetted against the fire. The American lines opened up. The German jerked forward then fell back as fire spread across his chest.

Flames licked across the tank into outlines of fire. The white infantry following the tank sprinted back toward the trees. A half dozen fell and skidded troughs into the snow. Nora caught herself silently urging the Germans on, faster and faster. The second tank scuttled back to the sheltering woods, and it ended. A feeble cheer somewhere to her right quickly hushed.

TWENTY-SEVEN

"I JUST LOST A BUDDY. My best buddy."

Nora read the words through a blur of tears. Putting his death on paper finally made it real.

"Will Davies wasn't a hero. He wasn't even a soldier. He was a reporter, a good one, who kept after a story even when it turned into war. The cost of his courage was his life."

She scratched a light for her cigarette. He'd laugh at the line about courage, but it was true. It took guts for him to admit his fear to her. No man wanted a woman to know he was scared. But fear didn't make him a coward. She hoped he knew that in the end.

Nora let her cigarette burn in the ashtray. He'd needed guts to force his fear aside and hit that beach in June. He'd needed even more guts to know when to quit.

"One kind of courage helped Will do his job at Omaha Beach in Normandy. Another kind of courage brought him to the snowy field outside Malmedy, Belgium, where he died last week."

She should have seen him before he left. He should have waited. Maybe he'd just had enough. The fight through the Hurtgen Forest had been hellish and skirmishing street-to-street in Aachen had shaken even Matthew.

"Will called it quits and was on his way home when he was taken prisoner. He'd seen too much butchery in three years as a war correspondent. He'd seen other men transformed into aficionados of violence, lovers of death. He had a wife and two sons who needed him, and finally he realized how much he needed them."

A teardrop blotched the page, and she blotted it with her handkerchief. He'd be a hero to those little boys but that could never stem their grief. Someday they'd learn how it was at Malmedy, but they'd never understand.

"A coward killed Will. In the bitter chill of a winter field, he shot down dozens of unarmed Americans standing with hands in the air."

Nora closed her eyes and let her head drop into her hands. All the way back to Paris she'd recoiled from the hatred in the eyes of GIs. It wasn't just the massacre of Will and the other men which fashioned those hard and merciless eyes. The bloodletting in those bitter villages and forests had sucked the last ounce of mercy from every man. Maybe that's why Will had quit the war—to save his compassion.

She sighed, wishing she'd made him understand that the last time she saw him. It took a brave man to see all that death and still care. Surrendering to indifference was the easy way out.

Biting a pencil, she summoned up their last day together. He hadn't gloated like many reporters over communiqués listing the tonnage of bombs dropped on Germany. He glanced at the paper and shook his head. He'd started to look beyond battles and said each sortie of bombers made the peace more difficult.

"Will knew that war breeds hate and fear. He took no joy when our bombers flattened the towns and cities of Hitler's Germany. He figured each bomb of destruction ignited fresh

flames of hate and fear. And he knew extinguishing those fires was the only way to achieve real peace.''

Nora tugged on the pencil and remembered the argument over dinner that last night. Some had called Will a softie, reminding him that the Germans asked for it by starting the war. To Will every government deserved some blame. He said the only way to avoid another world war was to find a better way to settle differences. They accused him of favoring world government and settled down to a discussion of Uncle Sam's chances against the Russian Bear. That was the next fight, the reporters agreed, and as soon as we wrapped up Hitler, it would be time to go after the Reds.

"Will Davies was a hard man to lose. He had the courage not to surrender to hatred or fear. We need men like Will Davies, and his like is always hard to find."

She tossed the pencil on the desk and rolled out the column. Will deserved a better eulogy than she could write for him. He'd given her so much, taught her so much. He'd always been willing to take her just as she was.

Dried tears stiffened her face and she rubbed her cheeks to erase the trails. She didn't want Norm Cox to see tear streaks when she gave him the column. He owed his new job as IP's Paris bureau chief to Will's death and could barely hide the delight in his new power. Cox was a cold son of a bitch behind his tasseled shoes and tie pins.

Nora grabbed her copy and stepped into the newsroom. No use worrying about yesterday's problems. Cox had edited the life out of her takeout on Bastogne, but New York raved about it, anyway. The censors probably would have axed out the heart, too.

ALLIANCES

Cox paused slightly before looking up when she stopped at his desk. She met cold eyes and passed him the column on Will. "I'm going upstairs to sleep."

He held up a hand. "Wait till I read this, Nora. In the meantime, you could clean out the desk in the private office."

She spun around without giving him the satisfaction of a frown. After years of calling her Seymour, he'd suddenly discovered her first name to put her in her place. He actually tried to assign her the overnight shift until she threatened to tell New York that would finish her column. In ten days Cox had managed to strip the newsroom of every iota of camaraderie and instill a new tone with all the liveliness of a boardroom. "Battlegrounds" was the only defense she had left.

Clearing the desk didn't take long. She tucked a couple of full notebooks into her bag and grabbed a handful of pens. Cox could sort through the bureaucratic garbage himself. He wasn't a reporter, anyway, just a born paper shuffler. She dumped the stuff on her new desk in the corner and sat down. Cox loved giving an imperious summons, and she didn't have to wait long for this one.

He studied her copy when she got to her desk. "Nora, I'm afraid this really won't do. This section about lovers of death reflects badly on all of us. And a bit lower it sounds like Davies advocated world government."

He pushed the column at her, but she didn't take it. She waited for Cox to look up instead. "What's your beef, Norman? Are you telling me the censors won't like this?"

His eyes narrowed as she plunged ahead. "Or don't you like it?" She slapped her hand on the desk, and he jumped. "Look, Cox, Will is dead. Let him have his say before everyone forgets him."

Cox pushed back in his chair and straightened his tie. "You're obviously distraught, and understandably so. But I'm surprised at you, Nora. Even I have admired your grace under pressure. I take it you'd rather I make the necessary changes?"

Nora hid fisted hands in her pockets. Losing her temper wouldn't work with Cox. "The same kind of necessary changes you made with my copy on Bastogne?"

He snapped forward and anchored his elbows on the desk. For a long moment he stared at his clasped hands. "I can't spare you right now. But once the German offensive is mopped up, you'd better take a rest in London. Better yet, New York or wherever you're from back home. You've had a trying time."

He lifted the column from the edge of his desk. "That's evident from this and the piece on Bastogne. I must exercise my best judgment in editing your copy before submitting it to censorship." He dropped the story on his desk. "And you must respect my authority."

Nora wanted to slap him but didn't have the strength. This was the price she paid for losing her distance. Will's death and the terror of Bastogne had drained her vitality and blunted her anger. On a better day, she could have won this fight. Today she couldn't even get started.

Tears prickled under her lids. She nodded and swung away before Cox could see. She snared her bag and escaped out the door. Another reporter stopped to congratulate her on the Bastogne story but she brushed by him and left his "Terrific" hanging in the hall.

The elevator doors closed the world out, and she sank against the wall. Could it get worse than this? Will was dead but not Matthew. She got word from him just a few hours ago.

As the elevator shuddered to a stop at her floor, she wiped away the tears. No, this was the worst it could get. The hiss of opening doors mocked her lie.

CONSTANCE FOLDED ASIDE her newspaper and reached for the teapot. "Another cup, Jane? The pot's still warm."

Jane Ludwig dropped the newspaper shielding her face and nodded. "I say, may I see the *Guardian*? There's not a decent letter in the *Times*."

Constance leaned back with a cup in her lap when Jane buried herself behind a fresh newspaper. Feeble winter sun streamed through the window to splash across the brilliant colors of the Oriental from Wickenden Square. In another few months the garden at Corniche would push out radiant blooms, and she wouldn't need to gaze at a carpet to lift her spirits on a dreary Sunday afternoon. But would Corniche ever be her home again? Peter was coming back for her, but he'd never said where they would go.

She finished the last crumb of toast and sighed. Would she go with him? The question had hung over her like a poised ax since she saw him off at the railway station. If she went, the ax would sever her ties with everything she cherished—family, friends, country. And if she told him no, the ax would chop the slender thread of hope that his love gave her.

Lighting a cigarette, Constance realized that's why she'd asked Jane to call this afternoon. In all of England, only Jane knew about Peter, and only Jane had common sense enough to accept her affair without recriminations. She wanted to ask Jane's opinion but couldn't quite find a way to broach the subject. For all her school chum's professional admiration of Peter

Ryan, she still harbored a parochial grudge against Americans. *"Hadn't they come in and taken over the country? If we're not careful, they'll finish the job by taking over the world."* It was nonsense, of course, but a good many sensible people shared Jane's fears.

A rattle of newsprint brought Constance's eyes up to Jane. "Look at this—a full column in the *Guardian* and you never said a word."

Constance frowned at the accusation in Jane's eyes. "What should I have told you about?"

"This." She thrust the paper into Constance's lap and swung around to point over her shoulder. "Right there." Her finger stabbed a column. "This new peace organization. What do they call it? There it is—United Nations—and it's to meet in San Francisco in April."

Jane huffed back to her chair and Constance scanned the story, heart sinking. Jane, big on organizations to solve the world's troubles, was ever after Constance to become involved with one or another. But joining this new one required more than good intentions. Only representatives of invited governments might attend.

She handed the paper back. "Perhaps it might do some good."

Jane glared. "Is that all you have to say on the subject? Really, Constance, I am disappointed." She set the *Guardian* down and folded her arms. "It's the very thing for you, you know."

For a moment, Constance only stared. Then she laughed. "Oh, Jane, that's absurd. I've no credentials for such a post. And even if I did, I can't rush off to San Francisco at the drop of the hat."

Jane pushed out her jaw. "Why not? You've no responsibilities here with the children in New York, Jeremy in India and Peter in Europe. And of course you've the credentials. I haven't forgotten *Judgment*, though I know you'd prefer I did. Every word was true then and it's true today. You've a sight more credentials than half the idiots at Whitehall."

Constance widened her eyes at Jane's vehemence. The idea was ridiculous, but she could tell by the way Jane folded her hands that her friend only paused to marshal more arguments.

"I've given this a great deal of thought." Jane waved her hand. "Oh, not this United Nations. I've been thinking about the best use of your talents." She arched an eyebrow. "You're rather bad at shelter work, though you try hard enough. And, anyway, the worst of that is over, thank God. Now we must think about the future and what you might do to make it better."

The words echoed what Peter had said. Jane shared his approach—see a problem, find a solution. Perhaps it was a course in medical school. Constance studied her hands as Jane plunged on.

"They'll be looking for a sop to throw the women— we got the vote after the last war, remember. And with your connections, you could easily become a delegate. Then we'd have a voice, a say, if you will. You could be our advocate among all those wretched men who think only of power and alliances and bossing everyone around. You could speak up for the children, for the refugees, for the poor rotters who starved before and will starve again unless someone stops it."

Constance glanced away from her friend. It was too ridiculous. Imagine pretending to know enough about things to make speeches! And yet she had once. She had made speeches and people had listened. And she had written *Judgment* and seen it discussed. But when the world hadn't immediately refashioned itself along lines she approved, she'd retreated.

She raised her eyes and considered Jane. This strong woman didn't retreat from the wretched poverty of the East End. Nor did Peter. Nor even Jeremy. It was only she who retreated when faced with an obstacle, preferring to claim failure rather than trying harder and yet again harder.

Jane must have sensed her line of thinking because she leaned eagerly forward, eyes blazing, awaiting an answer.

Constance smiled. "I'll consider it."

TWENTY-EIGHT

MATT SIGNALED HIS DRIVER to start the jeep and turned back inside Lou's command post. The sergeant, framed by lantern light, managed a thin smile. Winter fighting had etched deep lines in Lou's face, and Matt wondered again about sending his friend back for a longer rest. Lou's pride had more stamina than his body, and he'd be forty-five next month. Maybe if he approached the subject sideways.

"You look beat, Lou. Seen the doc lately?"

The sergeant straightened his shoulders. "What eats me no doctor can fix. I got a bad case of replacements. These new fellows are so green I got to wipe their noses and rock 'em to sleep every night." He shook his head. "Wish I had one like Mendoza to anchor the squad."

Matt nodded. The little fisherman's death had left a big hole in the battalion. Mendoza was the last of the old-timers. They'd lost too many veterans of Africa, Sicily and Normandy in the Ardennes' bitter woods. Lucky veterans caught a white boat home. The unlucky earned a gold star for their wives or mothers. And after two damned months, the First was back where it had started—fighting for a bridgehead across the Roer.

He shook Lou's hand and walked out into the chill night. At least it wasn't snowing anymore. Everyone blamed muddy roads for slowing the advance, but Matt figured German resistance would stiffen more before the Wehrmacht finally shattered. Inside their Fatherland, the Krauts fought harder than ever. But that couldn't last. Even snipers harassing Allied lines had started giving up.

The moon peeked through clouds to cast shadows as Matt hopped into the jeep. He told the driver to head for battalion headquarters. The jeep swung a tight circle into the road and left Lou's squad behind.

And after the Third Reich crumbled, then what? He sniffed cold air. The Pacific, probably, which meant learning a new way of fighting to battle another tenacious army. He eased back into the seat and cleared his mind. Better finish one job before starting the next.

Clouds blanketed the moon, darkening the road ahead. He rubbed an ache in his neck. God, he was tired of fighting.

The thought strayed into his mind uninvited, startling him. He grabbed a handhold as the driver rounded a curve. Before he could examine the new idea, a muzzle flashed on his left and the windshield disintegrated. The driver screamed and slumped over the wheel.

The jeep tilted and Matt dove for the ditch. A spray of lead chased him, tearing a seam of fire up his side. His chin plowed through gravel before his slide stopped. The jeep crashed through brush off on the left.

Mud sucked at his cheeks as he lifted his head just enough to breathe. He fought his mind past the burning pain in his leg and shoulder, forcing his ears to hear. The jeep's engine still growled somewhere on his left. Carefully he eased his head down, turning his face toward the threat. The throb of his wounds pounded through his head.

For endless minutes he lay still, learning the night sounds, listening for a noise that didn't fit. The driver must be dead. If he was, the Kraut would come looking. A fitful breeze stirred over him, rustling creaks from the trees.

His eyes adjusted to darkness, and he memorized the slant of the ditch. Blood soaked through his jacket and puddled near his mouth, splattering parted lips. He sipped shallow breaths and sensed the bulk of his .45 near his good arm. The dull ache weakened his left side. Could he even use it?

A skittering rock decided it. He willed his muscles to relax into a mimicry of death. Angling eyes up, he waited. He'd waited for this moment since Tunisia.

A boot squeaked. A shadow loomed. He held his breath.

I don't want to die.

The thought screamed through his mind. The German bent over him. Matt's heart raced with panic. Rough fingers prodded bleeding flesh. Matt fought down a scream.

Don't let him win.

The hand withdrew, leaving searing prints that burned into his shoulder. The German grunted and turned away.

Matt released the air strangling his lungs but stayed still. The sniper had to move on. Anyone coming by would see the jeep. He just had to wait. He started counting, pausing between numbers.

Matt stiffened when his jeep roared on the left. Wheels hissed across slick pavement. A dim stream of blackout lights danced across the ditch. On grinding gears, the jeep gunned off into the night.

His body relaxed and mud cooled his face. Dull pain nagged his side, weakening his will. Help seemed so far and lying here so easy. The edge of his vision clouded. He strained his eyelids open.

I don't want to die.

He sucked air hard, breathing a mouthful of his own salty blood. He spat into the mud. Rolling onto his side against the weight of his wounds loosed a hoarse cry, but he made it. His right side still worked.

Cold seeped through his clothes, numbing his good side. Linemen had strung communication cables down this road only a few hours ago, lines stretched thin through these woods. Probably no one had heard the shots.

Anchoring an elbow, he propped his chest up and tried to get a leg under him. Pain bolted from shoulder to calf and he collapsed.

In a little while, he tried again. Edging out an elbow, he pulled himself up and threw out his hand. He clawed mud and made a few inches, but it was no good. Cables laid in roadside ditches were easily cut. Good linemen laid cables back from the road.

Angling a knee, he straightened his good leg and pushed himself back against the wall of the ditch. He winced as he flung himself over, swinging an arm up toward level ground. His good hand grasped a root and he tugged, grunting with pain, until his shoulders flopped out of the ditch.

His good foot propelled his legs over the edge. His fingers slid forward and found nothing. Angling his foot and his hand, he pushed and pulled himself away from the ditch. Again he felt. Again he moved. Again he rested.

Finally his fingers found a cable. Two. And two more. He worked the knife from his pocket and tugged himself onto an elbow. Sawing through cable took too long.

Wire frayed against his hand, scratching deep. He hacked with the last of his strength and felt the cut. Only a few strands held.

A few strands weren't enough to keep a division's communication network operating. Somewhere up there an officer would roust a lineman from bed and send him out to troubleshoot the problem. Matt let himself go limp. If he could wait, he wouldn't die.

FLIERS SURGED into the equipment room, banging open metal lockers and grabbing flight gear. Tim took his time emptying his pockets. He didn't want to fly this mission. If Dresden was so all-fired important, why was the city still standing? And how come the Russians didn't do the job if the Red Army was only seventy-five miles away? A couple of fellows whistled when they saw the distance to target on the map in the briefing room. His Mustang could easily make the round-trip, but the bombers would be pushing it on the way home.

He fastened his flight suit and pulled on his Mae West, ignoring the nervous chatter around him. When the briefing officer said fighters would split into two groups, he knew what his assignment would be—strafing. Major Nixon's group always strafed. And that crap about "targets of opportunity" disgusted him. Why didn't they just come right out and say they wanted the fighters to blast anything that moved? Targets of opportunity meant that passenger trains and civilian trucks and columns of refugees were fair game.

After adjusting the leg straps, he shouldered into the parachute and stuffed an escape kit into his oxygen mask. He carried his goggles, oxygen mask and dinghy out to the waiting jeep and climbed in. Maybe he could fake engine trouble somewhere over Holland and head back to base. A few eyebrows would raise when his Mustang checked out mechanically, but with his record, no one would dare call him chicken. Escaping today wouldn't solve the problem tomorrow when he'd be ordered to strafe again. He'd already tried getting into another group, but Nixon wouldn't let him go.

The jeep ferried him across the apron toward the waiting Mustangs. As he started down the row toward his fighter, someone caught his elbow and tugged him roughly around.

"I've been meaning to have a little chat with you, Chase." Nixon smirked up at him behind narrowed eyes. "I pulled you into number-two position last time just to make sure, and there's no doubt about it. You aren't what I call trigger-happy."

Tim shifted the gear in his arms and glanced around. The other fellows crouched on wings, leaving a pool of privacy for Nixon's little chat.

Tim shrugged. "I've got five kills to my credit, if that's what you mean."

Nixon stepped closer. "You know damn well that's not what I mean, Chase. Maybe you'll go after the Luftwaffe, but you don't have the guts for the job on the ground. I won't stand for it."

He'd been waiting for this. Last time up he made sure to lay on the fire when Nixon pulled him into number-two position. The only target they found turned out to be a couple of stray cows wandering down a country road, so it hadn't mattered much. Somehow he hoped slaughtering cows would take care of it, but Major Nixon wasn't stupid. He must have seen how Tim held back from firing until the last minute. He laid off pretty quick, too. Tim sighed. "Is that all, sir?"

ALLIANCES

Nixon folded his arms. "Listen good, Chase. I hate gutless bastards who crybaby about innocent civilians. I won't have any in my group. Your old man may be a big shot in Washington but that won't make any difference. If you don't do your job today, I'll court-martial your ass and no chicken-shit isolationist Daddy will save you. Understand?"

Tim struggled to keep from slugging Nixon and managed a stiff nod. Father had nothing to do with this. All his life he'd fought ignorant bullies like Nixon. The major glared again to make sure his message got through, then left Tim alone.

Flying toward Holland, he worked hard to forget Nixon's threat. He fell back on the routine of his cadet days, constantly monitoring instruments and scanning for Messerschmitts that wouldn't appear. The Luftwaffe couldn't strike anywhere near the Channel anymore. It was all the Germans could do to get a few planes airborne over the Fatherland these days. Hitler's new jets caused some concern, but the Allies dominated European skies.

Holland's coast sped by below, and Tim's group rendezvoused with other fighters waiting for the bombers over the Zuider Zee. Nixon's voice squawked into Tim's ear, ordering him up to number-two position again. He maneuvered the Mustang into place without thinking. He glanced down at the expanse of gray water and tried to remember the name of the story about a Dutch boy and ice-skating that he'd read as a kid.

Engine vibrations pounding his feet altered pitch slightly. He adjusted the fuel mixture feeding the twelve-cylinder Merlin until the motor hummed evenly. All during the Bulge he'd been itching to fly, wanting to give guys like Matt a hand. At least they had easier going now.

Matt must be somewhere in Germany. Everybody else was. Maybe Nixon would feel different if he knew about Matt. No one called Big Red One chicken shit.

A chill crept over him. Shit, forget Nixon. He pulled off a glove to test the warmth from the cockpit heater. A well-aimed kick might boost it up. His eyes strayed over the penciled date jotted on his hand above compass readings for navigation. What was special about February 14? It wasn't the day he met Hillary. He'd never confuse January 30 with any other day. Could it really be only a little over a year since he met her? It felt as if he'd known her forever. It felt as if she'd been dead forever.

Nixon's voice intruded again. "Here come the bombers. Remember, after the heavies deliver our Valentine's gift, we stick around to make sure the Krauts remember it."

Shit. Valentine's Day. A stab of regret left him feeling like a jerk. Did the Germans let sentiment interfere when they bombed Bastogne on Christmas Eve? Nora's story about it finally opened his eyes to the terror endured on the ground and made him doubly glad he'd switched to fighters. Though that city was filled with troops, the Germans hadn't strafed Bastogne. How could he avoid strafing today? Maybe Father would understand—*he would understand*—but Matt never would. Could he stand having his brother believe him a coward?

A screech of interference from German radar shattered his thoughts. Far below, the smooth ribbon of the Rhine sliced through Germany, and Tim didn't have time to worry anymore. That bank of clouds in the north could hide a squadron of German fighters. He kept glancing north until the formation cleared the threat. A thin blanket of clouds veiled the ground, but weather wouldn't be a problem today. Outlines of fields and roads showed through.

Black puffs of flak thrust up through the clouds but fell short of the formation. That must be Leipzig. A few minutes later, he spotted the Elbe as the formation swung south. A dark tower of clouds appeared ahead, and he squinted against the sun to judge the distance. Maybe the weather was on his side, after all. But no, clouds didn't boil up like that. It was smoke, dense black smoke.

He risked a glance up as the Fortresses' bomb bays dropped open. It was Dresden, then. He tightened his grip on the stick and scanned the smoke. The Germans had an airfield near Dresden, though no one knew whether it was operational. It didn't look like it. Now was the time for Messerschmitts to jump them.

He flicked his eyes at the strings of bombs dropping from the Fortresses. Roiling smoke swallowed the flash of their impact. Tim glanced at his watch. In ten minutes his group would break away from the formation. Nixon stuck to the bombers on their pass over the city and into the slow arc of their turn. Tim's eyes returned to his watch again and again as the minutes slipped away. All too soon Nixon waggled his wings and twisted away from the Forts. Tim followed him down.

The altimeter swung wildly in the descent until Nixon eased out of the dive at ten thousand feet. The major avoided the heaviest smoke as he circled back over the city. Tim didn't have to find targets. That was Nixon's specialty, but maybe he'd strike out today. Or maybe luck would guide them to a troop train or airfield instead. That might satisfy Nixon.

A second circle turned up nothing of interest, and Tim came close to thanking God when Nixon barked over the headset. "The fields along the river. Follow me in."

The major's Mustang pulled up and rolled into an attack dive. Tim hesitated only a moment before swinging after him. The ground rushed up in a blur as he followed Nixon's fighter. Glowing lead streamed out from Nixon's wings as the plane leveled off for short moments before starting to climb.

As Nixon's fighter cleared his gunsight, Tim squeezed the trigger on his stick. His fire tore down toward the bodies sprawled in the field. Someone down there dashed into his gunsight, weaving wildly across dead grass. He released the trigger but the form pitched over headfirst. Too late. He glanced back at a long spill of blond hair.

His stomach heaved as the Mustang climbed. He followed Nixon's tight circle as the major swung around for a second pass and nosed into another dive. But when Nixon's Mustang cleared his field of fire, Tim left the trigger untouched and searched for the girl. Motionless figures whizzed underneath, and he couldn't pick her out. On the third pass he spotted her. She hadn't moved since his first time over.

Nixon's voice crackled into his headset and his anger broke radio discipline. "Remember what I told you, Chase?"

Tim acknowledged with two clicks of his radio button. To hell with Nixon. He didn't kill civilians, dammit. Not anymore. Even the five he'd sent down for Hillary bothered him, but at least they'd asked for it. Just as he was asking for a court-martial. Living down that disgrace would be easier than living with himself if he kept strafing.

ALLIANCES

Tim scanned the compass. Hell, there wasn't even any antiaircraft fire. Only the column of smoke flawed the winter sky. When Nixon led the group back over the city, Tim saw there wasn't much left of the city center, only burned-out hulks surrounding embers glowing red in the noon sun. He couldn't even pick out the streets under the rubble. And what about bomb craters? There weren't any. With all the bombs those Fortresses had dropped, there should be plenty. He visualized the tumble of bombs, a mix of explosives and incendiaries, mostly incendiaries. And where were the military targets? He hadn't seen a ruin large enough to have housed a factory. He hadn't seen anything but residential blocks, street after street of homes and apartments.

Dresden fell behind as Nixon turned north, following a highway far below. Tim hoped anyone down there heard them coming as the major called for an attack on a speeding truck. He waited the interval and nosed after the group leader, but the angle was too steep. Tim corrected his dive and waited for Nixon to do the same. Pressure built in his ears with the sudden loss of altitude. Nixon still didn't pull out of his dive.

Tim snapped on his mike. "Too steep, Major. Pull up."

His headset crackled just before Nixon's Mustang smashed into the road. Flames billowed up. Tim jerked the stick back as the blast reached for his plane. The nose came up sharply. Burning air clawed his tail as the Mustang climbed. He checked his mirror. The rest of the group climbed after him as their target careened on down the road.

TWENTY-NINE

LONDON'S FADING TWILIGHT cast a sickly pallor over Tim's face as he slumped in the chair by the window. Nora sipped her drink and studied his hollowed cheeks and sunken eyes. He hadn't looked this bad when she'd seen him the day after she arrived from Paris. At least that evening he talked. Tonight Tim hadn't said another word after muttering thanks when she handed him a Scotch.

Her eyes flicked over the table, noting the empty glass and cigarette burning in the ashtray. Whatever it was, he needed help. She drained her glass, pulled the desk chair next to his and touched his hand. "Tim? Is there anything I can do?"

He let out a ragged sigh and looked up. "Can you make me forget? I keep seeing her run into my gunsight and my finger's still on the trigger and then she'd dead." His eyes looked vacant. "I know they're Germans, but they can't all be Nazis. She wasn't a Nazi. She was just a kid."

His face crumpled, and his head fell into shaking hands. Nora frowned. She squeezed his shoulder. "I don't understand. Who are you talking about?"

A shudder ran over him. "I don't know. That's funny, isn't it? I didn't even know her, but I killed her. Probably killed a bunch of others, too, but they were already down. She was running away when I got her."

Nora kept quiet this time, gently rubbing his back to convince him she wanted to hear. Full darkness settled on London's chimneys before he continued. She pulled the blackout shade and snapped on a table lamp. He squinted against the sudden light and gulped a couple of deep breaths.

"After Hillary died, I couldn't bomb anymore. But I couldn't quit, either. So I switched to fighters because my enemy would come at me in a Messerschmitt. It'd be simple—him or me."

Nora nodded. But something had gone wrong for him. She touched his hand, urging him to continue.

"At first that's how it went. But then things eased up for us. We about wiped the Luftwaffe out, so not as much fighter escort was needed. Some of us were ordered to find targets of opportunity." He glanced away. "To strafe."

She squeezed his hand. "And you think you killed a German girl by accident?"

His head snapped up. "It was no accident. None of it. Everyone knew Dresden was different. The target was too far. A bunch of Fortresses ran out of fuel coming back and ditched in Belgium. And the briefing was sketchy about what to hit. The city center, they kept saying. Even the mix of bombs was different. I never carried that many incendiaries."

His eyes stared past her. "God, it was hell down there. The RAF hit Dresden twice before we went in. It was still smoking. After the Forts dropped their bombs, my group took a couple of low passes over the city. I couldn't make out the streets under the rubble. The buildings were shells, everything inside had burned out. We could have stayed for hours. There was no antiaircraft and no German fighters to intercept us."

Nora remembered Bastogne and shivered. Tears spilled from Tim's eyes, and he wiped his face against an upraised arm. "Along the river we saw people and dove after them. Mostly they just lay there, but not the girl. She tried to run. That's when I cut her down."

He remained fixed on a private hell she didn't understand. "I wanted to see you 'cause I couldn't see Matt. I had to tell someone who'd understand that this was different." He brought his eyes back to meet hers. "It was wrong. That's what made it different."

Nora shook her head and reached for his hand. "You didn't mean to kill her. Maybe you didn't. And anyway you had no choice. You were doing your job."

"Don't tell me that. That doesn't matter." His voice rose, and he struggled for control. "That's no excuse. I knew it was wrong and I did it, anyway."

He shook off her hand and sank back into the chair. His shoulders heaved, and he closed his eyes.

Nora wanted to cry when she saw tears roll down his cheeks. Why did he keep torturing himself? "Stop it, Tim." He looked up, startled. "Don't tear yourself apart. It's over now."

He stared past her again. She grabbed his hand and squeezed hard. "Timmy, listen to me. Walk around London. Look what they did here. Don't blame yourself."

He shook his head and focused his eyes on her. "I've seen it. It doesn't make us right. It just makes us as bad as them."

WHEN HE WAS GONE, Nora sat for a long time without moving. It couldn't be true. Tim misunderstood somehow. She couldn't believe he'd been ordered to strafe civilians. That sounded like something the Germans would do. Look at what they'd done to Will. But Tim's last words kept floating through her mind, a haunting counterpoint to her denials. *"You survived Bastogne. Did the Luftwaffe strafe civilians?"*

Nora pushed out of her chair and paced the hotel room. Tim's guilt tore him apart. He wasn't the boy she'd met a year before or even the man she'd seen three weeks ago. Whatever happened over Dresden must have been different. In dozens of missions he'd learned what was routine. And he claimed Dresden differed from all other missions he'd flown.

She turned off the light and opened the blackout shade. Leaning against the casement, she let the truth seep in. If she believed Tim, she had to do something. What happened to him wasn't right. The torment Tim suffered was not of his own making. He'd been promised one kind of war and made to fight another. How naive that sounded.

But it was true. Everyone shouted slogans about good versus evil and freedom versus slavery, but in the end it was just death and more death.

The memory of Tim's anguished tears flooded back, and she smacked the casement with her hand. She could find out, at least. She could dig out the truth, for her own sake and for Tim. But she had to work fast. Cox expected her back in Paris the day after tomorrow.

She swung away from the window. Maybe Connie would help. She must have sources at the air ministry. Nora glanced at her watch. Connie never went to sleep this early. She grabbed her keys, trotted up two flights and knocked hard. Jiggling keys while waiting, she slid inside as soon as Connie cracked open the door. "I need your help, Connie. It's important."

Nora stalked across the room and dropped into one of the chintz-covered chairs. Without asking, Connie poured drinks and carried them to the table. Pushing framed pictures and delicate figurines aside, she set the glasses down and eyed Nora over narrow reading glasses. "What's the trouble?"

Grabbing a Dunhill from Connie's pack, Nora sighed. "It's Tim. He's half crazy, Connie. He flew a mission to Dresden and strafed a girl on the ground. He says she was a civilian."

Connie raised her eyebrows but Nora plunged on.

"That's not all. He thinks the Dresden raid was different, and he claims the city had no military significance. The whole point was to terrorize civilians. From what he said, there's not much left."

She sat back and let the words sink in. Connie sipped her drink and studied the amber liquid in her glass for long moments. Finally she looked up. "What do you propose to do, Nora?"

Nora stabbed out her cigarette and sat forward. "Just find out what happened. Tim didn't volunteer to kill civilians, Connie, but it looks like he has. I want to know why."

Connie knotted her fingers and glanced away. "What do you want from me?"

The indifferent tone of the question hung in her mind for a minute, but she forced it aside. "You can help with the legwork. Make some calls. You know the right people. Find out if the Dresden raid was out of the ordinary. If it was different, find out why."

Connie lifted a small china piece from the table and passed it to Nora. She set it on her palm. Delicate and beautiful, a young couple reclined, innocent and trusting in their love.

"Jeremy bought that for me in Dresden on our honeymoon tour. It's a beautiful city."

Nora raised her eyes from the small figures and met the plea in Connie's. "*Was* beautiful. Tim says it's gone, gutted by fire. And a whole lot of people like these two burned up with it."

Connie jumped out of her chair and walked to her desk. "What possible good can come of this?"

Taking her time, Nora leaned back against the chair, still cradling the Dresden figures. "All I want is the truth. That sounds corny, but so what? It's still the best reason I know."

Connie paced back to her chair. "Sometimes I wish we could all forget the truth and simply cherish our illusions. Truth doesn't grant peace of mind. We didn't ask for this war, but we're winning it."

Nora carefully put the Dresden lovers back on the table and leaned forward to grab Connie's arm. "Listen to yourself, Connie. Do you really believe that garbage you wrote for *Manhattan*?"

Connie shook her off and walked away. "Did they leave us any choice when Europe was overrun?"

"I don't know what the choices were then. What I do know is that you can't be inhuman to save humanity."

Nora could see by the pain and grief in Connie's face that she was torn. Finally, hugging her arms across her middle, Connie nodded.

THE NEXT AFTERNOON when Connie showed up at the IP newsroom, Nora borrowed the bureau chief's office to compare notes. She was running out of time. Everyone she talked to clammed up when she brought up

Dresden. Officials at SHAEF just referred her to a days-old communiqué announcing the raid. The fliers she tracked down weren't too helpful, either. Mostly she talked to bomber officers who said clouds and smoke obscured the ground.

She flipped open her notebook and glanced at Connie. "What did you find out? Let's start with the targets. I've got railroads as the primary target."

"No one mentioned railways to me. Of course, I spoke to RAF chaps. Were yours Yanks?" At Nora's nod, Connie sighed and pulled a sheaf of papers out of her bag. "Everyone seems to have a different target. One chap mentioned a Gestapo headquarters, another an ammunition plant and a third a poison-gas works." She checked another sheet. "But the fellow I know best said Dresden wasn't on the air ministry's list of targets, at all. He said the list included all significant military targets."

Nora raised her eyebrows as she noted the information. "American planes came in last—450 Flying Fortresses. Fighters had orders to attack columns of soldiers, trucks and locomotives in the railyards."

Connie sorted through her sheets. "Yes, that's what I have. First came 244 RAF Lancasters about 10:00 p.m., followed by 529 more Lancasters at 1:30 a.m. Your chaps arrived just after noon, I'm told."

Nora jotted down the information. It didn't add up to anything more than a big raid. She raised her eyes and met Connie's frown. "What's wrong?"

Connie's lip trembled. "Do you know what a firestorm is?"

Nora shook her head.

"Apparently in some of these raids..." Connie took a deep breath and started again. "When a rash of small fires links into one massive fire, a firestorm results. The air heats to six hundred degrees or more, and violent updrafts cause gales that suck everything into the inferno."

"Are you saying that happened in Dresden?"

Connie nodded and glanced away. "I know a man who flew in the second wave. They spotted the fires of Dresden two hundred miles off. The city was a sea of fire, he said, the streets etched in flame."

Nora sat back and searched Connie's face. Her eyes looked old and very sad. "It wasn't intentional."

Connie met her eyes without wavering. "I'm afraid it was. The bomb load was designed to start massive fires. The first wave carried one huge explosive to smash windows and tear through roofs. The rest were all incendiaries to start fires." She glanced at her hands. "Dresden was an ancient city of half-timbered buildings."

Nora shook her head. "I can't believe it. I just can't believe what you're saying."

Connie's eyes turned stern. "I didn't want to believe it, either, but I must. Our chaps started it. The RAF dropped more than six hundred thousand incendiaries on Dresden."

Nora cringed away, not wanting to see in Connie's eyes what she'd seen in Tim's. Connie touched her hand. "One fellow said it was to please the Russians. Another was more honest. He said the point was to show the German people the price they would pay for continuing to fight. Dresden is only the beginning."

Nora raked fingers through her hair and bent over her notebook. "What about casualties?"

When Connie didn't answer, Nora looked up to find her eyes closed and her hand covering her mouth. Connie's hand dropped slowly. "I talked with a fellow at

BBC who monitors foreign broadcasts. Berlin claims thirty-five thousand dead. The Swiss put the number of dead to twenty-five thousand.

The pen dropped from Nora's hand. That was twice the population of her hometown. Gone. Just like that. In one night.

She swung around to a typewriter, rolled in a sheet of copy paper and checked her notes. Without glancing at Connie, she started to write. The lead came easily.

She lifted the paper and turned to Connie. "Does this sound right: *'Allied air chiefs chose Dresden as the first German city to endure deliberate terror-bombing of civilians designed to ensure a quick end to the war in Europe. A total of 1,200 bombers made three sorties over the city on Feb. 13-14, igniting a massive firestorm that killed 25,000.'* Is that how you add it up?"

Connie nodded and sat forward. "You're mad to think censors will allow you to publish that story."

"They can't stop me if they don't see it."

Nora scanned her notes and started in again, fueled by building anger. Why should they get away with it? The men who wrote up Tim's orders wouldn't suffer. More likely they'd get medals and be lauded by the press, held up as the heroes who'd won the war. The big shots got away with it because they always made little guys do the dirty work.

Connie leaned over the desk and scanned the sheet in the typewriter. "How do you propose to get this story out?"

Nora ripped out a sheet and started another. Maybe the big shots wouldn't get away with it this time. All the American censors were in France, but all the news was routed through London on its way to America. No one in London even read copy from Paris before sending it on to the States. Why bother since anything coming from Paris had already been censored?

She waved a hand around the office. "Do you see any censors? All the Americans are in France and your guys only check stories intended for British publication." She flicked the page in the typewriter. "A Paris dateline means it's cleared censorship. This one's going straight to the States."

"Nora, are you sure this is the right thing to do?" Connie touched her shoulder gently. "Have you thought about what could happen?"

Nora shrugged and checked her notes again. She'd be breaking an IP rule by using a Paris dateline on a London story, although getting a big scoop might square things with New York. Breaking censorship would absolutely finish her in Europe and probably finish her chances for a special correspondency.

She glanced up at Connie. "Yeah, I'll be in big trouble."

A smile softened the concern in Connie's eyes. "Trouble, yes. I remember when I didn't give a jot for the uproar, either. The regrets came later."

Nora frowned but shook off the warning in Connie's words. She'd regret it more if she didn't try.

Connie picked up the story and started to read. Her smile faded as her eyes zigzagged through the sheets. "It is beyond belief somehow and yet I'm not surprised at all, really. Why should we be immune to savagery and excess?"

Nora read through the pages and penciled in changes, but the story stood up under editing. She craned around to see who was left in the newsroom. She asked Connie to wait and walked over to the teletype machine. Rose looked up with a smile.

"This just came in from Paris. Would you get it right out?"

Rose nodded and pinned the story to the board above her keyboard. Nora watched the teletype girl send the first page. Connie came out of the bureau chief's office. Nora gave her a smile. "I could use a drink. What about you?"

THIRTY

THE LAST MESSERSCHMITT dodged right. Tim kept after his prey, firing a steady stream of glowing tracers that punched holes through the German plane. His Mustang followed too close, but he didn't care anymore. The German pilot was asking for it, and so was he.

A shudder ran over the Messerschmitt. Tim stomped the rudder and banked hard. The German plane exploded into a glittering cloud of flaming pieces. A gust of pressure buffeted his Mustang and white-hot pain sliced into his leg. A searing bolt flashed stars into his eyes, and he screamed.

"Major Chase. Tim. Shit, answer me, man."

MacVinner's plea screeched through his headset and brought him back. The altimeter unwound as his Mustang curled lower. Tim eased the stick back until the plane leveled off at fifteen thousand feet. He glanced through the canopy and spotted MacVinner's fighter about a thousand feet above.

He punched his radio button twice and finally looked at his leg. A jagged strut torn from the Messerschmitt pierced his thigh. He fought nausea and forced one hand to release the stick. Biting a fingertip of his glove, he pulled his hand free and gently examined his leg. He followed the strut with careful fingers and discovered a portion protruded from the Mustang's airframe.

"Shit."

A hiccup from the engine instantly recalled his hand. He adjusted the mixture and waited for the engine to respond. Nothing.

He snapped on his mike to answer MacVinner. "I've got engine trouble. Let's head home."

He swung a loose arc to the west. No need to get his wingman worried about the wound. The prop wash set the strut vibrating, and he gritted his teeth against the building ache in his thigh. He didn't see much blood and didn't really need that leg. He could work the rudder with his right foot if necessary. He'd be clumsy, but that was okay. The engine's hiccup bothered him, though. It was a long ride back to base.

MacVinner's voice crackled again. "You coming up?"

Tim throttled up, preparing to climb. The increased speed tugged the strut in his leg, and fresh blood seeped from torn flesh. The engine sputtered for a moment and changed pitch as a cylinder cut out. The temperature gauge looked fine, so he pulled the stick. The Mustang's nose tilted up, but the climb seemed more like a crawl.

He radioed MacVinner. "Not sure I can. Hold on. I'm punching off the external tanks."

He switched over to his main fuel tank and dropped the auxiliaries. The loss of weight buoyed the plane for a moment but not enough. "Can't get her up, MacVinner."

His wingman swooped a tight circle and came up beside him, flashing a thumbs-up through his canopy. Tim nodded and checked his map and compass readings. They'd clear the German border in a few minutes. His leg throbbed and sweat popped out on his forehead. He turned off the cockpit heater and blinked his eyes. He felt a little woozy.

"You okay?" The voice in his ear brought him back. "Major Chase, do you read me?"

Suddenly the oxygen mask threatened to smother him. He clawed it off before answering MacVinner. "I took something in the leg." The engine coughed. "Shit, I'm losing another cylinder."

A rhythmic clank started under his hood and echoed through the cockpit. The engine vibrations under his feet reassured him until the Mustang started dropping. He twisted the fuel mixture knob again, knowing it wouldn't help. He glanced down at a blanket of green firs.

He snapped on his mike. "Something's rattling around up there. I'm losing power. Start looking for an airfield."

MacVinner's Mustang shot forward and climbed away. Tim throttled back to ease the pressure on his thigh. Each throb loosed a spark of pain. He forced himself to breathe normally and tried to pull the strut out of his leg. A grunt escaped and his eyes teared, but he couldn't free himself.

He loosened his shoulder straps and told himself not to worry. Scanning the horizon, he found a speck that could be MacVinner. No Messerschmitts got this far west anymore. He checked the engine temperature gauge again. Still fine. That Merlin didn't need to hit on all twelve cylinders to get him down.

The hillsides below fell away, and the ground opened into small fields. He was clear of the German border and over Belgium. The engine coughed again. He let the Mustang find its own level at seven thousand feet. He punched the radio buttons, searching for chatter, but heard nothing. The growing dot in the west had to be MacVinner coming back. A crackle over his headset confirmed it. "Found one. I buzzed 'em, so they must be searching for our frequency."

Tim grunted. "Keep talking, MacVinner. I can't."

MacVinner's chatter couldn't drown the drumming in his ears. He ached everywhere now. Another voice cut in on the radio. Tim let MacVinner do the talking. He widened his eyes to keep his lids from slipping down. Sweat trickled salt across his lips as the altimeter dipped under four thousand feet.

The Mustang slipped lower, and MacVinner followed him down. Tim watched the altimeter unwind. Under twenty-five hundred feet now. The engine coughed again, and the plane dipped. He tugged the stick to keep her level as the fighter slowly sank toward earth. He checked the countryside below and spotted a road that might be wide enough.

"I'm going to try for that road."

Tim pushed the stick until the Mustang settled into a gentle glide. The altimeter swung under one thousand feet. The road drew closer, empty but lined with poplars. He bit down hard as pain stabbed up from his leg. The engine hacked, and whatever clanked under the hood began to grate against something. He kept the fighter's nose steady and released the landing gear at five hundred feet.

The grate in the engine worsened as the shadow of the plane spread across the road below. A breeze stirred the highest branches just under his wings. A hundred yards ahead, a wagon rolled out of a field and into the road. A small figure in red held the horse's bridle.

Tim jammed a hand against the throttle and yanked the stick back. The Mustang's nose lifted as the engine screamed. The left wing brushed a treetop, and he knew it was finished. With the last strength in his wounded leg, he slammed the left rudder to the floor. The right wing came up sharply to send the fighter cartwheeling over the trees and into the field.

NO MATTER WHAT HAPPENED NOW, the Dresden story was worth it. Nora turned her face toward the passenger window to watch the sun rise and smiled as dawn edged into the fields of France. Maybe revealing the truth about the raid would help ease Tim's suffering. Publishing that truth was a fitting requiem for Will.

The car flashed past a clump of stone houses. The driver braked and turned onto a wider road. "Next stop, Paris, the City of Light."

Nora laughed. "You mean they've turned them on again?"

The GI threw her a smile. "I got that out of a guidebook. Maybe I'll get lucky and still be here when the blackout ends."

She sighed and arched her head against the seat. She wouldn't see the lights go on in Paris, that's for sure. If she guessed right, unpacking would be a waste of time. Last summer SHAEF had suspended the reporters who violated censorship by broadcasting from Radio Paris on Liberation Day. No way she'd be that lucky. Losing credentials and being sent home in disgrace sounded more like it.

A short laugh whispered out. Somehow the best part was knowing how bad the story was for her career. The distinction of her Bastogne pieces and "Battlegrounds" could never outweigh the crime of ignoring the censors. Throwing the special correspondency away for a story like Dresden freed her of that stale ambition to claw her way out of the pack. *Knowing* she could have had the job provided satisfaction enough. The rest of the world would quickly forget the scandal her story caused. She wouldn't. She'd never forget how great this moment felt, how free and light and reborn.

The driver dropped her outside the Scribe, and she watched the car pull away before shouldering her duffel into the lobby. The clatter of silverware from the dining room meant waiters were getting breakfast tables prepared. Leaving her bag with the concierge she wandered through the tables toward the kitchen and begged a croissant. She couldn't face Norman Cox on an empty stomach.

Nora stopped in the hall outside the IP office. One part of her dreaded the confrontation with Cox, but she wasn't afraid. She'd spent the flight from London preparing for this moment. Behind the door, the jangle of a telephone pierced the silence.

She pushed open the door. Cox and Decker huddled in Will's old office. Cox bellowed and jumped for the door.

"Have you lost your mind?" His face flushed to purple as he raged toward her. "Do you know what you've done?"

Nora nodded and stepped around him, heading for the coffeepot. She carried her cup to her desk and sat down with her breakfast. Cox just stared at her for a minute, then stomped up to hover at her shoulder. She bit into the croissant and washed it down with coffee.

Cox sputtered and dropped into a chair. Her indifference stopped him cold, and she wanted to laugh when he flapped his mouth a couple of times without making a sound. She finished the croissant and wiped her fingers. "Why don't you start by showing me the cables?"

A fresh blaze lit his eyes. "No, let's start with this." He dragged a paper from his shirt pocket and tossed it on her desk. Before she could unfold it, he gave her the gist. "They've shut us down—suspended our filing privileges all over Europe."

Her surprise must have shown because Cox's face twisted into a sneer. "You *didn't* know, did you? You never figured your stupid stunt would finish us all. Did you think you'd get away with it? Well, Seymour, you haven't. They yanked your credentials first thing. You're through covering this war or any other."

Nora dug a cigarette out of her purse and lit up. This was bad. She honestly never expected SHAEF to go after IP as a whole. She'd slipped the Dresden story past the war desk by using a Paris dateline, knowing the editors in New York would assume the cable from London originated in Paris and had passed the censors in France.

She blew out a stream of smoke. The whole thing looked trickier now. New York might forgive her for breaking censorship since the censors rubbed a lot of editors wrong to begin with. But getting the whole organization shut down in Europe!

She stabbed out her cigarette. "Okay, Norman, let's find Colonel Logan. I'll explain IP knew nothing about it. Maybe he'll let us off the hook."

Cox snorted with a bitterness that stopped her halfway out of her chair. "You aren't getting off the hook, Seymour, with SHAEF or anyone else. I have a letter of resignation ready for you. And if you won't sign it, you're fired."

She sank back down and forced herself to meet his eyes without squirming, masking her pain and surprise.

"Fine. I'll sign it. Now do you want my help getting you out of this jam or should I just clean out my desk?"

Decker sidled up beside them with a questioning glance for Cox. The bureau chief nodded, and he pulled up a chair. "I don't understand you, Nora. You know the censorship rules. Hell, you made sure I knew before I came over here."

Nora patted his arm. She liked Decker and wanted to set him straight. "This isn't about breaking censorship. That's a good excuse to get rid of me, but that's not why SHAEF's doing it. The brass can't admit to deliberate terror-bombing. It doesn't fit their idea of honor or duty. They'd like to forget what we did to Dresden and now they can't. At least, not yet."

Decker shook his head. "I still don't get you. The Germans did worse. You know what they did to Will. You were at Bastogne. Why'd you do it?"

Nora sighed and glanced away. There were lots of reasons, including Will's death and Bastogne. But Decker couldn't see because he didn't want to. Maybe part of what Connie had said about cherishing illusions was true. The only conscience Nora had to live with was her own.

She met Decker's eyes and shrugged. "I knew how."

CONSTANCE PASTED an attentive look on her face but let her mind drift away from her parents' dining room. It was out of her hands now. Nora had flown back to Paris at midnight, so she wasn't on hand to quake when the first thunder of anger rolled in from America. Constance's friends at the air ministry had rung up to bluster threats all afternoon, but the furor here would die down. The Yanks had a different bone to pick with Nora.

ALLIANCES

She cut another piece of roast beef and nodded at her mother's "Isn't that so, Constance?" Nods were all Mother required at table since she preferred to dominate the mealtime discussion.

At the memory of Nora's courage, the beef turned to ashes in her mouth. Nora would find hell to pay but perhaps her gamble would be worthwhile in the end. Certainly Constance found it worthwhile. For her, the good of it would be determined after dinner, when she would ask Father to secure her an appointment to Britain's United Nations delegation.

Constance returned her father's smile and sipped from her water glass. She'd forgone wine tonight, not trusting false courage to do the job. If he agreed, she'd have Nora to thank for her post, Nora and those poor creatures in Dresden. She'd been a coward too long, but no longer. Nora's outrage at Dresden stirred old memories of her own horror of Flanders, and somehow she relived her own journey from ignorance to outrage. Last night she thumbed through *Judgment* for the first time in years, and that finished it for her. In the end it wasn't Peter or Jane or Nora who convinced her. It was her own words that did the trick.

The maid cleared the table with a clatter of dishes and whispered apologies. The time had come. Constance waited until her father selected his afterdinner cigar and her mother stepped back from her chair.

"I'd like a word with Daddy." She met the old woman's stern eyes and upraised eyebrows. "I'll join you directly."

She fought back a deep sigh when her mother swept out of the dining room. Her father sniffed his fat Havana as he poured a glass from a crystal decanter. "A bit of port, m'dear?"

"No, thank you, Daddy. I prefer brandy." She selected a snifter from the sideboard and splashed in a hearty measure. After a furtive gulp, she returned to the table.

Constance liked watching Randolph Adair's ritual lighting of a cigar. She rarely saw him at it anymore and only knew of it from childhood fishing trips. Daddy had always broken his one-a-day rule when he took them fishing, but he never violated the ritual. First a proper cut off the end and then lighting with a wooden match held the proper distance to avoid further roasting of the tobacco. Turning off ashes to achieve the proper burn capped his procedure.

She rolled fine brandy over her tongue as she waited. Daddy's daily cigar meant a precious moment of solitude, and she felt a bit guilty for butting in. Parliamentary duties and life with Mother managed to steal most of his time. But only Daddy could give her what she needed now. His first sip of port signaled his readiness to hear her out.

"I've a favor to ask, Daddy. A very large favor."

He glanced over his glass without speaking, but his eyes invited her to continue.

She knotted her hands around the glass. "Perhaps I'm going about this all wrong. How do you think things will be once the war's over?"

He puffed his Havana and blew out a steam of fragrant smoke. "Winston expects things will continue much the same. A bit of icing knocked off the top, no more."

"But what do you expect?" She sipped enough to moisten her tongue. "You've been a public man for forty years. How do you think it'll go?"

ALLIANCES

The cigar burned unnoticed in his hand. "I anticipate, and perhaps even welcome, an early retirement from parliament. When the next election is called, we'll be swept from office."

His words surprised her. Not the content, really, but the equanimity he admitted. Perhaps he'd finally tired of politics. No doubt he'd aged a century since 1939. "You usually agree with the PM."

"Not as often as you'd think, m'dear. We've had some jolly rows, you know." He drained his glass and settled back into his chair. "He's wrong again now. However necessary, the war is unpopular. The people will fight it, but in the end, they'll have our guts for garters. And that's as it should be."

Constance stared into her glass and wondered if she should reconsider asking his help. She'd expected a fight, but now, well, she didn't know what to expect from him. She always thought he'd gone into politics from some archaic belief in noblesse oblige. But if that were the case, Daddy would scream bloody murder before losing his seat to the other side. She couldn't turn back now.

When she looked up, he wore the tender smile he'd saved just for her in her childhood. She glanced away but he called her back with a gentle question. "What is it you need from me, Constance?"

She traced the damask flowers on the tablecloth. "A posting, Daddy. I'd like your nomination for the United Nations delegation. I know you don't approve of the idea. I do, though, and I'd like a chance to make it work."

A rich chuckle spilled out with cigar smoke. "Had enough grubbing in shelters, have you? Think you're ready for the trenches, do you?"

She met his eyes and nodded. "Something like that."

His eyes half closed. When he cocked his head to study her, she wilted inside. He thought her a fool. Perhaps she was. "Daddy, I . . ."

He waved his cigar with a flourish. "Not another word, m'dear. You'll make an admirable delegate. In fact, I considered asking you myself. Somehow I thought you had other plans."

She flushed. "Well, there'll be a bit of shuffling with the twins and Jeremy, of course."

He smiled. "Of course."

He wouldn't hear her thanks and just retreated with an enigmatic smile behind a wreath of smoke. A fit of coughing took him as she slid open the door, and she spun about. "Daddy, are you quite all right?"

He regained his breath with a huff and set aside the cigar. "Absolutely peachy, I assure you." He folded his hands on the table and glanced away. "I do wonder, though, about your doctor. Will he approve?"

The words froze her. What did he know about Peter? She'd been so careful. She straightened her shoulders and looked him in the eye. "I believe he will, Daddy. He's a wonderful man."

"So I've heard."

She resisted the urge to run to his side. "Does Mother know about Peter?"

He shook his head and surprised her with a smile. "She's not mentioned it. I assume she would."

His silence stretched into a limitless gulf that Constance couldn't bridge. There was no need to plead for his understanding. Peter *was* a wonderful man. What she'd found with him should be celebrated.

He picked up his cigar and a box of matches. "I should like to meet him someday." The match flared, and he carefully brought it within range of his Havana. "I expect to see him next time he's in London."

"Then you will." Constance felt the smile growing inside before it reached her lips. What a rare scene that would be. Somehow she looked forward to it. "Thank you, Daddy."

He nodded and closed his eyes, sinking back with his cigar and his solitude.

THIRTY-ONE

CONSTANCE SLID THE LETTER into the envelope and sealed the flap. It was better this way, better for Jeremy and better for her. He hated scenes and now wouldn't face one. He'd learn of the divorce as he breakfasted and have time to compose himself before facing the world. But perhaps her news wouldn't ruffle his composure at all.

She glanced at the framed photograph on her desk, studying Jeremy's rigid pose. His unhappiness showed plainly in the sliver of life caught by the photographer, and yet only now could she recognize Jeremy's stiffness for what it was. As miserably as he'd failed her, so too had she failed him. Perhaps he'd welcome this letter and give a long overdue sigh of relief.

Constance caught her own sigh before it escaped. Yes, there was the pain of admitting her part in the failure of their marriage. How much easier it would be to drape herself in the complaints of a wronged woman. But that would be terribly dishonest and cowardly, and she'd finished with all that. From this day forward, she would take each step because it was right for her. Never again would she let the opinions of others dictate her choices.

She walked to the window and looked down on the gray rain-washed streets of London. Peter was right for her, even though choosing him meant saying goodbye to so much she loved. More than anything, England was her past, and a future with Peter meant great happiness and adventure and starting fresh. America was the place for new beginnings, with its brashness and energy and everlasting hope. Even the twins felt that.

A bus splashed red through the puddles below, and she smiled. She imagined their delight when her letter reached them in New York, announcing not the summons home they expected but a reprieve that meant they could finish the school term. Her visit in March would be the time to explain about Peter and the divorce. The news would certainly hurt, but they were almost adults. She must learn to treat them as such and accept their decisions. Geoff and Adair could decide themselves where to live and with whom. At least she knew that they liked Peter. If their affection survived the trauma of watching their parents' marriage dissolve, then all would come right in the end. She was confident it would.

Constance walked back to her desk and shuffled the letters. Strange that announcing her decision to Peter was the hardest. She'd hushed the small voice that wondered in the recesses of her mind if Peter would shy away now that she'd chosen him. Peter loved her and wanted her and would come back for her. He'd said so, and so he would. Whatever hurt the world delivered would never shake the truth of his love and hers. Whatever pain she must endure as this part of her life ended could be borne because the certainty of Peter's love was a promise for her future.

She gathered a stack of folders into her arms and carried them to her bed. Now that she'd settled her personal affairs, she could get on with her new public life. She had so much to learn before the United Nations conference in April and so much to think about. She glanced at the subject headings on Whitehall's briefing papers and selected three to study. The men in England's delegation would argue incessantly over the rest, but Jane was right. Someone must think about refugees and agriculture and health.

Her excitement grew as she scanned the pages. Let the others look for peace in a new generation of treaties and alliances. They would fail again, as they'd failed for centuries, because they couldn't envision true peace. Peace came from inside, growing from the seed of good intentions through the sapling of good works into the sturdy timber of a better world for all.

Constance dug a pencil out of her bedside table and jotted notes as she read. Her hand trembled. So many would dismiss them as dreamers who searched for a paradise that couldn't exist. But this time, despite their derision, she *would* keep on. Every problem had a solution. She knew that now. That belief was Peter's greatest gift, beyond even his love.

THE DOOR CLICKED SHUT behind the nurse, and Matt sank into a chair beside Tim's bed. His brother's face seemed as pale as the crisp cotton of the pillow under his head, whiter than the bandages swathing his body. He leaned forward to touch Tim's hand, and the nagging ache in his shoulder returned. He cradled his slung arm against his mending thigh and gently wrapped his fingers around Tim's wrist. The boy's eyes might be closed, but the steady pulse and warm skin under his fingers reassured Matt.

His hand slipped down to cover Tim's as he studied the still face. Even if Tim woke, Matt knew there'd be no lighthearted gleam in his brother's eyes. The boy in him was gone for good, banished forever by suffering and guilt and senseless death.

He closed his eyes, wanting to siphon Tim's pain into himself. He deserved the broken body and ruined hopes that had fallen to his brother. He'd been the one who studied war and drilled himself in death. He'd been the one who threw their father's beliefs back in his face and joined his opponents. He'd been the one who pretended to despise butchery even as he gloried in it. Why couldn't he be the one who paid the price?

His shoulder protested against his awkward posture, but Matt didn't move. The German sniper who stitched him with bullets deserved his thanks for killing the part of him that loved war. The dregs of his addiction to death leaked out with his blood as he desperately scrabbled for life in that muddy ditch. But it wasn't just getting hit that did it. There was Nora. Looking at Tim, that's what scared him the most. With the burden of unnecessary guilt following so closely his loss of Hillary, would Tim fight for his life? No matter what the doctors said, Matt knew Tim wouldn't make it unless he wanted to.

The fingers under his hand stirred, and Matt looked up. Tim blinked and drew back his hand. "Matt? I thought I was dreaming. What are you doing here?"

Matt forced brightness into his voice. "Come to see the hero. You made a pretty spectacular landing to earn that medal."

Tim frowned and retreated behind closed eyes. Matt swore softly. What could he say to bring him around? The usual older-and-wiser relationship didn't work anymore. Without it, he wasn't sure how to approach Tim. Maybe jumping straight in would work.

He eased back in his chair and jockeyed his good leg across his knee. "I guess you had a rough time over Dresden. I'd like to hear about it."

Tim snorted. "Why? So you can pat my hand again and tell me it doesn't matter?"

"No. It does matter. It'll always matter to you, Tim, and so it matters to me. I want to know what happened."

For a long moment, Matt sat still under Tim's appraising eyes, forcing himself to meet their harsh judgment. This day had to come. Tim finally had to see him for what he was, just as Matt had finally seen their father for what he was. It hurt like hell to watch your towering hero wither into a mere man, but it was necessary. To succeed as your own man, you had to know the true measure of other men.

Finally Tim glanced away. "I killed a girl, strafed her. She wasn't the first civilian I killed. Hell, in twenty-five bombing runs there were hundreds probably. But she was the first I saw die."

Matt waited until Tim's eyes came back. "Makes you sick, doesn't it? Killing somebody like that kills something inside you, too. It's so easy to kill and so hard to live with."

Tim frowned, and Matt rushed past the question in his eyes. "I froze up my first time under fire. And then this kid next to me went down hard. Suddenly it was easy to squeeze that trigger. I almost couldn't stop. When it was over, I went out to see what I'd done. There was one guy out there I knew was mine. I rolled him over. His eyes were open, caked with sand but open. I puked."

Tim's head rolled against his pillow. "You liked it. You never said so, but I could tell."

ALLIANCES

Matt shrugged. "Maybe I did. At least it was easier to think so since I had to do it. And then I'd think about Dad, and I hated myself for liking it. I guess I always figured him for a coward, so if I didn't like it, I was a coward, too."

At that, Tim jerked, trying to sit up. Matt grunted as he pulled out of the chair. Tim's eyes widened. "Hey, you're hurt."

Matt waved away his concern and Tim continued. "Dad's no coward. He's got more guts than anyone I know. No one wanted to hear what he had to say, but he kept after them. Even after Pearl Harbor, he said it was stupid. And he's right." Tim rolled his eyes. "His way doesn't work, but he's right. You know what I mean?"

Matt smiled. "Yeah, I know what you mean."

Tim sighed and settled deeper into the bed. "After Dresden I thought about quitting. But I knew the stink they'd make would hurt Dad." He glanced away. "And you, too, of course. So I kept flying, but I stopped strafing. And I started taking stupid chances. I guess I wanted to die."

Matt grabbed for the reassurance in his words. *Wanted*, not *want*. But he had to make sure. "Do you still want to die?"

Tim stared at the ceiling and finally shook his head. "Not anymore. Dying's the easy way out."

Rubbing the stiffness out of his leg, Matt bent over the bed and gently squeezed Tim's shoulder. "Good. I couldn't stand it if you died."

Tim covered Matt's hand with his own. "Thanks. Hey, what happened to you?" His eyes brightened. "You coming home, too?"

Matt shook his head. "Not yet. The doc says I'm still fit, but not for fighting. I've pulled another desk job at SHAEF."

Tim's eyes teared, and he blushed. "Shit. That's still in the war zone. Be careful, will ya? Until you get home?"

Matt blinked away the wetness in his own eyes. "Sure. You're right about that, Tim. Dying's too easy."

NORA NODDED TO A NURSE and hurried down the hospital corridor. She'd hoped to have more time left in France so she could keep an eye on Tim, but the army had other plans. The phone call that morning had been brief and to the point: be ready with one bag at six tonight for transport to the States. She wanted to plead for a few extra days but knew better than to even try. Maybe the note she'd sent four days ago to Matthew would get to him before Tim was shipped home.

She shivered as she started up the steps toward Tim's room. At least he was out of it now. The doctors promised his broken bones would mend and the burns on his legs would heal, but he'd never play baseball again. That's how she liked to think of Tim—laughing in Hyde Park sunshine with the outcome of the game the only doubt troubling his mind. He could never go back to that day—none of them could. But at least he wouldn't go back to the fighting.

Pausing at the top of the stairs, she opened her mind to the thought she'd been pushing away for days. Matthew might die. That possibility never seemed real before. Everything else in her life had always worked out somehow, and she thought Matthew would, too. But Dresden had changed all that.

By turning in her resignation, she'd eliminated the one sure thing in her future. Tomorrow she'd get back to the States, return to an empty apartment in New York to wait out the war and wonder if she'd spend the rest of her life with empty arms. In her note she hadn't even told him they were sending her home in disgrace.

She stepped into the shadowed upstairs corridor just as the door to Tim's room opened. A uniformed officer limped into the hall, hugging a slung arm to his chest. Something about his shape warned her, but as she walked forward, she still wasn't ready. When the soldier lifted his head, Nora stopped in midstride.

"Matthew!"

He rushed the last steps to steady her and winced as they came together. Nora leaned into him, not wanting to see the bandaged arm. "Oh, Matthew, you're hurt."

He tilted her chin with his good hand and forced her to meet his eyes. "It's nothing you can't cure, sweetheart." His mouth closed over hers.

Nora clung to his kiss, needing the reassurance of his lips. *He was here. He was safe.*

For now.

She forced the thought away, wanting the kiss to last forever. All too soon he released her. She fumbled for words. "Did you... have you seen Tim?"

His mouth twisted into a grim line as he nodded. "Yes." He glanced around. "Let's get out of here. Find somewhere to talk."

She took his arms on the stairs, bracing his leg from the jarring punishment of the steps. Downstairs he traded words with a nurse before pulling Nora toward a door. She let him lead her outside into the feeble warmth of the February sun. In a dead garden awash with leaves, he pulled her down beside him on a mossy stone bench.

She cradled his arm without speaking. Finally he sighed and lifted her hand to his lips. "I guess Tim will pull through. He said dying's the easy way out, and he's right. Maybe someday we'll all be able to forget."

Nora touched his cheek. "Should we even try to forget?"

Matthew turned his face into her hand, rubbing his cheek against her palm. "Now you sound like Connie and my father and all the rest of the philosophers."

She eased her hand away and stood. "I don't think I want to forget, Matthew. I don't want to forget Will or Hillary or what's happened to Tim."

"You're right." He winced as he lifted a hip to free the cigarettes in his pocket. "But remembering doesn't stop it from happening again."

She refused the Camel and watched him light his. "Because men like you love war?" His head came up sharply, and she met the surprise in his eyes.

When his eyes narrowed, she withered inside. He was going back. He wanted to because he loved war more than he loved her. "You were talking about yourself that night in Paris."

He ground the cigarette under his heel. "Maybe. But that's finished now, thanks to you and Tim and the German who put my arm in this sling. When I thought I was done for, all I kept thinking about was how much I wanted to live."

Footsteps crackled dead leaves, and Matthew's driver came around the hedge. "Sorry, Colonel, but we'll have to hustle to meet your schedule."

Time to tell him. Nora waited until the GI walked away. "I'm going home. IP sacked me for the Dresden story."

"I can't say I'm sorry. I want you safe at home, waiting for me."

"Without a job, I'll have plenty of time to wait."

He pushed himself up, the slung arm making him awkward. He took her hand in his good one. "You'll get another job."

She tried to smile. He was always so damned certain. And he was right this time, too. She'd have her pick of good offers once word got around. But she'd never be a special correspondent. And maybe she'd wait forever. She dropped his hand and stepped away. "You may not come back."

His laughter surprised her. "They had their chance and won't get another. I'm going back to the war, sweetheart, but not to the fight. I'll be warming a desk at SHAEF until the peace."

Tears filled her eyes as she hid against his shoulder. She turned into his good arm, taking care not to knock the sling. He tugged her hair gently until she raised her eyes. "I'll be back for you, Nora. You can count on it."

She reached up and brought his lips down to hers. She wanted to believe the promise in his kiss. Something good had come out of this, something to wipe out the horror. She wanted to forget some of it, but not Matthew, never Matthew.

When his lips lifted from hers, she almost cried out. She couldn't let him go. There'd been too many goodbyes in this war. And then she saw the promise in his eyes.

"That ought to carry me through."

"You better go now, Matthew."

He brushed her lips as he pulled her against him again. She whispered in his ear. "But hurry back."

When he turned toward the hospital, she knotted her hands to keep from pulling him back. At the door, he paused and called back across the dead garden. "I'm counting on you, Nora."

As the door swung shut behind him, tears streaked wet trails down her cheeks. She took a deep breath. He was so certain. And so was she.

PATRICIA MATTHEWS

America's First Lady of Romance upholds her long standing reputation as a bestselling romance novelist with...

Enchanted

Caught in the steamy heat of America's New South, Rebecca Trenton finds herself torn between two brothers—she yearns for one but a dark secret binds her to the other.

Available in APRIL or reserve your copy for March shipping by sending your name, address, zip or postal code along with a check or money order for $4.70 (includes 75 cents for postage and handling) payable to Worldwide Library to:

In the U.S.	*In Canada*	ENC-H-1
Worldwide Library	Worldwide Library	
901 Fuhrmann Blvd.	P.O. Box 609	
Box 1325	Fort Erie, Ontario	
14269-1325	L2A 9Z9	

(()) WORLDWIDE LIBRARY

Breathtaking adventure and romance in the mystical land of the pharaohs...

YESTERDAY AND TOMORROW

ERIN YORKE

A young British archeologist, Cassandra Baratowa, embarks on an adventurous romp through Egypt in search of Queen Nefertiti's tomb—and discovers the love of her life!

Available in MARCH, or reserve your copy for February shipping by sending your name, address, zip or postal code along with a check or money order for $4.70 (includes 75¢ for postage and handling) payable to Worldwide Library to:

In the U.S.	In Canada
Worldwide Library	Worldwide Library
901 Fuhrmann Blvd.	P.O. Box 609
Box 1325	Fort Erie, Ontario
Buffalo, NY 14269-1325	L2A 9Z9

Please specify book title with your order.

WORLDWIDE LIBRARY

YES-1

CLAIM THE Crown

Carla Neggers

The complications only begin when they mysteriously inherit a family fortune.

Ashley and David. The sister and brother are satisfied that their anonymous gift is legitimate until someone else becomes interested in it, and they soon discover a past they didn't know existed.

Available in APRIL or reserve your copy for March shipping by sending your name, address, zip or postal code along with a check or money order for $4.70 (includes 75¢ for postage and handling) payable to Worldwide Library to:

In the U.S.	In Canada
Worldwide Library	Worldwide Library
901 Fuhrmann Blvd.	P.O. Box 609
Box 1325	Fort Erie, Ontario
Buffalo, N.Y.	L2A 9Z9
14269-1325	

CTC-H-1R

GILLIAN HALL

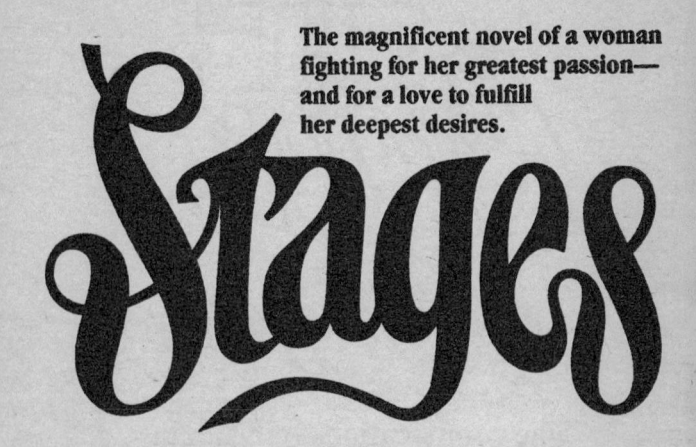

The magnificent novel of a woman fighting for her greatest passion— and for a love to fulfill her deepest desires.

Stages

The desire to break from an unbearable past takes prima ballerina Anna Duras to Broadway, in search of the happiness she once knew. The tumultuous changes that follow lead her to the triumph of new success... and the promise of her greatest love.

Available in MAY or reserve your copy for April shipping by sending your name, address, zip or postal code along with a check or money order for $4.70 (includes 75 cents for postage and handling) payable to Worldwide Library to:

In the U.S.	In Canada
Worldwide Library	Worldwide Library
901 Fuhrmann Blvd.	P.O. Box 609
Box 1325	Fort Erie, Ontario
Buffalo, NY 14269-1325	L2A 5X3

Please specify book title with your order.

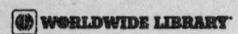

WORLDWIDE LIBRARY

STA-1